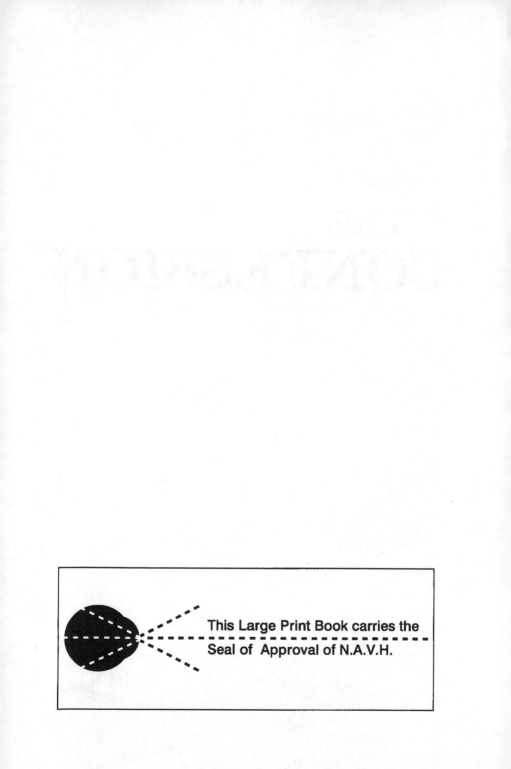

This Large Print Book carries the
Seal of Approval of N.A.V.H.

# THE
# CONFESSION

# THE
# CONFESSION

## OLEN STEINHAUER

**Thorndike Press • Waterville, Maine**

Published in 2004 by arrangement with
St. Martin's Press, LLC.

Thorndike Press® Large Print Adventure.

The tree indicium is a trademark of Thorndike Press.

The text of this Large Print edition is unabridged.
Other aspects of the book may vary from the original edition.

Set in 16 pt. Plantin.

Printed in the United States on permanent paper.

**Library of Congress Cataloging-in-Publication Data**

Steinhauer, Olen.
      The confession / Olen Steinhauer.
        p. cm.
      ISBN 0-7862-6568-X (lg. print : hc : alk. paper)
      1. Police — Europe, Eastern — Fiction.   2. Europe,
Eastern — Fiction.   3. Missing persons — Fiction.
4. Writer's block — Fiction.   5. Authors — Fiction.
6. Large type books.   I. Title.
      PS3619.T4764C75 2004b
      813'.6—dc22                              2004047882

FOR

K

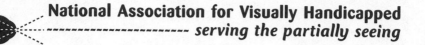

As the Founder/CEO of NAVH, the only national health agency solely devoted to those who, although not totally blind, have an eye disease which could lead to serious visual impairment, I am pleased to recognize Thorndike Press★ as one of the leading publishers in the large print field.

Founded in 1954 in San Francisco to prepare large print textbooks for partially seeing children, NAVH became the pioneer and standard setting agency in the preparation of large type.

Today, those publishers who meet our standards carry the prestigious "Seal of Approval" indicating high quality large print. We are delighted that Thorndike Press is one of the publishers whose titles meet these standards. We are also pleased to recognize the significant contribution Thorndike Press is making in this important and growing field.

Lorraine H. Marchi, L.H.D.
Founder/CEO
NAVH

★ Thorndike Press encompasses the following imprints: Thorndike, Wheeler, Walker and Large Print Press.

# ACKNOWLEDGMENTS

For their wise and informed criticisms, I thank my steadfast agent, Matt Williams, my friend, the author Robin Hunt, and my editor, Kelley Ragland. In fact, they are all friends.

For a clean, friendly place to scribble in a corner, then abandon all hope of work in favor of a drink, I thank the staff of Pótkulcs, who always made me feel welcome.

In my more studious moments, the Central European University kindly allowed me the use of its extensive research facilities, as did the Artpool Art Research Center, and for that I am grateful.

Some details of the labor camps are taken from a fascinating and disturbing collection of eyewitness accounts called *Voices from the Gulag: Life and Death in Communist Bulgaria*, edited by Tzvetan Todorov and Robert Zaretsky.

They are not to be blamed for the mistakes of my own imagination.

*You assemble the picture later, after all the bodies have been examined and the clues tracked down and all the facts have come to light. Or most of them. Or some.*

*It is 1956. The Comrade Chairman has been dead three years, and General Secretary Mihai has less than a year left to him. No one knows this yet, but Mihai knows. Maybe this knowledge shadows every decision he makes.*

*The year feels light after all those others, and once news of the Twentieth Congress in Moscow spreads, the pictures of Stalin disappear from the bookstores and post offices and living rooms. Soon, it's hard to find the old man anywhere in the Capital. Where his volumes of speeches were once shelved, there is now a stack of crisp little pamphlets by N. Khrushchev.* Stalin chose the path of repression and physical annihilation, not only against actual enemies, but also against individuals who had not committed any crimes against the Party and the Soviet government.

*You hear about Budapest on the radio — the Magyars are setting fire to Comrade Chairman*

9

Stalin's posters. They make a show of dancing in the ashes, in the middle of the street. The Hungarians are a surprisingly vocal lot.

The Poles have also made noises and faced tanks on what they call Black Thursday, setting off a ripple of discontent through their own young nation.

But at home it's a good time. Some of the old writers return to the shelves, and you're surprised, even, by what you read. In The Spark's editorial pages, citizens complain about hot water and trash disposal and crime. Their anger sweetens the air, and this irony is intoxicating. After war and the era of the Comrade Chairman, it feels like we're finally finding our own path. You hear it in the radio speeches, in the promises from Mihai's own lips, and from others in the political stratosphere. There's the old history professor, Bobu, and Kozak the Engineer who rants about the "thick Muscovites" in the Central Committee and demands a new, national path to socialism. Mihai gives up his First Secretary post and keeps only his Prime Ministership — a reminder of the progress to collective leadership. Truly, says an editorial, the Dictatorship of the Proletariat has never been so democratic.

All this is just background to the hope. Certainly now it seems naïve and unwarranted, but it was there. For a few months.

10

*Years may pass, but the memory of that hope always warms you. Future generations will not understand, but you would want to make the historic moment clear. Not for individual glory, nor opportunism. Only clarity.*

*Resolution 683 was first suggested by Mihai at the Fifth Party Congress of the Central Committee. 25 July, five months to the day after Comrade First Secretary Khrushchev's words to his own secret Congress, and two months after the Yugoslavs spilled the secret to the rest of us. Mihai announced with grave urgency his agreement with the First Secretary. Stalin's crimes. Stalin's mass terrors. Stalin's insidious effect on the development of socialism in this eastern edge of Europe.*

*In the newsreels Mihai purses his lips between thoughts, hands gripping each side of the podium, over the profile of a hawk surrounded by laurel. These pauses are heavy with meaning, and you want to think this signifies that his words are heavy with meaning, that this is a man convinced of the truth of his own words. But again, with all that follows, you wonder.*

*He proposes to right the wrongs of the Comrade Chairman. From 1945 to 1953, he explains, hundreds — no,* thousands *— in our own dear land were wrongly jailed in tiny municipal prisons, in medieval dungeons, in the labor camps of the western provinces. Under the ex-*

11

*press urging of the Comrade Chairman.*

*No one in the Committee chambers is hearing anything new. No one in the entire country. It's the telling, the act of speaking aloud, that is new. The Central Committee chamber — all 236 men and women — is silent. Mihai's dark hair is mostly white; he's not the young partisan he once was. He sighs significantly and tells the chamber that he proposes to release all political prisoners, effective immediately.*

*There is a polite pause. The room waits for a* but, *or a* however.

*The room erupts. Thunderous applause. A few stunned Committee members, unsure, lag behind. Maybe they're wondering where they will be in this new world of prisoners in the streets. But then they're swept up in the wave of clapping hands. The domed ceiling rolls their applause back down at them, and that only heightens their fever; the noise rises. Deafening. They're on their feet, stomping, clapping, shouting unintelligibly. And under this onslaught of approving mayhem, Mihai folds his speech in half, creases the edge, and slips it into a jacket pocket. In the newsreel, you can see the fatigue. Wrinkles clear under the harsh lights, eyes weathered and sagging. Maybe he knows everything. All that will follow. The applause lasts a full seven minutes. There are wet eyes — yes, even tears. The Amnesty has begun.*

12

# SUMMER

SUMMER

# 1

Packing up the dacha was a simple, silent affair. Three weeks' worth of clothes, damp underwear still hanging from the back porch, pens and paper, and all the books. I saw Flaubert and Dostoyevsky to the Škoda's trunk, then wedged my own novel beside them. The creased, sewage-colored paperback was a vainglory I still felt I could afford.

Stories begin this way, with the mundane details. Underwear, books, leaves. Because these are the irrefutable facts; they exist outside speculation. I'm in that dacha now, verifying everything, because while other points in time may be chosen, this is where my confession truly begins.

Then there were the empty brandy bottles, clanking on their way to the car, two full boxes. Magda had helped out that first week, when the conversation sank into mute glances and nods, pouring whenever our glasses were low. But after she walked out I had two weeks to tackle the bottles alone: a big, hulking thirty-seven-year-old

15

drinking brandy from tiny glasses, spending the days in front of blank sheets of paper at the table that looked out onto the dried forest, thinking only that, yes, my wife has finally left me.

And each morning I woke with a stunned head and a pile of still-empty pages.

Once everything was collected I made the slow walk through the bedroom, living room, kitchen. I even looked in the fly-infested out-house to be sure nothing was left behind. Methodical. This was the only way not to imagine her in the shadows and ignore the long walnut hairs left on the sofa. The kitchen stank of old, spilled liquor and the occasional gusts of forest decay through the open windows.

Locked the shutters, then the doors. No extended pause on the front steps, no re-flections while looking back on her family's dacha, nervously adjusting my rings.

It took a half hour to reach the main road, then I turned south, where the trees thinned into farmland and fields, and the sun caught on the dirty windshield. I tried in vain to dampen my mouth. Behind a de-tour, the road was torn apart, and an old woman poured a kettle of steaming tar into a hole while other women with kerchiefs on their heads leaned on shovels and watched. The Škoda's engine sputtered when I went too fast, and I remembered Georgi's comment when I'd first bought the car. He had walked around it slowly, a hand on his chin, then said: *I do believe that very soon socialist engineering will accomplish the dream of fitting an automobile into a shoe box.*

# 2

Her parents' modest farmhouse looked exactly as it had when I first saw it — 1935, October. I can mark only a few things in time. Magda was a lithe schoolgirl who spent the days in class being ogled by my best friend Stefan and me, and after some unbearable amount of time, I was the lucky one invited to her house for lunch on a Friday afternoon. Sixteen years old, and I was already hers. Storm clouds had overrun the sky then, like now. A warm wind rolled over the orchard-covered hills.

Teodor was outside, eyeing the car before I turned off the engine. His washboard face was crossed by scars and pits. Farming had done it to him, that or the 1949 collectivization push. At family gatherings there were always veiled allusions to commissars starving them out of their complacency.

"Ferenc."

"Teodor."

We shook hands, and he asked how long the trip had taken. He always seemed to think he could judge the value of a man or a day by the economy of travel.

"Two hours, about."

"Some good time, that."

"My daughter around here somewhere?" I asked.

Teodor nodded at the house, and as we approached it he spoke beneath his breath: "How about my daughter?"

"Your guess."

"Don't be smart."

"She's in the city, I suppose."

The old farmer opened the door for me, and Pavel, our black-and-tan dachshund, trotted up and let out a short bark.

Magda's mother's baked apples smelled sweet and fruity — it was all she knew how to cook. She came out of the kitchen, wiping fat fingers on her apron, and gave me a kiss. Pillow cheeks and thin lips.

"Hello, Nora."

"Hello yourself." She didn't need to ask the question; she only needed to look significantly over my shoulder at the empty doorway.

18

Ágnes stumbled out of the guest room holding a book and squinting through thick, black-framed glasses. "Hello, Daddy."

Fourteen years old and, even behind glasses and foggy with sleep, showing strong signs of her mother's lazy beauty. I could smell the boredom of these three weeks all over her.

We ate Nora's meager potatoes and paprika outside in the shriveling, bush-lined private garden, shaded by the house. A dusty breeze from the apple orchard made the napkins tremble on the worn wooden table. Teodor kept on with his questions about the condition of the road, the shape of his dacha, and, after these practicalities were out of the way, the writing. "Is your book still in print?"

"It's not," I admitted as I finished the meal. "Maybe once I get this other one finished, they'll print more, but not now."

"And when will this second book be done?" asked Teodor. "It's been — how long?"

"Four years," said Nora, but without judgment.

"It took ten years to get that first one out," I said.

"Daddy's going to write a proletarian

novel," said Ágnes. It was the second time she'd spoken since I arrived, and in her long grin I read a lovely irony.

"Like that man?" asked Nora. "What was his name?"

"I don't know what I'll write."

Magda's father leaned forward. "You mean you haven't *started?*"

I wanted to explain, again, that I was a militiaman. Maybe I had only one book in me — that was okay — and now I could go back to what I actually was. And lead, at least generally, a virtuous life. The brief celebrity had been good, the friends I'd made — the literary clique led by Georgi Radevych — and the supplemental income. Although the primary proceeds of the book went into the state bank, a personal allocation had bought the Škoda sitting outside, most of Ágnes's better clothes, and the big German radio set back at home. But now, the writing was probably finished. It certainly hadn't come at the dacha, once my wife had left me again, and the last two weeks had been an unproductive alcoholic misery.

But I said nothing. I forced a smile and looked at Ágnes in order to forget the old farm couple waiting for that next book.

# 3

Magda's father was still sturdy despite the weathering he'd taken over the years, and could probably even stand up to me, were it to ever come to that. He was nearly as big as I was, and I'd wondered often if this was part of Magda's attraction to me, that I was a large man, like her father.

We'd eaten the apples, which were blander than they smelled, and the women had gone inside. Teodor uncorked a bottle of northern red for us, but did not pour. This was the obligation of entering his house and eating his food: the talk. For a while, we only looked out at the thousand hectares he shared with nearly a hundred other families. Pavel burrowed frantically into clumps of hot earth.

"So it didn't work," he said finally. "What now?"

"The same."

"You wait for it to go to hell."

"Something like that."

Teodor gazed at the spindly bushes that separated their personal plot from the fields, then rocked his head from one side to the other.

This was the long silence in which Teodor worked. It made me — and he knew this — want to clarify that I wasn't simply admitting defeat. For the last four years I'd known what was going on. I'd seen it in her, in myself, and I'd done what I could. Maybe I wasn't bright enough to know what to do; maybe we were both stupid in such matters. So we listened to our friends and family, who told us we needed to get out of the city. We needed peace. Together in her parents' small dacha in the woods near Sárospatak, over the space of three weeks, we would find what we'd lost along the way. But Magda's patience had crumbled. *This is all too self-conscious,* she said before she left. *You can't force this kind of thing.*

"I don't think she wants to," I told him. "She's always the one to walk out."

"And you didn't chase her down, did you?"

I looked at my oversized hands, at the rings on each finger.

"You think you've got problems." He poured our glasses and watched as I swallowed mine quickly. "I got a letter from a friend in Warsaw. You know what's

22

been going on there? It's not in *The Spark*, I can tell you that." He tapped his glass on the table. "Demonstrations in Poznan, that's what. Back in June they had days of it. Workers out in the street because they were *hungry*. Then the troops came in, shooting. Seventy-four killed. Not by Russian troops, not like you'd think. But by their own boys. Polish soldiers killing Polish workers."

I poured myself another. He was right; I hadn't heard any of this.

"When that happens," said Teodor, "you get your bearings again. It's only in peace-time you have the luxury of divorce."

# 4

She kept Pavel on her lap as I drove, and the dog slept, blissful and mute. I asked her about tomorrow, her first day at school. She shrugged. "Did you study your French?"

"A little."

I had been hoping to get her into the French high school at the beginning of Yalta Boulevard. Her state-run school, the "Rosa Luxembourg," had never been much of an institution, even before the Liberation. But she'd failed the language test last May. "We can try again. There's no shame in a second chance."

She shrugged again, then after a moment asked the question, easily, trying to make it sound as if it hadn't been the only thing on her mind ever since I had shown up. "Mama didn't make it?"

I shook my head and watched the road, but could see her mouth moving as though she was chewing on something. Maybe she was.

"How did she get home?"

"What?"

"There's only one car."

I glanced into the rearview and noticed a hitchhiker with a small, hand-drawn sign: RELEASED FROM POLITICAL PRISON. I hadn't seen him when we approached, and that troubled me. "I drove her to the station."

"She took the train?"

"That's what I said."

I understood a fraction of what she was thinking. She could not fathom how anyone could calmly drive his wife to the train station and send her away. Not without some scene; some breakdown and reconciliation.

She nodded at the road. Her cheeks and forehead were very red from her three weeks under the provincial sun. I always insisted she wear a hat, but she thought she looked stupid in hats, which was untrue. And Magda's parents seemed to think any amount of sun was a virtue, that even when my daughter's pale skin turned red and crisp it was only a sign of health. She looked thin, too, and I rashly vowed never to leave her with them again.

"Did you have a good time?"

She grunted something incomprehensible.

"Well? What did you do?"

She pulled too hard on Pavel's ear, and the dog made a squeaking noise in his sleep. "Picked apples, bought apples, talked *apples*."

I laid a hand on her shoulder, then tugged her earlobe. "Miss me?"

She pulled her head away, but smiled. "Of *course* not."

# 5

They had been working on the Ninth District for as long as I could remember. Whenever I left town for an extended period, I fantasized that when I crossed back over the muddy Tisa and drove north, the roads would be smooth, the piles of broken concrete gone.

But now, as then, there were still three unfinished shells, and the road that wrapped around each unit of eight blocks had still not been paved. Long ago it had been plowed, some gravel thrown halfheartedly on it, but with each hard rain, the road slid into the ditches. Now that it was dry, the Škoda whined, climbing out of potholes, and crunched when it hit them. Pavel sprang up in the backseat, barking at a couple strays running past. Ágnes was unconcerned, but I calculated damages in my head. The six-story blocks of Unit 15 to our left, set at an angle to the road, were lit yellow by the descending sun, and I wondered if she was up there, watching us navigate the holes and turn off the road into the well of shadow between the buildings, trying to get home. At least I hoped this with every muscle in my tight, sweating hands.

Children at the next corner climbed over a hill of concrete slabs, and just beyond them two slumped, babushkaed women fed chickens in the heat that in the provinces had been almost invigorating; here, it was only stifling. I parked by two other, older Škodas and a Russian make I didn't know and grabbed our bags from the backseat. Ágnes took Pavel. As we stepped over dry rivulets, one of the women with the

26

chickens called to me: "Come arrest my brother, Comrade Inspector! I've been waiting a month!"

I measured out my syllables, as if for a child: "We've been through this, Claudia. I can't arrest your brother for drinking in his own home. Anyway, homicide inspectors don't take care of this. You have the number to call."

"See what I told you?" she said to her friend, who hadn't looked up from the chickens until now. "Just does his hours and goes *home*."

The friend shook her head, muttering something I couldn't hear. I started to tell Ágnes to hurry up, but she was already ahead of me, looking down on Pavel, his leg raised, pissing absently on the corner of our block, Unit 15:6.

The mailbox was empty, which was a good sign. The stairs had been recently cleaned, though nothing could get rid of the smell of boiled cabbage, and on each landing someone had set out leafy green plants. On the top floor, there were none. Our door was locked. The apartment felt stuffy, unlived-in, and I began speculating wildly. We opened the windows, the fresh air bringing in voices and the hack of a car coughing to life.

"She's not here," said Ágnes as she set Pavel on the rug. He did not run away, only peered around at the sofa and table and the wide German radio against the wall.

The bed didn't look slept in. But Magda made it up every morning; it told me nothing. The icebox, though, had fresh milk. Ágnes took out some water. She drank from the bottle and leaned against the counter, looking at me.

I hoped she wouldn't repeat the obvious, because if she did I was afraid I might shout at her. She didn't. She instead drank her water and left the kitchen, making *tsk tsk* sounds, calling for Pavel.

When she came across the note on the radio, I was still in the kitchen. The curtain was pulled, so it was very dark. Ágnes, from the doorway, said, "Daddy?"

I didn't answer right away, but noticed that she'd turned on the radio. Shostakovich murmured through the house. "What is it?"

"She left a note for you."

Something seemed to crack inside me. She had a small sheet of paper in her hand. It was almost weightless, and when I brought it into the light of the living room it shook in my hand. I unfolded it by the window and got a clear view of the angular script. I read it twice to be sure. Then I almost laughed. It was a telephone message. Stefan, my old friend and Militia partner, had called. While I was on vacation — if that's what it could be called — there'd been a case.

"Daddy?" said Ágnes. She sounded afraid, so I smiled and turned up the Shostakovich.

"It's nothing," I said, my smile now authentic. "Someone's been killed."

# 6

I slept on the couch, because this was where I'd been sleeping for months. The mosquitoes woke me, but I survived by pulling the sheet over my head and sweating. I heard her come in, saw the dim light from the stairwell as she opened the door, then smelled the cigarettes on her clothes when she passed. Pavel whimpered in recognition. She didn't look at me, and I didn't say a thing.

A thump to the head woke me. Ágnes's stern face was in mine — she was dressed. "We're going to be late," she said.

"Have you walked your dog?"

Her expression relaxed.

"Well then," I said.

I waited for the hot water to reach our floor, then shaved and gave myself a quick wash from the sink. I toweled off and went into the bedroom for clothes. Magda was still sleeping under a mess of sheets, her walnut hair curled against the pillow, and a bare, dirty foot stuck out below. I considered waking her, then realized she was probably already awake, playing dead until I left the apartment.

I drove Ágnes to a café in the center before sending her off to school. I always did this on first days — the drive and the breakfast were to mark something important. There was the usual mess of blue work clothes and old, quiet men in berets who perked up at the sight of a young girl. We sat by the window. "Are you nervous?" She shrugged and pushed her glasses closer to her eyes. "First days are exciting." But she didn't answer; she was becoming quieter as she got older. She was becoming more like her mother.

Emil Brod and Brano Sev were the only ones in the office this early, and Brano, behind his files, turned his round face with its three moles and gave the usual, polite half nod. The last time I'd seen him, the state security inspector had a mouth full of

30

metal braces, but now they were off, and his teeth, when he flashed a brief, self-conscious smile, were straight and true. It was a clever lie. We'd worked with him over a decade now, but like all the world's secret policemen, his world was run by a dark logic none of us was privy to.

Emil's blond hair was combed to a perfect part, like a schoolboy's. "You're back," he said, smiling.

"I'm back."

He sat on the corner of my desk. The smile wouldn't leave him. "So?"

He was one of the few I'd told. I shook my head.

Emil was the youngest in Homicide, only thirty. We'd given him a hard time when he was first transferred here — there were misunderstandings on all sides — but after a while he became part of the woodwork. "No decisions, I guess?"

"We wait."

"You know, Lena's still willing to talk with her. It might help."

I didn't want his crazy wife talking to mine. "I still don't think so."

"You hear about Leon?"

"What?"

"His mother died."

I looked up at him.

"Two weeks ago. We all went to the funeral, even the Comrade himself," he said, tilting his head toward Brano's desk. "Leon's taking it badly."

"I imagine."

"He adored Seyrana. I liked her a lot too."

"I never met her."

He shrugged in a way that suggested these kinds of events were beyond us all, then got off my desk.

There was nothing to do until Stefan showed up and walked me through the case, so I rolled a fresh sheet into my typewriter, gave the ring on my left pinkie a half turn, and stared at the page. I'd written the book on this, adapting my touch to the stiff T, the rusting carriage return, and its fragile, gray body.

A half hour later, the paper was still blank. I scratched a mosquito bite on my ankle, then typed a few words to get it going. But it went nowhere. I tapped my fingers on the edge of my desk and gazed at the ubiquitous portrait of Prime Minister Mihai — young, a wave of healthy hair, a smile that begged to be trusted.

Finally, Stefan stormed into the room, his satchel banging against the doors and clattering to the floor as he arrived at his desk. He was looking fatter than usual, and his shrapnel limp was stronger today, but he had a pink, lively glow above his sparse beard. "There you are," he said, out of breath.

We shook hands, a little formally.

"You get my message?"

"Magda wrote it down."

"Good, good." He rubbed a hand through his whiskers. He seemed to be deciding something. "What are we waiting for?" He got his satchel again, and I followed him out of the office.

# 7

I'd known Stefan since childhood. When you know someone that long, the actual circumstances of your introduction disappears. We went to school together, got into trouble together, and lusted after the same girls together. It was a joke, around the time of my marriage, that he'd never forgiven me for seducing Magda, because we'd both stared at her from across the schoolhouse, gauging our prospects. But by the wedding we weren't boys anymore. It was 1939 and we were preparing to meet the Germans, who had crossed over from Czechoslovakia and were ready to make quick work of us. Stefan was wounded that first week by a mine and sent back home. I survived the whole month and a half of useless fighting, all the way to the defeat in May. But by the time I returned home to Magda, and to the news that my parents had died when an errant bomb fell on their house, I was sick and mentally worthless. I had to begin anew.

I wrote about my condition in the novel, a few sentences about how the act of killing Fascists seemed to take away my humanity, and when the war was over I thought it would never return — I was surprised that those lines made it past the Culture Ministry editors. But the humanity did return, months after the war, with Stefan's help. He had become a police officer in the occupied Capital, and he continually came out to visit us at Teodor's house, trying to save me from my self-pity with the offer of a job. It took a lot of prodding, but by 1940 I accepted it, and two years later Ágnes was born. Two years after that, I was best man at Stefan's marriage to Daria Vídra, the first girl who'd ever slept with him. But by the end of the decade they had split up. He'd been alone ever since.

In the car, he adjusted the mirror and

went over the details. On Friday morning, a neighbor had smelled gas around the victim's apartment door and informed the building supervisor, who, when he unlocked the door, was almost knocked unconscious by the fumes. But he made it inside and turned off the stove by reaching over the body of the deceased. "His name's Josef Maneck."

"So it's a suicide?"

Stefan leaned into a sharp swerve around a trio of broom-sellers. "That's the easy answer, but I'm not sure. He'd been beaten up pretty badly."

"Any word on that?"

He stopped behind a cart overflowing with yellow squash. The farmer tapped his stick on the tired mare's rump. "The supervisor could only say that the victim was a drunk. I got the name of his bar."

"Nothing in the apartment?"

"I went through it once, but didn't find anything."

"And the neighbors?"

"Heard nothing, saw nothing. The usual."

We were in the last hot days of September, and everyone seemed to know this. Women wore uncovered heads and those tight, unignorable skirts that had become fashionable that summer; the men went without jackets. It was as if they were taking this final chance to soak up the sun. I saw a few familiar faces in the bookstore displays, then wondered how Ágnes was doing at school. "What now?"

"Let's hear from the coroner," he said, "then visit his watering hole."

He took a few more turns, scratched at his beard, and asked how the writing was coming. I told him the writing wasn't coming along at all. He didn't seem fazed. "So did the countryside do its magic for you and Magda?"

I shook my head. "I heard about Leonek's mother."

"Heart attack." He turned into the Unity Medical Complex parking lot. "Happens every day, and she was old enough." His eyes roamed the cars for a spot. "Leonek's fallen apart, though. Remember when Sergei was killed?"

1946: Leonek's longtime partner, with a bullet in the back of his head down by the Tisa.

"Same as he was then," Stefan said. "He looks like hell, he doesn't come into work half the time, and he can't even do the job when he does." He put on the parking brake, turned off the engine, and looked at

36

me. "That man wears his grief on his sleeve. It's not pretty."

He said this with more scorn than I would have expected. In the last years — since his divorce and the more recent death of his own mother — he'd been losing his ability to empathize with misery. I'd noticed this often and once made the mistake of mentioning it to Magda. Her answer: *And you can?*

In the basement morgue, the new coroner set aside his newspaper. "Markus Feder," he announced as he shook our hands with his rubber-gloved one. Yuldashev, the previous coroner, had moved back home to Tashkent in July. He'd done it in a hurry, without any announcement, and they replaced him with this redheaded child who delicately pulled back a white sheet covering the body of Josef Maneck.

Fifty-one, very thin, flesh loose over his limbs. There were black welts on his face, around his cheeks and jaw, and his skin was white except where the sun had browned his head and hands. His ears, lips, and the fingernails on his clenched hands were blue. Markus Feder repositioned the head for us to see clearly. "I cleaned the froth and blood off the lips, and we had to

37

change his drawers because of the defecation. I also pushed the tongue back in to get a look inside the mouth. See here," he said, and pulled open an eyelid. Around the cornea was a field of burst capillaries. "It was the gas, all right. Suicide."

"And what about these bruises?" I waved a hand at the face.

Markus Feder grimaced. "Somebody hit him, sure, but that was hours before he died."

"I wonder who," said Stefan.

"That, Comrade Inspectors, is your job." He covered the dead man with the sheet.

# 8

It had no name. Before the war, it had been named after the owner, but he had been shipped off somewhere when his bar was nationalized. Now, it was only CAFÉ-BAR and, below the sign, on a small white placard, #103. It was the kind of dingy place I would lurk in when I came back from the Front. In these places maimed veterans grumbled into their shot glasses and made menacing noises at anyone who looked whole. For the price of a drink you could learn their stories or see their scars. I had no scars to show but my gaunt body, though I grumbled too.

Stefan wrinkled his nose. There were a couple men in the back corner, hunched in the darkness over their tables, and we could smell them from the door. The bartender looked at us through round glasses, and said, "What, then?"

"Not much a of place you're running here," said Stefan.

"If you've come to complain —"

"We've come to ask questions." Stefan unfolded his green certificate to display the Militia hawk.

I stepped up to the bar. "One of your customers."

The man flinched, just slightly. My size does that to people sometimes.

"Josef Maneck," said Stefan. He climbed up on a stool and settled in for a long talk.

Café-bar #103's portrait of Mihai, suspiciously sandwiched between vodka bottles, was blackened by years of smoke. The bartender squeezed a dirty rag, and a few drops fell on the counter. Then he set it down and soaked them up. He looked at me. "Don't know any Josef Maneck."

"Sure you do," said Stefan. "About my height. But thin, very thin. A drunk."

"Oh," said the bartender, smiling, still looking only at me. "A *drunk*. *That* guy."

"This drunk's dead," I told him.

His smile went away, and he stepped back, holding the rag in both hands. "What did you say his name was?"

"Josef Maneck," said Stefan.

The bartender took off his glasses. He put them back on. "Maybe." When I leaned against the bar, he finally looked at Stefan. "Maybe I know him. Did he have a way of blinking? You know." He blinked a few times to demonstrate.

"When we saw him his eyes were shut," said Stefan.

He looked at me again, as if I'd confirm it. Then he peered past us at the dark corner. "Hey, Martin! Martin!"

One of the two figures shifted a little, the head rose, then swung slowly toward us.

"Martin, is your friend dead? The one with the blink."

I could just make out his features in the darkness — pink eyelids, wide mouth, high cheekbones. His face sat still a moment, then his lips parted. "Josef?" His voice was like gravel in a ditch.

"That's the one, Martin," said Stefan. He walked over. The second drunk, deeper in the blackness, didn't budge. "Did you know he's dead?"

"Josef?" Martin repeated.

I kept an eye on the bartender.

"Come on, Martin." Stefan stood over him now, his wide gut level with the man's face. "Why don't you tell us about your friend."

"He was crazy," the bartender whispered.

I turned to him. "How's that?"

"That man was trouble." He picked up his rag again. "Started fights all the time. Isn't that right, Martin?"

Martin, by Stefan's belly, closed his pink eyes and considered it.

"Did he start fights, Martin?" asked Stefan. "Is that what your friend did?"

There were pumpkinseeds in a dish on the counter, and I collected some in my hand. "Was he a good fighter?" I asked the bartender. "Did he win his fights?"

"That nut?" He shook his head. "Never. He was crazy. He'd start a fight, then get brutalized. Every time."

Stefan's voice: "What do you say, Martin? Could you have beaten him up?"

"He was a nut, all right." The bartender adjusted his glasses and looked at me. "So how'd he die?"

"Come on, Martin. It's your friend we're talking about! Give us some help."

I chewed on a pumpkinseed, but it was soggy, so I spit it out in my hand and dumped it back into the dish. I had heard enough, and the familiarity of this place disturbed me. It was all so obvious; there was no reason to be here. Josef Maneck was a drunk who had reached the end of his tether. He got into a fight and lost, like every other time. He stumbled back to his apartment and, faced with the reality of where his life had brought him, decided to finally end it. He turned on the gas and sat on the kitchen floor. I had seen enough of his kind to know it was the inevitable end.

Stefan was squatting beside the drunk, a hand on his frayed jacket, shaking to keep him awake. "Come on, Martin. You can do it. Tell me about your friend."

I scratched a mosquito bite on the back of my hand.

"Martin, tell me, did you kill your friend? Is that what happened? You can tell old Stefan."

"I'll be in the car," I said, but didn't know if he heard me. As I left, the bartender washed out the dish where I'd dumped my chewed seed.

# 9

He was in there a while longer, but on the drive back only said that there wasn't any-

42

thing to be learned from an alcoholic like that. We were in agreement.

Leonek had finally arrived at the station. He and Emil and Chief Moska were over by Brano's desk. That in itself was strange; no one spent time with Brano Sev. But through them we saw a tall man with a thin mustache leaning back against the desk, his long legs crossed at the ankle. His top half was animated, arms moving around in his well-tailored jacket, smiling, speaking in heavy, grinding syllables. He had a horrendous Russian accent.

Chief Moska, though, looked as weary as ever. I'd watched him aging since I joined the police force during the German Occupation, back when his particular bureaucratic genius found a way to hide Stefan's and my war records; he saved us. And then, when the Russians marched in and we were renamed the People's Militia, his hair went gray overnight. He waved us over. "Meet Mikhail, guys."

The Russian stood up to shake our hands. He did it somewhat stiffly, but winked at me as he gripped my fingers. He didn't wink at Stefan, and I'm still not sure why.

"Mikhail Kaminski," he told us both.

"From Moscow," said Moska, and I

think we all noticed then, if we hadn't before, the similarity between our chief's name and that capital. He seemed almost apologetic about it, his self-conscious smile revealing his two missing teeth on the left side. "Mikhail's here for consultations."

Brano Sev sat at his desk as passively as usual. Mikhail Kaminski was here to consult with Sev, no one else, but from that blank expression you couldn't guess it.

"All *consultation* means is a lot of dull paper-pushing," said Kaminski, smiling broadly to show us he wasn't about to start doing any of that foolishness. "Where's the closest bar?"

We all stared at his attempted joke.

"Seriously, though, I want everyone to feel free to approach me at any time. I'm from Moscow, you know, not the Moon."

This Muscovite wasn't from the Moon, but he was from Lubyanka. Even without his uniform, his KGB stripes were visible to all of us.

"Come on, guys," Moska said, knowing when to step in and clear things up, "we've all got a lot of work to do."

At his desk, Stefan and I looked over the coroner's report. A simple suicide was, in the end, only that, and I tried to explain this to him. "But why now?" he asked.

44

"Why does a man commit suicide now of all times?"

"Because it builds up. You don't know how it can build up in a man. None of us does."

He laid his chubby hands on the desk, spread wide. "But look around. Things haven't been this good for a long time. The market's fuller than ever before, political prisoners are coming back home, and you can read damn near anything you want. Why *now?*"

I slouched deeper into my chair. "Tell me about him, then. What was he before he became a drunk?"

Stefan moved some pages until he came to a typewritten sheet. "Josef Maneck, born 1905 in Miskolc. His family ended up in the Capital in 'twenty-five, when his father opened a frame maker's shop. The father died in 'forty-three, during the Occupation, and Josef took over his shop. He ran it for four years until, presumably because of connections, he became acting curator of the Museum of National Contemporary Art. In 1953 he was transferred to the Stryy Mineral Springs bottling plant outside town."

"A bottling plant?"

"I suppose he wasn't so good with the Culture Ministry. But he was no better on the assembly line. He was fired last year, for not showing up enough."

"That takes a lot of work."

"Arrested twice since for public drunkenness and fistfighting. Overnight stays."

"And you need a reason for him to kill himself?"

Stefan stared through the page. "I guess I do."

I noticed Leonek in the corner, at the coatrack, putting on his jacket to leave. He was a way out of this pointless conversation, so I did it, beginning something that would unravel so much. I asked Stefan to wait a moment, then went over to Leonek and told him I was sorry about his mother.

He looked surprised. "Thanks, Ferenc."

"Come over for dinner. Okay? Tomorrow night."

"Thanks, but no."

"Really." I put a hand on his arm to make my sincerity clear. "Magda's a good cook, you'll thank yourself for it."

He shook his head again, his leathery Armenian face looser and more lost than I'd seen it before, his dark eyes drifting. But he was considering it, I could tell.

"Six o'clock, okay? We'll leave from here, go get a drink, and be there in time to eat. It's settled."

"Why'd you do that?" Stefan asked when I returned.

"He just looks terrible."

"He'll work through it." Stefan spoke with that same cold edge I'd heard earlier. Then he went back into the details of Josef Maneck's miserable life, but by then I wasn't listening to a word.

Mikhail Kaminski left with Brano, loudly describing the glories of Moscow nightlife, and Emil and Moska left together. Stefan asked if I wanted a drink. I said no. "You want to get right back to her, do you?" He smiled. "Come on, spend some time with your oldest friend for once." But it wasn't going to work. I was stuck in thoughts of Leonek's dead mother, and of those days, long ago, in dark bars like the one we'd visited. After Stefan sighed and left, I called home.

"Hello, Daddy."

"How was your day?"

"What day?"

"Don't give me that."

Ágnes sighed. "It was satisfactory, Daddy. Very satisfactory."

"Your teachers? How are they?"

"Too soon to tell."

"And your friends? Are all of them still around?"

"You don't even know my friends."

I knew a few, but it didn't matter. "Your mother there?"

"She's downstairs, talking to that old woman again. Claudia. Want me to get her?"

"Just give her a message, okay?"

"I suppose."

"Tell her we're having a guest for dinner tomorrow. Can you do that?"

"When should I tell her you're coming home? She *always* asks."

"I'll be," I began, then realized I didn't know. "Tell her I'll probably be late. There's a lot of work backed up here."

"I'll tell her."

From her tone it was clear that Ágnes saw right through me.

I sat straight in front of the typewriter. I'd rolled in a white sheet, twisted my ring, and now I waited for something to come. After a while, though, it was too dark to see.

# 10

I knocked on Georgi's door after having walked down to the Tisa, trying to summon inspiration from the black water. The summer heat had brought out the smell of decay, and when the clamoring noise of a dogcatcher's van filled with its barking victims flew by, the stink became too much.

Georgi let out a rude exclamation, kissed my cheeks with his wine-stained lips, and pulled me inside. His face was red, and the smile lines that sprouted from his eyes were white. "Have you met Louis? He's leaving tomorrow! Come on, come on." There were a lot of voices coming from the kitchen.

"Louis?"

"The *Frenchman*." He reached up to my shoulder and urged me along.

They were up at this hour because they were always up — this is something they prided themselves on — ten or twelve men and women squeezed around a tiny kitchen table, drinking. Louis, the Frenchman, was in town, and everyone had made the pilgrimage to Georgi's to see this emissary from the West. I'd forgotten.

"Louis!" Georgi called, and a fat man with oily, tasseled hair rolled his head back.

"*Oui?*"

"*Mon ami*" said Georgi. "Meet another of our writers!"

"This is a nation of writers!" Louis shouted, then rose wearily to his feet and stuck out a hand. "*You're* a big writer."

He gave the kind of firm, rough shake

49

men give when they consider my size, then turned my hand so he could see my rings, my sentimental reminders of the war.

"Each finger, huh?" Louis grinned as he settled back down. "I bet those rings have got some stories to them. *Writers!*"

It was a kitchen of writers — Karel and Vera, Daniel, even Miroslav, and more — and I wanted none of them. All I'd wanted was Georgi, a quiet talk, and then some sleep. But Georgi couldn't do anything quietly tonight. His Frenchman was in town. His French communist poet — an existentialist, no less.

The Frenchman sat up and said a few words of a love poem by Paul Eluard that I did not understand, something about wasps flowering and a necklace of windows. When he paused long enough we knew he was done, so we clapped. He beamed. Karel got up, and I took his chair. Louis said, "Now that you're sitting I can face you!"

Vera and Ludmila laughed, and when they quieted, I saw Vera's big, drunken eyes holding on to me. Her black hair hung loosely down her back.

"They told me about it," he said. "This book of yours."

*"Oh great."*

"I hear it's autobiographical. That so?"

He spoke our language surprisingly well.

"Everything's autobiographical, isn't it?"

Louis laughed expressively, as though he were on a stage and had to project to the back rows. "Very good, very good!"

I hadn't said it to be funny, but they were all laughing with him, even Georgi, and I didn't know if this was because it actually was funny, or if they were trying to stay in France's good favors.

"I just finished an epic poem on the most glorious of all human desires: revenge. I swear, there is nothing more sincere. What about your book?"

"It's about my time during the war."

The Frenchman stopped laughing and put on a very serious face. "And what did you do during the war?"

"Killed people, of course."

Louis winked. "Me, I hid under my mother's skirt!"

Everyone laughed again, and even I cracked a smile.

# 11

The conversation was literary before it became political. It started with some French poets I hadn't read, then some Italians I'd read in translation, and finally came back home. Karel, Vera's husband, brought up August Menish, who had been released from internal exile two months before and was busy editing his prison memoir. "It's going to be incredible," he told us.

"That's what you told us about Brest's camp book," Vera said as she put out her cigarette. "And that ended up worthless." The smile on her gaunt philosopher's face was directed at me.

"Menish has the books behind him — he's got the evidence," said Karel. But no one was listening to him anymore.

Louis talked about the bus strike going on in Montgomery, Alabama, in the United States. A couple people waved his comments away, because we'd heard enough of the story from *The Spark* — further evidence of capitalism's racist underbelly — but Louis insisted that we listen. "You should hear this reverend they've got leading them. His name's *King* — a doctor, in fact. He's one hell of a speaker. He's putting nonviolent resistance on the map."

"That was Gandhi," said Ludmila. "The Americans would have you think they invented water next."

"Didn't they?" said someone I didn't know.

Miroslav pulled out a pack of cards to start the games, so I moved to the deflated sofa in the living room and half listened to Vera provoke Louis into a debate on existentialism — she questioned his credentials, which was something Vera loved to do. I stopped listening. On the far wall was Georgi's old poster for the Fifth Soviet Five-Year Plan, of kerchiefed women working in fields, below the enormous face of Stalin filling the sky, a chalk-scribbled beard over his wide chin. Georgi had been drunk when he defaced it, and everyone over that night — myself included — had applauded.

Georgi Radevych was known as a drunk and, briefly, as the author of a small volume of state-published poetry that made his name. He had used that momentary fame to secure his position as an arbitrator of all things literary. He gathered writers in his home and made them perform for him, and sometimes from these evenings self-published manuscripts emerged that bore his name on the front page. After my own little book came out, he showed up at the Militia station and introduced himself. I couldn't help but admire that. He had a card with the profession *poet* inscribed in cursive beneath his name. He invited me to his evenings, and over the last four years I had met almost everyone who did any worthwhile writing in the Capital, before forgetting their names. They came through his apartment, drank his wine, and performed impromptu readings under the gaze of his bearded Stalin. Even I got into the mood now and then and said some spontaneous lines, but those were rare intoxicated moments, and seldom worth a listen.

Georgi flopped into a chair and asked how the criminal classes were coming along. I told him about the dead man in the kitchen. He waved his red hands. "This is what passes for criminality these days?"

"Suicide's illegal."

"A sin, you mean. Just a sin. And a coward's way of breaking the law. You've got to stay alive in order to face the punishment. Tell me, Ferenc," he said, dropping to almost a whisper, "what have you got for my new collection?"

He had been asking for months. They were going to put out another volume of writings, dissident writings perhaps, on the theme of responsibility. He wanted a piece from everyone. Another basement-printed book — maybe just some stapled pages to pass around to friends and talk over in smoky living rooms like this one. "I don't have anything."

"Weren't you writing in the provinces?"

"I was trying to restart my marriage."

"And?"

I drank the wine, but it had a spoiled edge. I set it on an end table. Somebody in the kitchen turned on the radio, and we heard static until voices rose through it. It was the American station that you could sometimes hear from Germany, broadcasting eastward. In certain weather it drifted through. News and music and more news. Georgi's eyes closed as he meditated on the commentary on developments in Poland: negotiations between Moscow and Warsaw to end the unrest. "The Frenchman, he's staying here?"

He nodded, eyes still shut. "Been here two weeks. But tomorrow it's off to Prague, and then back home to Paris. A glorious tour of the People's Republics."

"There was no trouble, then? Him staying here? No knocks on the door?"

Georgi opened his eyes, then his hands, and spoke with the simplicity of spirit that reminded me that I actually liked him. "We're living in the most wonderful of times, my friend. And if we're not, then please, don't let me know."

# 12

"I'll tell you what I'm trying to do," said the Frenchman. He had come in after Georgi left and leaned forward on the edge of the chair. "I'm trying to grasp this situation we're in right now. It's unprecedented, you know, in human history. The entire planet is split between two camps, and the rest of us are intermediaries. We're the ones fighting it out. I want to find a way to express this puppetry. Because that's what we are. We're puppets of history, and we're playing out a tragedy. Those hydrogen bombs are ready to be dropped. There are enough idiots in the White House and the Central Committee to ensure one of those buttons is going to be pressed. And the longer the wait, the bigger the explosions — they'll put bombs into space before long. I'm not kidding, all our leaders are mad. In the West we vote them in, but the vanity only makes them more crazy. Don't you see? All our efforts are toward our own annihilation."

He was drunk, but this was something he'd thought about for a long time and needed no sobriety to express — just a listener.

"Now, I'm not trying to deride this situation. I'll leave that to the pacifists. It simply is, and I want to see it as clearly as I can. Without prejudice."

"So what's this?" I asked. "Your visit here. Research?"

He crossed a leg over his knee with some effort, then gripped his raised ankle. "Yes, maybe, in part. But I've spent a lot of time here over the years, and I always have friends to see. A very special one recently got out of the camps, thank God. This soil is in my heart," he said, touching his nose. "You should see the miles of paperwork I had to fill out in order to come here. Then the checks at the border, the soldiers who went through my luggage. They kept half the gifts I brought! I'll never see them again." He frowned. "You probably don't see it in the newspaper, but the East Berliners are running through the border like mad. Nobody can stop them. There's not enough room in the refugee camps."

"They just pick up and leave their homes?"

"They're desperate, Ferenc." He leaned closer. "You know what happens when I walk down the streets here? People follow me."

"State security?"

"No — *investors*. They want to buy French francs. They can smell it on me." He paused. "And do you know, Comrade, what Western money smells like?"

I shook my head.

"Soap," he said. "It's the smell of a clean body washed with Western deodorant soap."

I settled back, remembering the excuse for a bath I'd put myself through that morning, in the sink, and all those weeks in the dacha. "You're not a communist after all."

He smiled. "I'm a communist all right. I just haven't seen an ounce of real communism since crossing the Iron Curtain."

There was commotion in the kitchen; someone had won a hand. But it was a weak enthusiasm. They were getting tired.

"Georgi tells me you're having trouble writing," he said.

I was surprised Georgi considered it important enough to mention. "It's just not coming."

"But no ideas? Nothing at all?"

"A couple things, maybe."

He gave a fatigued smile. "You've heard, though, haven't you, that plot is dead?

"Is it?"

"I read it in *l'Humanite*, some editorial. Plot is a capitalist construct made to give lives a false sense of totality, so they can be valued like a wheel of Brie, then bought and sold." He grinned. "Luckily, I'm a poet. It doesn't affect me."

Vera and Karel appeared, and when she kissed my cheeks, I thought I heard her whisper, *Call me,* but wasn't sure. When she pulled away she smiled conspiratorially. Karel shook my hand. The others gave quiet greetings on their ways out, and I knew then that Georgi had told them all about Magda and me. I was too tired to be bothered by it. They filed by the sofa, asking why they never saw me these days, telling me to give them calls. Their requests for a call were entirely different from Vera's. They told Louis they would see him again, and, with an elegant bow, he said that this was undoubtedly true. And then, after what seemed like forever, they were gone. Georgi settled on the other corner of the sofa, and the three of us were silent for a while. Georgi laughed once, but when we looked at him he shook his head.

"*Alors,*" said Louis. He leaned into a standing position.

Georgi stood as well. "Staying?"

I shrugged.

"Tomorrow, then."

Once they were in their rooms, I got another glass of wine, lit a cigarette, and stretched out on the sofa. Vera was behind my lids. Almost a year before, at a Christmas gathering, on that same sofa, she lay on top of me and kissed me deeply. I could feel the weight of her slight body, her narrow hips, her small breasts against me. It was a wonderful kiss; I hadn't had one like that from Magda in a long time. Ever since then she had watched me when we were all together, and it had taken a long time to rid her stare of the heat that spread along my neck and cheeks. Now, though, her suspicions about Magda's and my problems had been verified. I rolled over.

# 13

Georgi woke me by shaking my shoulder. "Telephone." He was in a thick beige robe that had his initials *GR*, on the breast. "Your oaf." I knew then that it was Stefan.

"Magda said to try for you there. You're no longer sleeping at home?"

"What's going on?"

"Come see me at Josef Maneck's apartment. Here's the address."

I yawned. "What is this, Stefan? The man killed himself."

"Just get over here, okay?"

Georgi was frying eggs when I came into the kitchen. "Is the oaf requesting your presence?"

"Shut up, Georgi." I sat at the table and started filing the playing cards back into their boxes. The empty wine bottles still lined the counter, and every surface was stained by red circles. There was a sour stink in the air. Georgi brought over two plates.

"Want coffee?"

I nodded.

"Then make it yourself, I'm going back to bed."

I put some water on to boil and searched for the grounds.

"What do you think of Louis?"

There were enough grounds for a few cups. "He's all right."

"He told me that things here are looking pretty bad."

"In what way?"

"Says this won't last. This thaw."

"What does he know? He's a tourist."

"No, he's lived here before, and he's visited a lot."

61

"Well, then, he's a foreigner."

"Not really — his last name's Rostek. His grandfather's one of us, from one of those purges, you know, in the 'teens — if you could afford it, you went to Paris. His opa could afford it." Georgi brought his empty plate to the sink. "I worry too much in the mornings."

The water was boiling, so I added the grounds. The froth ran over, hissing on the burner. "Don't worry so much," I told him. "And don't listen to foreigners. They mean well, but they know nothing about our lives."

He considered that a moment, then got two cups out of the cabinet. "Give me one of those, will you?"

Josef Maneck's apartment was in the old town, a three-room, high-ceilinged place that had been his father's. Now it was no one's. The old furniture was still here, dusty chairs and cabinets and trinkets collected over too long a life. On the walls were faded portraits in ornate frames, and a few empty frames stuffed recklessly behind the sofa.

Stefan was sitting on Maneck's sunken mattress, reading a book. He showed me the cover — a state edition of poetry by someone I vaguely remembered — before throwing it on the dirty, knotted rug. "Josef liked his verse," said Stefan. "Pretty uplifting stuff for a suicidal drunk."

"Someone gave it to him. How long have you been here?"

"I spent the night."

He leaned forward with his hands on the bed and lifted his weight with a grunt. He passed me on his way to the living room and took a notepad off the coffee table. The top page had been ripped out, but Stefan had rubbed a pencil all over the second page. Not all the scribbled letters were recovered.

$$A - TO - ÍN$$
$$K - - R - 5 -$$
$$2 - 2. - 0 -$$

"Antonín," said Stefan. "The rest, I don't know — address and phone number, maybe. But I'm sure about the name."

"So he knew someone named Antonín. Does it really matter?"

"It could matter." His voice was trying to encourage me to believe, with him, that this suicide was more than it seemed. "I've been all over the place looking for an address book. Nothing. But I'll bet that if we can find Antonín, we'll learn something important."

I doubted this, but got up with him and handed him his hat from the coffee table.

# 14

Café-bar #103 had just opened, and the bartender, when he saw us come in, said with sudden, false brightness, "Comrade Inspectors, you've returned!" He set two somewhat clean glasses on the counter. "What will it be?"

Stefan climbed onto a stool while I stood beside him. "This Josef Maneck," he said. "Did you ever see him with other people? Someone named Antonín?"

The bartender's smile faded. "Not much business lately. Won't you have a drink?"

"We'll just take some answers," said Stefan.

"Give me a coffee," I told him.

"Coffee? Come on, Comrade Inspector."

"Palinka," I said.

He grabbed a bottle of apricot brandy from the shelf behind him. As he poured, he said, "Well," then corked the bottle and set it beside my glass. "The nut only came in alone. He was that kind."

"What kind?" asked Stefan.

"A friend of nobody. You know what I

64

mean." The bartender pushed his eye-glasses up the arch of his nose, then leaned an elbow on the counter. "He came in alone, ordered his drinks quietly, but as he got drunk he ordered them louder, like I couldn't hear." He shook his head. "We could all hear him."

I picked up my brandy. "So he always came in alone."

"Of course he did. No one would spend time with that guy, except maybe Martin. But Martin only did it for the drinks. Martin will do most anything for a drink. Sometimes I get him to clean up the toilet for a drink, and he does a hell of a good job."

"But did he ever talk to you?" said Stefan. "About anyone he knew. An Antonín?"

He put away the second, empty glass. "If he ever did, I wasn't listening."

The brandy was coarse; it burned my tongue. "What about Martin?"

"What about him?"

"You said Josef Maneck talked to Martin." I placed some koronas on the counter, more than the drink cost.

He looked at the money. "That's what I said. But I don't know what they talked about." He placed his hand over the coins.

Stefan looked at me, at the drink beside the bartender's hand, then at the bartender. "Where does this Martin live?"

He slid the coins off the counter. "That, I can tell you."

Around the corner, down an alley, and through a misaligned side door that did not shut all the way. There was a short, dark entryway that led to a curtain of beads missing half its strings. "Martin?" Stefan called through the beads. "You in there, Martin?"

We heard a horrendous, wrenching cough.

It was an old storage room, with a couple rusted shelves in the corner. I wondered for an instant how someone could end up in a hole like this, in a time of assigned housing. Then I saw Martin on a thin mattress, his back against the stone wall, trying to light a cigarette, but the matches wouldn't catch. No paperwork, that's how you ended up here. Lost, or sold for a drink. From a high barred window enough cold light came through to see the cockroaches scurrying from our entrance. Here, beneath the surface of the Capital, lived the lumpenproletariat — or, as *The Spark* would put it: *the underworld criminals, antisocial shirkers and prostitutes.* The place stank of feces.

We stayed on our side of the room. "Having a rough morning, Martin?"

Martin's face was swollen and red-veined. He dropped the matches, then leaned to pick them up again. "You got a light?"

"We've got questions, Martin."

I saw on the rusted shelves his only possessions — a pair of lopsided shoes, a frayed jacket, and an empty bottle of rubbing alcohol. I threw my lighter; it landed beside his bare foot. When his eyes focused, he made something like a grin and took it.

Stefan stepped forward. "Just a few questions."

He lit the cigarette and drew on it deeply, his whole body rising, then coughed again, lips wet.

Stefan squatted to his level. "Remember your friend, Josef Maneck? He talked to you, didn't he?"

Martin wiped his mouth with the back of his hand and took another drag. He nodded, maybe in answer to the question.

"Did Josef tell you about his other friends, Martin? Did he tell you about a friend named Antonín?"

The lighter was no longer in Martin's hand. I didn't know where it was.

"Surely he told you about Antonín. That's his oldest friend. Did he talk to you about his friends, Martin?"

That's when I noticed the source of the stink. In the corner, behind the shelves, were a few fresh turds. Martin had been too drunk to make it outside last night, or this morning.

"Stefan," I said, but he didn't hear me.

"Tell us about his friends, Martin, come on."

"I don't know," Martin said. He sat up a little, as if to look dignified, and took another drag. "He talked, yeah, but he didn't tell me nothing." His voice was strangled and labored, and I wondered how a man like that could keep taking breaths.

"Now we're getting somewhere." Stefan settled a little lower, on his haunches. "So what did Josef talk to you about? He bought you drinks, he talked to you. What about, Martin?"

"Nothing nothing. I didn't listen."

"You're not that rude, Martin. He told you about his friends, maybe, or how he used to be an art curator. Surely he talked about that."

Martin squinted, then nodded slowly. "Yes, art. He wouldn't shut up. Art."

"Of course he did. And he told you why he stopped doing that. Why he stopped being a curator."

Martin's next drag was aborted by a fit

of angry hacking that turned his face purple and ridged his neck with fat veins. Stefan looked away finally, and I caught his eye and nodded at the door. He shook his head and turned back.

"Why did he stop working in the museum, Martin? You know the reason. It was a good job, why give it up?"

"And you'll leave me alone?"

"Sure, Martin. Then we'll leave you alone."

He squinted again, trying to think it over. His eyes were red all the way through. "He couldn't."

"Couldn't what?"

"Couldn't live with himself."

"Why couldn't he live with himself?"

"Because."

I cleared my throat. The stink was making my eyes water.

"Because *why*, Martin?"

"He was terrible," said Martin. "A terrible person."

"How's that? How was he terrible?"

I stepped forward, and it shot out of me: "Because he was a goddamned *drunk*, for Christ's sake!"

They both looked at me, Martin with some hesitant surprise, Stefan clearly angry.

Then, just as I had done the day before, I turned around and left.

# 15

Since we had brought separate cars, I drove back to the station to wait for him. On the way, I saw wives in windows brushing off their shutters and waving away pigeons, and in Victory Square there was a procession of university students. They had signs — small, hand-drawn boards — that demanded accountability within the universities. LET US GRADE PROFESSORS, SO WE CAN TRUST THEIR GRADES! Along their edge, a handful of bored, uniformed Militia looked on.

I didn't regret my outburst; I didn't care what Stefan thought. I'd had enough of his worthless needling, because when I looked into Martin's decomposing features I felt like I was one with him again, in those black bars just after the war. Like I had never crawled out of that subhuman existence.

Leonek gave a smile for my benefit, but when I talked to him there was still that underlying misery. "You're coming over tonight, then?"

"New tie and everything." He flipped it up for me to see. It was green silk with small brown dots forming diagonal lines.

"I'm sure Magda will appreciate it."

Emil passed me on his way to Leonek's desk and gave a wink. "When are you going to invite me and Lena over for dinner?"

"When you get a decent tie."

Mikhail Kaminski had set up a chair across from Brano Sev, and they were hunched on either side of the desk, conferring over typewritten pages from the files of state security. Their voices were a distant rumble.

I knocked on Moska's door and waited for his voice: "Enter." He was sitting at his desk, large hands prone atop piles of papers, and I was struck by the suspicion that he had been sitting like that all morning, immobile, while outside children played loudly on the sidewalk.

I sat across from him. "What do you know about this guy?"

"Who?"

"Kaminski."

He glanced up to make sure I'd latched the door, then patted his shirt pockets and the coat hanging from his chair until he found a pack of cigarettes. He offered me one. We blew smoke simultaneously into the stuffy office. "Moscow sent him, but I only heard about it the day before he

71

showed up. What can I tell you?"

"You can tell me why he's here."

"Does he need a reason?" He didn't seem to like the taste of his cigarette, so he put it out. "You've heard about what's been going on in Poland. It wasn't so long ago they sent tanks into East Berlin and shot a lot of people. You think they want to do that here? They don't like sending in tanks, any more than we like receiving tanks." He readjusted himself in his groaning chair. "Kaminski apparently asked for this assignment. He was posted here after the war and claims he's in love with our country. Says he wants to help shepherd our path to socialism. I checked his file, and it's true — he was here after the war. I don't think either of us knew him, but he worked with Sev. And you know what that means."

It meant that, just after the war, Mikhail Kaminski from the KGB and Brano Sev from our own Ministry for State Security were partners in the quick cleansing of the Capital. It meant sudden disappearances in post offices, government ministries, and even the Militia offices — old friends of questionable loyalty vanished, replaced by fresh-faced automatons. Only Moska's deft juggling of paperwork kept our office relatively untouched. I said, "So this guy is an old hack."

72

"He's an ambitious prick. Be careful around him. He puts on a good face, but take a look at his hand when he talks. He's got a nervous trigger finger."

I smiled.

"How was your vacation?"

"Didn't get much rest."

"I don't think you mean that in a good way."

"I don't." I smoked his cigarette a while longer. "I think you're going to hear from Stefan. About me, that is."

He frowned.

"He's obsessed with this case, he's got us going all over the place for nothing."

"It is his case."

"Maybe." I put the cigarette out. "But I don't have to like it."

"Just bear with him, he'll figure it out soon enough. He's a good inspector."

"He can't seem to believe that anyone could commit suicide in these times."

"But you can," said Moska.

"Yes. I can."

# 16

Stefan was there when I came out. He didn't have his bag, and he was standing at his desk, shifting some papers around. When he saw me leave Moska's office he stopped trying to appear occupied. He gave me a firm look, then nodded at the door.

I followed him through the busy corridor, past uniformed militiamen walking with secretaries, and out to the front steps. It wasn't that hot, but Stefan was sweating.

"Yes?"

"I've had enough of this," he began, then stopped. When he started again, it came out clearly and without hesitation: "I've put up with you for a long time now, and I thought that going off to the provinces would help things. But it's only made them worse."

"Investigate the suicide. I don't care, really."

He raised a hand. "That's not what I'm talking about. This case is just another part of a four-year-long insult. Four years!" he said, shaking his head. "Ever since that shoddy book came out you've forgotten what we were to each other — we grew up together!"

He waited, for some kind of recognition perhaps, and it says something about me that I was stuck on his description of my book as shoddy.

"I've seen this coming for a long time.

Those friends of yours, those *writers,* they fill you up, they make you think you're infallible. But you certainly are not. You've ruined a marriage to a beautiful woman, you can't do police work anymore, and now you can't even write. What are you, Ferenc? What the hell do you have left to offer?"

I didn't know where all this was coming from — or maybe I did know, but I didn't know why now, of all times, he had to say it. We'd been drifting apart for a long time. "This is a load of crap," I said.

He started nodding very quickly, his second chin quivering. "Crap is right, Ferenc. You've crapped on our friendship for a long time. You've crapped on me. And now I'm going to crap on your future. Are you ready?"

I didn't know how to get ready.

"When you were at the Front," he said, "I slept with Magda. I had sex with your wife, and I wouldn't trade that single night for anything in this world." He tapped his head. "I keep it up here always. Why do you think I was so eager to get you this job? Misplaced goddamned guilt. I still valued our friendship. But I had your wife in your own bed, and I hope that knowing this ruins what little joy you still feel when you look at her."

He stood rigidly on the steps, his chin up, waiting. He was expecting what I would have expected: a fist. His resolution fluctuated as I watched him, his eyes blinked, his nostrils flared as he breathed loudly, the sweat now coursing past his ears, but I did not move. I wanted to. I wanted to throw myself on him and break his bones. I wanted my fist, with each of its five rings and a story for each, to crush him. It would have been an easy thing. But I just looked at him, then past him, to where the city kept moving along the narrow street, pedestrians and automobiles and a few horses pulling emptied, dirty carts.

"Well then," I heard him say. He took a step farther down, nodded briefly, and joined the traffic down below.

# 17

I don't know why I didn't hit him. He would have respected me for it. But the anger wasn't upon me yet — it was only shock. Maybe it was simply the residue of our decades of friendship, and that for a long time he had been so good to me — because of guilt or some other weakness. Or maybe I knew he was right: Ever since the book had come out I'd stopped calling him, stopped working to maintain our friendship.

I went back into the station, where Leonek and Emil and Brano were standing around Brano's desk again. Kaminski was talking, and they were all smoking, a soft cloud hovering above their heads. My phone was ringing.

"Daddy?"

"Yes," I said, for a moment unsure who it was. "Yes?"

"Mother wants to know —"

"What does she want to know?"

"When you'll be over for dinner. With this friend of yours. That's how she said it — *that friend of his.*"

My watch took a second to focus. "Tell her seven. We'll be there at seven."

"Daddy?"

"Yes?"

"This friend of yours, he's a cute one?"

It was a joke, I knew, but I couldn't rise to it. "I'll see you at seven."

"Here," said Kaminski, as I approached. He held out a cigarette. I took it, noticing the small pin on his lapel. A red rippled flag. "I was telling the guys about the Komsomol."

"The youth brigades?" I asked. I didn't

care what he was talking about. I just wanted some noise.

"You know them," he said. Everyone knew about the Komsomol. Even *The Spark* carried articles of their industrious exploits in unclaimed regions on the other side of the Empire. "I went to the virgin lands in northern Kazakhstan after my years here, to help farm. Such good soil. Terrible climate, but what soil!" He held his gangly hands out, palms up. "You know what it's like to work with your hands like that? It's a dream. That's what it is. I coordinated the work, and I ate with these fine young people in the fields, then we all went back to work, such hard work, and at night we ate around a campfire and sang revolutionary songs. You have to imagine it if you weren't there. Fifty, a hundred passionate young people singing songs about their hopes and dreams for the future. No, I don't think you can imagine it." He shook his head. "Over here, maybe it's different. But in the Motherland, we're in this together. We build everything from nothing. That's socialism. It's the collective spirit that moves us on. Do you understand?"

I lit the cigarette finally, and visions of Stefan — stretched naked over my wife, grunting, his flesh sweating — only now began to fade.

"The peasants," he said, "they brought us *flowers*. Can you believe it? Maybe you don't know real peasants here, but you don't get flowers from Kazhak peasants for no reason. They knew we were there to save them, that we were there to save the Union. Khrushchev had told us to make the plains arable. And for the sake of humanity, that's what we did. Not me personally, of course, I was only there a couple years, mostly administrative; but we did it, all of us working together. Last year we worried that everything was ruined by the drought, but this year, I'm told, the wheat yield is going to be unprecedented." He shook his head again, this time with admiration. "They're still doing it now. They sing their songs at night and work all day and hope for better things. And better things are happening. Just wait."

It was a peculiar thing to see. This man from Moscow had us surrounding him in a corner of the office we never visited, had us listening to him as if he were our kindergarten teacher. He had a sparkle in his eye, and a lively voice, and when you didn't pay too much attention to what he was saying, you could feel his excitement yourself. Emil and Leonek were transfixed. Brano stared, his face revealing nothing.

Kaminski was a real orator. A tremor ran through my body. It was a terrible, magical feeling.

Then I noticed the index finger of his right hand. Moska was right; it twitched. And I remembered that the word *administrative* meant a lot more than paperwork and long lunch breaks.

# 18

At a nearby bar filled with workers sipping vodkas and beer, I ordered a couple brandies for us. Leonek reached for his wallet, but I put a hand on his elbow to stop him. A warm shower had fallen on our way there, and the place was humid with wet bodies and drooping hats. We squeezed into an empty table in the center.

I wanted to say something, to get this started, but nothing came to me. We drank in silence, him looking over the crowd, blinking, his dark face reminding me of what little I knew of his background — childhood in an Armenian village, until the Young Turks started butchering his people, then the life of a refugee until he landed here with his mother.

"I'm sorry," I said finally.

"You already told me."

"I would have liked to make the funeral. Were there a lot of people?"

He shrugged. "The guys came, and her friends from the neighborhood. There were enough."

"That's good." I sounded a little stupid. "How old was she?"

He looked at his glass on the table. In the voices and sweat of all the men around us I remembered the clean, sweet-smelling Italian, then, inevitably, Stefan's disgusted face.

"She pushed her way through so much." Leonek looked at me. "Even when the Turks killed my father, she kept a level head. Through Yugoslavia, to Bulgaria and Italy, then here, she kept everything together. I wanted to stay back home and fight. But they would have killed me too. She knew this. She made me come with her."

I thought I should say something, but what do you say to that? I noticed then that he'd shaved, he looked clean, and this was something I appreciated.

"I even considered moving to the Armenian Republic a few years ago. Can you imagine that?" A smile finally split his face. "But this is my world now, not Central

81

Asia. I wouldn't know what to do in Yelevan."

I agreed.

"You remember when Sergei was killed?"

I nodded.

"It was her again. She was the one who made me let it go, to stop looking into his murder. I was angry at her a long time about that. He and I were close — we were the two foreigners in the station house. Sergei was a brother to me. You know that."

I did.

"At first I didn't understand. But she understood." His thin hands were on his glass, his fingers tapping. "Then people in the other offices were sent away — suddenly, with no warning, their desks were empty. Remember that?"

We all remembered that.

"Only then did I start to understand. She always knew. She saved me."

She had saved herself as well. An old woman who knows how to survive knows that her son had better stay employed. Back then it was truer than ever. We all learned a degree of blindness — first during the Occupation, and then after the Liberation.

The door banged open, and five laughing students barged in. They had pink faces and shoddy clothes. "Five brandies!" shouted the first one, with an attempted mustache shadowing his lip. They gathered around the bar, talking animatedly. The workers looked at them a moment, then went back to their drinks.

"School must be going well," said Leonek.

"Demonstrators," I told him. "They were in Victory Square today."

"How about that." He turned in his seat to face them. "This is something, isn't it?"

I shrugged.

"Remember how it used to be? No one would think to demonstrate. And look at them now!" His face pulsed as he considered it. "God, I wish I was young."

"You are young."

"We're both young," he said. "We should be out there too, standing next to them."

It was good to see him pleased by this thought. "You going to make up a sign?"

"Why not?"

"What would it say?"

He put his chin in his palms, elbows on the table — he really did look young. "I don't know. Isn't that amazing? I've got no idea. What about you?"

"I'm not the demonstrating kind."

"What does that mean?"

He was waiting, eyes big. "I have a wife and a daughter," I said. "If I get thrown into jail, how would they fare? I don't want my girl to grow up fatherless."

He opened his mouth — something was ready to pop out — but then he shut it. He said, "Maybe that's why I should do something. No one depends on me anymore."

"Maybe." But then I remembered what men like Mikhail Kaminski and Brano Sev would use to keep demonstrators from forcing Russian tanks to roll down our streets: interrogations, informers, secret police, and prison camps.

# 19

I drove us through the busy evening streets, stopping for busses and trams and bicycles, until we were back among the unfinished towers of the Ninth District. We parked half in a ditch, and I worried that I wouldn't be able to make it out later on. Claudia was outside with her chickens again — she stopped to give me a severe nod. She was still waiting for me to pick up her drunkard brother, and no doubt Magda had been filling her head with advice to pester me. But this time she chose silence.

Ágnes opened the door. She wore a knee-length dress I had never seen before, with a pattern of purple-and-yellow flowers. She stood on her toes to kiss my lowered cheek. "Do you remember Leonek?" I said. "Leonek, Ágnes."

Leonek kissed her hand, and, over his head, she winked at me.

"Where's your mother?" I asked.

She nodded toward the kitchen, then Pavel trotted in from the bedroom and gave Leonek two high barks.

Magda's hair hung over her face as she brushed a plate of chicken bones into the trash can. When she looked up at me, I could hardly see her through the strands. She brushed them away with her wrist and smiled. It was the first time we'd really seen each other for a while, and momentarily it was as if nothing bad had ever passed between us in the provinces.

Then it came back to me: Stefan, his choking breaths beating out of him as he writhed over her breasts, her clean smooth belly, her face.

"You're late," she said.

"How was the train?"

"Well, it got me here."

I went to a cabinet for the wine as she washed the plate off in the sink and set it with other dishes on a towel. "You know Leonek, right?"

"Sure, yeah. I don't remember the last time I saw him. A year ago?"

"His mother died recently. So he might be a little strange."

"I see."

"Come on, then."

Leonek stood up stiffly when we came out, Ágnes folded on the sofa beside him. He kissed Magda's hand with purpose. It reminded me, if I needed the reminder, that Magda was really quite beautiful; she could still stop a man in his tracks.

# 20

The silence hung over us as we dug into the bean soup, then the paprika chicken, forks and knives scraping plates, glasses pressing to lips, quiet gulps, water and red wine. I saw Ágnes place a sliver of chicken in her lap, glance to the side and toss it to Pavel, who silently gobbled it. When she looked up again I gave her a sharp shake of the head. Magda glanced at Leonek, who was focused on his food, then looked at me. I smiled, but she

86

didn't. I said the most benign thing that came to mind: "A Frenchman told me recently that plot is dead."

"What?" Magda asked, leaning forward as if she hadn't heard.

"Plot. He says that no one's doing it anymore."

She grinned. "In the West maybe. Was that Georgi's poet?"

"It was."

Leonek looked up. "What are you talking about?"

"Literature," I said.

"Oh." He nodded at his plate.

Magda tried. She told us about the hourlong line she'd stood in, waiting for beef, but when she reached the front, all that was left was chicken.

While she spoke, Stefan's pale flesh came to me again, and I couldn't muster any comment. Neither could Leonek.

But her stamina was high. She launched into a description of her factory. "Textiles, we even make the Militia uniforms. Well, the shirts at least. Lydia works opposite me on the line, and she makes jokes about undermining quotas every time she leaves for a cigarette. You should meet her sometime, she's hilarious. I'll set you up."

Leonek smiled politely but said nothing.

I leaned down and scratched the mosquito bite on my ankle.

Magda watched him return to his plate; it was almost empty. "Would you like some more?"

"Thank you, no," he said through a mouthful. "It's very good."

"I told you it would be," I said. At the end of the table, Ágnes was bent toward the floor, feeding Pavel, but I no longer felt like reprimanding her.

Magda refilled our wineglasses, then turned to me with round eyes and tilted her head in Leonek's direction.

"Are you on a case now?" I asked.

His tongue searched behind his lower lip. "The city's pretty quiet. Except for those students, maybe."

I couldn't see Ágnes at all; she had vanished behind the edge of the table.

"Students?" asked Magda.

I shrugged. "Demonstrators."

"Oh."

"Otherwise," said Leonek, "not many homicides."

Magda spoke again, but slowly. "On the way home today, I saw two men in front of the cinema. I've never seen them before. They were pretty destitute. They had long coats, both of them, and through the flaps

I could see their old prison shirts. Striped, you know?"

Leonek seemed to wake a little.

"They looked menacing to me, standing with their hands in their pockets, and when they watched me pass I was a little scared. I don't know what they were thinking."

I said, "I can imagine what they were thinking."

"No — not that. I know that look. They were thinking something different." She paused. "But you can't really read faces, can you?"

"Sometimes you can."

"They've been through a lot," said Leonek.

We both turned to him.

"After the funeral, I talked to one of them in a bar." He thought a second, eyes glazed, then returned. "Slavery. That's what it was. And after years of being watched over by guards, after the malaria and executions — yes, that's what he told me: They often executed men in a field near the barracks. After all that, what can you expect from someone?"

Ágnes was in her chair now, paying attention. She stared at Leonek with something approaching wonder.

"Remember in August?" he asked me.

"Just before your vacation. There was that Ukrainian. He came back from the camps and beat his son to death because he'd become a clerk for the Central Committee."

"Lev Urlovsky," I said. "He was at the Vátrina Work Camp."

"Yeah." He leaned forward. "When we arrested him, he showed no remorse. None at all. It was strange to see."

"After killing his own son?" said Magda. "That's horrible."

"Ágnes," I said, and it took a second for her to hear me. "Ágnes, take Pavel for a walk."

She sighed loudly, but got up and left the room. Pavel followed, nails clicking on the floor.

"You don't know," said Leonek. "You just don't know what they've been through. The Turks were going to take my father to prison, but they shot him instead." His hands settled on the table, on either side of his plate. "Maybe he was lucky."

I heard the front door open and slam shut.

# 21

The two wine bottles were empty, so I went to get another from the kitchen, and when I returned, Leonek was leaning back in his chair, legs stretched out beneath the table, frowning again. Magda shrugged. When I filled his glass, he took it absently and pressed it to his lips, but did not drink. Then he set the glass back on the table and looked at Magda. "I'm going to do it," he said.

I was almost afraid to ask. "Do what?"

He turned to me. "I'm going back into the files. I'm going to investigate Sergei's murder."

"You're sure?"

"Why not?" He drank some wine. "I told you before, there are no more responsibilities for me. This is the only responsibility I have left."

"Who's Sergei?" Magda asked.

"You met him a couple times during the Occupation."

"My partner, Sergei Malevich." Leonek put his elbows on the table. "He was killed just after the war. Shot in the back of the head."

"I think I remember. The Russian, right?"

We nodded.

"He was nice." She looked at Leonek. "And it wasn't investigated?"

I spoke up. "He was looking into the rape and murder of a couple girls in a synagogue. We knew who had done it, everyone

91

knew: Russian soldiers. But we couldn't do a thing. Sergei was insistent, though."

"Because *he* was Russian," said Leonek. "It tore him up that everyone in the Capital thought of Russians this way, as rapists and murderers."

Magda refilled our glasses.

Leonek took another drink. "He wanted to prove either that the killers weren't Russian, or that if they were, a Russian could bring them to justice. You remember that night?"

I did.

"He called me," said Leonek, "then I called you. He wanted us to meet him down by the water. There was that thick fog, and by the time we showed up he was dead. It was unreal. We could even hear the gunman running away, but couldn't see more than a foot ahead of us."

"Is there anything left of it?" I asked. "In the files. After so long, it'll be hard to follow the leads."

"I can at least try."

"What about his family?" Magda asked. "Wasn't he married?"

"His wife and son, Kliment, moved to Moscow." Leonek smiled. "Kliment became a militiaman too."

Magda stared at Leonek, cheeks flushed,

and I realized then that she had been doing most of the drinking. She was a little drunk, and maybe I was too.

Leonek looked into his glass, then popped his head up. "This is really good wine!" I guess he was drunk as well.

I heard the front door open, saw Magda's face turn to me, flushed and radiant, and that was when it bubbled through me, and over me.

I was in the present. I was not thinking of later that evening, when we would be alone again and the strained silence would keep us far from the one sad subject that was the only thing we could ever think about. I was in the present, where I was generous and could forget a single night almost two decades old, because marriage and all the years, and Ágnes — they were so much bigger than one carnal act. I could see her cheeks redden; her smile warmed me. I saw my daughter watching from the doorway. Our guest smiled at all the riches I had in this house, his admiration all over him. And that's when I thought, hopefully, that Magda and I still had a future together.

"Leonek," I said. "That really is a nice tie you're wearing."

He looked down, flipped it with his fingers, and we all laughed, even Ágnes.

You can read it all; it's no secret. The Magyars have grown loud. Because if they scream enough, they might get their Nagy with the mustache like two paintbrushes, just as the Poles have their Gomulka. And after a momentary face-off, the Empire bows its head and allows Imre Nagy to control their path to socialism. You read this, and you wait. And for a while you're encouraged — who isn't? Collectivization is halted in the Hungarian plains, and People's committees are formed to air complaints. The Spark calls these moves bold, unprecedented. The sun shines on the Magyars, and even over here in the Carpathian basin the clouds are dispersing. Kozak the Engineer opens the Tenth Central Committee Meeting with a declaration of solidarity with the revered Comrade Nagy. Mihai does not condemn the phrasing, and his silence is greater than any words. Bobu the Professor asks for an investigation into the benefits of trade agreements with nations outside the socialist neighborhood.

Yet just as quickly, the cooling begins. In their enthusiasm, Magyar workers seize gov-

94

*ernment buildings and form revolutionary councils. Bobu says nothing, and even Kozak stares quietly at his podium. Nagy announces the end of the one-party system in the Hungarian People's Republic. Breaths are being held; the oxygen grows thin. The Magyars decide to take their soldiers out of the year-old Warsaw Pact and ask to be united with the nations of the West. Exhale. The Empire mobilizes. Russian tanks reach the edge of Budapest. The lack of air makes everyone a little crazy — there are barricades in the streets along the Danube, then the tanks move in. The American radio gives instructions on guerrilla warfare. The radios of the Empire shout of imperialist-financed counterrevolutionaries. And in the Budapest streets busses are turned over and rifles disseminated and Magyar students and Magyar workers line up at the barricades. Nagy calls for quiet and calm, but he is whispering to a hurricane. On Radio Budapest he says,* Today at daybreak, Soviet troops attacked our capital with the obvious intent of overthrowing the lawful democratic Hungarian government. *Then Radio Budapest sends an SOS signal and drops quietly off the air.*

*Here in the Capital the silence reigns. But it is a tense silence, like the one that hangs over a failing marriage. No one in the street can smile cleanly, and even you hear whispers about the tremblings beneath the surface. Here, the only shouts are unheard: the epidemic of workers calling in sick. One day someone is at the factory, the next day he is not. Then there are five gone, then twenty. This is not the news that reaches* The Spark, *but is passed along on the street and in bedrooms and over drinks. You hear it once or twice — you're not sure anymore who from, or when — but then it is common knowledge, the whole country is part of the secret society that has only one weapon at its disposal.*

*The radios whine like sick animals when the electronic jamming functions, and whisper orders for street-battle tactics when it doesn't. While that other capital is aflame, this capital is silent. There is a secret society of discontent with its hand on its only pistol, waiting to fire.*

# FALL

# 1

This confession is becoming longer than I would have expected, and has still hardly begun. But the details that precede and surround the story are necessary for understanding what follows, because crimes are not committed without precedent. Even the most banal details come together and gain power and lead murderers to their final, defining acts.

Through the weeks following that dinner, the writing began. I tried to ignore the news from Budapest and focus on words during the early-morning hours in the empty office. The typewriter rattled, and the sluggish T stuck. A few words came, interrupted by long periods when the blank sheets just hypnotized me. Then, gradually, thoughts began to coalesce. Magda's parents' farm before the war, the long journey home after the war, the discovery that my family was dead, then the move to the Capital, black bars and fevers of depression. By November, as the weather cooled, I was typing a regular, controlled flow. Marriage was the only subject for me now, and it was becoming the story of how time can erode a marriage from the center. I wrote about our early, flush months, the month-and-a-half war-time separation, then the strange, inexplicable disconnect when I returned. I was a different man even after such a short war, one who had to find his way back to the world of human feelings, to the joys and fears of a family man. That short war had changed Magda as well. I wrote of Ágnes, and how her birth drew me back into the marriage, so that the marriage was the one thing that sustained me. I wrote nothing about Stefan because he was incidental, just a symptom of a real ailment. I showed my pages to no one.

Mikhail Kaminski continued to work with Brano Sev on the files of state security, his trigger finger always more active than the others. These security officers had the appearance of clerks, poring over sheets with numbers and paragraphs and photographs. When they left, we could only imagine what they did: converse with informers on park benches, drag victims into interview rooms, strong-arm trouble-some students into the silence of utter submission. Leonek speculated that they were deciding which ones of us to get rid of, though Emil and I shrugged that off as paranoia. Once I overheard Kaminski laugh and say to Brano: *Those bitches will wish they never heard of nonviolent resistance!* I only understood this later.

There was one more incident with Stefan. I was out drinking with Emil and Leonek on a Friday night, and Stefan appeared, already a little drunk. He sat with us and joined the conversation, which slowed once he arrived, but he kept looking at me significantly. Sometimes he smiled, and he kept taking my cigarettes. The others didn't seem to notice this, but I did, and when he got up to use the toilet I followed him into the bathroom and, without a word, hit him on the back of the head. His face fell into the mirror, leaving a long crack that as far as I know is still there. I returned to the table and finished my drink, and when Stefan appeared again he was padding a bloody spot on his forehead. The fact that Emil and Leonek said nothing only proved that they understood everything.

We changed partners. I was to work with Emil, and Stefan would work with Leonek. "A temporary measure," Moska explained in his dim office. "Nothing to worry about." He looked at the paperwork on his desk rather than at me.

"How long?"

"What was that?"

"How long is temporary?"

"Does it matter?"

He was right — it didn't matter. No one in the Capital was committing murder. Leonek noticed this aloud. "When people are focused on something great outside their borders, they don't have enough attention to kill each other." Revisiting Sergei's case was making him philosophical. Or something else was.

First he had gone through the station's file cabinets, all of them, then barged in on Moska, demanding to know where Sergei's files were. *Expunged* was the answer. Leonek sneered the word. "Cleaned *out*, that's what he told me."

"They were destroyed?"

Leonek flattened a hand on a stack of papers beside his typewriter. "Not quite. I had to go to the central depot. Do you know where that is?"

I'd never even heard of a central depot.

"Just outside the Seventh District. A *warehouse*, no less. Stefan came with me, and after two days, running back into town for unpredictable signatures, this greasy bureaucrat finally gives them to us. *Reluc-*

tantly." He sank into his chair and straightened the pages. A few inches thick — a couple hundred pages, I guessed. "A lot of this is useless," he said. "Forms, certificates, the like. But there's something here. I'm sure of it."

He had the same surety as Stefan, when he had insisted that no one in the Capital could kill himself — a stubborn, peasant conviction.

Georgi called to invite me and Magda to a party. "More foreigners in town?" I asked.

"No foreigners, but it is for them. For the foreigners."

"The Magyars, Georgi?"

"I'll support our Hungarian comrades the only way I know how."

"By drinking, you mean."

"Such a cynic. Remember, Ferenc, you're Magyar-blooded too. Bring Magda."

"I don't know. Haven't seen her much."

"Where's she been?"

"Out with a friend from the factory. A Lydia." This is what Magda would tell me when she returned home, often after Ágnes went to bed, as she passed me on the couch: *I was out with Lydia again.*

But I had never asked where she had gone, or whom with.

"You know I'm still waiting for your literary contribution."

"You'll have to keep waiting. Nothing's ready."

"But you're writing?"

"I seem to be. Finally."

By the time we hung up, he sounded positively thrilled.

# 2

On November the fifth, a Monday, Emil and I were sent to look into a disappearance. A Party official, attached to the Health Ministry, had come home to find his wife missing. "So she left him," I said.

"I'm likely to agree," said Moska. "But what I think isn't important."

It didn't sound particularly interesting, or perhaps I was just feeling lazy. I pointed out that homicide inspectors shouldn't be wasting time with missing person's cases. But Emil knew his regulations: "She's connected to the Party, and it's been three days. After three days it goes to us."

Moska seemed impressed. He explained that she had left no note, but did leave a mess in the kitchen. "Silverware all over the floor."

"What about her clothes?" I asked.

"A few dresses taken." Moska paused, as if unsure. "I told him you two would be over to see him today."

Because it was close, we walked to Comrade Malik Woznica's apartment down by the Tisa, where the colder winds blew. Built on old bomb-damaged buildings, these were the new riverview homes filled with apparatchiks and officers. There was a noticeable lack of cabbage smell in the stairwell, and the doorbell, instead of buzzing, emitted a soothing sequence of three tones. Emil smiled when he heard them.

A white-haired man shorter than Brano, but three times heavier, opened the door and started speaking immediately: "Comrade Inspectors, so very good. Please please, yes, come in, yes, right this way. A drink? Come on, a drink between friends. Yes?" His smooth face was pink beneath his sleep-deprived eyes, and as he spoke his chubby hands flew around. It wasn't nervousness, I didn't think; it was simply too much energy. "Come, come, sit, no, yes — take a look. Isn't it a lovely view?"

He left us standing at two large, double-paned windows, gazing out at the Tisa. The river changed colors depending on the sky, and today it was gray. The Georgian Bridge, off to the right, crossed into the dilapidated Canal District and continued to the southern bank.

"All Mag and I see are more blocks. What's your view like?"

"Come by and see for yourself," said Emil. "It's breathtaking."

On a wall, beside the old portrait of Mihai, was an austere photograph of Comrade Woznica and his wife. She was much younger. Her nose turned up, and her eyes were spread a little wide, but even through the formal pose you could tell what had attracted him to her. What had attracted her to him — besides the comforts of Party lodging — was less apparent.

Woznica returned with a tray of glasses that tapped together as his overexcited hands shook. We joined him around the coffee table. Vodkas, with fresh limes squeezed into them. Despite all the improvements, I couldn't remember the last time I'd seen a lime.

"So," I said, after we'd touched glasses to health, "can you tell us about your wife?"

Woznica took a deep breath that seemed to drain his energy. "Well. This happened three nights ago —"

"Friday night," offered Emil.

"Yes, yes." He leaned back into the sofa. "I had returned from a special meeting of the Pharmaceutical Section — distribution problems, very troublesome — it was late for me. Eight at night? Yes. Eight, eight-thirty. I came in and called for her. *Svetla,* I called. That's my wife. Svetla. There was no answer. Very surprising. But I went into the kitchen, and that was what worried me. The cabinets, yes, they were open — *all* open. And the pots and dishes and forks and spoons — they were all over the floor!" As he talked, his hands were on his knees, the sofa, his glass, his chin, his ear. "I called her name loudly — *Svetla! Svetla!* But still no answer! I ran through the apartment, checking everywhere, but no, she was nowhere. And now, three days later, still no Svetla."

Emil set down his empty glass. "Her clothes? We were told —"

"Yes yes," he answered, nodding and flushing. "I should have said before. Some dresses were missing. Whoever took her is prepared to hold her a long time."

I shot Emil a glance; he caught it.

"What about the neighbors?" Emil asked. "Have you talked to them?"

"I have, Comrade Inspectors, I have."

He seemed proud of his foresight. "But the downstairs neighbor, Comrade Ioana Lipescu, is so terribly deaf she never heard a thing. She's very old — her husband, who I knew from the Ministry, died a year ago. We live on the top floor, and these walls keep out noises. I was going to talk to the family on the ground floor, but to be terribly honest, I don't want word getting out. At least, not until we've found her. For a man like me . . ." He finally ran out of words.

"Of course," said Emil.

"And relatives? Are there any we can speak to?"

Woznica opened his hands. "Feel free to speak with her father, but he returned to Russia a year ago, after we married."

I took out my notepad to make this seem like a bureaucratic question. "You and your wife — how well have you been getting along recently? Any arguments? Disagreements?"

He took it very well. A sad smile came over him, and he shook his head more slowly than I would have thought him capable. "Comrade Inspectors, my Svetla is an angel. Truly. I don't say this as a husband; I say it because it is true. She is very agreeable. We are always of a like mind on all issues." The smile was gradually disappearing. "My Svetla, you have to understand, she has a weak constitution. This has been a hard year for her, the last months — yes, six months — spent in bed. In June I took her to the baths at Trebon, I thought it would help. And for a little while, yes, it seemed to. But then she suffered more, the poor thing. She's too weak to get up on her own, you understand? I have to help her exercise in her room so her muscles — so they don't *degenerate*. In the Health Ministry we know how to take care of people. I know you ask the question because you are good investigators, you have to ask. But my Svetla, were she to decide to do so, is too weak to pack her clothes and leave me." The smile was returning, though his eyes were wet. "And why should she want to leave me? I give her everything I have. I nurse her. She is my little angel."

# 3

We took a quick survey of her windowless bedroom — a vast, too-soft bed, half-full wardrobe, wide-mirrored vanity filled with all kinds of blush and mascara and lipsticks. If she had left on her own, she wasn't interested in doing her face. On the outside of the bedroom door was a pale square with four screw holes where a lock had once been. Woznica explained: "The previous tenants had, yes, a child. Sometimes, you know, they had to lock him in."

I could never imagine locking Ágnes in her room.

"What do you think?" Emil asked as we walked back to the station.

I stopped for a crowd of teenagers in exercise shorts to jog by. "How can he be fat with so much energy?"

"If you can afford it, anything's possible."

Emil was the one militiaman who knew this firsthand. Lena had brought an unnationalized fortune to their marriage, and though they lived among the rabble, one look at Lena gave them away. She visited the station in current Western fashions, new hairstyles, and though she wore little jewelry, the long neck beneath her black, bobbed hair was hereditarily built to support a string of pearls. Her drinking problem, and the fact that he had saved her life, were the only reasons any of us could figure for her choosing a clumsy peasant like Emil for a life mate.

"It looks like shell shock," he said.

"Those shakes?"

"Was he in the war?"

"That would be a long time ago."

He shrugged. "Let's check his file."

Files on public officials were kept in the basement of the Central Committee on Victory Square. We caught a bus from Woznica's neighborhood, got out at the vast circle of roads around a huge statue of a man and woman holding up a torch, and made our way to the columned Central Committee building. Before it stood the Lenin of all capitals, a recent gift from Our Friend, arm elevated like the couple in the middle of the square, stepping into the future, the wind raising his jacket. A guard stood smoking at the small side door, beneath the emblem of the hawk at rest. The sight of our Militia certificates did nothing to excite him.

The records room was down a dark, musty corridor, and Miloš the old Slovak record keeper, wasn't known for his helpfulness. Beneath a large, smiling Mihai, he scratched the gray stubble on his cheek. "I don't imagine you have the proper forms, do you?"

"What forms?" I asked.

Miloš opened his hands. "Read your regulations, comrades. Article seventeen-fifty. Permissions for all Militia inquiries must

111

be prefaced by signatures from your superiors. Isn't that old Karl Moska?"

Emil shook his head. "Subsection three," he quoted: " 'This article pertains to investigations not previously authorized by Militia decrees G-34 or G-72.' These are blanket decrees which cover Homicide Department work."

Now I was impressed.

Miloš shoved a thumb over his shoulder at the wall of black drawers. "Don't mess them up."

Comrade Malik Woznica, his brief file told us, was forty-eight years old and married to Svetla Levin (daughter of a Russian tailor who had moved here with the Red Army). He had been suffering from an unknown neurological disease for the last decade. The doctor's report offered no answers, but speculated that the cause might be found in a mining town where Comrade Woznica had spent two years as Party boss before developing his condition. The water in that region, said the doctor, was known to have been contaminated by mercury, and the town was almost famous — in the medical community, at least — for its cancer rates. As for Comrade Woznica, only morphine seemed to help the condition. I wondered aloud if Woznica was hooked on his medication.

Emil shut the file. "The way he was jerking around, I'd say he hasn't touched it for a long time."

"Maybe she took his prescription with her. For herself."

"Or to sell. But she couldn't move in the first place."

"Give me the name of that doctor, will you?"

Back at the station, I called Dr. Sergius Brandt's office at Unity Medical, but his secretary curtly informed me that the doctor was out of town. "When will he be back?"

"Tomorrow."

"I'd like an appointment."

I listened to static while she, I assumed, examined his schedule. Emil was on his own telephone, checking in with Lena. He was smiling.

"Two weeks."

"What?"

"The doctor will be able to see you in two weeks. Wednesday the twenty-first."

"This is official business," I told her. "I'm not a patient, I'm a Militia inspector."

"Comrade Doctor Brandt is a busy man."

"So am I. I'll be there at noon. Tomorrow."

Before she could protest, I hung up.

113

# 4

Ágnes showed off her athletic uniform that evening. They'd just arrived at school for the Pioneers' new fitness campaign. Like the students I'd seen in the street: white short-sleeved shirt and shorts that stopped just above the knee. "Aren't those a little revealing?" I asked. She modeled in the living room to a Prague Symphony rendition of Mahler, her milky legs goose-stepping. "Where are your glasses?"

No question could faze her. She demonstrated the new, scientific exercises — sharp bows from the waist, arms out, bent, forward, down. When she stopped finally, her face was as red as the Pioneer scarf.

We went in to help Magda with dinner, but she was already plating it. While we ate, Ágnes went through the eleven-point Pioneer pledge she was supposed to memorize: "*One:* We the Red Pioneers honor our socialist motherland by wearing this red scarf. *Two:* We the Red Pioneers value learning as it advances the wisdom of our motherland. *Three:* We the Red Pioneers respect our parents —"

"That's a good one," I said.

"*Shh*," Ágnes warned. "You'll throw me off. *Four:* We the Red Pioneers love peace and the Soviet Union, and hate all warmongers. *Five* . . .”

She stumbled over number seven, the one about loving and respecting work and all working people, but otherwise did a fine job. It was impressive enough to provoke a smile from Magda.

"You coming tonight?" I asked her.

"What tonight?"

"Georgi's party."

She gave an exaggerated expression of anguish, as if she'd forgotten, then shook her head. "I'll stay here. I don't want to leave Ágnes alone."

"I'm fine by myself," she muttered through a mouthful.

"She's old enough. Come on, you'll enjoy it."

She raised her eyebrows at me: no contradictions in front of the child. "Really. I'd rather spend some time with my daughter." She turned to her daughter. "We'll do something nice. Girls' night."

Ágnes shrugged and went back to her plate.

# 5

In addition to the same ten from my last visit, there were twenty more crammed into that small apartment. Georgi had painted a red banner that hung over the kitchen door: ARTISTS OF THE WORLD, UNITE!

"You like?" he asked me, his drunkenness clear from the first glance.

"It's clever," I lied.

Georgi stumbled through to the kitchen. Someone had opened the window over the sink to cut through the smoke and humidity of so many sweating bodies, and a brandy was shoved into my hand. I noticed Vera — the hard stare and red lips playing on the edge of her glass made her unavoidable — then the others, squeezed tight: pairs and threesomes in heated conversations and lonely drinkers peering around in anticipation or nodding off.

"Did your Frenchman make it out all right?"

Georgi leaned close, looking baffled. I repeated myself. "Ah! Louis sent word from Paris! Come, come!"

I followed him back to the living room, pushing past faces that said *Ferenc so good to* and *Where have you been hiding* and *I've been wanting to talk,* until we had reached the bedroom. There was a young couple on his small bed, half-dressed. The girl tugged her bra strap up to her shoulder; the boy blushed. I didn't know them, and neither, apparently, did Georgi. "Who did you come with?"

There was some confusion as they buttoned their clothes and tried to manage an answer. "We just . . . well, everyone knew about . . . it was . . . *no one,* okay?" The boy, a Gypsyish southerner, finally stood straight. "Is there a problem with us being here?"

Georgi gave me a sidelong glance. "I don't like my bed being soiled by other people's fluids."

They were edging along the wall toward the door. The girl's lipstick was smeared to her chin. "No need to get all heated up," said the boy.

"I'm not heated," said Georgi. "It's just my friend here. He's a little protective. He keeps breaking people into little pieces. I don't know what to do about it."

Both of them looked up at me, and when I laid my hand over my rings and cracked my knuckles, they bolted.

Louis had sent a picture postcard of Notre Dame, with a question mark and an exclamation point scratched beneath it.

*My dear Comrade! Here in the bourgeois capital looking for ways to take back my surplus value. Thoughts of my days with you warm me in this cold place. Please look into coming to Paris, where I can show you the hospitality you've shown me.*

The scribbled *Louis* at the bottom was illegible.

"He's got your sense of humor," I said.

Georgi put it back in his bureau. "You going to the Union meeting on Friday?"

"The Writer's Union?"

"What else?"

"Haven't been to one of those in years."

He squeezed my knee. "That's because you're a sweetheart. You stopped going when they kicked me out."

I shrugged. "Coincidence."

He patted my cheek and gave a bleary smile, then raised his glass. "To our Magyar comrades-in-arms. Kick those bastards out!"

I allowed myself a slow, quiet intoxication. It was a gift for writing again, for surviving

Stefan's stab at collapsing my marriage, and for not thinking too deeply about Magda's late nights out, *with Lydia*. I swept through the rooms and back again, caught by half conversations about Budapest and Moscow and Washington, DC, and the Suez, and about writing. Stanislaus was working on a series of poems remembering the end of Stalinism, and Bojan was in the final edits of a surrealist memoir — a "dream book." A couple artists were ridiculing Vlaicu, probably the most popular state painter at that time. A journalist I'd never met before provoked a few words on what I'd been writing and seemed genuinely interested in my vague answers, which helped my mood. There were more students, a few making out, and another young couple in a corner, telling Georgi loudly that there would be a strike very soon. "Citywide," the girl said earnestly. "It will be unambiguous. They'll know how the People feel."

Georgi was humoring their optimism, but an older painter whose name I didn't remember asked how they expected to get word around. "How are we supposed to know when to strike?"

"We won't need to utter a word," said her boyfriend. "The government will tell everyone when to strike. All they need to do is close down one demonstration. Just one. Then the People will react."

The painter laughed, and the ensuing argument lasted a long time, all shouts and condescending one-liners.

Then, very late, as the party was clearing out and I thought I'd avoided it, Vera cornered me.

She had made herself up very well: Her dark hair hung loose down her back, and she'd worked hard on blackening her eyes. Red sweater and one of those tight skirts I'd seen a lot of in the summer. Stockings and heels. I'd noticed all this when I first saw her in the kitchen, but now, drunk and a little aroused, I couldn't ignore it.

"Where's your lovely wife?"

"Home. Your husband?"

"Writing, *somewhere*. Why don't I ever see you anymore?"

"We run in different circles."

"That's a shame."

Vera had studied philosophy in Switzerland during the war, and returned to teach and marry her childhood love, Karel. But over the years their fights had been as public as her subsequent affairs. When she turned her attention to me the previous Christmas, no one knew about the problems in my marriage, but Vera's philosopher eye had been able to divine our secret without much trouble.

I tried to change the subject to the one still lingering around us — the fighting in the streets of Budapest — but she stood on her toes and leaned close to my ear.

"Don't bore me," she breathed. "I expect better from you." Then she rubbed a hand down my tingling arm. "Do you have a cigarette?"

I lit it with a match because I'd never replaced the lighter Martin had taken. She stared at me through the smoke. I said, "Ágnes is doing some fitness program now. They gave out uniforms."

"She's a pretty girl. Are the boys showing interest?"

"I hope not."

She picked something off her lip with her long nails.

I started rambling about wanting Ágnes to go to a foreign school in order to learn languages. "The French high school is exceptional, but they won't take her unless she passes the exam. She's not studying her French."

But Vera wasn't listening. She gazed at the living room, which was empty except for the young couple we'd caught in

Georgi's bed. They were on the sofa, and the girl was determined to smear her lipstick again. Vera stroked my back. The drunkenness slid up to my scalp. When I turned back, she was back on her toes, our faces close, and her lips were on mine. I could taste smoke and bitter lipstick in her long kiss, then her tongue sliding against my teeth, probing deeper. Her hands held my head still.

It was Christmas again, her body pressed on top of mine, her saliva filling my mouth, hips shifting over me.

I held on to her waist and pulled her closer.

Then I let go. I pushed her down by her shoulders. She looked up at me, licking her lips. "You want to go somewhere?"

I shook my head. I even said no — either to make it clear to her, or to myself.

I could tell by the sudden widening of her jaw that her teeth were clenched behind her lips. "Ferenc, I'm not going to wait forever."

"I know."

"Once a year, that's not enough for any woman."

I looked at her a moment more, at her hard, determined expression, then gave her shoulder a squeeze.

# 6

Ágnes listened to a staticky American crooner while she half read a civics schoolbook on the sofa. Pavel was asleep beside her. She wrinkled her nose when I kissed her. "You stink. Are you drunk?" When she took off her glasses to examine me, she seemed very much like a grown woman.

"No, I'm not drunk." But I slurred the last two words. "Why aren't you in bed?"

"I told Stefan to come see us more often. Is he all right?"

"Stefan was here?"

"He called. But not for *you*. He wanted Mama."

I opened my mouth, then shut it.

"After she talked to him she was crying. Is something wrong with Stefan?"

I looked around. "Where is your mother."

"She went out."

"What about girls' night?"

She put her glasses back on and returned to the book. "I guess she meant other girls. She went to see her friend Lydia." After a moment, she looked at me again. "Daddy, are you all right?"

Later, as I lay on the sofa in the dark, a sheet over me, staring at the ceiling, she arrived. First the key clicked in the lock, then light spilled in from the corridor. I waited until she had locked it again. "Where were you?"

I heard her gasp, then the keys being set down. "Out. With Lydia."

"Come over here, Mag."

"I'm tired."

"This is important."

Her shadowy form moved over to me, and I sat up. I patted the sofa for her to sit.

"Where were you?"

Her profile was black, but I could see her thinking about it. "I told you, Ferenc."

"We've got to talk about this."

Her profile tilted so she was looking at her hands. "I just need to figure everything out. I don't know what I want anymore." She paused. "I can only do this on my own. Can you understand that?"

I put a hand on her knee.

"Don't. Please."

I took back my hand. "We used to talk about these things together."

She turned to me, but I couldn't make out her expression as she stood up. "Yes. We used to."

# 7

The next day, Emil and I walked back to Woznica's neighborhood and split up at the Tisa to canvass the local shops for information. I talked to a fishmonger, two bakers, a keysmith, and two bartenders, all with no luck. They had never seen Comrade Woznica's wife — him, yes, but never her. "Not once?" A shrug and a shake of the head. Maybe years ago, they couldn't be sure. The second bartender, a man nearly as large as I, with a shock of black hair marked by little thinning spots, had never even met Malik Woznica. I took the news with a handful of pumpkinseeds and turned to go, but recognized a figure hunched by the far wall. The name took a moment to materialize, but it did come, along with a cool wave of repulsion.

"Oh god *damn,*" he said when he saw me.

"Martin." I didn't stick out my hand because I didn't want to get that close. His dry nose was peeling.

"Comrade Inspector," he mumbled, then finished his shot. "You've found me, now I must go."

"I'm not looking for you. Josef Maneck's case is over."

"Tell that to your goddamn friend." He started to stand, wobbled, and settled back down.

"Is that why you're in this neighborhood? Has the other inspector been asking questions?"

"Don't tell." This time he made it to his feet and put a purple stump of finger to his lips. "Don't say I was here. Be a pal?"

He didn't look back as he tumbled out the door.

The bartender told me he'd been coming in there a week, maybe more, and I knew then that Stefan was still obsessed with that old suicide. The thought brought some small satisfaction. Stefan, perhaps, was spiraling into darkness.

Emil met me at the Georgian Bridge, and as cars passed we huddled against the cold and compared notes. It had been the same for him — they'd seen the husband but not the wife. "Talked to Woznica's pharmacist, though."

"Tell me."

"Picks up his morphine every week, like clockwork. He told me those first weeks he'd been suspicious — it's no small amount for one man."

"What convinced him?"

"How big Woznica is. And how extreme his condition. The pharmacist said it's gotten worse this half year or so."

"So he's been taking more?"

"I asked him that. It's increased, yes, but only because of his tolerance. In essence, Woznica's been on the same dosage for the last five years. But it's no longer helping — we've both seen how he shakes."

We leaned against the iron rail, the wind battering us, and faced the Canal District.

"How about Svetla?"

Emil shook his head. "Hasn't seen her. And listen to this: He's never filled a prescription for her."

"Never? A sick woman?"

Emil buttoned his jacket higher. "I think we should visit Comrade Woznica again."

But he wasn't in. On the way back down, we spoke with Ioana Lipescu. She was in her seventies, with a little red hammer and sickle pinned to her blouse. She had a great toothless smile that remained with her as she served us tea and sweet breads, but she could offer little more. Woznica hadn't lied — she was nearly deaf. But she had fond words for Svetla Woznica. "*Beautiful* — you've seen? Such a gorgeous girl. Some of those Russians can be. You wouldn't think

127

so. But I remember she had a mouth on her. Before she was sick, yes. She knew how to complain, you can be sure."

"Complain?" asked Emil. "What about?"

She had him repeat it a few times, then placed her spotted hands on her knees. "You know how they are. This city's not Moscow, we don't claim it is! We like easy living. She liked to dance. Out all the time, what a frustration for him."

A weak constitution, an angel. Now, a dancer. A complainer. I leaned forward. "When did you last see Svetla?"

"Oh, I don't know, a long time. Could it be six years?"

"Six months?" Emil offered.

"Six months, yes." She adjusted her pin and licked her gums. "I used to dance. Oh, I used to dance."

"I bet you did," I told her as we got up to leave. Then I repeated it. Louder.

# 8

The corridor on the fifth and highest floor of Unity Medical was as crowded as Georgi's party. Old babushkaed women, a farmer with a leg ending in dirty bandages at the knee, pregnant girls, fevered children, and

128

young, chain-smoking men pacing as best they could. There was a smell of decay, of rotting, but I couldn't locate its source. I wondered how the hospital corridors in Budapest were looking at that moment.

We had avoided the nurses' station at the end of the corridor, where a heavy, smocked woman leaned into a telephone, trying to slow the flood of patients.

The third door on the right had a corroded bronze nameplate: DR. SERGIUS BRANDT.

The doctor didn't seem aware that we had entered. He was bent over a young, pregnant woman in a chair that faced the door, one hand beneath her blouse, holding her swollen belly. She looked past his shoulder at us, reddening beneath her freckles. "Doctor," she whispered, but he wouldn't be distracted. He shifted his hand and hummed a few bars of something. *"Doctor."*

He straightened, tugged down his white lab coat, and turned to face us. His glasses magnified his eyes, and his short-cropped white hair was thin and soft. "You," he ordered us, *"wait."*

We remained by the door as he finished with the woman, whispered some kindness, accepted a bottle of white wine from her, and kissed her cheeks. When she passed

129

between Emil and me, she kept her eyes on the floor.

The doctor sat and made a few marks in a folder, then closed it. Behind his head was a framed photo beside his medical certificates: two blond boys — twins, perhaps his. Almost in the corner was a tiny, framed Mihai — put up as an obligation. He took off his glasses. "You can see I don't have a lot of time, Inspectors."

"We'll try to be fast," I said. Out of habit we pulled out our certificates, but he waved them away. "We want to know about one of your patients."

"Then ask."

He had a way about him. His curtness was commanding, yet not insulting. He was a man living under the weight of great responsibilities.

"Comrade Malik Woznica," said Emil.

"And his wife," I added. "Svetla."

Doctor Brandt started to reach for his file cabinet, then stopped. "Of course — Malik Woznica suffers from nerve problems of indeterminate origin. This is public record."

I stepped closer to the desk. "We understand that his condition's become worse in recent years."

The doctor frowned, then got up and left

the room. When he returned he held two yellow folders — one thick, the other nearly empty. He opened the thick one, replaced his glasses, and read over the top page. "Who told you his condition was worse?"

"His pharmacist," said Emil.

Dr. Brandt shook his head. "Ask someone with an education, okay? I've examined him regularly for five years, and his condition has plateaued. I've increased his morphine dosage, but only to counteract his tolerance. There's been no change in his condition."

"What about his wife?" asked Emil.

There were only a few sheets inside the thin file. "Last time I saw Svetla Woznica, she was fine. A sore throat, nothing more."

"How long ago was that?" I asked.

He looked for a date. "Eight months ago."

When he saw our surprise, he took off his glasses, and his eyes shrunk.

"I'd ask what this is about, but I'm hearing too many terrible things these days. God knows there's no reason to compound them."

On the drive back to the station, I went over the particulars again: "Svetla Woznica, a woman too weak to leave the

131

house, disappears with some clothes, leaving the kitchen a mess. Malik Woznica is also ill, and requires morphine in order to function." I stopped behind a pair of coffee-colored horses that would not move, no matter how much the farmer in front of them pulled the reins. "And now, we have contradictions."

Emil stared at the swishing tails. "The family doctor can't verify her condition, because he hasn't seen her. The neighbor thinks of Svetla as a *complainer*. Not how her husband describes her at all."

"Maybe that's just nostalgia," I said. "On his part, or hers."

A couple other farmers had joined the first. They pulled on the reins, pleaded with the horses, and struck their ribs with sticks. Behind, another Škoda's horn blared.

"And Comrade Woznica's own condition has worsened over the last half year."

"Which is almost the amount of time," Emil said, "that the good doctor has not seen Svetla Woznica."

Their patience at an end, the farmers beat the horses on the rump, the ribs, and the face. Some bystanders joined in, one of them a teenage boy in his exercise uniform. There were more horns screaming behind us.

"For a half year," I muttered, and by saying the words aloud, it crystallized in my head. "Svetla's been taking her husband's morphine for the last six months. She's an addict."

"And Malik Woznica's been protecting her."

"Nursing her. But it still doesn't explain her disappearance." I tapped the horn to hear it squeak. "When Comrade Woznica gets home from work, we should be there to greet him."

The horses would only move after blood had been drawn. It flowed along their rib cages and over their eyes. One bucked, then shot forward, the other following, and a crowd of men and boys with sticks and boards chased after them.

# 9

Kaminski was waiting for us. He'd already assembled Moska and Stefan, both of whom looked worried, and after we arrived Leonek sauntered in. The Russian waved us over to Brano Sev's desk, but Sev himself was nowhere to be seen.

There was a demonstration, he told us, in one of the housing units near the Tisa.

"Hooligans." He shook his head. "Now, we've no plans to do anything to these people. Let them shout their heads off. We just need a show of support out there, to make sure they don't set fire to themselves." A smile, a half laugh, then he opened his hands, the right index finger jerking. "A lot of our regular Militia have called in sick. I don't know. The flu or something. And we need more warm bodies out there. Can you spare an afternoon?"

Moska waited for the affirmation that didn't come, then said, "They can spare an afternoon."

Within the half hour, all of us — except Kaminski — were in the dim rear of a van, rattling through cobbled streets. There were no windows, so we looked at each other and at our hands.

"Where's Sev?" asked Leonek.

Moska shrugged.

Stefan and I were preoccupied by our mutual vicinity. The cut on his forehead had healed and disappeared. His beard had grown out in a blond mess, and I wondered what Magda thought of it. I tried not to wonder about anything else. Emil, beside me, was quietly accepting this new aspect of his job. Leonek cracked open the rear door and nearly tumbled out. We pulled him back in. "We should have turned left back there," he said in a high whisper. "I bet they're just taking us to prison."

"No one's going to prison," I said.

"Sit down," Moska said as we clattered through a pothole. "You'll hit your head."

"I'll get out of here is what I'll do." But after a moment he sat down again.

The demonstration wasn't as large as Kaminski had us believing. There were maybe fifty students and workers milling around the entrance to an apartment block, a few with signs that said SOLIDARITY and EYES TO BUDAPEST and FIRST HUNGARY, THEN US! There were murmurs of anxious conversation, and groans whenever more militiamen arrived in white, unmarked vans like the one we'd taken. Some were in uniform, some not. Kaminski was on the edge of the crowd, speaking with a commander from another district. He smiled when he spoke, opening his hands and moving them around in explanation. The commander then walked to a van and spoke to three young militiamen — boys, really — who began gathering short black clubs from the van.

More groans from the crowd, some wor-

135

ried faces. One stared at me a long time, a stout man with oil stains up and down his work clothes. Farther back was a student who I thought I recognized from Georgi's. I stood beside Moska. "What's going on here?"

But he didn't answer. His repulsed expression was clear enough.

"I'm not touching that," said Leonek when a club was offered to him.

"Orders," said the boy.

Moska touched Leonek's shoulder. "Take it, Leon."

Stefan stared at his own club, as if he'd never seen one before. "It's like the Americans say."

"What?" I asked.

"On the radio. They say that we club and shoot demonstrators. I was beginning to doubt them."

I put my own club under my arm. It was stiff and awkward. Then I looked at all those faces looking back at me. I saw some fear, but primarily hatred. Particularly in the students. A few in the back were trying to start a chant. *Russia out of Bu-da-pest!*

A couple others picked it up, but it was a weak effort; our presence was draining their resolve. But as it went on — *Russia out of Bu-da-pest!* — the repetition began to endow them with courage. I noticed a familiar face in the rear of the crowd, open mouth shouting, helping raise their excitement. Round cheeks, straight teeth, three moles: Brano Sev, only half-disguised in a blue worker's cap. He and a few others raised fists above their heads, their voices turning to mist. But I could see only him.

Wives and mothers leaned out of windows and shouted for their men to come back in. From above they could see there was no escape through the ring of militiamen and white vans. But no one heard them. The chanting rose, the students shouting bravely, taken by a fever, by the knowledge that this was their moment of glory — they would not stop shouting until the last Russian tank had left Budapest. Then — a *thump* on the van beside me. The raised fists held rocks that began to rain on us. Brano Sev's piece of ragged concrete cracked a windshield.

The commander bellowed something that must have been an order, because we were all moving forward, clubs held tightly, to round them up. The chant dropped off, and when we reached the demonstrators their open hands tried to push us back. Palms pressed into my chest, faces flashed by. Someone was behind me, stopping my

137

retreat, and we were in the midst of them, in faces and hands and shouts and sweat. Someone hit me in the jaw, and I instinctively struck out with my club. The snap of bone. A student dropped at my feet. I looked around for Emil or Leonek, or anyone, but saw only angry workers and students climbing over each other to get away. Above, women covered and uncovered their faces, screaming. This was too much. I pushed backward through the crowd, outward, elbowing anything that tried to stop me. Something hit the back of my head and I swung the club again, turning, and saw a militiaman floundering on the ground, his ear bleeding. I pushed through them, but the crowd seemed to go on forever, hysterical demonstrators and militiamen, who swung their clubs as if such a small tool could bring silence. Then I was out, and Kaminski stood shouting at me. I couldn't hear his words, only saw his large mouth, spit-damp, his own club pointing me back into the riot. He reached for me. I grabbed his shoulders and flung him against a van and kept going.

I crossed the street and stood in front of an apartment door, then sat down. Windows slammed shut above me, then I heard gunshots. I thought I would be sick, but wasn't. From where I sat, I saw a row of white vans, bloody men being thrown into them, and a block where women cried from their windows. Two unconscious bodies were carried into a van. I stared at my rings.

After a long time, the vans started to pull out, beginning their journeys to the prison infirmaries. Stefan and Emil appeared, beaten and numb. They noticed me and turned away. Then they parted without words. Leonek was shouting at Moska, some incomprehensible stream of abuse. Moska said nothing, then started across the street toward me, leaving Leonek to his anger.

"You got out," he said. He looked back. There was a smear of blood from his ear to his collar; it wasn't his blood. "Kaminski is after you. Says you attacked him. Says you refused to fight." He brushed his shoulder with a hand. "Sounds like you just fought the wrong person."

"Did I?" My hands were between my knees. I didn't know what had happened to my club. "Did you see Brano?"

He turned to me.

"Sev was dressed up like a worker. This was all a setup."

Moska grimaced, but didn't say anything

for a while. As the last van left, we saw what remained: a bloodstained sidewalk with spare pieces of clothing — a torn shirt, a shoe, some hats. A crying woman knelt over a hat, and a few dazed militiamen stood perfectly still.

"To dirty us," said Moska.

My hands were dirty. My clothes were dirty.

Moska sat down next to me. "A trial run, to implicate ourselves. So that if they want to use us later, we won't hesitate. You, though," he said, but didn't finish his sentence. He stood up and said something that, at that moment, struck me as utterly strange: "I wonder where my wife is right now."

# 10

It took an hour and a half to walk back to the station. I wasn't thinking of Malik Woznica anymore. He and his morphine-addicted wife were nothing to me. A few busses passed, but I didn't flag them down. Brano Sev had helped organize a demonstration in order to close it down. The absurd logic of state security was difficult to grasp.

If I were sent to prison — this is what I

remembered telling Leonek — Ágnes and Magda would be alone, maybe even harassed. I would not be able to protect them. But I couldn't take a club to those people. And Kaminski — I'd attacked him. That, perhaps, was my one regret. But it wasn't a deep regret.

I didn't go inside the station. I found my car, waited for the ignition to catch, then drove fast.

Magda was putting away groceries in the kitchen. "Ágnes is with a friend," she said absently. Her hands shook as she closed the cabinets.

"Are you all right?" I asked.

"Of course I'm all right." I was glad she didn't look at me, because I was not all right.

Pavel followed me as I turned on the radio and went back to the kitchen. But instead of the usual Russian composers, or even staticky American crooners, I heard a Hungarian voice speaking slowly and clearly, giving news of the continued fighting in Budapest. Then another voice asked Soviet soldiers why they were killing their Hungarian brothers and sisters; why, after suffering Stalin for two decades, they were now serving worse Stalins. Magda looked up, surprised and, it seemed to me, terrified.

"You've been listening to the Americans?"

"No," she said abruptly. Pavel let out a sharp cry; she'd stepped on him.

"Christ, Mag, I'm not going to arrest you for it." I forced a smile to show that this was true.

Pavel scurried, whimpering, into the other room.

Magda turned back to the counter so I wouldn't see her face. "Maybe it was Ágnes," she said, then: "No, it was me."

"Doesn't matter. Just turn it back to something mundane when you're finished."

She nodded at the wall. "Of course. Yes."

I wanted to talk it all out with her, to tell her what had happened. I wanted her to touch me and say that I'd done right. But she wasn't listening today. She was somewhere else. She was distracted by her own decisions.

When the telephone rang, I turned down the Americans, who were calmly asking Russian soldiers to lay down their arms and disobey their officers in the interests of justice.

"Ferenc."

"Emil?"

"Look, Ferenc, we've been talking."

"Who?"

"Us. The guys. We're not going in tomorrow. We're calling in sick."

He sounded like he'd been drinking,

which was what I should have been doing. "All of you?"

"Stefan, Leonek, and I. And you, Ferenc."

I paused before answering. "I guess it should be all of us."

"Good."

Magda was throwing something away; I could hear paper crunching. "Just tomorrow? There's the rest of the week, Thursday and Friday."

"No decisions yet. But we can discuss it tomorrow."

I still wasn't completely sure, but the thought of that office was more abhorrent than the fears for my own family. After I hung up, I raised the volume again and said to Magda, "I'm staying home tomorrow."

"You're —" she began, and looked closely at me for the first time since I'd gotten home.

"I'm calling in sick."

Then a high squeal filled the apartment as the radio-jamming went into effect.

# 11

I called the Militia switchboard in the morning and coughed through my lie. The operator took it as easily as she'd taken all

143

the other calls that morning, finishing with a knowing *Take care of yourself* that meant more than a warning about illness.

Ágnes and Magda left together, and I sat with Pavel and the newspaper. My coffee became cold. Although the fighting in Budapest would go on for a few more days, it was evident to *The Spark* that the battle was over. *The Hungarian agitators of reaction are shrinking back into their bullet-riddled holes.* They were defending from broken windows. And the Americans, despite their proud radio talk, were staying out of it.

There were only a few lines about the demonstration:

> **Yesterday, an unwelcome scene appeared on our streets. Hungarian and other foreign elements staged a counterrevolutionary riot that quickly exposed their violent intentions. Four brave members of the People's Militia were injured restoring order.**

I was preparing to take Pavel for a walk when the telephone rang. It was Moska. "How are you feeling?"

I hesitated. "Sick. I feel sick."

"So do I, Ferenc, but I can't do anything

144

about it. Other than Brano and Kaminski, this place is deserted."

"Oh."

"Listen. Your disappeared woman has been found."

"Svetla Woznica?"

"Third District. Central train station. Ferenc, they picked her up for prostitution."

"For what?"

"When they brought her in, someone noticed the missing person's report, so they called over here. Are you too sick to pick her up? I can't leave the station."

"Can't they drive her over?"

"Too short-staffed. Seems half their men are out with the flu."

The Third District Militia station had been moved when its previous home — the old royal police station on Bishop Albert Street, later Engels Street — caught fire in 1952. The cause of the fire was never fully proven, but five Party officials who had, before the Liberation, been high in the Peasant Party were blamed. The charge was subversion, and they were executed. The new station was a concrete slab built on the ruins of a bomb-damaged apartment building. Flat-faced, four floors. It stood out on a street of Habsburg homes. Above double doors, a blue sign told visitors in flat, unadorned letters: MILITIA, DISTRICT III.

The old desk veteran who took me to the basement cells muttered about all the young men who had called in sick. "Forty-three years, and not a day missed. What's this? They don't fool me. Not one minute. *Lazy.*"

I wondered if he really believed that. "What about this girl?"

"She wasn't even hooking for money," he said as he turned on the corridor light.

"What?"

"Ticket. She was selling her goods for a train ticket. Can you believe it?"

"Where to?"

"Does it matter?"

Svetla Woznica was behind a steel door with a barred view-window. She was curled up on the cot in the back corner, and though I didn't look close, her bedpan smelled of fresh vomit. From the ceiling, a fluorescent light buzzed.

When she rolled over to look at us, at first I didn't recognize her. Her upturned nose was ringed by a purple bruise where someone had hit her, and above her thin cheeks her eyes bulged out.

"Svetla Woznica?"

She used an arm to help sit up. Her hair was chopped strangely, as if with gardening shears. "You've come." Her voice cracked.

"You going to take the whore?" asked the veteran.

I squatted beside the cot. Her skin, where it wasn't bruised, was as white as a corpse's. "Can you leave us alone?"

The veteran hesitated. "You're not —" he began, then shrugged and walked out, closing the door behind him.

Svetla's smile exposed a few missing teeth. "Want a good time, mister?" The Russian accent was more apparent now. "You're very big, aren't you?"

"How long has it been?" I pointed at her bruised forearm.

She looked at it too, and shrugged. "Yesterday morning. You got some?"

I tried to lay out the questions in my head, but the stink was distracting me. "Svetla, tell me why you left your husband."

Her mouth opened behind her closed lips, as if she was going to be sick again. But she found her voice. "That prole bastard." She rubbed her face. "Do you know? Did you get it out of him? Of course you didn't." She trembled in a way that reminded me of him. "He had the drug. It was for him. Then when Papa went back to Moscow Malik said, *Svetla, you want a try? It's very nice.*" She closed her eyes. "It was

147

nice, just like he said. But he didn't say how you need it. Because that," she said, tapping her temple, "*that* was his plan. First a little, it's for both of us. *Svetla, we share.* Then all of it, all the medicine for my little Svetla." She was remembering with her expressions, half-crying, half-laughing. "You know how it is? At first it's very good. And then it's better."

I watched her bruised nose, her squinting eyes, understanding slowly. "The morphine?"

"First morphine, yes. Then pills and needles with no names — names I don't know. I'm a whore, not a doctor. Not like Malik."

I swallowed.

"At first, you know, it was not bad. Then he said, *You need rest, my Svetla. I know a spa in Southern Bohemia.*"

"Trebon."

She shook her head. "But we didn't go to Trebon. I knew, I could tell he was driving to the mountains. To that dacha." She covered her mouth with a hand, eyes big. "That was," she said. "That was when it was very bad. He wanted to know what he could do to his little Svetla when no one could hear. He found a lot of things. He's imaginative." She uncovered her mouth.

"And when he wasn't doing his things, he moved me around. That prole's so smart. He said *Svetla, we exercise you so you don't have bedsores, we make sure you don't die.* Like a very smart doctor."

I started to say *Why?* but I didn't know what that meant, or what the answer could be.

Her smile was wide and thin, and flattened out her emaciated face as she read my mind. "I wanted to go home. I *want* to go home." She glanced at the steel door. "Malik, he wanted a quiet wife. He said, a *good* wife. He made me a good wife. *You stay here, Svetla, with me.* In that room with the lock. And no windows. He showed his love with a needle and his prick. You know what I mean? He dressed me up, put all that makeup on my face, and gave me this lovely hairstyle." She touched her chopped bangs. "Needle and the prick." She looked very tired. "And now. Now you take me back, I know. I know this. I'm a crazy whore, but I'm not stupid."

# 12

I signed the forms and took her and her small bag of clothes into my custody. We drove along the Tisa as I tried to make up my mind. It was his word against a morphine addict's. He'd gotten rid of the lock on the bedroom door, and she had taken the rest of the morphine and the other drugs he'd used to keep her incapacitated. There were no witnesses. Malik knew all of this, and that was why he had felt secure enough to face the People's Militia when regulations required our entry — and, ultimately, to use us to retrieve her.

"How did you get away?"

She lifted her forehead from the door window. "Svetla's not stupid. I told you this, now listen. I even have control, a little." She smiled crookedly. "I just didn't take it — the pills, no pills. Simple. Very hard, *da*, but simple. The medicine under the bed and Svetla playacted. After a week, just a week, I was stronger. Maybe Svetla shouldn't have brought the medicine with her, but I did. Now here I am, back on the medicine."

"But the lock. You were locked in."

She considered it, then spoke slowly, "God unlocked the door for me." She looked at a passing bus. "It was a miracle, you know? But not so strange. God wanted Svetla to get away, so she did. But first I looked for a knife, you know, to kill him.

Malik is a clever prole. So clever. He took away all the knives. The whole kitchen, no knives! Such a clever prole."

Malik forgets to lock her door, or maybe he's decided there's no longer any need, then she tears the kitchen apart in her desire to kill him.

I stopped at the central bank, and while she waited in the car, humming to herself, I stood in line and withdrew a quarter of the money from my account, more than half of it in rubles. Then, at the train station, I bought a sleeper cabin to Moscow, both beds so she would be alone.

I found the conductor and pulled him aside. Using both my Militia certificate and a stack of koronas, I commanded him to keep a close watch on her. "She's not to leave the cabin, you follow? You bring her meals. She's to stay on the train until Moscow, where someone from the Soviet Militia will pick her up. You are also to hold this," I said, handing over an envelope heavy with rubles. "You will give it to the Moscow militiaman. He knows how much to expect. This one," I added, handing over another, "is for the border guards. She does not have papers. You're still with me?"

He started to protest, but I leaned over

him to make it clear that we both knew what was and was not possible at the frontier.

I gave Svetla a third envelope of rubles, in case something went wrong once she was on the other side. That was when she finally understood what was happening. She started to cry, fell on her knees, and pressed her bruised, wet face to my hand. Some old women in the ticket line looked at me with scorn, and a few men smiled.

# 13

It took a while, and the operator had to call me back, but finally I was speaking, in very poor Russian, to the switchboard operator of the Moscow Militia. She was stern-sounding, but when she heard the name she brightened. *Immediately.* There was no one in the office around me, and Moska's door was shut.

"*Da?*"

"Comrade Inspector Kliment Malevich?"

"Moment."

I was trying to not think about Svetla's story, the details she never quite spelled out, and to ignore the knots in my stomach when I didn't succeed.

"What is it?"

I hadn't spoken to him since he and his mother had left almost two decades ago. He had been a fat child then. "Comrade Kliment Malevich?"

"*Da.*"

"I was a friend of your father's. In the royal police."

He hummed into the phone, unsure of what to say.

"My name is Ferenc Kolyeszar."

"I think I remember." He sounded young. "Didn't you . . ."

"Yes. Leonek Terzian and I discovered your father's body."

That seemed to reassure him. "Okay, Ferenc. How are you?"

"As good as can be expected in difficult times."

"Truly."

"And yourself? Your mother?"

"I'm excellent, but my mother's been dead five years."

"Was it easy for her? I hope."

It was obvious to us both that I was no good at small talk. "Tell me, Ferenc. Tell me why you've called."

I described the situation in as much detail as I could, so he would understand the necessity of what I was asking of him.

"Who's this husband of hers?"

153

"Doesn't matter."

"So he's political." He paused. "And I do what, exactly?"

"You give her a ride, that's all. Find out where her father lives and drive her there." I told him the exact number of rubles he would receive.

"You don't need to pay me, Ferenc. I'll do it."

"Consider it expenses — what's left over is a tip. And if the conductor gives you one ruble less, break his knees."

Kliment laughed.

As I hung up, Moska came out of his office with a half-eaten sandwich, wiping a spot off his tie. "Where's the Woznica woman?"

I swiveled in my chair. "Who?"

"Jesus, Ferenc." He brought the sandwich down to his side. "Tell me."

"Wasn't her. Some hooker I'd known from before. I took her back to the Canal District and told her to stay away from trains."

He didn't know whether or not to believe me. But he had other things on his mind. "I'm sending you back there. To the canals. I've got a real murder for you."

"I think I feel my illness coming back."

Moska didn't smile. "Come on."

He settled in his chair and watched me

sit across from him. "Do you know what you're doing, Ferenc?"

I shrugged a forced unconcern.

"I was as disturbed as anyone by yesterday. You know that."

I did know.

He picked up a typed sheet. "If you need to talk it over, okay? Just come to me. I'll do what I can from my side, and if you need anything, let me know. Don't ruin your career."

"Thanks."

He looked at me a moment more, then read from the sheet, his tone back to its usual efficiency. "Augustus II Square, number three. A burned body." He handed it over, and there wasn't a lot more. No identifying traits, just a body in the center of the Canal District. It had been called in anonymously and not yet verified. "You're the only one around to take the case."

"I can't pass it on to someone else tomorrow?"

"Stefan's still wasting time on that suicide, and Leonek's working on a dead case — not to mention he thinks I hid Sergei's files." He shook his head. "That kid doesn't have the slightest idea how a bureaucracy is run. Anyway, when Emil gets over his flu, he can help you."

155

On my way out I passed Kaminski and Brano Sev in the corridor. Brano looked again like himself — he'd gone back to the long leather coat, and his somber mouth was too small to ever form a shout.

"So you're feeling better," said Kaminski. There was no more levity in his manner. He'd run out of it.

"Yes."

"A lot of sick guys today. Me, I've got a sore back. Stumbled carelessly into a van. You, though," he said, his trigger finger tapping his thigh, "You were quite sick yesterday. Very ill. It was obvious in everything you did."

"I'm okay."

Brano nodded at my hand, which held the folded sheet. "But you're shaking. You're not quite recovered."

"Looks like we should keep an eye on him," said Kaminski.

I pressed my lips together until they formed something meant to look like a smile.

# 14

The anxiety collapsed upon me on the front steps, the bright sun spotting my vision. I had bribed state employees of the railroads, frontier guards, and even a Moscow militiaman. I'd aided the wife of a Party official in leaving the country illegally. Yesterday, I had walked away from the scene of battle, and in the process attacked a member of the KGB.

I reached the empty sidewalk and found my car. I had trouble getting the key into the door, then into the ignition. My joints were heavy, gummed up. I leaned my head on the wheel and took deep breaths.

A burned body would not walk away. I could wait for tomorrow. Or the next day. Or forever.

There were only a few farmers in the markets I passed, looking bored and alone. No children, and all the window shutters were closed. A general, unspoken strike had descended on the Capital. Just as the students had predicted.

I turned on the radio and settled into the sofa. There was a show of song and recitation for the fortieth anniversary of the founding of the Communist Party. *There is nothing secret about the Party — we all know what it is.* I wished the day would end. I lit a cigarette, and in the smoke saw Svetla Woznica sick in her cabin, racing toward the Soviet border. *It's all of us. It's me; it's you.* I saw an empty city, shutters closed, then another one filled with tanks and gunfire and shattered windows. *The Party is a tree in the desert; it's a star at midnight.* Magda beneath Stefan's sweating white body, half-listening to the Americans' radio broadcasts, then stumbling home and muttering some guilty words about Lydia, but feeling only the ache in her groin.

*Be happy. A great Party means you are never alone.*

Ágnes showed up with Pavel, and I realized I hadn't noticed his absence. He sprang onto the sofa and climbed on me. His breath stank as he licked my chin. Ágnes brought a cup of water from the kitchen.

"Why are you home so early?" I asked.

She sat on the floor and squinted — her glasses were nowhere to be seen. "Not enough teachers," she said. "Sick. They tried to teach us anyway, but by lunchtime they saw it was no use."

"You took the bus back?"

"Had to wait forever. But Daniela came along. Wasn't so bad. Where were you? I thought you were sick too."

"I had to work." My cigarette was burned down, so I carried it to the kitchen, dropping ash along the way. Ágnes changed the radio station.

"Daniela told me about this," she said by way of explanation.

So we sat together on the sofa and listened to the Americans. It was a day of injustice, they said. Although sporadic fighting continued in some areas of the city, Budapest was now clearly lost. Imre Nagy was hiding in the Yugoslav embassy. I put my arm around Ágnes, and she leaned into me. Pavel was quiet in her lap. When the news began to repeat itself, I turned it off.

Around six, as I was cooking eggs for dinner, Magda showed up. She seemed disheveled somehow, as if she'd put her clothes on backward. But they looked fine. She sat at the kitchen table and watched me with surprise. I didn't think it was because I was cooking.

"Why didn't you tell me?" she asked finally.

"What?"

"Yesterday. The demonstration. Why didn't you tell me about it?"

I stared back at her. "How did you know?"

"Word gets around."

I wondered if Stefan had shed tears when he'd told her the story. I set a plate in front of her. "You weren't in a listening mood."

After dinner, we put on the Americans again, sitting together like a proper family, until the screech of jamming overcame it. As I turned it back to music, I told Ágnes that, whether or not everyone else listened to this station, it was still against the law. It should not be discussed outside the family. "The volume should remain low," I said. "And afterward, always change the station. You understand?"

"I knew all this before, Daddy."

"Now it's more important than before."

She nodded, and so did Magda.

We put Ágnes to bed, then drank wine in the living room. We didn't talk, but for the first time in weeks the silence wasn't strained. I didn't know why. I was too exhausted to dwell on her and Stefan or even the mistakes I'd made these last two days. I was blank. I was disconnected from everything around me, even all that we had learned from the radio. It was disturbingly like the blankness I acquired on the battlefield, where all tender emotions are kept at arm's length, so they will not harm you.

But then she smiled and nodded at the bedroom door. "You want to sleep in a real bed tonight?"

I did.

We undressed and got beneath the sheets

in the dark. At first we did not touch, then she slid against me, and I could feel that she had not worn her nightdress. She buried her face in my chest in a way that made the blood rush into my head. It had been so long since she'd held me like that, and I stroked her bare, warm ribs with the tips of my fingers. But it was no use. After the initial flush of excitement, my body wouldn't stay up for it. Everything receded to arm's length. I kissed her ear and let her go. She rolled away from me, her cold heels just touching my shins, and began to cry.

# 15

The students had been right. A general strike can arise spontaneously out of the malaise of discontent triggered by a single act, and when this happens it seems that the entire population has found its voice at last, one that rises above all the little voices in *The Spark*. But the students were wrong to think a strike can last without organization. No leaders came from the Sixth of November Strike. No Imre Nagy. Even Kozak the Engineer stayed quiet. So over the days that followed, the streets became fuller, the shop counters staffed, the shutters open. Because despite our proud talk at parties and clandestine meetings, all any of us wanted was some food on the table and a little security. When on the twelfth *The Spark* proclaimed that the imperialist-financed counterrevolutionaries in Budapest had finally been crushed completely, we were all already back to work.

Emil came back first, on Thursday the eighth. We took his Russian Zorki camera over the Georgian Bridge and parked in the lot on the edge of the canals and walked the rest of the way.

The lumpenproletariat of the Canal District was still on strike. We crossed arched stone bridges over stagnant water and heard our footsteps through the ancient alleys. A few old women in black scurried behind their doors.

Augustus II Square was in the flooded Deeps, the center of the canals. It had always been the most crumbling, waterlogged area of the district, and recent fires had turned a lot of upper floors into charred shells. We paused at the summit of a bridge and tried to figure out how to reach the dry curb. My leap was just short, and I landed shin deep in icy water. Emil, lighter and more agile, arrived unscathed. One more long alley, my shoes squeaking, and we were finally there.

Two centuries back, it had been a tanners' square, and there was still an eroded wooden sign depicting the shape of a cow's flesh, removed and flattened. Below it, a man's black shoe floated in the water. But number three was an old, aristocratic residence. Its front door was missing, and beside its frame, the anonymous caller had been kind enough to mark it with a white chalk x.

In the entryway, the temperature dropped and a decomposed rug slopped under my feet. Emil cursed as he slipped and almost dropped the camera. I lit a match to see better. The cracked walls were blackened by moss. Light came from a doorway up ahead. I blew out the flame.

The smell hit us first. I'd smelled charred flesh during the war inside burned farmhouses. Its pungency is different than any other burned substance, but in a way I still can't describe with words. The room was vast and circular, its edge raised like a walkway, everything lit by the shattered glass roof above. In the corner was the stone lip of a well, probably dug so the servants could avoid mixing with the tanners in the street. The lower level of the room was now a circular pool coated with pieces of shattered glass and fragments of colored stone that had once been part of a mosaic. A bacchanal scene of nymphs and satyrs with chalices of wine and grapes. All that was left was a hoof here, a breast there, and pieces of purple grapes scattered through the water. A Roman scene — here, in the middle of the Carpathian basin.

Emil pointed to a black mound curled up on the dry edge, facing the wall. The stone floor beneath it had been discolored by heat. That indescribable smell filled me as we approached, and I had to focus to quell my stomach.

Emil snapped a picture.

I crouched and examined as best I could without touching it. Gender unknown. Folded up fetally, arms together, black hands pressed tight as if praying. That, at least, made some kind of sense. A final prayer. Then I noticed the lump around the wrists. "Tied up," I said, and Emil took another photo. There was more charred rope around the ankles.

I didn't know if the body had been alive or dead when it was burned, but it seemed to mean something that the body was only two feet from the ledge that dropped off into water, and salvation.

Emil circled the room, shooting and

looking for clues. I started to do the same, but I wasn't seeing anything clearly. "Emil."

He heard the tone in my voice. "Go on. I'll be out in a minute."

I squatted on the steps outside. The chill froze my wet feet, but I was more worried about my stomach. I stared at that lone shoe beneath the tanner's sign and tried to steady myself, the fall light making everything too crisp and too gray. The nausea was more than it should have been; it was proving how weak I really was.

A flaming body, bound and twisting, so close to the water. One roll, that's all it would have taken. The tragedy was magnified. Then, inexplicably, I remembered earlier that morning, waking up next to Magda for the first time in months. That first rush of joy was tempered as she rolled over, smiling, and said, *I'm going to call in sick again.* She didn't remember at the moment of waking that she'd told me she had worked her full shift.

I walked through the water and retrieved the shoe. Black, unadorned leather, not very worn, right foot. If I needed it in the future, I wouldn't want to come back to search for it.

"Nothing," said Emil from the doorway.

He noticed the dripping shoe in my hand. "Let's get out of here."

Back at the station, I called Markus Feder and told him to send his men to pick up the body. "You think I've got men here? I've got no one. Your corpse will just have to wait."

# 16

By Friday we were fully staffed, except for Kaminski, who had mercifully disappeared. But even in his absence I had the feeling he was in some other room in the Capital, trigger finger flicking, calculating my demise. Kaminski's eyes — Brano Sev — worked at his desk, silent, his back toward us, but he was aware of everything we did. He knew that each of us wanted to smash his head against his steel file cabinets for what he'd made us do at that demonstration. But none of us touched him.

Emil had developed the pictures in his darkroom at home, and Leonek joined us to look them over in a café, far from Brano Sev.

Our first choice was still closed, its metal blinds pulled down, so we went a couple streets farther to a crowded, smoke-congested bar on October Square. We leaned on the counter as Emil passed around the photos. "Bad light, a little blurry. But you get the idea."

We did get the idea. Leonek squinted the blackened human mass, and the smell came back to me, cutting through the living bodies all around us.

There were photos of empty corners, the dry well, and fragments of decadent Roman life underwater, "It's an empty crime scene," I said.

Emil drank his coffee, "Except for a shoe."

"It was outside the scene. And I'm not walking all over the Capital with just a shoe, not when half the stores are still closed."

"Then we wait for the coroner."

A table became free, so we took it. Emil asked Leonek how his investigation was coming.

"Not well." Leonek leaned close, arms on the table. "But I've learned a lot. Sergei kept good records of his interviews, and I've got a list of names. He had tried to talk to the families of Chasya Grubin and Reina Westreicher, the two dead girls, but they wouldn't tell him anything." He frowned at this. "Why would they? He was

167

Russian. So I looked them up. The Westreicher family got out soon afterward, to Austria. The Grubin family — only the brother and the grandfather are still here. The grandfather's a little crazy, I can't get much out of him. And Chasya's brother — Zindel — is in Ozaliko Prison. He's in for political crimes — a societal menace, they told me."

"Can you talk to him?" asked Emil.

"I filled out the paperwork two weeks ago, but now — now, I don't know." He coughed into his hand and waved to the woman behind the counter for another coffee. "Corina!" he called, but she didn't notice him. "Sergei interviewed a lot of Russian soldiers, but that was a decade ago. They're all back home. So, like you, I wait."

"What about Stefan?" My voice cracked. "Is he helping you?"

He tilted his head from side to side. "Now and then, yes. He's still working on that suicide."

"Looks like a suicide to you too?"

"Stefan hasn't convinced me otherwise. He's talked to a lot of people, but none of it seems to lead anywhere."

"But why is he so convinced?"

Leonek blinked at me, as if he'd said too

much already. "Why don't you ask him yourself?" He went to the counter and ordered another coffee.

# 17

Homicide investigations work in starts and stops. Clues move them forward; the absence of clues takes the drive out of them. When this happens, you move on to the next case, or complete paperwork.

Markus Feder called to say he'd received the body but wouldn't have anything for us until Monday. The waterlogged shoe in my drawer was useless until then. Emil and I had neither another case nor backed-up paperwork, so, to avoid Moska thinking up more paperwork (something he had a great talent for) and to keep myself from dwelling on the train that had by then reached Moscow, I helped Emil pick up his wash from the laundry. We carried the tied bundles to his apartment.

He lived a little farther back from the Tisa than Woznica, but still clearly in the upscale Fourth District. Lena's money had paid for the entire top floor, for renovations, and no doubt the functioning elevator as well. The view, as Emil had promised, was breathtaking. Red clay-tiled roofs crisscrossed in a jumbled mix that reflected how the Capital had grown over the centuries: piece by piece. I could spot the ragged shards of a couple buildings not yet rebuilt from the war. Beyond were the two spires of the Georgian Bridge and the roofs of the Canal District, speckled by holes. To the left, low plains rose eastward to the Carpathians.

They had lived here for seven years, and after Emil's grandfather died, his grandmother came to live with them. She had passed away three years back, and since then this space big enough for five families had housed only two people.

We settled into the plush, modern sofas — thick white cushions shaped like boxes — and began to drink. This was a serious thing with Emil. When he first joined the Militia, he had been a child who couldn't hold his liquor, and a bullet in the stomach had slowed him even more. But eight years with Lena had seasoned him, and now he treated drinking as a respected ritual. There were the thin, openmouthed glasses that felt ready to shatter, the polished tumbler into which he delivered crushed ice with an elegant silver spoon. "You develop a taste for it," he told me. "The ice has got to be crushed, at least that's what they say. Then the gin. Wait a minute — it's got to get to *know* the ice. Then the vermouth. This," he said as he shook the mixture with both hands, "is something special. They drink it in New York City."

He called it a martini, and it tasted like flowers.

"The place I go to ran out of olives a few days ago, but you get the idea."

I smiled.

The first one put me over, and the second kept me moving. Lounging in that huge living room, gazing at the painting above the radio set — a stern, white-bearded old man — I thought I could get used to this. Leonek had told me once that Emil's home had always made him uncomfortable, but I couldn't see why.

Were I not a little drunk, I might have kept quiet about it. But by the third drink, as we were touring the apartment and he opened the door to the darkroom, he asked. I told him everything. He switched on a red overhead light as I talked and touched the prints hung up to dry like clothes. Images of the burned body, snapshots of Lena that made her look younger than she really was, views of the countryside. His face darkened as he listened, the red lights deepening his cheeks. "So I called Moscow. It's been arranged."

"What are you going to do when Woznica finds out?"

The gin was making me unconcerned. "Don't tell. He won't know."

Emil waved that away. "A couple well-placed questions, and he knows it all. Have you thought about this?"

"You think I should have handed her back?"

"Of course not. But there are other ways."

"What ways?"

"Go after him. It's possible."

"It's not possible. He might as well be a politicos."

"What about papers? You could have gotten papers from Roberto in Supplies. He's got connections, and he's helped me out before."

"It would have taken too long."

Emil closed his eyes as he considered possibilities. Then he opened them. "Maybe you're right."

In the living room, Emil described the effect of the Hungarian uprising on his marriage: "Lena's starting to go crazy."

"She's afraid?"

"Not of the Russians. Not that. She wants children."

I looked into my empty glass, fearing for any child with that woman as a mother.

"We've been trying for years. Once it did work, but —"

"Miscarriage?"

"Four years ago. I don't want her to go through that again."

"What does this have to do with the Magyars?"

"Nothing, not really. She's just feeling her mortality. She needs to give her love to someone other than me."

"Watch out she doesn't leave you."

He went silent, so I looked over at him. He was staring into his glass. "Each of us has his own marriage, Ferenc."

Lena showed up with a shopping bag on her arm and a smile on her face. "The very comradely Inspector Ferenc Kolyeszar. How did Emil ever get you here?"

Her beauty was beginning to wear from her drinking, but there was still something about Lena Brod that gave the illusion of a woman in her prime. She glided over in a cloud of perfume, her dark hair stroking my cheeks as she kissed them. "You're looking well, Lena."

She winked at me, her mascara thick but precise. "When are you going to bring your *extremely* well looking wife over for dinner?"

"Soon. Very soon."

"I *hope*. What are you drinking?"

I looked blankly at my empty glass, then at Emil.

"Martinis," he said. "Here's yours." He was already pouring it.

The conversation turned to shopping. Lena had recently traveled to Paris, and it saddened her when she had to shop here. "That's the tragedy of our situation, do you realize? Look at this material." She showed us a black blouse she had found. "It's so thin. And do you know how many colors I had to choose from? *Two*. Black and blue. Doesn't that tell you something?" Then she began a monologue on the virtues of capitalist department stores, her hands turning continually in her lap until Emil put his own hand on them.

"I don't think Ferenc cares too much about shopping."

She touched a red nail to her chin and looked at me.

I shrugged.

Lena stood up. "I'll let you boys discuss homicides, then." She grabbed a bottle of vodka from the bar and marched into another room.

"She okay?"

Emil took a sip. "She'll be fine."

174

But there was nothing more to talk about. He fell into one of his unself-conscious silences, distracted by other matters, and it only made me self-conscious. So I reached for my hat.

I drove slowly and carefully through the early dusk. The apartment was empty. I lay down in the empty bedroom. It was still a lovely novelty: a bed. Its breadth was amazing, the even firmness of the mattress, the headboard. I breathed in deeply to cleanse my head, and caught a faint whiff. I was unsure. I rolled facedown and sniffed. I thought it was the drunk, webbed parts of my imagination, but no — this was a very definite, heavy stink: sex. I put my nose into the duvet, then pulled it back and smelled the sheets. Its strength went to my head. I'd slept with Magda those last couple nights, but we'd slept beside one another, touching only hands.

I considered, briefly, taking it all out on Stefan as I should have done before. Our years of friendship meant nothing in the face of this. I could drive to his apartment, whether or not she was there, and beat him until there was nothing left to love. But I used the only real weapon I had. I grabbed the spare pillow, took an extra sheet and blanket from the wardrobe, and made up my bed again in the living room.

When she saw it that evening, she did not say a word.

# 18

On Monday morning, we found Markus Feder chain-smoking in the corridor outside his lab. He didn't stop as we approached. "Rough weekend?" Emil asked.

Feder put a hand to his red hair as if he'd forgotten something. A few passing colleagues looked at him. "Comrade Inspectors," he began, "what do you know about this body already?"

"Nothing," I said. "Bound wrists and ankles. Burned in the Canal District. I've got a shoe in the car, but I don't know if it's the victim's."

Feder dropped his cigarette and stepped on it.

There was a lump on the examining table that he didn't uncover. He washed his hands in the sink and talked loudly over the water. "It's a man, all right. The bone structure's clear enough." He shut off the faucet and went for a towel. "Height, five-nine, average. I'd guess he was balding, but can't be sure. He was killed about a week ago." His hands were dry now, so he turned to us. "Inspectors, both his arms and legs had been broken."

"By the heat?" asked Emil.

Feder shook his head. "The victim was tied and gagged. Then his legs and arms were broken. Probably with a simple household hammer. And then the victim was dragged a long distance by his broken, bound arms. The way the bones are separated and the muscles stretched, I can't imagine how far he was dragged. Very far. And, finally, the poor bastard was doused with benzene. And lit. There are carbon monoxide particles in the lungs — he was burned alive."

We stared at the lump on the table. There was that smell again, though the ventilation kept it to a minimum.

"He couldn't roll over," I said. "Into the water."

"Your victim's arms and legs were useless. All he had was jelly and bone shards." Another cigarette hung from his lips, unlit.

Emil looked a little sick.

"What about his shoes?" I asked.

"His left shoe," said Feder as he lit his cigarette and started for the door. "It melted into him."

"His right shoe?"

Feder shrugged and passed through the swinging doors.

Emil suggested we stop for a coffee, and over our cups we said nothing, thinking of muscles contracting uselessly and bones crunching. I could feel it too, in my legs, and this is the imagination that had made me believe I could write; this was how I could feel Stefan's weight on Magda's dry skin, could see his twisted face at the moment of climax.

The first cobbler, an old professional with half-moon glasses, turned the shoe over in his hand. First the heel, which was worn at an angle (he disapproved of this with a shake of his head), then the mold of the toe, the sewing around the lace holes, and finally the compressed insole. He handed it back to me. "I don't know this work, and I don't think I want to."

"But it's not a factory shoe, correct?"

"Absolutely not. Unskilled work, but hand-made."

The second cobbler was a young man on the other side of town. He wore a tailored jacket and wide red tie. His name was Petru Salva. "Comrades, this shoe was not made in the Capital. You may be assured of that."

"Can you be certain?" asked Emil.

Salva held the shoe up on his fingertips and touched a long nail to the toe, the laces, the border with the sole. "This threading is absolutely provincial. No doubt about it."

"Which province?"

"Difficult to say, Comrades. Extremely difficult. Each village with its own cobbler has a style individual to that one cobbler. It's *idiosyncratic*."

"But you," I said, "you're very familiar with such things. You can find out?"

Petru Salva tugged the end of his jacket. "Of course, Comrades. I imagine I'm the only one in the Capital who can. I will make inquiries."

"It's much appreciated."

"We all do our part." He smiled. "The times require it."

"The times do," I said.

We did not get our answer until Thursday, and on Tuesday I suggested we help Leonek. "Another set of eyes is what I need," Leonek told us. "I can't see straight anymore." He handed over a thick stack of pages.

They were interviews with Russian soldiers conducted in mid-1946. The questions were simple — *Where were you on — ? Where was Comrade Private — ? When?*

179

The answers were direct. *The bar, Comrade.
Asleep, Comrade. Fishing in the Tisa, Comrade.* After a while I couldn't see straight
either. Nothing pointed to anything; these
were good boys who fished and slept and
drank. Yet Sergei's questions continued, as
if he were filling in pieces of an outline, but
could not find its shape.

Sergei had been an impressive militiaman. It wasn't easy to trust a Russian,
but with him it was possible. He was earnest and straightforward with everyone. He
had a simple view of justice from which he
never deviated. When the girls turned up
dead in that synagogue, it crushed him. It
was a Russian crime, and only a Russian
could set things right — he told us all that.
He went off on his own, feverishly plowing
through interviews, then Leonek and I
were on the foggy bank of the Tisa, and he
was dead.

Emil drifted to sleep over his stack. I
went back to reading. *Buying cigarettes,
Comrade. Fishing in the Tisa, Comrade.* The
Russian boys were all doing the same
thing, day after day. *Asleep, Comrade.* The
same things, no complications. The same
words. The answers began to look as if
they had been scripted. *The bar, Comrade.*
Scripted and agreed upon and practiced

until they were rote.

I handed Leonek the pages. "They're all lying."

"Of course they are." Something crossed his face when he looked at me.

"What?"

"Nothing. Listen — I need to get to Zindel Grubin, Chasya's brother. They're ignoring my prison interview request. Do you think you could get me into Ozaliko? Moska would never help me. But maybe he'd help you."

"Try him yourself. Moska's not hiding anything from you. He even told me that."

The look crossed his face again. Something like disappointment, or shame. "Forget it."

My phone rang.

"Ferenc?" The line was staticky.

"Yes?"

"Ferenc, this is Kliment."

I realized there had never been a need for me to struggle through Russian with him. "Good to hear from you. Tell me."

"Without a hitch, Ferenc. She's with her father now. There were a lot of tears."

"You get all the money?"

"No broken knees. But it looked like she needed it more than I."

I couldn't quit smiling — not that day,

or the next, as we continued our haggard reading of Sergei's interviews.

# 19

Petru Salva called Thursday morning. Perhaps for our benefit, he had attached his Party pin to his lapel and dusted his portrait of Mihai. He held the shoe — cleaned now, and polished — by the heel and the toe as he spoke. "The inquiries have been made, Comrade Inspectors. The verdict is in. Notice this, please." He turned the toe to face us. "The corners of the leather are uneven. Very sloppy. And this." He raised it so we could see the bottom of the heel. "Nine nails to hold the heel in place. Wear this shoe for six months, it will fall off. Guaranteed."

"But where is it from?" asked Emil.

Salva placed the shoe on the counter. "There is a cobbler in the Fifth District. A friend of mine. He has had much experience touring the provinces in order to nationalize the means of shoe production. But provincial cobblers are a notoriously uncooperative bunch, if you get my meaning." He was smiling again. "My friend has seen this work before — once you see such terrible work, you don't forget it."

"Where?" Emil repeated.

Salva's smile spread. "There were hundreds of possibilities. You see, each village is like a little pompous ego. But my friend —"

"The village," I said.

His smile went away.

Drebin was an hour out of town, its sign half-buried in the long grass, just past an enthusiastic billboard that said in large red letters: THE PARTY'S POLICIES EXPRESS THE INTERESTS OF THE WORKING CLASS AND THE WHOLE WORKING NATION!

It had once been a farming village, then, after collectivization, a tractor factory was built in one of the fallow fields and workers were moved from the Capital to run it. The blocks constructed to house them — two identical concrete towers — overlooked the tin-roofed village homes and Orthodox church. Earlier that day, a rain had turned the white walls gray. Along the main street lay all the stores — bakery, bar, grocer's, butcher, post office, and cobbler. The tiny cobbler's workshop was filled with leatherworking tools hanging from hooks. Scraps of leather covered the floor, and the old cobbler sat at a wide wooden table covered with finished shoes. He took off his glasses and smiled toothlessly. "Morning."

"Morning."

"What size?" he said, looking at the shoe in my hand.

"We haven't come for that," said Emil.

"Repair, then? Here." He reached for the shoe, and I let him have it. He replaced his glasses as he turned it over. "My work," he muttered, then tapped the heel on the table and examined it again. "What's the trouble, then?"

We pulled out our Militia certificates. "Can you tell us who you made that shoe for?"

The cobbler chewed the inside of his mouth.

"We're trying to identify a dead man," I said. "He was found in the Capital, but his shoe was from here."

The cobbler went to a low shelf where some cheap notebooks lay. "In the Capital, huh? Size forty-one," he muttered, then opened a notebook on the table.

Emil eyed a hand-drawn poster with the shape of a cow's hide, like the tanner's sign in the Canal District. I read the labeled sections over his shoulder — *the back, the bend, belly, side and double shoulder.*

"Oh Lord," said the cobbler. He was shaking his head over his notebook. He checked the shoe again, then went back to the page. His face had lost its color. "Oh poor Beatrice."

"A woman?" I asked.

He took off his glasses and rubbed his nose. "Beatrice is the boy's mother. Antonín," he said. "Antonín Kullmann. That's whose shoe this is."

# 20

He didn't trust us to deliver the news properly, so he closed his shop and led us. He would only say that Antonín was a good man who lived in the Capital but still remembered where he came from. He would never trust one of *those* overpriced cobblers. Then he fell to muttering, shaking his head and sucking on his gums. People paused to watch us pass, and a few greeted the cobbler, but he didn't hear them. The housing blocks watched over us as we turned onto a dirt road lined with face-high metal fences. We stepped around puddles like lakes. The cobbler entered the fifth gate on the left and kept moving up the front steps. "Beatrice!" he called, then knocked.

A fat woman with squinting eyes and red hands opened the door. "Frederik." As she kissed his cheeks she noticed us at the bottom of the steps. A curt nod.

"I need to talk to you, Bea."

She pulled back to look into his face. "Come in, then."

Frederik followed her, but before he shut the door he held up a finger. "One minute."

Behind him, the muted sound of Antonín's mother: "*What*, Frederik?"

Emil kicked the dirt. "I've never gotten used to this."

"It's hard."

"More than that." He took a deep breath. "I feel like I'm giving myself the news for the first time. I've seen the body, I know it's dead, but only through someone else can I feel it. Does that make sense?"

I was looking at the twisted rose branches that lined the house. Dead branches: Winter was fast approaching. "Yeah."

"Leonek is very cool about this. I let him take over and do the talking."

"Then, if you'd prefer —"

"I would."

This was one of the many things I liked about Emil: Unlike me, he wasn't afraid to broadcast his weaknesses to the world.

The door opened, and Frederik, chewing on his gums, nodded us inside.

It was what one would expect from an old woman living alone: claustrophobia. Insecure tables and bureaus and porcelain-filled shelves, and walls of family photographs with hazy borders. A jigsaw of rugs covered the wood floors, and through a door I saw a pile of wet clothes in the tub, more hanging from a line. In the living room, where Beatrice sat on a sofa staring at the wall, there was a waist-high marble sculpture of a naked woman with an arm stretched over her head. I wondered how that had gotten there.

"Sit down," she muttered.

There were enough chairs to accommodate one of Georgi's get-togethers. Frederik sat next to her and put his hand on the hands clenched between her knees.

"How?" she said. "How did my son die?" It was impossible to judge her face or voice. Her deep-set eyes rested on Emil. "You must tell me."

Emil looked at me.

I spoke: "First let me give our consolations, Comrade Kullmann. We understand how difficult this must be."

"Don't tell me you understand. This is regular for you. Just tell me how my son died."

"He was burned," said Emil.

She looked at him again, as if she knew it was hardest for him. "It wasn't an accident, was it? *Tell me!*"

Emil opened his mouth. His *no* was too quiet to hear.

But she heard it, and asked me, "Why was my son burned? Do you know this? Old ladies in the provinces are harder than the ones in the city. You can tell me."

"We don't know anything yet. That's why we're here."

Frederik shook his head, sucking. "They don't know anything." He squeezed her hands tighter.

"Did you hear from your son much?" I asked.

"Hear from him?" Her head popped back. "He was my *son,* Inspectors. Look around you. Everything you see is from him. He knew about family. Antonín had his faults, but ignoring his mother wasn't one of them. Let go of me, Frederik."

The cobbler returned his hand to his own knee.

"Then perhaps you can help us out."

Maybe it was my size, or the way I chose to hold her gaze, but she shifted on the sofa to face me. Despite the others, it became a dialogue. "He called me a few weeks ago, Inspector. Not a rare thing, but unexpected. It worried me."

"Why did it worry you?"

"Because he didn't have a reason. He

only called to say he loved me."

"He didn't do that usually?"

When she smiled, her eyes shut and her cheeks swelled. "He always said he loved me, Inspector. He usually called for other reasons. He liked to give his mother things."

"So you heard from him often."

"Let me tell you about Antonín." She leaned back into the sofa. "He's a good boy. He reveres his mother. He works hard — you probably don't even know what he does, do you?"

I shook my head.

"He's the most important painter in the Capital."

I noticed that Emil was recording everything in his notepad. "Go on."

"Do you know how he became so important? No? He worked for it. Out here, he got no education at all, and everyone expected him to be a cooperative farmer like his useless father. Or a factory worker. But my Antonín is better than that. He loved art. And when you love art in Drebin, you had better leave. So that's what he did. He left, with my blessings, at the end of the war — he and his wife — and after only a few years he had his very own shows. Can you believe it?"

I had been on the periphery of the arts in the Capital for a long time now, and the name Kullmann did not ring a bell. But Antonín . . . "He was married?"

Her face settled. "Zoia Lendvai. That tramp left him the same year as his first show — nineteen and forty-eight. For a *clerk*. You can bet she kicked herself once my Antonín became famous."

"Do you know the name of the clerk she married?"

"I don't care. My Antonín survived her treachery, that's all that matters. See that?" She pointed to the marble nude. "Antonín made it for me. And here." She pointed at a small framed painting. It was peculiar — a simple image of tree branches, black winding lines on a white surface, and where the black and white met my eye could not quite focus. "That's an early one, when his genius was first apparent. He's still big, no matter what they say, certainly bigger than that big-headed friend of his, Vlaicu." She put her hands together. "My Antonín."

Then it hit me. *Antonín:* the repetition dug deeper into my memory. The name on Josef Maneck's notepad. "Tell me," I said. "Do you know Josef Maneck? He used to be a museum curator."

"Know him? Well, of course. I haven't talked to him in years, but *he* was the one to recognize my boy's genius. He put up my son's paintings — that's all it took. The rest, as they say, is history."

My hands were cold as we shook her hand at the door and nodded at Frederik.

"Catch my boy's killer, Inspectors."

"We'll try," I said.

"And say hello to Josef for me."

"We'll do that," said Emil.

# 21

On the drive back I explained the connection to Emil. He frowned at the fields. "Why was his name on Maneck's notepad?"

"They were probably friends. What's Antonín's address?"

Beatrice had given it to us with Antonín's extra key. "Karl Marx fifty-nine."

K — — R — 5 — : K. Marx 59.

The apartment was another one near the Tisa, but in the Second District, and on the ground floor. It faced a small, overgrown courtyard through barred windows. Books had been tossed casually around, clothes strewn on the chairs, and a smell of fried eggs lingered in the kitchen. Emil brought out his pistol.

It was soon clear that the apartment was empty, though someone had eaten there not long ago. There was no sign of forced entry.

"Another spare key?" Emil suggested.

"Or Antonín's key."

The apartment had been treated roughly, but not destroyed; I didn't think anything had been taken. Someone had slept in the bed recently.

Emil looked through some canvases leaning against the wall. Family scenes: dinner tables, children in a lake, an overfull Trabant driving to holiday. The signature was quite legible: *A. Kullmann.*

We went through the apartment and came up with little. Whoever spent the last few days there had left only old food in the kitchen — potatoes, eggs. There were crushed cigarettes on a plate beside the chair in the living room, and a couple books on the floor around it — a volume of Kandinski's writings on the spiritual in art, and a book on Socialist Realism. Our anonymous man was a reader — that was the only thing we learned.

A small room with a large window housed the studio. Empty tubes of oil paints littered the floor with crumpled newspapers. A couple canvases — more family scenes — had been destroyed with a knife. "When artists get frustrated, watch out," said Emil, then stopped at the canvas on the easel. It was empty except for the image of a hand, a couple inches wide, that had been painted in the center — or, it had been begun. The brushstrokes were awkward — they trembled — as if Antonín had been terrified when he painted it.

I looked around the corridor. Clean enough, and empty. The buzzer on the only other ground-floor apartment was marked SUPERVISOR, but there was no answer to my ring. An old man came through the front door as I was heading back, and I asked if he knew the building supervisor.

He squinted up at me. "Supervisor?"

I pointed at the door.

"Yes, some time ago." He pressed his temple with a finger. "I suppose, yes."

"And now?"

He shrugged with opened hands. "Haven't had one for I-don't-know-how-long. What can you do?"

"How about here?" I nodded at the open door. "Antonín Kullmann. Did you know him?"

"How could I? A man like that doesn't talk to us."

"A man like what?"

"You know. Didn't have time to talk to us proles."

"Bourgeois?"

He touched his temple again. "You're not kidding."

"Did you ever see anyone else go in there? Another man, perhaps?"

"I didn't look. I'm no spy, you know. Why did you say, *did?*"

"Did?"

"You said, *Did* you know him. Is he gone now?"

"He's dead."

"Ah." He nodded. "So his apartment's free?"

# 22

It was getting late, and Emil had plans with Lena, so I told him I'd see him in the morning. I called home using Antonín's phone. Ágnes had received a red ribbon for her fitness aptitudes, and was being chosen as a group leader. "The Pioneers are funny. I don't think I understand half of what they tell us, but the sports aren't bad."

"What about your French? How's that coming?"

"Our Pioneer chief said that French was below me. That's what he said word for word."

"Well he's not your father. I expect you to study tonight."

Her grumble broke apart through the telephone lines.

"Your mother around?"

"She's going to be late too. I told her not to be out with more than three friends."

"Why not?"

"Aren't you supposed to be in the Militia? They even told us in class about the new law. After dark, more than four people together can be arrested for hooliganism."

"I see. Can you make yourself dinner?"

"I'm not a *child*, Daddy."

I found a tin of orange juice in the refrigerator. I was no longer particularly interested in finding out who had stayed here. If it was the killer, he hadn't left obvious clues. In the morning I'd call in the lab coats to dust for prints, but for now I could do nothing. So I focused on who Antonín was. In some desk drawers were newspaper clippings chronicling his shows. He'd had his first one in the Museum of National Contemporary Art — Josef Maneck's place — in 1948, and soon after became a regular fixture of the state-owned museums. There were even clippings from a German newspaper praising his early work, some of which traveled to Paris and Köln as part of a series of "international friendship exchanges." I knew a little German, and could muddle through an article about him, published in 1954, that described "the rise and fall of Antonín Kullmann." According to the critic, Antonín had burst upon the socialist world in 1948 as a full-fledged genius "by any regime's standards." His compositions were ahead of their time and utterly original. But in 1952 that changed. Antonín, in the statement that accompanied his 1952 Köln East/West Friendship Exhibition, claimed to be reinventing himself. But to the German critic it was not a reinvention, but an eradication of the Antonín Kullmann of the earlier exhibitions:

*The flat, insipid Socialist Realism of this Kullmann seems to give doubt to the idea that the soul can rise above totalitarianism. He has given up art for the pleasures of submission.*

Some of our local critics, on the other hand, felt his genius was continuing to grow "by great schismatic leaps."

Once I started looking, I found papers everywhere. Reams of typewritten sheets — half-written artist statements, catalogs for upcoming exhibits and, in the bottom drawer of the bedroom bureau, typed drafts of letters. I took them to the living room and settled into the sofa.

Antonín had been a meticulous man. In his correspondences he seemed to work out different versions — sometimes three variations of one letter — before sending them off. There were some addressed to gallery owners and critics — a couple names I recognized — and one was to his ex-wife, Zoia. It was dated 1 November, two weeks ago, about a week before his death, and there was only one draft. The second, presumably, had been sent.

*My dear Z. I've tried, and I've failed so often. The times we've spent together are the happiest of my life, but I've made clear that this is not enough. I have to be firm about this, or we will go on with these dishonest rendezvous.*

*You know what's brought this on, this sense of my mortality, and yet you will not succumb. Why? I again offer myself to you and ask you to leave him. He's never made you happy in the way that I have. We can leave together. We can go west. I will take care of everything.*

*Please, don't think of this as desperation. These are only the words of a man who knows the one thing he wants, and must have it at all costs.*

*With love and shame, Antonín.*

The entire letter was nullified by a large red **X**.

I went through everything, but could find no replies to his letters, and no address book.

I looked again at the trembly hand on the studio's easel. It was green-tinted and the paint was very thick. I touched it and jerked back as the small hand smeared onto my index finger. I washed it off.

The pictures on his walls were scenes of socialist utopia — one by the famous Vlaicu, the others by himself, though in one corner I saw the "new" Kullmann and the "old" Kullmann side by side. First, a factory scene of determined, muscled men at work. Nothing new. The second one was entirely different. Two men sitting at a table in a dark room, and on the table was a pig's head, with black flies hovering over it. But the pig's head glowed, casting fly-shadows on the wall and lighting the men's faces. I didn't know if I liked it or not. It left me with an unsettled feeling.

I bought a cheese sandwich from a store in the neighborhood, then looked at the painting again as I ate, sitting at Antonín's typewriter. I rolled in a fresh sheet. But nothing came. I typed a few useless words and found myself surprised that the T did not stick. Its ease almost disconcerted me, and the whole machine felt too foreign, too perfect. I finished the sandwich, grabbed the Kandinski book, and settled into the chair again. Although Kandinski was not actually banned, he was certainly in disrepute, and the only places one could find his works were the used bookstores with their spare selections of dusty, twenty-year-old paperbacks like this one. I didn't make it much further than the introduction, where Antonín or the other man had marked some lines that still stick with me:

*Our souls, which are only now beginning to awaken after the long reign of materialism, harbor seeds of desperation, unbelief, lack of purpose. The whole nightmare of the materialistic attitude, which has turned the life of the universe into an evil, purposeless game, is not yet over.*

I woke to the key turning in the lock, and for an instant didn't know where I was. The floor lamp was still on, and I had to blink to adjust to the light. On the other side of the room, the apartment door opened a little, stopped, then closed again.

I ran. The glass front door was easing shut, and in the dark street a figure bounded away. I skipped over craters in the sidewalk and shouted for the runner to stop. But despite his visible limp and the bag bouncing on his shoulder, he was small and quick, turning the next corner, then the next. By the time I stopped to catch my aching breath, he was gone.

# 23

I drove through the Friday morning work crowd up to the Sixth District, to Unit 21, Block 10. The entryway was one of those dismal greens that give the feeling of being underwater, and the elevator was broken. So I climbed to the fifth floor and knocked. Stefan was in his underwear. "This is a surprise. Finally decide to finish me off?" He was smiling, but when I stepped forward, he stepped back.

I peered past him. "Have any coffee?"

"No."

"Then I'll buy you a cup."

I waited for him to dress. His view was like ours: blocks upon blocks; up, sky. He lived the same way ever since Daria left him; he lived like the bachelor he would always be. This, I supposed, was why he and Magda used my marital bed.

I considered talking to him then. We could have it all out in the open and start settling things finally. But when he wandered out of the bedroom and found his shirt under a sofa cushion, I changed my mind. Magda had said she was making her own decisions, and this, in the end, was the only way. It was not up to him, or to me. He pressed a hand against his swollen belly to flatten the wrinkles of his shirt, but it didn't help. What did she see in him?

In the car, he leaned forward and frowned. "That your engine? You need to have it looked at."

"It's fine," I said.

He shook his head. "I'll take a look if you want. I just hate to have cars going around sounding like that."

I stared at him until he shut up.

We went to the same place he had been going to for years. Café-bar #338. A dark workers' hole almost in the Third District where Turks drank coffee from very small cups. "Why don't you try another bar?"

He shrugged. "Why should I? I've brought Leonek here. He likes it."

"*Leonek* likes it? I wouldn't think so."

"Because of the Turks? Come on, Leonek's a bigger man than that. These guys didn't kill his family."

"Well, neither of you has any taste."

We got coffees and rolls and settled on knee-high stools around a low table. A thin Turk with a little beard raised his cup to Stefan, and Stefan nodded back. "Out with it," he said to me.

"I've found your Antonín."

"Antonín?"

"You know what I'm talking about."

He knew, but it took a moment to settle into his skull. "*My* Antonín?"

"Antonín Kullmann. He was found in the Canal District, burned to a crisp."

His tongue moved around his teeth, then he swallowed. "So that was Antonín."

"I talked to his mother, in Drebin. He was an artist, and Josef Maneck showed his stuff. He has an ex-wife named Zoia who's married to a clerk. He was trying to get her back."

Stefan folded his hands beneath his chin.

"I think the killer came by last night, but I lost him."

"The killer?"

"Maybe."

He finished the roll and ordered another coffee from a barmaid with striking dark eyes. Then he watched me a moment. "And you're bringing this information to me?"

"It's a case."

"You're right."

"And I can be a big man too."

"I'm glad."

We returned to Antonín's apartment and went through everything again. There was nothing new, but Stefan was thorough as he read the letters and examined the newspaper clippings. I pointed out the letter to Zoia mentioning the *sense of my mortality*. "He may have known he was going to be killed."

"Uh-huh," said Stefan. He looked at the cigarettes still dirtying the plate beside the chair and read their brands. "This one's yours?"

"Yeah."

He examined the bed, then went on to the bureau. The clothes were good quality, expensive, and I wondered if Lena Brod would approve of them, or if I was too much of a prole to know the difference. As he searched he told me what little more he had learned about the dead curator, Josef Maneck.

"Before he was sent to the bottling plant, he was doing very well for himself. The Culture Ministry gave his museum a significant percentage of their budget."

"Why?"

He straightened. "This is where I become embarrassed. It was because of his contribution to the art world, having brought some genius — an A. Kullmann — to the attention of the public." He shrugged. "I never followed up on it."

"You should be embarrassed."

"Anyway," he said as he went back to searching, "in 'fifty-one the heavy drinking began and just got worse. He drank throughout the day, hid it from no one, and after he'd drunkenly insulted enough Ministry officials, they sent him to the bottling plant. The drinking didn't stop."

"Did you catch up with Martin again?"

"He disappeared."

"I saw him hiding from you in the Fourth District. What did you do to him?"

Stefan smiled. "Maybe I was a little pushy."

"What happened after the bottling plant?"

"Josef survived. That's a mystery, how he made ends meet. I suspect someone was helping him out." He appraised the living room as he walked to the paintings on the wall. "Probably Antonín. Hey — this is good." He took down the one I'd noticed and brought it to the window, turning it so the pig's head became even more illuminated.

"Josef made this guy famous."

Stefan turned it in the light. "This painter made himself famous. Josef just came along for the ride." He shook his head. "I've never seen anything like it."

"Here's another one."

I brought him the factory scene, and when he took it his head slipped back, as if afraid of catching something. "What happened to him? This is trash."

We held the paintings side by side. Beneath each signature was a year. The good one was dated 1949, the factory scene last year, 1955.

Stefan grunted. "It's criminal. That's what it is. Someone with this much talent, and he sells his soul. To make *this*." It was more than he could bear. He tossed both paintings on the sofa and reached for his hat.

# 24

Emil, sitting on the edge of Leonek's desk, looked surprised when we entered together at noon. Leonek did too.

I called the forensics lab to give them Antonín's address. Emil appeared as I hung up. "You guys together, then?"

"For the moment. Can you see about this Vlaicu guy? He might know something."

"Already did. He's having a show."

"When?"

"Tomorrow night, seven o'clock. Have you heard about Malik Woznica?"

I peered up at him.

"He came by yesterday. Looking for us. Seems to think you found his wife and didn't give her back."

"What did Moska do?"

"Told Woznica he was mistaken — it was a wrong ID. What else could he say?"

"I better talk to him."

Emil shook his head. "Don't. I started to, but he put his hands over his ears and told me to leave his office."

I called the civil records office over at the Ministry of Justice and spoke to a man with a guttural Polish accent. "This is Militia Inspector Ferenc Kolyeszar. I need some information about a divorce and a marriage."

"We close at three."

"It's one now."

"Then you've got plenty of time to come over."

"I'd rather not. The name is Kullmann. Antonín Kullmann. He divorced his wife Zoia Lendvai in 'forty-eight."

There was a long, phlegmy sigh, then a bang as he set the receiver down.

I wedged the phone between my ear and shoulder and watched Emil sitting opposite Leonek, where they pored over more interviews, muttering to each other now and then.

"Antonín and Zoia Kullmann," said the unhappy clerk. "It's right here."

"Good. Is there any mention of who Zoia Kullmann married afterward?"

"Of course not. This is a divorce certificate."

"I want to know who she married. It would have been the same year, or the next."

"You're really going to have to do this yourself. I'm busy here."

"Comrade," I said. "This is a direct request from Colonel Mikhail Kaminski, from Moscow. I suggest you take care of it."

Another pause as the threat registered, and he envisioned everything it signified. "Moment."

Moska came out of his office with a sheet of paper and went over to Brano Sev's desk. I hadn't noticed Sev's arrival.

He had the silence of all those in his field, and I wondered if he had heard me use Kaminski's name. Moska showed him the paper, then they conferred quietly. After a minute or two, he straightened and returned to his office, going out of his way not to look at me.

"Please tell Comrade Colonel Kaminski that there is no record of a Zoia Kullmann or a Zoia Lendvai remarrying in 1948, or any year since then."

When I hung up, Emil dropped his pages and came over. "I'll tell you what," he said. "You bring Magda to this Vlaicu show, I'll bring Lena, and beforehand we can all have dinner at our place. That way we won't look so much like a couple of *flatfoots*."

"Flatfoots?"

"It's American," he said proudly. "American for *cop*."

# 25

There really was no getting out of it, and since, for once, Magda wasn't occupied with Lydia, we arrived at the Brod household at five. Ágnes was happy to see us go. "Have a good time!" she called from the door, and that only made me worry. Lena's olive, floor-length dress seemed a little much for the occasion, but Magda complimented it with sincerity.

"Come now," said Lena as she used her pinkie to wipe excess mascara from her eyeball. "*You* need nothing to help you shine. When you're as over-the-hill as me, you've got to buy your beauty."

Emil opened a bottle of champagne.

We drank in the living room and listened to a sweet-voiced American singer on the record player — Sarah Vaughan, Emil explained — and began to loosen up. Despite her apprehension when I had told her our plans, Magda was awed by the size of the apartment and the glittering rocks hanging from Lena's ears. "Tell me," she said after her second drink, "what is it like to travel out of the country?"

"Haven't you been?" asked Lena.

Magda shook her head.

Lena took a deep breath before launching into a description of the glories of international travel. She had been to Paris, Rome, Zurich, London and Stockholm, and had found each one more enchanting than the last. "Except, perhaps, London," she said as her lip began to twitch at the corner. "Well, it's obvious, the problem with that town, isn't it? It's filled with the *English*. What a dry, dour race. Do you know, not *one* person in all of London looked at me crossly? If I bumped into someone — you know what they did? They *apologized*. Can you believe it? The entire nation, and not a single testicle among them. But," she said, looking sadly into her empty glass, "Westminster *was* beautiful."

Emil had gone with her on a couple trips, but admitted he seldom had the urge to leave. "I used to love to travel. But I don't anymore. Not sure why. Anyway, it takes twice as long for me to get a visa. I just slow her down."

Lena stood to refill our glasses. "They seem to think I couldn't *stand* to leave the country for good if my husband wasn't with me. They don't know much, do they?"

Emil slapped her thigh as she passed, then held up a finger. "Let me show you something." He went to another room and returned lugging a large reel-to-reel recorder.

"Not *that*," muttered Lena.

He set it heavily on the coffee table and plugged in a microphone. He flipped some switches and the reels began to turn, the tape sliding through metal gears and heads to the take-up reel, humming.

"I don't hear anything," I said.

Magda leaned close. "I think I hear something."

"It's recording," said Emil. He returned to his chair. "Just act normal. I haven't had a chance to use it yet, and I want to see what we sound like."

It took a few more drinks to act normal, to pretend that the big humming machine in the middle of the room did not exist. But we did normalize finally, touching on the Magyars, which was the only subject that could effectively silence Lena, then the Sixth of November Strike. "It's a shame," Emil said. "I would have liked it to do something in the end."

"You don't think it did?" said Magda. "I was under a different impression."

"What was your impression?" I asked her.

"I don't know. I don't mean it accomplished anything really *apparent*. More than anything it set a precedent, don't you think? It's clear that, if another crackdown like that comes along, there's an option for people. Striking is an option."

"But striking's always been an option," said Emil, leaning into the debate. "It's been done enough times in East Germany, in Poland, Czechoslovakia, and, of course, Hungary. It took a long time for us to get around to it."

"Everything takes a long time here," Lena said.

"But it's something," said Magda. "It's late, but it's something."

We all looked as the end of the tape emerged from the recording heads and flapped in the full reel.

Emil rewound the tape and rethreaded it. He was grinning. "Now we can find out what we really sound like." He tugged the switch.

At first, there was little conversation — half phrases and spare words — and then the clink of glasses and muted drinking. Then I was saying something about Ágnes, and the sound of my voice gave me pause. "I sound like that?"

Emil shrugged. Magda stared at the reel-to-reel. "Of course you do," said Lena, leaning close to the speaker as her own voice chattered about something insignificant, and I could see the disappointment in her face.

Magda talked and Emil talked and when my voice appeared again I was still surprised by the lilt of my deep voice, the singsong quality. It was effeminate and soft, as if it did not want to offend. It was an embarrassing realization.

Then Magda was talking again — . . . *there's an option for people. Striking is an option.*

We had the same thought at the same time, all four of us. But it was Emil's machine, so we waited for him to do it. He rewound it again, rethreaded the tape, and pulled the switch to the marker that said ERASE.

# 26

Most of the art admirers were choked around the drinks table, far from the paintings. It was an older crowd than I was used to, white-haired members of the Culture Ministry with red pins wedged in their lapels, their wives, and only one beard in the whole room. The wood-framed paintings were more of what we'd seen at Antonín's: the virtue of the working life. Young, fresh proles working wrenches on machines and pushing shovels into the hard soil. Names like *Comrade M. Harvests a Record Yield* and *A Five-Year Plan in Four*. Emil and I had to shove to get drinks for our wives, and when we returned a couple of officials were flirting with them. One worked in the Interior Ministry, and though he wore no leather coat, he knew the effect the name of his ministry, which had long ago been put in control of the Ministry for State Security, had on people. He whispered it. The other was in the upper ranks of the Pioneers. Magda mentioned we had a daughter. "So how does she like it?" he asked. "We try to give young ladies the confidence to make their lives an active, purposeful affair."

"She loves it unequivocally," Magda lied, and brought up a weekend camping trip that Ágnes returned from in tears, but left out the tears.

"So which one is Vlaicu?" I asked.

The Interior Ministry official nodded at the one man with a beard. He was noticeably younger than the rest, and already drunk. He shook hands and nodded at their comments and laughed. He knew how to work a room. "Would you like to meet him?" the official asked.

All six of us migrated over and cornered the artist. "More admirers, Vlaicu," said the official.

When we shook hands, Vlaicu's brilliant, green eyes shifted over to Magda. "What do you do?" he asked her.

She smiled and shrugged. "I work in a textile factory."

"Aha. So what do you think of my representations of factory life?"

She gazed at the walls a moment. "A little clean, maybe."

He laughed and clapped his hands together. "And what about the rest of you?"

Lena held her drink to her lips. "I sit around."

Emil said, "The two of us are militiamen."

Vlaicu nodded in mock-admiration and asked if it was a difficult job.

"Tiring," I said. "You should paint our work. It could be interesting."

"Maybe a little sensationalistic."

"Paperwork? Trust me. It's not sensational." The two officials had wandered off, and Emil seemed to want to get this going, so I said, "We're working on a case regarding someone you know."

"Oh yes?" He bobbed his eyebrows. "Someone sinister?"

"Antonín Kullmann."

His eyebrows dropped. "You've found him? Where is he?"

"He's dead," said Emil.

Vlaicu's eyes flicked back to me as his lips twitched, ready for this to be a joke. But our expressions convinced him otherwise. "I can't believe it."

It was real shock, I had no doubt. His hands floundered out to the sides, and he stepped forward, then back. Magda and Lena went off for more drinks.

I grabbed his arm lightly. "Come on."

We made it through all the greetings of the crowd and out to the dark, chilly sidewalk.

"Can you tell us about him?" asked Emil.

The hand that brought the cigarette to his mouth shook. "Of course. Yes."

I said, "How long has Antonín been missing?"

"Two weeks? Maybe three. I've been so busy. We had drinks together."

"You two close?"

"Not really. State painters drink together because the others won't drink with them."

"Did he tell you anything about fearing for his life? We have a letter of his that suggests this."

Confusion crossed his face, his eyes losing focus. "No, nothing. He didn't discuss his personal life much. Except his love life."

"Did he have much of a love life?"

"Well, he didn't have a lot of women, if that's what you mean. But love . . ." He scratched his beard, still confused. "Well, he had found it."

I said, "Zoia."

"Exactly. But she left him."

"She remarried, didn't she?"

"Yes, yes," he said. "A clerk."

"We couldn't find the record of the marriage."

216

"Probably because she changed her name. She thought Zoia was too provincial a name. So she changed it to Sofia." He grinned around his cigarette. "*That's* a provincial name."

"Do you know the name of her husband?"

"Mathew Eiers. Never met him, but Antonín hated the man. Eiers probably hated him, too, because he was still trying to get Zoia back." He blinked at the sidewalk, then looked at us. "You don't think Eiers —"

"We don't think much yet," said Emil. "Does the name Josef Maneck ring a bell?"

"Sure. Curator-turned-drunk. He was before my time, though. He and Antonín still talked sometimes. I think Antonín felt sorry for him — I mean, without Josef maybe he would've never had a career."

"Did he help support Josef?" I asked. "Financially, I mean."

Vlaicu held up his cigarette. "Wouldn't surprise me if he did."

A low figure came limping out of the darkness. It was Stefan. He raised a hand when he saw us, and Vlaicu looked briefly worried as he realized there were now three of us.

"Why didn't you invite me along?" asked Stefan.

I shrugged.

Stefan looked at Vlaicu. "This is the artist?"

"I'm the artist, yes."

I could smell the alcohol on him, probably from his favorite Turkish bar.

"Why don't you go say hi to Magda," I told him. "We'll be in in a second."

"Magda's here?"

"Why do you think I didn't invite you?"

I watched his face carefully, trying to read anything from it. I read confusion, maybe a little surprise, but I wasn't sure. He went in.

"You guys come in all types," said Vlaicu.

"About Antonín," I said. "Is there any way we can get in touch with his friends? Some you know?"

"I didn't know his friends. I have a feeling he didn't have any. Not the easiest guy to get along with."

"No one?"

He rubbed his beard. "Might try a Nestor — Antonín mentioned him last time we talked."

"Who?"

"Don't know his last name, but when he and Zoia moved to the Capital they roomed with this Nestor. An overeccentric painter, Antonín told me. He was released from a work camp last summer — that's all

I know." He looked at the sidewalk again, rubbing his arms. "I need another drink."

# 27

Stefan was at the drinks table with Magda, while Lena entertained three officials in a corner, one hand fluttering over her head in an imitation of something mysterious. Emil went to save her. Stefan and Magda didn't seem to be talking when I approached them, and I turned this over in my head throughout the rest of the night, trying to ascertain any meaning, but finding nothing. Stefan told me he had been watching Antonín's apartment, but without luck — no one had approached it. "What about you?"

"I've got Antonín's ex-wife's name. She changed it to Sofia, and married a clerk named Mathew Eiers."

"You got that from the records?"

I nodded at Vlaicu at the end of the table, filling up a glass with wine. He noticed me looking and wandered off.

Magda whispered in my ear: "Can we go?"

"In a little while."

"We should talk."

"Later," I said.

I tried to give each painting a good look. I took my time, cradling my drink, and examined the brushstrokes. I knew Moska did a little painting, but I'd never tried it, and I was always impressed by that much attention to detail. In writing, it was simple to change a word here and there. With painting, each little mistake seemed unfixable. I told this to Vlaicu, and he shrugged. "You paint over it. It's the same thing." He'd regained his easy drunkenness. "Painting's a breeze. Writing is too literal. Everyone knows exactly what you're saying, so if you make a mistake, everyone sees it."

Stefan and Magda kept their distance from one another. Magda chained herself to the drinks and smiled and nodded at the old men who ogled her. Stefan lingered around Emil and Lena, getting more drunk himself, pointing with his cigarette hand at the paintings and laughing. Vlaicu asked him what he thought.

"Of this?" He pointed at a picture of workmen pouring tar for a highway.

Vlaicu shrugged.

"It's the most useless thing I've ever seen. How can you live with yourself?"

Vlaicu smiled thinly. "Lay into it, Comrade."

So Stefan did. He called it empty and re-
dundant. "Why not use a camera? Save
you time. But don't make other people
look at it; they look at this dirt every day."

"Maybe that's my point," said Vlaicu.

"Your point? Paint a pile of dog crap
next. We see it daily on the sidewalk, you
know."

"Don't you think labor has meaning?"

"It's to get a job done — that's its
meaning." Then he leaned forward and, in
a whisper high enough for a few of us to
hear, said, "You've sold your soul, Comrade
Vlaicu."

No one expected the artist to swing. His
fist caught Stefan's jaw, then they were on the
ground, tangled, throwing punches as best
they could. I pulled Stefan off, and some officials took Vlaicu into their protection.

Outside, I noticed how drunk Magda
was. She was laughing about the fight,
leaning on Lena's elbow, then she started
to cry. Lena patted her head like a mother.
Stefan said nothing as he stumbled back
into the darkness, and the rest of us piled
into Emil's car.

Surprisingly, Ágnes was on the sofa,
snoring. Pavel, dozing beside her, woke up
and trotted over. "He needs to pee," I said.
Magda wandered off to the bedroom. I

carried Ágnes to her bed, then took Pavel downstairs. He crapped on the front steps, and I wondered what a painting of that would really look like.

Magda lay in bed staring at the ceiling.

"You said you wanted to talk."

She shook her head. "Stefan," she said, but could hardly get the word out.

"What about him?"

"He told me days ago. When you were at Georgi's. That he told you."

I sat on the edge of the mattress. "He hasn't told me everything. Are you going to tell me?"

She tried to look at me, but her eyes crossed and uncrossed, so she returned to the ceiling, then shut them. "It was a long time ago, Ferenc. You were gone. I couldn't —"

But I was standing up again and leaving. If she wasn't going to be honest about the present, about everything, then I didn't want to hear.

# 28

Her hangover lasted all Sunday, and she stayed in bed, the lights out and the blinds drawn. I brought water and lunch, but whatever she took in she immediately threw up.

"Don't tell me she drank last night," said Ágnes over breakfast.

"Sometimes it happens."

"Maybe I should start drinking."

"Maybe you should take Pavel out for a walk."

Magda was able to get a small dinner to stay down, and as she ate in the dark room she asked what she had said last night. "I don't remember at all. But we spoke."

"You didn't say anything, really."

"I said something."

"Do you want to say something now?"

She considered it, frowning through the pain. "We should talk, yes, but I can't. Not in this state."

"Have you figured out what you want?"

She looked at me, her expression still painful. "I wish I knew, Ferenc. God, you don't know how much I wish that."

I pulled the blanket to her chin.

Ágnes was rolling a ball across the living room floor for Pavel to bring back, but the dog was uninterested. She stood up, retrieved it from the corner, and came back to try again. "I think we need a new dog. Pavel just isn't working out."

I sat on the sofa. "What kind of dog would work out?"

"Something larger, that's for sure. Pavel can't keep up when I run."

"Maybe we could make some wheels for him."

"Wheels and an engine."

"Tell me about school. Is it going better this year?"

She nodded into her chest. "Better than last year, yeah. I learned about cosmonauts."

"Cosmo*what?*"

"Cosmonauts," she repeated just as incomprehensibly. "People who go into space. The USSR has big plans for putting us in space. Communes on the Moon."

"Don't hold your breath," I said. "I'm still looking into the French school. But you've got to pass that exam."

"Maybe I should stay where I am."

Her hair needed a trim. "I thought we'd decided to give it another try."

"I've made friends this year. I don't want to just leave them."

Then she pulled her foot toward herself and started playing with her toes. You learn a child's behaviors so they become simple clues to the inner life. I wanted this school for her, but knew that nothing would come of it if she didn't want to go.
"What's his name?"

"What?"

"The name of the boy you're in love with."

*"Daddy."* She glared at me, but her mouth was smiling.

# 29

I arrived at the office early and found Mikhail Kaminski hunched over my desk, hand on his forehead, absorbed in a slim stack of typed pages. He'd had a haircut since I'd seen him last, his mustache was trimmed to a razor's width, and his coat had large shoulders that rose as his elbows spread on the desk. Then I realized what he had before him.

"What the hell are you doing?"

He looked up, blinking, and smiled as if suddenly recognizing me. "Ferenc!" He tapped the sheets with that trigger finger. "You're really very talented. I had no idea." He pushed himself back in my chair, scratching the floor, and crossed his hands in his lap. "Why don't you sit down?"

There was something in his voice. So I took Emil's chair. "You've been going through my things."

He nodded at the papers. "How do you do this? I mean, all I write are reports. They're so dry. But you, Ferenc, you've got a way with words. How do you do that?"

"I work at it. Now please put them back where you found them."

He lifted the top sheet and read aloud: "*She moved through the world as if nothing was worth her effort, but she nonetheless influenced the outcome of situations. The proper word, or a subtle gesture, and someone was filling her empty glass with wine.* You see what I mean? I feel like I've known this woman before. You've nailed it just right. I'm impressed." He tapped the pages again. "Impressed, and a little disappointed."

"Disappointed?"

"I'm not an artist, not like you. But like anyone, I enjoy a good read. I know what I like. It's a shame to see your great talent wasted like this."

I waited.

"This," he said, laying his hand on my words, "It's so . . . so *unreliable*. All this — how should I put it? — this *me me me*. You understand?"

"I don't think I do."

He crossed a leg over his knee. "Who do you think would be interested in this, Ferenc?"

I shrugged.

"There's my point! No one, except for yourself. You should be writing about subjects that unite people, subjects we can all relate to! For example, there's a wonderful Soviet writer, whose name I can't remember now, but he wrote about the building of a dam in Siberia. Now *that's* a story! You see the human drama of people working together for a great aim, and when you read it, you feel a part of that endeavor. And when, in spite of foreign saboteurs and some nasty hooliganism, the dam succeeds, you can't help but clap and feel the same pride those workers feel. But this," he said, abruptly changing tone. "This is about you, and only you. And this relationship — this marriage — what depressing people! The story about the dam, *that's* what people want to read. I ask you again, who would want to read your story?"

I wanted to reply, but there was no satisfactory answer.

"I'll tell you who," he said, lowering his voice and leaning closer. "People who revel in their pain. You see what I'm saying? Healthy people want to read about camaraderie, about healthy love, about how to be valuable to their society. They want lessons on life. What does this teach them? How to fail in life. Do you plan on publishing this?"

I was wordless. Then, finally, I managed:

"I don't know. Maybe."

"Well. I wonder. This stuff is bourgeois, cosmopolitan. It's *rootless*. This sort of thing could be dangerous."

"For me?"

"For the city, for the country, and yes, I suppose, even for you. Keep it to yourself, Ferenc. That's my little bit of literary criticism. Keep these kinds of thoughts to yourself, and for the rest of us explore the things that people really care about. We want healthy writers. Healthy writers are concerned with progress, enthusiasm for life, human industry. Unhealthy writers . . . well, they're the kind of people who walk away from battle when their country needs them. They attack their superiors. Am I making myself clear?"

I nodded, my fingers fiddling with my rings.

"Good," he said, still smiling. He patted my shoulder. "Keep at it, you're very good. And I look forward to reading your great proletarian novel one of these days."

I watched him walk away, his casual stride, and all the organs in my exhausted body hardened into heavy rocks.

Kaminski wasn't there just to critique my fiction. He greeted each inspector as he arrived, as if they were all old friends who had been unfortunately separated from him for a while. Then Moska came out of his office and asked us to gather around. "New regulations," he said. "We've fitted all the Militia cars with two-way radios. We're later than a lot of cities getting this done, but the funding came through, I think for obvious reasons. From now on, whenever you go out on a case, you're supposed to use one of our cars rather than your own. So we can keep track of you."

Kaminski shook his head. "It's so you can call for help whenever you need it. The streets aren't as safe as they once were, we all know this." He must have taken our silence for agreement, because he clapped his hands together, grinning hugely. "You may have wondered where I've been the last week and a half. Out west in Budapest, as they say. You'd be surprised how good things are now. They've cleared up the barricades, it was a mess. Busses turned over, set on fire. It took some real pigs to do that. But you'll be happy to know that now it's peaceful, and they're busy rebuilding. It's becoming almost normal."

Brano Sev gave a lesson in the garage, all of us bent over the open doors of a new Mercedes. "You pick it up like so. Press here and speak. The reply comes from here." He pointed at a small speaker grille. "When a message comes in, you do the same thing. Pick it up, press, and talk. But remember that when you press the speaking button you cannot hear what the central office is saying." He turned it on by flicking a switch. A red light glowed and we heard static. He pressed the button, silencing the static. "Central, this is a test. Can you hear me?"

When he released the button, a garbled woman's voice said, *This is Central, Sev. We hear you fine.*

"Who's that?" asked Stefan.

"Regina Haliniak. She's new."

"A new girl," he said, smiling at the rest of us. "Cute?"

Brano looked at him, expressionless, and switched off the radio. And I stared at Stefan, disturbed that, with Magda, he could even joke about a voice on a radio.

When we got back to the office, there were two notes on my desk: one from the lab, saying that they had clear prints from five different people in Antonín's apartment — I could pick them up whenever I wanted; the second was from Moska, asking to see me in his office.

"Ferenc, you were looking for the Kullmann woman?"

"I'm going over today. But her name is different now."

"Yes, yes. I know. Sofia Eiers."

"How did you know?"

"Because she's just been reported dead, Ferenc, and the only names I learn are those that don't matter anymore."

# 30

The Eierses lived out on the edge of the Fifth District. These low homes were still as they had been for a hundred years: a stone suburb of clay-roofed houses that were charming because of their style and infuriating because of their plumbing. Emil had decided to stay behind, and Stefan sat in the Mercedes passenger seat, switching the radio on and off, listening to bursts of static.

"Just turn it off, will you?"

He did, then watched the homes pass. "What do you think of this case?"

"I don't know what to make of it. An art curator is killed, then his prize artist. Now, the artist's ex-wife."

"I'd like to know why Josef Maneck started drinking," he said.

"Back to that."

"He was doing well for himself, he was

respected. Martin said he couldn't live with himself — why? Maybe Eiers knows."

Mathew Eiers looked nothing like a clerk. He was a dark man with broad, massive shoulders, and at home he wore a tight-fitting undershirt that showed off his thick biceps. Which made it all the stranger to see him burst into tears at unexpected moments. I offered him a cigarette. He shook his head. "And please, don't smoke in the house. Health."

He had laid Zoia, or Sofia, on their bed, and at the foot of the bed was a weight bench. Above the bed, on the wall, was a crucifix. She was dressed in a short, fashionable black dress. I nodded at it. "Is this what she was wearing, when . . . ?"

He straightened the hem over her thigh. "It is." Then he started to weep.

She looked a little pale, but asleep. No great beauty, she had a certain peasant attractiveness. Short, dark hair and a rounded chin. I sat on the edge of the bed and looked at her arms, her hands and neck, seeking clues, but I didn't want to touch her. There was some discoloration around the neck, a bruise. "Do you know what caused this?" I asked.

He leaned over her. "I didn't notice that. What — what do you think?"

"I don't think anything yet, Comrade Eiers. Please sit down and tell us what happened."

Mathew Eiers settled on the weight bench, tears under control now. "We spent the weekend in the country with my parents. She was in a good mood, she *liked* to travel. You know, we had a good time every time we traveled." He looked at her closed eyes. "We got in late last night. This morning was, well, as it always is. Blessed. I went out to buy the paper, and when I returned she was —" He looked at me. "But I don't under*stand*."

"You found her here?"

"In her chair, in the kitchen. I tried to make her heart start again. I've heard of it. You hit right here." He pressed a hand to his heart. "But it didn't work. *Nothing* worked. So I cleaned her off and put her to bed."

"You cleaned her off?"

"Her face." He touched his own. "She had . . . fallen. Into her breakfast."

"What was it?"

"Porridge. She eats it every morning. It's *good* for her."

Stefan had been standing in the doorway, keeping notes. "Did you eat the porridge as well?"

"Never," he said, holding down the sobs. "I eat yogurt. Fresh yogurt from the country. It's for the *bones*." Then he looked again at his wife, sniffing. "Oh Lord. You don't think it was . . . ?"

"We should check on it," I said. "Tell me. Were the doors unlocked when you went for the paper?"

He shook his head. "I locked the front door when I left — I had to use the key to get back in. I checked the back door, too, after I found her. *Both* were locked."

We looked into the bag of oats, but if it was poisoned, we'd never know without the lab.

"You know," I told him, "we were planning to come see your wife today before hearing about this."

"What?"

"About her ex-husband, Antonín."

He straightened and his voice leveled off: "What does he want?"

"He's been murdered, Comrade Eiers. Before he died he had been in correspondence with your wife. He mentioned in a letter the sense of his mortality. It's vague, but perhaps he knew who was going to kill him. Perhaps she knew."

"Or maybe you know," said Stefan.

Mathew Eiers glared at the floor. "I

would have liked to do that."

"To kill him?"

He looked as far from tears as we would ever see him. "I didn't, no, but I *could* have. She still saw him now and then. Sofia thought I didn't know, but husbands know these sorts of things, right? They didn't make love, I'm sure of that, but she wasn't honest to me about it. I could either do something about it or not." He shook his head. "I didn't."

"Why not?" asked Stefan.

He concentrated on the floor and spoke slowly: "Because I didn't want to lose her. Sofia had left him for me. She could choose to go back just as easily. I knew this. It didn't matter how evil he was."

"Evil?" I said. "Isn't that a little strong?"

"That's what Sofia told me. She used that very word. She never told me why, but she said that his evil deeds had made him a star in the Capital. His *fame* was at a terrible price."

Stefan didn't seem to understand. "But if she thought he was evil, why would she still see him? Why would she go back to him?"

He smiled for the first time. "Come on, Comrade Inspector. Don't be naïve. You don't go to bed with someone because you

235

know they're pure. And sometimes you don't love purity. Sometimes you do everything precisely be*cause* of impurity. Sometimes you can't help it."

We let that sit a moment. The living room was stuffy; he'd sealed it against unhealthy drafts.

"Let's try some names on you," I suggested. "Did Sofia ever mention a Josef Maneck?"

"Maneck died some time ago, didn't he? He was a *business* associate of Antonín's — you know, the art business — before he fell off the wagon."

"Any idea why he did that?" asked Stefan.

"What?"

"Fell off the wagon."

Mathew shook his head.

I cleared my throat. "How about a Nestor?"

"Nestor Velcea?"

Stefan wrote it down.

"I never met him, but Sofia called him the greatest artist she'd ever known. She and Antonín lived with him their first year in the Capital, until he was sent away."

"To a work camp," I said.

He nodded. "Yes. I suppose he got one of those summonses from Yalta Boulevard. You know — *document check*. She never really told me the details of what happened — it was a sensitive subject. Understandably."

"Understandably," I said. "But he's supposed to have been released."

Mathew frowned. "Really? From the way she praised him, I wouldn't mind meeting this guy. His paintings are supposed to be better than Antonín's early work, but I've never seen them. He was a little weird, she told me. He refused to show his work in public and didn't even sign his paintings. A little mixed-up in the head, maybe."

Stefan cut in: "I still don't understand why your wife thought of Antonín as *evil*. Didn't she say why?"

"My wife wasn't a gossip, Comrade Inspector. She stated her opinion and left it at that. I respected her for it."

While Stefan retrieved the bag of oats, I used the bathroom. There was another crucifix beside the mirror, and on the floor was a book by an American weightlifter named Atlas. It was all in English, but there were photos of this massive man throughout, showing how to lift weights, which kinds of food to eat, and how to live in order to grow into a healthy old age.

I drove Stefan back to the station, then took my writings out of my desk and put them into my satchel, not looking up as Kaminski strolled in. The Russian positioned himself by the door, hands in his pockets, watching us a while before speaking. "There was a little confusion today. We tried to reach all of you by the new radios, but had no luck." He held up his hands. "It's a new system, we understand this, and there will be bumps along the way. But, guys, the radios have to be left *on* in order to function. This only makes sense, doesn't it?"

"But what about that noise?" asked Stefan. "They hiss like mad all the time."

"Then you turn the volume down," Kaminski explained. "Not all the way, but some. The call-in will be loud enough for you to hear it." He took a step toward my desk. "Any questions, Ferenc? I can get Brano to show you how to use it again."

"No thanks."

"It's no trouble," said Sev, rising from his own desk.

"I get it. Really."

# 31

The next morning, I took the tram into town. The car would be a burden if I wasn't

238

going to use it. Then we set off for Unity Medical. Emil drove, I sat in the passenger's seat, and Stefan sank into the back. The radio hissed quietly.

"Kaminski's got something planned," said Emil. "All this with the radio. I don't know what it is."

Stefan grunted. "The Americans said they're rounding up demonstrators in Budapest. They're making them identify their friends and sending them all to prison. *That's* what he was doing out west in Budapest. He'll do it here, too."

Emil touched the radio and turned the volume up — static filled the car — then down. He drew his hand from the radio. "Do you think they can hear us through this?"

We all looked at the hissing box, its red light burning, and said nothing else until we were out of the car.

Markus Feder was in a better state. "Three visitors at once, I should be pleased."

The lab was clean and empty. No tables with lumps beneath sheets, no indescribable smells, just the faint lingering odor of ether. He had a clipboard in his hand.

"First, these fingerprints. I asked the boys to pass them on to me, so I could check them with the corpses. Out of five sets from Antonín Kullmann's apartment, two were identified as you two, Ferenc and Stefan. I checked the remaining three: One is Antonín Kullmann's and one is Sofia Eiers's. Here's the unknown one," he said, passing over a card onto which eight prints had been transferred to ten boxes.

I waved it. "The guy I chased."

"Tell us about Sofia Eiers," said Stefan.

Feder raised a hand. "Thanks for giving me an easy one this time. The boys checked the oats first, and they came up clean. I hadn't even gotten a chance to look at the body yet." He smiled. "Didn't you guys notice the marks around her neck?"

"I did," I said, but sounded overeager.

"Well then. It might have suggested something else. The girl was strangled. The killer came up behind her and used his whole arm. Leaves fewer marks, just a welt, but breaks the trachea pretty quickly. As soon as I saw her it was obvious. You said she was found with her face in her breakfast?"

"Yeah," I said. "That's what made us think —"

"Don't worry about it. The thing is, there was a single thumbprint on the back

240

of her neck. Again, I checked, and it's from that one you have in your hand. He must have decided she looked better in her porridge."

I looked down at the card.

"Looks like your killer's starting to get a heart," he said. "No more barbecues."

If the doors were locked, that left two possibilities — either Sofia Eiers knew her murderer and let him in, or the murderer had been waiting inside the house since before breakfast time that morning, hidden. He had broken into the house, perhaps over the weekend, while the Eierses were in the country, and waited. Once Mathew stepped out, he killed Zoia and left, locking the door behind him.

Mathew Eiers wasn't at home — his office, it seemed, would only give him that first day off to mourn his wife — so we talked to the neighbors on each side and across the street. One family had been away for the weekend as well; on the other side, a single man who was terrified by the sight of us had been around that weekend, but could not remember seeing anyone out of the ordinary. A teenage boy opened the door to the house across the street and gawked at us. His parents weren't in. I didn't bother asking why he wasn't in school.

"We wanted to know if you'd noticed anyone going into the house across the street last weekend. Anyone at all."

He looked at the three of us gathered around his doorway, then up at the bright, but cold, sky. He was chewing gum. "Anyone?"

"Yes," I said. "Anyone."

"I didn't see him go *in*, if that's what you mean."

"Who are you talking about?"

"The recruiter." He chewed with an open, smacking mouth. "I was out getting the mail when I saw him. He said he was going to come back."

"When?"

He shrugged and smacked his lips. "Before he knocked on their door I asked what he was doing. He was recruiting for a trip to the provinces. A Party project. To build a dam, or a dike, something like that. I said I might be interested. He told me that once he finished that side of the street he'd come back. I went in and waited, but I never heard from him." He seemed a little dejected by that missed trip to the provinces.

"What did he look like?" asked Stefan.

"The recruiter?"

We all nodded.

The boy gazed into the sun. "Well, I

guess he was shorter than me. Not much, not a real shorty, but not big. And he had blond hair, kind of brown, but mostly blond. He didn't walk so well. Looked like his knees didn't work right. He wobbled. Oh!" he said. "This is good." He raised his left hand, wiggling his fingers. "The guy was missing his pinkie. I noticed that. It was just a little stub. I was going to ask about it, but I didn't want to be a jerk."

"Of course you didn't," I said.

"That the guy you're looking for?"

"If he comes back, give us a call." I wrote the station number in my notepad and gave him the page.

"And when you find him," said the boy, "tell him I'm still interested in that trip."

On the ride back to the station, a crackly voice shot over the radio.

*Comrade Inspectors Kolyeszar, Brod, Weselak.* It was Kaminski.

We looked at each other. "Emil," I said. "You know how to work it."

*Comrade Inspectors, please answer.*

Emil lifted the mouthpiece. "This is Inspector Brod."

"Press the button!" said Stefan, his face right up with ours.

He pressed it, the radio silenced, and he repeated himself. He released the button.

*Thank you, Comrade Brod. This was just a check. Out.*

"Good-bye," said Emil, but because he didn't press the button, no one back in the station heard him.

I didn't feel like crowding in with the proles to get home, so I took one of the station's Mercedes. After listening a while to the hiss, I turned off the radio and paid attention to the pedestrians streaming from shops and offices, a river of hats. The case was giving me an overwhelming feeling of dissatisfaction. I still couldn't get Antonín Kullmann's murder out of my head — the stretched sinews, splintering bones, the benzene — but that was only part of the dissatisfaction. Because beyond this case was so much else — I could not grasp it all in my big hands. The roads widened, and the buildings grew, then I was back in the blocks.

I entered our unit from the south side, and across the field saw Magda stumbling through a group of parked cars. I put the heel of my hand to the horn and almost pressed, but didn't. It was the dissatisfaction; it was everything. She'd never seen this car before — she wouldn't notice me hanging behind her.

She left our unit on Tashkent Boulevard

and boarded the Number 15 tram. I couldn't remember exactly where that went. But as I followed it through its stops, crossing beneath the electric lines strung over the road, the route became clear. It cut around the city, into the Sixth District. As the tram approached Unit 21 my hands went cold on the wheel, and when the tram stopped and moved on without letting her off I actually laughed out loud. This was stupid. I was ready to turn back, when, just before the Third District, she got out. My fingers went cold again.

She even looked around. Like someone afraid of being followed. She crossed the street and paused — one more look around — before entering Café-bar 338, the small Turkish haunt where I'd bought Stefan breakfast last week, the one Stefan went to every day without fail.

Then I did turn back.

# 32

In the morning, I sent Emil out to see if he could find any files on Nestor Velcea, Antonín and Zoia's old roommate, then looked up as Leonek rushed in, ecstatic, his grin larger than any I'd seen in a long time.

"He's dead! I can't believe it — what luck!"

"Who?" I asked.

"The old man! The girl's grandfather!"

Tevel Grubin, grandfather of Chasya Grubin, one of Sergei's dead girls. One of two family members still in the Capital. "I don't see how that's great news, Leonek."

He tapped his head with an index finger. "Think, man, think! There's only one family member around to go to the funeral — the one I need to interview. Zindel, Chasya's brother. He'll be let out of prison — there's no reason they would refuse him!"

"They don't need a reason, Leon."

"They've got to let him. I'll lodge a complaint if they don't."

"That always does the trick."

"Don't be ironic, Ferenc. Can you come with me?"

"To the funeral?"

He tilted his head. "I need you there. Just your presence. I'd ask Emil or Stefan, but they couldn't intimidate a fly."

As I agreed to it, my phone rang.

"It's been signed out," said Emil.

"What do you mean it's been signed out?"

"Day before yesterday someone signed out Nestor's file. Guess who."

"Tell me."

"Brano Sev."

I waited for Emil to return, and in the meantime told Stefan about the file. I went out of my way to be brusque with him, but he didn't seem to notice. So we watched Brano Sev at his own desk, his back to us as he went through more files. This was how we always saw Brano Sev: a man at a desk with files. The times when he left his desk to do the more heinous acts that state security required, for us he was simply gone. He did not share his cases with us, though we knew that he was aware of everything we worked on.

Emil arrived flush from the cold. "Did you get it?"

"I was waiting for you."

"For me? Why?"

I looked at the floor. "I don't know."

Like every other time anyone approached his desk, Sev instinctively closed the file in front of him. "Ferenc."

I started to lean on his desk, but changed my mind. "I need to look at a file you've got. Nestor Velcea."

For the first time in my life I saw Brano Sev's face form an expression of surprise. "Why are you interested in Nestor Velcea?"

"His name came up in an interview, I just want to see if there's anything to learn."

Sev turned to his wide file drawer, hesitated, then opened it. It was stuffed tight with files and papers, and when he found the Velcea file he had to use both hands to keep from pulling out the ones around it. He kept hold of it as I held the other side. "Do me a favor, will you?"

"Sure, Brano."

He licked his thin lips. "Tell me if there's anything useful to your case."

When I nodded he let it go.

I opened the file on Stefan's desk, and he took over, passing us things he thought were of interest. A photograph from before his incarceration — a blond young man with curls around his ears, good-looking. His data sheet said little. He had been born in the Capital in 1919, which made him thirty-seven now — my age. His profession was marked by the word *various*. *Painting* was listed under "PASTIMES," along with *reactionary political interests*.

There wasn't much else. His family had been transferred south after the war, which perhaps explained why Nestor never had regular work. He didn't have the residence papers to allow him a job assignment in the Capital. But he had stayed nonetheless, to work on his painting and eke out a living.

His decade in the Vátrina Work Camp, number 480, from 1946 to 1956 was just a line on his résumé — the details would be in a file at the camp itself. Behind the work camp fingerprint card with its ten swirls of black ink, Stefan noticed a sheet, just a brief description added after the Amnesty, in September. A physical description gathered from an informer named "Napoleon": *Limping due to damage to right leg, loping walk. Damage to left hand — small finger missing.* I looked at them looking back at me, then grabbed the fingerprint card from my desk, the prints taken from Antonín's apartment. They matched Nestor's.

We had the name of our murderer.

When I took Nestor's file back to Sev, he closed another file on his desk. "Tell me," I said. "Why is state security interested in the file of an artist?"

Brano Sev slid Nestor's file between the others in the drawer. "Just a routine check on amnestied prisoners. We do this sometimes." But he didn't look at me when he said that. He only looked at me when he said, "And you? Anything of interest in his file?"

Knowledge was not something Brano Sev deserved from anyone — if he could lie, so could I. "No," I said. "Nothing."

# 33

Thursday morning in the empty office, while waiting for the others to arrive, an idea came to me. I had the Militia operator patch me through to Ozaliko Prison, named after a sixteenth-century nationalist whose name was dredged out of history soon after the Versailles borders were drawn. A man sounding sick of his job answered the phone. "This is Inspector Ferenc Kolyeszar from the Militia Homicide Department."

"Hello, Comrade Inspector."

"Do you still have a man named Lev Urlovsky in custody? He was brought in last summer."

"Urlovsky?"

"Exactly."

He went through his files. "I see, killed his own son?"

"That's the one."

"That particular bastard will be here for another week or so, then he's off to the provinces."

"Labor camp?"

"Labor?" The functionary grunted. "Sure. Labor."

It was a long shot, but he and Nestor were at the same camp during the same period, and it wasn't unreasonable that they might have known each other. Or that they still knew each other. I told him I'd arrive in the next few hours to fill out the request for an interview.

"As you like."

Footsteps exploded in the station. I knew, even without looking, who it was.

"*You!*" He was at my desk, leveling a cool, stable finger at me.

"I see you're back on your medication."

Malik Woznica swung down a fist that made my typewriter jump. "Where is my Svetla?"

I tried to seem concerned. "You haven't heard from her yet? And no ransom notes?"

"Don't talk to me like that! What did you do with my wife?"

"I think my chief told you, Comrade Woznica. I haven't found her. A prostitute was mistaken for her, but really, your wife's no prostitute."

He breathed heavily, not used to so much exertion, and when he spoke his teeth were clenched. "Comrade Inspector

Kolyeszar. You signed the papers authorizing her leave. We have your name on a paper that says you took Svetla Woznica into your custody."

"I was mistaken." I said this smoothly, but it was just the coolness of immediate shock. I had forgotten about that form.

"No, you weren't mistaken, Comrade Kolyeszar. But you did make a mistake. You thought you could go against Malik Woznica of the Health Ministry. You thought you were above the rules." He put another unshaking hand on the desk. "I'm going to finish you off."

Then he walked out. There was no sign of his illness at all.

# 34

I didn't wait for the others. I got into one of the Militia's Mercedes and sped north to Ozaliko. Woznica's hands did not shake, but mine did, and they threw the car off a little when I took wide turns. The Militia radio buzzed through tinny speakers, and a few times I heard voices. Leonek informed the station that he was heading over to the Fourth District Militia station, and Regina Haliniak thanked him for his update. I lifted

252

the mouthpiece and even pressed the button before changing my mind. Sev would learn where I was going, and wonder why. He would want to know why I was speaking with a prisoner at Ozaliko, and for the moment I didn't want him knowing anything. He'd had the file of my killer, and that meant Kaminski did as well. They were just two heads of the same Hydra.

The face of the man who sounded sick of his job matched the voice. His features sagged depressingly, in direct contrast to the smiling Mihai on the wall. When I told him I had called a half hour ago, he made no move to suggest that this rang a bell. He handed me the forms on a clipboard and asked if I needed a pen. But I already had one.

It was a three-page form requesting all of my personal details, with open spaces to fill in my reasons for seeing the prisoner. I labored over that, wanting to explain it without bringing up Nestor Velcea's name, though I knew that, were Sev interested, he could figure it out easily enough. But there was no reason to make it easy for him.

The clerk took back the clipboard and ignored me as I stood waiting. "What now?" I asked.

He looked up again. "You'll be contacted."

I drove all the way to the station before changing my mind. I was afraid that Woznica would be there again, waving forms at Sev or Kaminski, awaiting my arrival. I was afraid that Kaminski was finally done playing with me, that all this time he had only been waiting for a free cell in Yalta Boulevard, where I could think about what I'd done on the Sixth of November. So I instead parked by October Square and asked Corina if I could use their telephone. She looked over to Max, cleaning glasses behind the bar, and he shrugged.

"Hello?"

"Vera. It's me. Ferenc."

"Well, this is a surprise."

"Are you busy?"

"Just looking over some lectures for a class. Want to drop by?"

"Can I buy you a coffee? I'm over at October. Max and Corina's place."

At that point I had no intention of sleeping with her, or I believed I didn't. I just wanted someone to talk to, and she was the one person I knew would be at home. But she was also the one person who would want more from me than a talk.

She looked as though the cold had taken a decade off her age, and when she sat I waved to Corina for another coffee.

"Shouldn't you be hunting criminals or something?"

"Just don't feel like it right now. What lectures were you working on?"

Corina set down the coffee. Vera thanked her, pulled some long black strands behind an ear, then leaned close to me. "You don't really care about that, do you?"

I could feel her warm breath on my face. "I do, actually. I'm interested." And that was true.

She leaned back. "Well, Marx, if you must know. His critique of Plato's *Republic* — Marx considers it largely a defense of the Egyptian caste system. Which, you can imagine, Karl wasn't too happy about."

"I can imagine."

"Some of my students are relatively critical of Plato, but I like to point out how similar, in a way, social Marxism is to Plato's theory of forms. In essence at least — because society is moving toward a predefined goal, a pure idea."

I looked at her, eyes wide, until she understood.

"You don't know anything about Plato, do you?"

"About as much as I know about Marx."

"Which is nothing."

I nodded. "So teach, professor."

She looked at me a moment, trying to decide, then slid the ashtray to her left. "Plato or Marx?"

"The first one."

"Well, it's really very simple. Kindergarten level."

"That's just right for me."

She looked at me another moment. "Plato felt that for everything there is an essential form that is more real than this reality."

"Like souls?"

"No," she said. "That's a common mistake. He uses the story of the people in a cave, with a fire blazing. On the walls are the shadows — these shadows are us. Our world is on the walls. And the people sitting around the fire are the ideal."

I nodded.

"You're sure you haven't heard this before?"

I had, but I wanted her to do the talking. "Just tell me, will you?"

"Okay. An example: For all apple trees, there is a single, perfect apple tree on which they are all based, but never equal to."

"Like God making us in his image."

"Something like that."

"All apple trees aspire to this perfect version?"

"Maybe. But it makes more sense for people." She pointed at me. "Behind Ferenc Kolyeszar there is an ideal Ferenc Kolyeszar. Do you aspire to it?"

I sank back into my chair. "Of course I do. Don't you?"

"Of course I aspire to the perfect Ferenc Kolyeszar," she said, smiling, then shook her head. "No, I don't aspire anymore. I used to believe all that. I used to think there was an ideal Vera Pecsok who was the perfect wife. I worked on it a long time. But the closer I got in action — because it's only through your actions that you can become anything — the less happy I was. The less like myself I felt. So either the perfect Vera was not the perfect wife, or there was no perfect Vera." She shrugged. "I prefer believing there's no perfect Vera, and that with each new action I become someone slightly different."

I tugged my lip. "So why are you teaching this? If you don't believe it."

"Because they let me," she said as she took out a cigarette. I lit it. "I used to teach six classes, now they've whittled me down to two, and seem to have forgotten I'm teaching under quota. Plato's forms are safe. Because, as I said, behind every socialist state lies utopia — that's the similarity I was talking about. And that utopia is what we're all aspiring to. Right?"

We drank our coffee in silence for a while. She had me thinking of that, too: Was there an ideal Ferenc that I should be trying to become? An ideal husband and father, an ideal militiaman? A great writer?

She said, "When I was studying in Zurich, a professor of mine had a theory about women in wartime. He said that, in times of war and revolution, when their men cannot protect them, women see their lives stripped bare. They understand, with utter clarity, that they are alone, as we all are. Most women also see that this life, with this man, is not what they wanted. It's just something they stumbled upon. And only in the clarity of this vision do they find the strength to change their lives. So they leave."

I watched her thinking about this. "Is that true? Do women leave their men in wartime?"

She raised her shoulders. "It happens."

"A professor told you this?"

"A professor, yes. He was also my lover."

"Oh."

"So why did you call me, Ferenc?"

"I'm not sure."

"Of course you are. That *I don't know* is the oldest, and worst, excuse."

"I guess I wanted this. To talk to you. We never do."

She placed the sugar spoon into her empty cup. "Talk isn't what I want from you. Don't try to make me into something I'm not. Okay?"

"But you're not anything," I said. "You told me that."

She touched a red nail to the back of my hand. "You're a fast learner. Did you know Karel's going to Yugoslavia on Saturday?"

"No, I didn't."

"A Writers' Union trip. A representative of our men of letters. He's very proud."

"He should be."

"And I'll be alone for a whole week."

The conversation didn't go much further because she was not very interested in it, and maybe I wasn't either, so I went home and waited for my family. Ágnes showed up first, but she didn't feel like talking either. She'd had a bad day, and all I could get out of her was that she would prefer to remain in her room for the rest of her life. Magda's mood was no better, and when after dinner I tried to talk to her it was no use. None of the women in my life wanted to talk that day. I told Magda that I'd had coffee with Vera, but it didn't faze her. She didn't know about the Christmas kiss or the more recent one, and I didn't know if knowing about them would have made any difference.

# 35

Emil was in the office, waiting with a slip of paper. "Results," he said, smiling.

The previous night a militiaman in the Second District had spotted Nestor Velcea near Antonín's apartment, but had been unable to catch him.

"How did he know about Velcea?"

"I filed a bulletin on him," said Emil.

"Oh." My secret was no longer a secret.

We drove over to the Second District station, and the switchboard operator used the new radios to call for Laszlo, the militiaman who had seen Nestor. Emil and I waited on the stiff corridor benches, listening to the heels of secretaries rattle the floor.

"It's no longer who," said Emil. "It's *why*."

I nodded at my rings, twisting them. "That's right. Any ideas?"

"Art and art. How much further can you take it?"

"A particularly grisly murder and two less grisly ones. An evil painter and two people who knew him. And the artist Nestor Velcea, a work camp prisoner who's killing them."

"Yeah," he said. He was staring at his own hands, too.

Laszlo was gray on the sides and seemed too old to be walking the streets with the young men. And he was. He had recognized Nestor right away from Emil's description, but had been foolish enough to shout before he was close. "That guy didn't even think about it," he said, grunting. "He was gone before I finished saying his name. Even with that limp he can *move*."

It was a wasted trip for us, and so was the subsequent visit to Antonín's apartment. There was nothing to suggest Nestor had returned to it — perhaps Laszlo had scared him on his way there. We spent the afternoon canvassing the neighborhood, but no one remembered the limping man short one finger. Back at the station I was relieved to find neither Sev nor Kaminski nor Woznica. But I did find Leonek in another of his ecstatic moods.

"They're letting him go! Didn't I tell you they would?"

I settled behind my desk. "Who?"

"Aren't you listening? Zindel Grubin, that's who!" He rapped his knuckles on my desk. "They'll lock you up and kill you, but they don't want your funeral unattended. You're still coming, right?"

"Sunday, is it?"

"You can pick me up."

After the others had left, Stefan arrived. I told him about our misadventures, and he nodded thoughtfully. Then he sat down to finish some paperwork.

I could have walked over and hit him again — it was a thought that still ran around in my head — but when you learn something over time the anger dissolves into the days, so that in the end you're too tired; the anxiety has dulled you. He also seemed tired, and I wondered if the guilt was keeping him from sleep. We'd had such affection for each other for so many years that there had to have been guilt. Or if there was no guilt, just a low burning hatred of me that he sublimated through the exertion of sleeping with my wife.

My inaction haunted me more than the infidelity. I knew how I was supposed to react: I was supposed to rage into a violent destruction until everyone around me was stunned. I'd seen enough husbands who had done that, men I'd put behind bars. I'd sympathized with them, and always thought I might do the same. But like Mathew Eiers, I did nothing.

Was this a reflection of my love for Magda? If I couldn't become irrational and brutal about this, then where did I draw the line? Because of my size, I'd seldom had to use my strength. The threat was always enough. But this was something that could not be assuaged by a threat.

No: I couldn't become violent because in the end it didn't matter. Magda and I had been growing apart for a long time, and this was just the uglier side of what already existed. The only thing that truly angered me was her nonchalance. She was sleeping with my oldest friend, and when Ágnes became aware of it — as she no doubt would — what would it do to her?

Stefan lounged at his desk sleepily, and I finally began to gather some strength to brutalize him. He was helping to chip away at my family, and for that there was no forgiving him.

But before I could turn the feeling into action, he stood up, stretched, and told me he was beat — he was going home.

I bet you're beat.

# 36

In the empty office I typed. It was in the form of a letter, and the only way I could write it was to think of it as fiction. It was addressed to "My dear wife" and listed, in detail, the reasons why the letter writer was leaving her. Why he was taking their child with him, why there was a reality to be faced up to and this lie could no longer be lived. He did not wish to hurt anyone, he said, but had no choice. He was sick of her evasions and the way she risked the family they had carefully tended for the past decade and a half. He didn't understand why everything had failed in the end (he was gracious enough to take some of the blame), but he had stuck it out with the faith of a monk. He knew there was something higher than simple happiness, and he wished she understood this as well. But she understood nothing. So he would leave her, and take their daughter with him.

I tugged the sheet out of the typewriter and folded it into my jacket pocket without rereading it.

"More egocentric writing?"

Kaminski was in the doorway, arms crossed, smiling at me.

"You put in the hours, don't you?"

I reached for my overcoat. "Sometimes."

"You know what's been on my mind lately, Ferenc?" He came over and leaned on my desk. "Kazakhstan. Remember me telling you about it a while ago? Well, the numbers are starting to come in, and it turns out I was right. We *succeeded*." He smiled, his thin mustache rising. "From that area alone we're harvesting twenty *million* tons of wheat. Twenty million! Sixty million from all the new regions, one hundred twenty-*five* million tons from the entirety of the Soviet Union! What do you think about that?"

He waited for an answer, so I nodded.

"It's better than that, my boy. It's a god-damn *miracle*. The largest yield in the history of the USSR." His smile was expansive, and I made a halfhearted attempt to match it, but just as quickly it went away. "These kinds of things don't impress you, do they, Ferenc?"

"It's impressive," I said.

He shook his head. "No it's not. You're only interested in the individual. Something you proved on November the sixth.

Put you in a group, and you'll always be the oddball, won't you?"

I didn't answer.

He pursed his lips and nodded at me. "How's your case coming?"

"Slowly."

"I thought so. It's because you don't work well in a team. It's all over you. Maybe you should find a different line of work, Ferenc. Maybe I can help you out with that."

I swallowed, too visibly. "What kind of work."

"Does it matter?" He shrugged. "You're a man who likes art. A fan of Vlaicu's work?"

"Not really."

"But all you boys went to his show. Now, that's a surprise. You don't see a lot of militiaman going in for art shows. It's a little eccentric. But Stefan sure made an ass of himself, didn't he?"

Although when he spoke his tone was light and conversational, his face, with its hard cheekbones and lips, did not match it. I didn't know if he just wanted to scare me, or if there was a point to this. State security has always worked by diversion, and to imagine you know what any officer is thinking is pure fantasy.

"You do know, don't you?"

266

I swallowed. "What?"

"That you and I will be face-to-face someday soon. I'm not the kind of man who forgets insults. Who ignores it when a man under my supervision embarrasses me in public."

"I . . . I know."

He drummed his long fingers on my desk, but kept staring at me. "There's a reason you're not eating your own waste in a prison cell right now."

I wanted to ask for the reason, but my tongue was too heavy to move.

"This is the only reason you're allowed to return to your family tonight. What do you want to ask me?"

My tongue was lead.

"Come on. You can do it."

"What," I managed. "What is the reason?"

He held up a finger. "No, Ferenc! No!" He shook the finger. *That* is the wrong question. The correct question is: *How do I stay out of a prison cell even after having humiliated you in public, Comrade Kaminski?*"

My dislodged tongue shifted. "How?"

He opened his hands. Smiled. "Simple, Comrade Kolyeszar. You work. You do your job to the best of your limited abilities. Bring in your killer, and perhaps, through the virtue of your good labor, I'll find a way

267

to rise above the insults of the past."

I nodded, and right then all I wanted in this world was his forgiveness.

But he'd had enough. He waved me away. "Go on, Ferenc. Say hello to Magda and Ágnes for me." He winked. "Send them my love."

# 37

"Your dinner's in the icebox," said Magda. "In the future, let me know if you're going to be late."

"Sure."

"And there was a call. Someone named *Vozka?*"

"Woznica."

"That's it. I asked him to leave a message, but he just wanted me to tell you he'd call back. He was insistent that you know."

"Where's Ágnes?"

"In her room."

I paused outside her door, again trying to shove Kaminski's threats down into the darkness. To my surprise, she was on her bed studying French, wearing her glasses, Pavel lying beside her. She pointed at the book so I would see.

"Very nice."

She sat up and crossed her legs beneath herself. "I think maybe you're right, Daddy. The French school may be a good idea." While she was trying to sound enthusiastic, it wasn't working very well.

I sat beside her and put my arm over her shoulder. "So it didn't work out with him?"

"With who?"

"This boyfriend you won't tell me about."

Her eyes grew large, and her face colored. "There *is* no boyfriend."

I stroked her hair, then gave her ear a tug. "Okay, then. Let's talk about the French school."

The next set of tests was scheduled for mid-December. She had a month to work on her language, which didn't seem like much time to me, but she was optimistic. "Then I can start in January."

"If you pass."

"I'll pass, all right."

Her optimism was infectious.

The dinner was cold, but good. Pork schnitzel and fried potatoes. Magda's cooking seemed to have improved recently, and I wondered if this was how she worked her guilt into something manageable. She lit a cigarette and sat across from me. "Did you take some money out of the account a couple weeks ago?"

"I did."

"Why?"

I looked at my fork. "Georgi needed to borrow it."

"You could have told me, you know."

"Sorry. We'll get it back by the beginning of the month."

She exhaled a cloud. "I believe that."

I tried to smile at her, but could only dream of a world where money was my only concern.

# 38

Sunday was bright as Leonek and I waited in one of the new cemeteries. The ones in the center had been filled to overflowing by the war, and the overflow had been directed to these modern expanses in the outer districts. There was no fence around this one, and the graves were flat stones in the grass. Name, dates, and sometimes a rank. Nothing more. The graveyard's flatness was made more noticeable by the narrow shed on the edge of the grounds, and the block towers in the distance. There were two trees, though they were no more than twigs rising hopefully out of the grass toward a white sun that warmed nothing. A man with a shovel stood beside a pile of dirt.

"No one here yet?" Leonek asked him.

The groundskeeper's weathered face buckled when he shut his mouth tightly. "No one ever comes early to a funeral."

"Well, we do."

Between us was a rectangular hole, well dug, and a slip of stone that read.

GRUBIN TEVEL
1856–1956

"Tevel was a century old," said Leonek. "Good for him."

"One lousy century to live through," I said.

We retreated to the closest of the two saplings, which made us feel less exposed.

"You know what you're going to say to him? You only get one chance."

"I never prepare an interview. I'll know what to ask when I'm asking it."

A cold wind buffeted us, then died down. In the distance a hearse drove toward the cemetery. It moved slowly along a gravel path through the graves and stopped near the groundskeeper. He and the driver heaved a cheap casket out of the back and placed it beside the hole.

"Where's your mother buried? Not here."

"Other side of town. It's a small grave-yard, out of the way. Lots of trees. Not like this."

After a while, five mourners appeared on foot. They were all in black and, I saw as they neared, stooped and old. Two men in Hassidic garb, three women with ceremonial scarves covering their heads. Neighbors or friends from the Jewish quarter. They waited beside the casket, muttering and occasionally shooting us mistrustful glances. One of the men — he seemed to have the serenity of a holy man — approached the casket and opened it; inside, the body was covered by a shroud. He said some Hebrew words over it.

At first we were afraid that Zindel Grubin would not arrive. Then Leonek spotted the reflection of sun off a white car coming toward us. We left the tree and waited with the others, and all of us watched the car stop behind the hearse. Three men were in the front seat, Zindel Grubin between two beefy men who walked him over silently. The old ones moved forward to greet him.

Zindel had a thin face and big ears on either side of his shaved head. His thick-lipped smile seemed a little unsure of itself as he bent to receive hugs.

The hearse driver opened a leather-bound book and said a few words. This was the official eulogy, the one that would go into the record books. He awkwardly inserted *Grubin, Tevel* where blanks appeared in the text. The guards retreated to the tree we'd left and started smoking. They had no worries — there was nowhere for Zindel to hide.

Afterward, the old man who had opened the casket stood over the enshrouded body and began to read outlines of Hebrew. Leonek and I glanced at one another. Everything was a mystery. One of the women cried, but briefly, and Zindel stared at the shroud as if trying to see through it.

After the words were said, we helped Zindel and the groundskeeper lower the casket into the earth. It was surprisingly light.

The mourners talked briefly with Zindel, and we waited behind them. Leonek stuck out his hand and introduced himself. "My condolences," he said, as Zindel hesitantly took the hand. "Look, can we talk?"

Zindel let go. "That's up to my keepers, I suppose."

The guards were still smoking by the

tree. "We'll say I'm a cousin. Come on."

He put a hand on Zindel's shoulder, and Zindel, to my surprise, did not shake it off. I stood beside them as they talked, keeping an eye on the guards, but I was all ears.

"I read you're in for sabotage. Is that right?"

Zindel smiled. "I wish. I was passing out leaflets at the barracks outside town, to the soldiers. That's what they call sabotage these days." He looked back at the mourners. "Being a Jew didn't help, it never does. You know, I'm told the entire neighborhood wants to move to Israel. I didn't think it was possible, but someone in the Interior Ministry said they're considering shipping the whole neighborhood off. Does that sound realistic to you?"

"No," said Leonek. "Doesn't sound realistic at all."

"Are you one of the tribe?"

"What?"

"Are you a Jew?"

"Armenian."

"Ah." Zindel nodded. "Well, that's not so bad either."

"Listen. I've come to talk about your sister, Chasya. Can you tell me about her?"

Zindel shrugged. "She was sweet," he said. "My sister was a doll. That's why they went for her. Russians see something that's pure, they want to piss on it."

"What about Sergei Malevich, the inspector who was investigating her murder?"

He shook his head. "Another Russian."

"He was different."

"Maybe to you, Inspector, but not to me. He's a good talker, that Russian, he even made me doubt myself, but in the end I was smarter."

"You didn't know he was killed."

I looked over in time to see the doubt come into Zindel's face. "Who killed him?"

"The Russians killed him when he was investigating the case. Because he was different."

He frowned at the pile of dirt beside his grandfather's open grave.

"That's why I'm here," said Leonek. "He was killed because he had figured out who the murderers were, and I'm trying to sort it all out. To get a little justice finally."

Zindel smiled at the word, as if it were a joke.

"I need you to tell me what you remember."

He said he didn't remember much, but he did. He remembered the night when

Chasya didn't come home, so he went to her friend Reina's home. It turned out that she was missing as well. He went into the streets — it was raining that night, he said — and looked in all the corners and alleys he knew they sometimes wandered to. He found her other girlfriends, but all he learned was that they were last seen heading home. "I had nothing to go on but my feeling. Fear. That something terrible had happened." So he and his father went out again and started asking strangers. It was a rare thing in those days to talk to strangers, and after the suspicion died away they finally got a lead: A shopkeeper had seen two young girls talking with some soldiers at the corner of Polska and Josefov. "I suppose those streets have different names now."

Leonek nodded. They did.

"So we stuck to that area. We passed the synagogue several times — it was boarded up, and we didn't think to look inside. But after we'd exhausted all our other options we walked around it until we found a door where the boards had been ripped off. It was very late then, and we didn't have a flashlight. So Father lit matches. It didn't take long to find them. They were lying between the pews. Raped. Their throats slit."

He stepped over to the edge of the grave, glanced at his guards who were looking back at him, and turned to us with a strange smile.

"Think I should jump in? Would that get them off my back? No," he said as he wandered back. He nodded at the mourners. "Those poor old mothers would get piles from sitting shiva so long."

They filed reports and complaints in rapid succession. Or at least Zindel did. His father, after seeing the bodies and learning what had been done to them, was unable to function. He stopped going in to work, and his wife had to take over everything. For weeks there was nothing from the authorities, and in that time Zindel investigated on his own. He got descriptions of a couple of the men — there were four in all — and brought his descriptions to a tired Militia clerk, who shrugged and put them in a drawer. "When I left I'm sure they went into the trash." By the time Inspector Sergei Malevich showed up at the apartment with an earnest expression that could not fool him, he even had a name: Boris Olonov. "He bought his bread from the same woman every day, that's how I learned who he was. But after he killed my sister he didn't come to the neighborhood anymore. I never got my hands on him."

"And you didn't tell the inspector his name."

He shook his head.

Leonek's voice stuttered with irritation. "That was a mistake. You don't realize what a mistake it was."

Zindel seemed surprised by Leonek's sincerity. He glanced at me, then said, "If I'd given him the name, would it have brought my sister back? Would anything have happened to Boris Olonov?" He shook his head. "Nothing would have happened. Except the Russians would have known everything I knew."

"My partner might have lived."

"Maybe," he said. "But I wouldn't be so sure."

# 39

Zindel returned to the custody of his captors, each one holding an elbow to guide him to the front seat of the white car. They squeezed in on either side and drove back to Ozaliko.

"Does it help?" I asked as I started the engine.

"Not really. Maybe. I don't know."

Leonek drew his finger along the windshield and looked at the dirt on his print. "I can file a report on Olonov, at least that. He might be the one who killed Sergei. But he's somewhere deep in Russia now, I'm sure, forgetting about the two dead girls and Sergei. I can't touch him."

I changed gear. "Maybe you can."

He looked at me.

"Kliment. He helped me out recently on a case. He might be willing to look around."

"*Kliment* helped you on a case?"

"He's a good man."

"Like his father," said Leonek, watching the blocks go by. A smile spread across his face. "Yes. This could work."

We had a few drinks at his tiny, tin-roofed house. It was dirty; ever since his mother had died, it seemed, no one had cleaned a thing. Except for the bedroom. The bed was made and the sheets starched, and all the surfaces had been dusted. "This where you live?" I asked him, and when he realized what I was asking, his face darkened in an uneven blush.

With our third round of brandies, Leonek turned on the radio. It was set to the Americans. These days they were

279

calmer, reporting on international events with a steady, tempered voice and leaving the vitriol to their guests, exiles recently escaped from the Empire. There was a writer from Kiev who chronicled in painful detail the interrogations he had faced at the hands of the KGB. He described the use of heat and cold on the flesh, the simple effects of clubs struck repeatedly against his legs. I wondered what simple tools Kaminski preferred, then wished I hadn't. I said, "You listen to this a lot?"

Leonek touched his glass to his chin. "It's the only thing I listen to."

I left just after dusk, feeling a little vibrant from the drinks, and I didn't want this pleasure to be undermined by Magda's silence or by dreams of Stefan sliding over her body, so I drove into the Fifth District and slowly turned up and down the narrow streets, stopping generously for pedestrians. My hands and feet knew where I was going, but I was in no hurry. When it occurred to the rest of me, I tried to deny it, but then I was parked in front of Vera's building and could no longer fool myself.

If I wanted to justify it, it would have been no problem. But I didn't try to justify it. That would have made what followed into part of a game between me and Magda. That would have trivialized it. So I held the loose banister as I ascended, thinking only that it was a lovely building where Vera and Karel Pecsok lived.

She opened the door, started to say *hello,* then stared.

She was half-dressed, as if getting ready to go somewhere. A brassiere and a black skirt over stockings, her hair tied in a bun on the back of her head.

"*Well,*" she managed, along with a smile.

"You busy?"

"Just wondering what to do with my night. Come in."

Vera's beauty lay less in her physical appearance than in her ferocity. Long, hungry fingers that pulled off my jacket and hat, large eyes that roamed over my chest, arms, face. Her brassiere was loose on her white, bony shoulders. She was so thin. She took my jacket away and reappeared in a blouse with glasses of red wine, smelling of lavender.

"You surprise me, dear," she said. "You always surprise me."

"I was in the neighborhood."

Her lips were the only fat part of her. They stretched when she drank, and her strong teeth made clinking sounds against the glass.

She turned on the radio. I was relieved to hear no Americans, just some tamed Soviet pianist tapping through a countryman's scribblings. I realized I was still standing, somewhat foolishly, in the middle of the room. I moved to the edge of the couch. Vera settled next to me, a hand on my back and her thigh against mine.

"Don't feel strange, Ferenc. I don't want you like that."

"How do you want me?" I said this quietly.

"Silent. But I want all your strength. You'll need it."

I finished my glass and held it out. "For strength."

She got up and refilled it, but before returning the glass she leaned down and kissed me on the mouth. Full, hard. It was in her kisses that her ferocity was most evident. She looked me in the eye, her voice a whisper: "You're going to enjoy yourself."

Her kiss had already convinced me, but I still drained my glass.

The Soviet pianist was having a fine time of it.

We kissed on the sofa for a while. First she initiated it, then I did. We were like those kids monopolizing Georgi's couch, smearing lipstick and saliva. Hands groping, my fingers pressed beneath her brassiere, over her tall nipples, then slid up her skirt. She flinched and pulled my hand out. A smile. "Your rings hurt." I took them off.

We were out of our clothes quickly, but it was not simple. It was more complicated than I had imagined. Their bed was wide enough for two couples, and we shifted positions often, twisting in a mad clockwork. She rolled to face the sheets and held her backside high for me, then turned over and brought her knees to her ears. She slid down and took me in her mouth. The gymnastics were strenuous. She brought me to the edge many times, then changed everything completely. I was sweating freely. Once or twice she expelled a brief orgasmic shout, then took a breath and kept on. She dragged her tongue over the moist inside of my thigh, then bit me. I flinched. She said, "Wait."

There was a drawer beneath the bed. She took out a frayed purple belt, part of a lost robe, and crouched on the bed, her long white body glowing.

"Tie me up."

I used the headboard and her wrists and a knot I'd learned in the army. It was secure, but would not bind. I paused to consider her beneath me, arms above her head, her long hair scattered over the sheets. Her rib cage tightened behind thin flesh as it rose and fell. She was so small and breakable.

I used her facing up, then facing down. She squirmed and made noises I'd never heard from any woman before. Once she trilled a consonant, then grunted. I could just make out the words that followed: "Hit me."

I struck her rear end with my open hand and heard the pleasure come out of her mouth.

*"Harder."*

I did, smacking until she was bright red, then I kissed her. I kissed anything I could reach. I licked and gnawed her until she made that sound again. Then I did, too.

# 40

I have to step back and apologize for the details. They are uncommon for a confession, and I only use them after the greatest deliberation. But to understand all that follows, the whole web of circumstances must be explained, because otherwise nothing can really be understood.

We smoked in bed. At first we were too

exhausted to speak, and the only sounds were our breaths. She crept away while I stared at the ceiling, where little spots were moving rapidly, joining, separating. I was not thinking of what we'd done; I wasn't thinking of Magda. I was too exhausted. Vera returned with the wine bottle and our glasses.

"Well," she said, standing naked and smiling.

I accepted a glass. "Well."

She sat beside me, back against the headboard, and took a sip. "What did you think, Ferenc?"

"I'm speechless."

"That pleases me." She rubbed her wrists and lit another cigarette. "You don't know how long I've been waiting. Much longer than since last Christmas. Karel — well, that's what happens in a marriage, isn't it?"

"What?"

"Repetition. The same two positions. Then one. You start to do it just because the other one happens to be in your bed. Boredom. There's no other reason." She took a drag and exhaled it into the air. "What about you and Magda?"

"We haven't had sex in over a year."

"*What?*"

The ceiling was moving again. I'd said too much. But no — after what we'd just done, how could that be too much? I felt something huge shift inside me. The world was an entirely different place.

"Oh," she said as she stroked my cheek. "You're crying."

She held me until it passed. I never suspected such patience was in her. Her bony chest was against my nose. She still smelled of lavender, but now it was mixed with the smell of me.

I'd seen a man buried that day, a man who'd witnessed a hundred years of what humanity can do to itself. Now I was in a married woman's bed, weeping. This is what humanity can do to itself.

# 41

I did not forget where I was, but that morning it was still a surprise to see Vera's sleeping face behind the nest of her black hair. I started to dress.

"You're going?"

"To work."

She got up on an elbow to watch me tie my shoes. "Should I ask?"

I looked at her.

286

"If you'll be coming back. Karel's out until Friday."

I didn't know if I would come back, if it was a good idea or a horrible one, or if by tonight I'd even want to. "You'll be here?"

When she shrugged, the sheet came off her shoulder. "I've nowhere else to go."

I kissed her forehead, then, almost as an afterthought, her lips.

Georgi was waiting for me on the front steps to the station, hat in his hands. He looked like he hadn't gotten much sleep, and I assumed I'd missed a party. We shook hands.

"I've got worries, Ferenc."

He took a folded envelope from his pocket and handed it to me.

It was a summons to appear, the next day, at the state security headquarters on Yalta Boulevard. The reason: DOCUMENT CHECK.

I took him to a café and fed him brandy. "It could be nothing, Georgi. You know this. It could just be a document check, like it says."

"Don't tell me that. Rubin Blazkova — you know him? A forger, but that's beside the point. He received a summons two weeks ago. No one knows where he is anymore. You've got to help me." He could

287

hardly hold his glass.

It surprised me how calmly I was taking it. I suppose I was trying to counterbalance his fear with cool, rational words. When I sat in certain positions I could smell Vera on me, and I wondered if he could smell her, too. "I'll come by tonight, okay? This isn't until tomorrow morning, so I'll work on it today." I patted his cheek. "Don't worry so much."

"I'm a poet, remember? I can't take torture."

"Nobody can take torture, Georgi."

"That doesn't make me feel any better." He finished his drink and shook his head. "I don't want to end up like Nestor Velcea."

I looked at him. "What?"

"I don't want —"

"Nestor Velcea — you *know* Nestor Velcea?"

He shrugged. "Of course I do. Didn't you meet him?"

"What?"

"He was at that party, a couple months ago. When Louis was in town — that's why he was there, to see Louis. The two of them go back a long way." He paused, looking at me. "I'd never met Nestor before, just heard of him. Friend of a friend, you know. He was in the camps — *that's* where I don't want to end up." I must have done something shocking with my face, because he leaned forward, for the moment forgetting his own terror. "What is it?"

All I could manage was: "Friend of *what* friend?"

"Well, the poet Kaspar Tepylo, of course."

# 42

Brano Sev was at his desk. I pulled up a chair.

"Ferenc," he said.

His flat, round face was eternally young. He was somewhere in his forties now — none of us knew his exact age — and in those years all his deeds had done nothing to his face. It must have been useful for him, having an innocent face to hide his corrupted hands. "Listen. I have a friend who's been called in for a document check. I want to know what this is about."

He considered the directness of my request, turning it over in his head, looking for motives. All state security men work the same. "That's confidential information."

"It's important I know."

"Why?"

"Because he's my friend."

"And what would you do with this information?"

I paused. "Ease his mind."

His fingers stroked some blank papers on the desk. He sniffed the air — perhaps he smelled Vera. "Let's suppose it is what the summons says: a document check. Then everything is fine. But if there is something more involved, something that takes a longer time . . . if that's the case, then what will you do?"

I was walking into a trap. I could see this. But I couldn't just stand up and leave. "I'd tell him to prepare himself."

"That's a lie, Ferenc. We both know it. You would advise him not to go, perhaps even to leave the country. It's what you did to Svetla Woznica."

In the silence that fell between us the shock settled into my bones. Nothing I did was a secret, nothing had ever been. I looked into his eyes, but couldn't keep up my strength. He had the ability to hold a stare indefinitely, and I imagined, as my stomach turned over, that this was the way he looked at his victims in the interview room.

"Ferenc," he said quietly, "maybe the fear has gone to your head. I wouldn't assume to know what you're feeling. But I am aware of everything you do. This thing with the Woznica woman was child's play to figure out — her release form and a few questions at the train station were all it took. I know, but more importantly, so does Comrade Kaminski. I'd worry less about your friends and more about yourself, and your family. This friend of yours, this Georgi Radevych? He's a drunk and a fraud, certainly you can see this. He's loud and stupid. You're not stupid, Ferenc. You're just confused."

I opened my mouth to reply, but he was turning away from me again, opening a folder.

I leaned over the toilet bowl and waited for the sickness that didn't come. I couldn't still myself. Then I sat down and tried to breathe regularly. There was graffiti scratched into the gray-green paint of the stall, and I focused on the men with enormous penises and large-breasted women bowed to service them. I closed my eyes.

When you know you are being watched, every movement takes on great significance. My stumbling walk down the corridor to the bathroom had been on a stage, with a crowd of thousands watching. Bent over the bowl, there was laughter, and when nothing came, hoots and catcalls. I was never alone, and never would be.

# 43

I called a friend of Leonek's with connections to Yalta Boulevard, but he could do nothing. So I took a long walk through the city, trying to work out the puzzle of the impossible. And I ended as I began: powerless.

I wanted to just call him. He would have understood. But Georgi deserved better. When he opened the door it was hard to look at all the hope in his face, so I turned to the floor. When I looked back, the hope was gone.

We got drunk. There was a long night ahead of us, so we tried not to drink too quickly, but once we'd started there was no stopping us. I held up a finger and said I needed to call home, because I'd stayed out last night and had forgotten to let Magda know.

"Slept somewhere else?" Georgi frowned.

"Where were you last night?" said Magda.

"Busy. A case. Sorry I didn't call, it was irresponsible. But I'm not going to be home tonight either. I'm over at Georgi's."

"That's fantastic."

"He got a notice."

"A what?"

"He has to go to Yalta Boulevard tomorrow. A document check."

"Well, I," she began, then inhaled. "Oh Christ. You don't mean . . ."

"I'm going to stay the night with him. Look, it's probably nothing."

"Yes. Yes, right. I hope so. Can't you do anything for him?"

"I've tried."

"Give him my love."

It was the first time in memory she'd ever offered Georgi such a thing. But Georgi smiled when I delivered it, and said, "I always liked that woman. Haven't I always said that? Because it's true."

"You've always said it."

"But listen. Was it Vera last night? I can see it was Vera. I might be going off to some cold prison, but you and Magda need to make up." He raised his glass. "For the good of the country."

"You should be talking to Magda about this."

"It's a two-sided thing, a marriage."

"You've never been married."

"True, true."

"Anyway, I've been trying for too long.

293

As far as she's concerned, we're no longer man and wife."

He didn't like the sound of that. "She *told* you this?"

"She's sleeping with my oldest friend, isn't that enough?"

Georgi, for the first time in his life, had nothing to say.

I brought the brandy from the kitchen. We went at it.

He was resolute in his doom. I admired him for it, and told him. He grimaced. "You know, this is the way heroes go down. They smile agreeably as they're led to the wall. They sing a song as the bullet comes at them."

"Don't say that."

"I'm past the terror. You should have seen me this morning."

"I did see you this morning."

"I mean after I talked to you. I threw up in an alley and wept on the tram. You know what I wanted more than anything? A wife to cry to. That's what I wanted. Why can't I settle down? What's my flaw?"

"You've got no flaws, Georgi."

He winked, then leaned forward and tapped my knee. "Fill me up, okay?"

We drank until early morning, then slept where we sat. He cried a few times when he was very drunk, but held on for most of the night. After a short rest, we had coffee, and he leaned his head on my chest a moment. I put my arms around him. No tears, just a momentary loss of strength. He washed himself thoroughly, because, as he said, he didn't know when he'd get the chance again. Then I drove him to Yalta Boulevard, number 36. An unassuming beige façade: a prewar administrative office. The only difference now was the crest above the door — the hawk with its head turned aside — and the simple sign: MINISTRY FOR STATE SECURITY, CENTRAL.

A handsome, uniformed guard standing just beyond the heavy wooden doors read Georgi's summons. He smiled serenely and told me I could not enter. I started to protest, but Georgi squeezed my arm. "Let's not make trouble." He kissed my cheeks and passed through the inner doors alone.

I waited in the car, watching women pass in their winter scarves, and kept looking back at the door with the hope that he would come bursting out, grinning with wild relief. Maybe I could have sent him out of the country. Buying someone passage east was no problem, but Georgi would have only been safe in the West. That was beyond my means.

After a half hour, I started the engine and drove.

# 44

The poet Kaspar Tepylo shared a room with a minimalist painter. There were canvases of large blue squares on red backgrounds stacked in a corner and a bowl of cigarette butts beside a jar of dirty brushes. "Never live with a painter," he advised me. "The messes are incredible."

We walked through to his sparse bedroom, a mattress and desk covered with neat stacks of paper. A few books were lined up beside a radiator that didn't seem to be working. He offered me the desk chair as he settled his tall, thin frame on the corner of the bed. He scratched a concave cheek. "So what is it, Ferenc?"

Like everyone, he was a friend of a friend, an unsuccessful poet who was assigned to work on construction sites and scribbled lines at night. "I need to talk to Nestor Velcea."

"What's Nes been up to? I haven't seen him in a while."

"I just need to ask him some questions. It's about a case."

"What kind of case?"

"A murder."

"Oh." He stood up and found some cigarettes on the desk. "I haven't seen him since, I don't know, early September. He stayed here for a while after he came back from the camps. Here in this room."

"Then he left?"

Kaspar nodded. "Told me he'd found a place. But he never gave me the address."

"Any ideas?"

"I've asked around, but he's not staying with anyone I know."

"Tell me," I said. "What's he like?"

He ashed on the floor and sat back down. "He's different now than he was. More withdrawn — which for him is saying a lot. He never told me what happened in the camps, but he's got a terrible limp. And he's missing this little finger here." He held up his left hand and pointed at it, then took another drag. "I asked, but he wouldn't tell me. He just smiled. To tell the truth, he made me nervous."

"But you let him stay here?"

"I couldn't turn him away, could I? I remember how he was before he was sent away. He was supposed to have been a good painter. A lot of promise."

"You didn't see his paintings?"

He shook his head. "Never let me. He always said they weren't finished, but I think he was just scared of criticism. I suppose that's why he didn't spend time with other painters, just writers. He said he found painters boring."

"But he used to live with Antonín Kullmann."

Kaspar shrugged. "When you're broke you have to make concessions."

"Why was he sent to the camps?"

"Your guess is as good as mine. Nestor was never political. He couldn't stand the idea of painting for political reasons. It was all propaganda, he said, no matter who was making it. I think he was a little too insistent on this, but to each his own, right?"

"I suppose."

"And he told me he never signed his paintings. This was strange, too. How did he put it? Yes: He didn't want his identity to overshadow the integrity of the work. I think I know what he meant — but again, it's a little extreme."

"So when he was picked up, it was a surprise?"

"To everyone. A few of us filed a protest at Victory Square, but that did no good." He looked at his long ash. "Until the Amnesty, we heard nothing." He tapped the cigarette, and the ash dropped to the floor. "You know, he has family in the provinces. The south, somewhere, I'm not sure. Maybe he went back to his village."

"I don't think so," I said.

"Why not?"

I got up and took my hat from the desk. "Get in touch with me if you hear from him, will you?"

# 45

I could only hold off thinking of him for moments, and in between those moments I imagined him in a cold concrete cell, suffering the light of a bare, dusty bulb hanging from the ceiling, then facing interrogators with complicated electrical equipment that attached to the tenderest parts of Georgi's body. Clubs striking his legs; heat and cold on his flesh.

At the station, Leonek stopped me on his way out to say that Kliment was "a mensch, a real mensch." He had agreed to track down Boris Olonov. But I couldn't share his excitement. On my desk was a message from Ozaliko informing me that I had an appointment with Lev Urlovsky at ten the next morning. I folded the message into my pocket and sat down. I tried to focus on this artist who had returned from the camps to kill his old roommates and an art curator. But it didn't work, and when Kaminski and Sev strolled in and began talking by Sev's desk my distraction gained material form. Kaminski wandered over. "Hello, Ferenc. Did you give my wishes to Magda and Ágnes?"

"Sure."

"Are you working hard?"

I looked at him.

"I believe we had a deal, Comrade Kolyeszar."

"Yes," I said. "I'm working hard."

"Good to hear." He returned to Sev and bent over the desk and read something Sev was pointing at, but I couldn't quite see them anymore. I could hear him laughing, saying *Good good,* but could no longer make out his features.

I took the tram home. It seemed unbelievable that the other riders could chat and smile or simply doze in their seats. I wanted to shake them out of their ignorance — didn't they know what was going on, at that very moment, on Yalta Boulevard? But they knew. They knew that they could be next. I could be next.

I took a bath, sinking into the murky,

cooling water, thinking still of electricity. Ágnes knocked on the door. "You going to be in there forever?"

"Just until I'm clean."

She knocked again. "I don't know if I can wait that long."

So I toweled off and went to the bedroom to lie down. She bolted past me and slammed the bathroom door shut.

Magda came once and settled on the edge of the bed. "Was it awful?"

"Of course it was."

"Did he seem . . . I don't know. In good spirits?"

I turned my head, the pillow crackling in my ears, and looked at her. "What do you mean, *good spirits?*"

"You know what I mean. It's Georgi we're talking about."

"I don't know," I said. "No good spirits today."

She got up to finish dinner.

We didn't tell Ágnes, because there was no need yet. She talked about the rope-climbing exercise that she and Daniela had apparently excelled at. The Pioneer chief — a man with the unlikely name of Hals Haling — brought them to the head of the class as examples of the female ideal of fitness, then awarded them with lengths of knotted rope.

"I suppose you were proud," said Magda, trying to smile.

"You'd suppose, wouldn't you?" Ágnes said into her plate. "I mean, it's all kind of stupid in the end, isn't it?"

"What is?"

"Climbing ropes. All we did was climb up so we could come back down. What's the point in that?"

I managed a smile of my own. "That's pretty perceptive, Ági."

She nodded formally at me. "Thank you, Daddy."

"You can take it further, though, can't you?"

She shrugged.

"Why get out of bed each day when you're just going to get back in at night?"

"Well, that's certainly a reason not to make the bed in the morning," she said, making a face at Magda.

"Or why," I continued, "should you eat a meal when you're just going to crap it out later?"

"*Ferenc,*" warned Magda.

Ágnes was grinning. "That's a good question, Daddy. And why should I study French when I'm just going to forget it anyway?"

"*That,*" I said, "is a different issue altogether. You really need a course in logic, sweetheart."

But the levity only lasted until we'd cleaned up the plates and headed into the living room. Ágnes insisted on listening to the Americans, and we heard a report on Bulgarian work camps. An emigrant described slave labor and casual killings in hushed tones that made us lean close to hear. The commentator apologized for his guest's too-quiet voice, but explained that, while in a camp, a guard had crushed his windpipe with a boot. Then the radio whined like a sick animal, and I turned it off.

# 46

There were only a few white hairs left on his head, but a plume of them rose out of his blue prison collar. He had big eyes, one smaller than the other, and long fingers with darker hairs covering them. He looked exactly as I remembered him from last summer. He placed his hands on the table and waited.

"Lev Urlovsky?"

He nodded. No smile, no sound.

"Do you remember me?"

He nodded again. "Ferenc Kolyeszar. You and your friend Leonek Terzian found me out."

"Not me. I only came on the case when they went to get you."

"You're modest."

"Still no regrets?"

"Nothing that keeps me awake."

"Vassily was your son."

He moved his hands together until the thumbs touched, then dragged them apart. "*Was*, yes. Until he decided to join the regime that took away my life."

"Part of your life. You were at the camps for — how many? Five years?"

"Seven."

"Seven, okay. But you were free again — it was over."

He chewed the inside of his mouth, looking at his hands. "Inspector, if you think my life was given back just because they let me walk around this beautiful city, then you're more stupid than even you look. Just because it's another day doesn't mean that yesterday never happened."

It was an elegant way to put it, but he'd had a long time to think over his reasons for bludgeoning his son to death, and maybe only elegance could justify it. "I'm here to ask about someone else. Someone you were in Vátrina with."

He leaned forward, just a little.

"Nestor Velcea. Does the name ring a bell?"

He leaned back again. "The Romanian."

"Romanian?"

"He sat in with the other Romanians when there was time — there wasn't much time. Very tight, those Romanians."

"But you knew him?"

"Sure I did. He had nothing against Slavs. I had nothing against Romanians. We all had the same enemy."

"The state."

He closed his eyes as he nodded.

I opened my notepad on the table. "You were friends?"

"Not hard to be friends when you're treated as we were."

"You talked."

"When we weren't too exhausted and beaten."

"So tell me about him."

Urlovsky opened his nostrils and took a deep breath. I wondered how old he was — sixty? Sixty-five? Or was he one of those who returned from the camps looking twenty years older than they were? "He used to draw on the wall. With a piece of coal. Anything you asked for. He had fantastic hands, at least until they took off that finger." He touched the pinkie on his left hand.

"Who took it off?"

"The guards, of course. First time he did a sketch on the wall. They took him in the yard and cut the thing off. But that didn't stop him." He smiled. "That Romanian was something."

"I've heard he was a great artist."

"Talent, yes. So much talent. But he was worse than me."

"Worse than you?"

He tilted his head. "*Worse* is the wrong word. He was stronger, that's what he was. He could sustain his hatred in a way most of us couldn't."

"His anger against the state."

"The state, sure. But not really."

"Then who, really?"

"The bastards who put him there."

"State security."

"Them, too."

I looked down at my empty page and sighed. "Tell me, then, who Nestor Velcea was angry with."

"Who shouldn't he be angry with?"

The guards would allow me to beat him if I wanted, but I didn't think it would work. He had been through a lot worse than I could give him, and had held on to all his rage. "Josef Maneck? Was that someone?"

"Might have been."

"How about Antonín Kullmann?"

He looked me in the face, as if judging me. Then he nodded, big eyes holding onto me. "These names, they do ring a bell."

"Why did he hate them?"

He frowned, as if reassessing his judgment. "Why do you think? They put him in there."

"He was sure about this?"

Urlovsky leaned back. "Not at first, no. A lot of us only figure it out later. For me, it took almost a year before I realized who did it. My ex-wife. You know why? Do you know why?"

I said I didn't.

"She wanted the dacha — that's why. I told her it was in my family before we were married, and it would stay in my family. I spent my summers in that dacha as a child. But she wanted to vacation in the countryside, so she made a phone call to Yalta Boulevard." He shook his head and smiled. "A crafty bitch, that one."

"Why didn't you kill her instead?"

"She was already a bitch; I couldn't do anything about it. But my son, I could stop him from becoming one. I'm his father."

"Let's get back to Nestor. Why was he turned in?"

He pursed his lips. "That boy was talented, and he knew it. It made him vain. He thought they'd done it out of jealousy." Urlovsky turned his palms to the ceiling. "I don't know, maybe he's right. But it takes a bold man to suggest that."

"Your wife did it for a house."

"You can live in a house. A house is security. What's art? Each time Nestor made his pictures on the wall, one of us used a wet rag to clean it so the guards wouldn't see." He patted the table. "It's pretty stuff, art, but it just wipes away."

# 47

On the drive back, I considered what Urlovsky had said. Josef Maneck and Antonín Kullmann had turned in Nestor Velcea because they were *jealous* of his talent — Kullmann didn't want to compete against a better artist. I didn't believe it. I couldn't imagine someone doing such a thing when the reward would have been so undependable. Was Nestor so self-centered to really believe this?

Moska was posting notices on the bulletin board behind my desk when I came in. "There was a call for you. That friend of yours — Georgi?"

I ran to the phone.

"My blessed friend! I'm in only one piece, and I've got an appetite that could stall a Volga."

We met in a restaurant near his apartment. It was an old place that writers in the prewar days used to fill with smoke and wine and literary arguments. Behind the bar were grainy photos of well-dressed men in stiff collars at tables, a few wearing looser, more artistic clothes, toasting the photographer. The great Romanian poet Eminescu sat next to our national poet, Pasha, and not a single blow was being exchanged — Georgi pointed this out as we edged our way to our own table. He was positively buoyant, and waved to people he recognized, then ordered cutlet and a long series of sides that came to him like flashes of inspiration. "Roasted potatoes! Yes, and . . . peppers!"

"You *will* stall a Volga."

He winked at me. "I'm just so happy to be alive."

He was too distracted by everything around him — the smells, the décor, the

309

women. Only after he had dived into his food could he, between mouthfuls, begin to tell me.

"I thought it was over. You can be sure of that. They stuck me in a cell without a word. It was no bigger than a water closet. I remembered the prayers Mother taught me when I was a child. Pieces, though, never an entire prayer. And in that little concrete room I whispered whatever I could remember. Do you know, I even worried that if I couldn't remember a single prayer from beginning to end, God wouldn't take me? I thought my soul would be doomed because of bad memory!"

He laughed at this, fully, expressively, though it didn't seem particularly funny to me.

"Time stops in a cell without windows. You know this, it makes sense, but when you're in it, it's a whole new reality. So I waited. There was nothing. No food, no voices, no sounds at all — they're sound-proof, those new cells they've got. Incredible." He took another mouthful and spoke as he chewed. "But they kept the lights on. Even at night. I couldn't even *guess* the time."

"So they didn't talk to you?"

"I think it was the second day I heard

310

from them. The guards woke me up and took me to another room on the next floor up. It was an office with a desk, and a chair in the middle of the room. I was told to sit down. Then the guards left. That room was *not* soundproof. I could hear someone shouting in the next room. *No no, please no* — that sort of thing. Christ." He shook his head. "I was crapping my pants, you can believe it."

"I believe it."

"Then he came to me. Tall guy, he smiled a lot. Russian. He walked around my chair and started talking. Conversationally. As if we were old friends."

"Okay."

"He talked about nightspots in town. He was fond of The Crocodile — you know that place?"

"A nightclub?"

"Russian-run nightclub. I've never been there. He suggested I go on Tuesdays, like he does — when some vaudeville act does their comedy. This is the conversation he started with. I suppose it was to relax me, but it didn't. Then he started talking literature. Seems he's a fan of our writers. He brought up some names, then he said he'd been reading your old novel recently."

I reached for my drink, my fingers cold and

my rings heavy. "Did he have a mustache?"

"Yeah. A thin one. He asked if we were good friends, but I told him we were just acquaintances. I didn't want him to ask too much."

"Good."

"But he knew we spent a lot of time together — of course they'd seen you bring me to them."

I waited while he dug into the peppers, then spoke through a full mouth.

"But he left that alone for a while, and asked about my poetry. He wanted to know why I hadn't published anything for years. He'd seen my old book, thought it was pretty good."

"What did you tell him?"

"Well, I certainly didn't suggest he read my self-published pieces. I told him I wasn't inspired much these days."

"Did he believe it?"

Georgi rested his wrists on the edge of the table. "Ferenc, I have no idea what he thought about anything I said."

There was a lot of noise in the restaurant, voices and clattering dishes and scraping silverware.

"After a while he asked about you again. He asked if I'd read anything you'd written lately. I said no. He told me he'd had a peek, and that it was brilliant stuff. I didn't ask him how he'd gotten his peek."

"I know how he got it."

"You know this guy?"

"He works out of our station. I know him. Go on."

Georgi stretched an arm over the back of his chair. "He also praised your Militia work. The man was full of praise, I tell you."

"It's his tactic. He's good at it."

"Don't I know. But he asked about the case you're working on. I said I didn't know anything about it. *But you've helped him?* he asked. *Helped him find Nestor Velcea?*"

"He said that name?"

Georgi nodded. "I didn't think it possible, but I was even more terrified than before. I said I hadn't helped with anything, and he shook his head. *Come now, let's be truthful.* He had me in a corner, you see?"

"He did," I agreed.

"I had no choice."

He waited for me to agree with that too, so I did.

"He was staring at me, with those eyes. I admitted I might have helped once."

Now it was coming out.

"He pressed on about it. How had I

helped? What did you need? So I told him you were looking for someone else, not Nestor. I made up a name. God help me, I did."

"What was the name?"

"Gregor Prakash."

"Who?"

He shrugged. "I don't know. I told him he was a painter I'd never met. A formalist. And the Russian asked what information I'd given you. By then it was easy. The lie was begun. I told him that Gregor lived over in the Fifth District, and if he was any kind of painter at all, he'd go to the bar on the corner of Republic and the Eighteenth of January."

"Incredible," I said. "And he bought it?"

"What do I know?" He picked up a cube of roasted potato with his fingers and popped it into his mouth. "All I know is he sent me back to my cell. This morning a guard took me out to the street and told me to keep walking."

I paid for the lunch, and we walked toward Victory Square. Georgi bought a couple fried doughs from an old man in a kiosk. We crossed the streets, passing the ideal socialist couple holding their torch, and entered Victory Park. I didn't know why Kaminski didn't just come to me for this information. He could have learned the details of the case from me — I saw no reason to hide such things from him. But no — I'd already hidden information about Nestor Velcea from Sev. And why? Brano Sev knew: The fear had gone to my head.

"So when are you going to have that brilliant writing ready for me?"

We were on a bench, staring through the trees at the Culture Ministry building, which had been white, but was being painted gray by a crew of workmen on scaffolding. "You're still going to print it?"

"Of course."

"This experience hasn't frightened you away from your publishing?"

Georgi licked his sugarcoated fingers. "All it's done is remind me how much I like being alive." He held up an index finger. "Alive, Ferenc. Not one of the walking dead." He placed the finger in his mouth, and sucked.

# 48

I called to tell Magda about Georgi's safe return, and that I might not be in that night either. Then I called to be sure Vera was in. There was no longer any hesitation. On the drive over I wondered if Magda knew about Vera, and I wondered if she knew what I knew about her. It was all a hopeless puzzle that could only be solved by two adults sitting face-to-face and speaking the truth. But neither of us was adult enough to do that yet.

Vera was fixing dinner when I arrived. She had strapped a soiled apron all the way around her narrow waist, down to her bare knees, and she held her wet hands like a surgeon's. She got on her toes and kissed me, her wrists holding my neck.

I tossed my coat on the bed and found her bent over the open oven. I held her hips and rubbed myself into her. She groaned, reached back, and parted the apron. She was naked underneath.

Afterward, we had pork and zucchini by candlelight. The candle seemed out of place. It was something that belonged to the world of romance, but what we did could not be called romantic.

"You like the wine?"

"Delicious."

"Did you know that Karel's going to be gone another week?"

"Is that so."

"Seems the Yugoslavs are fond of his poems. He's been invited to Split to give a reading and take part in their 'Week of Culture.' That's what they call it."

"So what do you have planned for the Week of Culture?"

"I'm planning to stay in, entertain a guest."

"Someone I know?"

"Maybe."

That night we did the closest thing to making love we would ever do. We stroked one another's bodies, as if comforting the flesh, and kissed more than we ever had. For a long time we just lay together, embracing, sometimes whispering tender words. She said beneath her breath, "I don't have to say it, do I?" and I told her she didn't. She smiled and slid under me and took me in herself. She didn't need to tell me she loved me, and by the next morning I was glad she hadn't.

We ate toast and jam with our coffee. I noticed, with a little shame, that Vera looked a mess in the mornings. Some women are this way. In the afternoons and evenings, they're radiant. But catch them before they've had a chance to put themselves together, and their looks turn to ash. Magda always looked like herself. Her hair could be pillow-pressed and her makeup gone, but there was an essential beauty to her that always came through. Vera looked as if she had taken off a mask.

"This is nice," she said. "Isn't it?"

"The coffee's good."

"I mean, this. Breakfast, sunlight coming in, sitting here with you." She nodded into the cup she brought to her face.

"You're right," I lied. "It's wonderful."

"Remember what I said before about us not talking?"

I nodded.

"Well, I forgot to mention that sometimes I'm wrong."

I smiled at her smile.

She watched me a moment. "You've never asked me about my Swiss professor. Not interested?"

"I knew you'd tell me when you wanted."

"I want."

I leaned back in my chair.

"It was very strange with him," she said. "I was a virgin — Karel and I had only kissed before — and this professor was forty-five. Very experienced. And very . . . unexpected. He had what he called *toys*."

"Toys?"

"Handcuffs. A riding crop for horses."

Stupidly, I said, "He rode horses?"

"He'd never ridden one in his life."

I put down my fork.

"It's strange for a girl when her first lover uses all that Western decadence. It makes her feel dirty, but she also learns to love the filth."

"Did you?"

She nodded. "But after a while it frightened me. I felt like I didn't have any more control of myself. I ran back home like a little girl. That's what the professor said when I told him I was returning: *You're just a scared little girl.*"

"So you ran home and married Karel."

She looked at her hands on the table, at her tarnished wedding band. "I married him as fast as I could." She blinked, eyes damp. "And I still don't know." Then she smiled. "Want to learn some more philosophy?"

"Next time. I have to leave."

She raised an eyebrow. "Sounds like someone thinks he's going to get a next time."

I gave Vera a proper kiss good-bye, but when I made it to the car and sat behind the wheel, I stopped. I was suddenly very heavy, a swarm of leaden feelings buzzing in my limbs. I did not want to return to Vera again, and I did not want to go back to Magda the way things were. We had both avoided our problems for so long that I doubted we even deserved happiness any-

319

more. I hated our immaturity, and knew I had to be the one to start climbing out of it. I had to try to be mature, to face at least part of this problem. Immediately.

The Militia radio hissed through the Sixth District — no one was talking today — and on the stairs to Stefan's apartment I noticed the brown drops. I leaned down and touched them — dry, blood.

I took the steps two at a time and saw that his door was ajar, but not broken. I took out my pistol. There was no sound. Then I kicked the door. It popped open and the first thing I saw was more blood on the wall. A brown burst. It was on the wall and sofa and rug, where Stefan lay. He was facedown, one hand extended awkwardly as if reaching for the pistol that lay between him and the sofa. His head was turned to the side, eyes open, mouth pressed against the blood-soaked rug.

The building was unbelievably silent. No noise from other apartments, only my footsteps squeaking against the floor and rug as I leaned over him. Then my head cleared a little, and I checked the other rooms. They were empty, but the bedroom window, despite the cold, was open.

I sat on the couch and looked at Stefan. I looked at him a long time.

# 49

Through the bad phone line Moska's voice had no air to work with. "No, don't say it."

"Let's get some people over here."

"Immediately."

The fifteen-minute wait lasted forever. I looked over the apartment again. There were dry crusts of bread beside two bowls of fish soup and a half-empty bottle of wine.

Who had been eating with Stefan?

I grabbed the phone and dialed. No answer. There was a telephone directory in the kitchen, and I flew through it, frantic, until I found Galicia Textiles. The shift head didn't want to get her, so I had to become a brusque militiaman rather than a terrified husband.

"Ferenc? Ferenc, what is it?"

"Are you all right?"

"Of course I'm all right. Why wouldn't I be?"

I couldn't catch my breath.

"Ferenc, are you okay? Is something wrong?"

"No," I said. "Everything's fine. I'll see you tonight."

I hung up and sat in the living room, heard the dry blood crackle beneath me, and rubbed my face in my hands. I hadn't told her, because she would have to deal with it all day at the factory. I would tell her tonight and make it as easy as I could. I would tell her at night so there would be fewer hours to go through before the respite of sleep.

Looking at the body, thinking suddenly of Stefan's guilt and the years of loneliness since Daria had left him, another wave of dread came over me. I squatted beside him and lifted the pistol to my nose. No smell at all — it hadn't been fired. He had not taken his own life.

Moska arrived with Leonek and Emil. They were in almost as bad a state as I was. Leonek paced furiously from corner to corner, picking up crumpled greasy wrappers and overfull ashtrays, then setting them back down, disappointed that they gave him no answers. Emil crossed his arms by the door, speaking occasional mysteries — *It smells like baklava, can you smell that? Stefan's wrist is bent, what does that mean?* Moska marched into the bedroom and emerged a while later shaking his head. "Can someone tell me what's going on here?" No one touched the body.

When you're faced with a corpse, you fight the instinctual urge to look at it by staring at the smoke-stained curtains, the frayed sofa cushions, the grime in the unwashed rugs. It would be a blessing if you noticed the sunlight or the bright colors of the quilt that Stefan had hung on the wall to remember his mother by. But the brain is clear enough to know such details are a lie. Somewhere in the room lies a dead man with a bullet in his belly. So what I remember from that day is the detritus of Stefan's life, and because of that his bloated body is that much clearer.

After a while a kid from Materials showed up and took photographs. We watched him and drank the rest of the wine.

"Someone else was here," I said. "Stefan had a guest."

"Is that who killed him?" asked Leonek.

Emil was in the bedroom, grasping at more inexplicable details he would take with him to his death, but Moska was within earshot. He set his wine on the kitchen table, beside the soups. He and Leonek waited.

"I don't know. I don't think so. The door

was open when I arrived, and Stefan's behind it. Seems like Stefan opened the door for the killer. If his dinner guest had done it, he'd be dead in the kitchen — the meal wasn't finished."

"This Nestor Velcea came to the door?" asked Moska.

"Looks like it."

"Nestor was hit, too," said Leonek. "He left his blood on the stairs."

"Or it's the guest's blood," I said, rubbing my temples to try and clear my head. "But Stefan's gun hasn't been fired. If that's Nestor's blood in the stairwell, he and the guest were shooting it out."

Leonek went over the details again. The uneaten food, Stefan lying in a different room, the open bedroom window. "Or Stefan argued with his guest. The argument took them into the living room, and that's where it happened. The murderer left by the window to avoid neighbors in the corridor."

"The blood on the stairs," said Moska. "Somebody went out the front door with a bullet in him."

"There were at least three people — that's a fact," I said, as we stood beside the photographer. Stefan's skin, beneath the blood, was so white. "One of them left by

324

the front door, and it looks like the other climbed out the window."

"You don't know for sure," said Moska. He looked at me, then settled into a frown that suggested there were other ideas that had not been touched on yet.

"What?"

He shook his head.

A flash blinded everyone momentarily.

"I don't know anything for sure," I said. None of us did.

Emil emerged from the bedroom, nostrils wide. "What's going on here?"

We watched Feder's men cover Stefan with a sheet, heft him onto a stretcher, and precariously make their way down the stairs.

Sev was waiting in the station to offer his cool condolences. "I know you two were close. Let me know if there's anything I can do." But his face was not cool — his lips were uncontrolled; they twitched.

Leonek and Emil waited for orders. I sent Emil to grill Stefan's neighbors and told Leonek to keep a watch on Antonín's old apartment.

I called Georgi. He listened in silence as I explained in detail why I needed to find Nestor Velcea. "Is Louis in town?"

"Still in Paris."

"Try and get in touch with him. If they were friends, he may know something. And ask around."

"I'll try."

"Try hard, Georgi."

I had too much energy. I kept getting up from my desk to walk up and down the corridor, and ignored people who nodded at me. Then I returned to my chair and picked up the telephone. I hadn't thought about it until that moment. I didn't know where Stefan's ex-wife, Daria, was now, but I knew his father had a telephone. The operator connected me with the Pócspetri number, not so far from Magda's parents' house.

"Yes?"

He was a heavy man like his son, and, like his son, he lived alone. "Franz? This is Ferenc."

He paused. We hadn't talked in a long time. "Ferenc Kolyeszar? Well how are you?"

"Not well, Franz. I've got some terrible news."

He wept, and I pulled the telephone away from my ear and waited. The two of them had grown apart since Stefan's mother's death, and I suspected this was at the root of his tears. He didn't ask many questions, because like most farmers he knew the details were unimportant — only the results mattered. By the time I told him that the funeral would be on Saturday, his tears were under control. "I wish I could make it. But if I don't get these onions to the market, I'll be dead, too."

Around three the photographer showed up with shots of Stefan on the floor, facedown, the blood-soaked wall, food laid out for two, dirty stairs.

# 50

I put Ágnes to bed and sat by her side as she sniffed the air and asked me, very seriously, to stop drinking so much. "You're worried about me?"

She sank into her pillow. "Not *worried*. I just don't like you stinking. You smell like those Romanians who play music in October Square."

I turned off the light.

Magda handed me a plate of cold chicken when I came out. "I'm going to bed."

"Stay up a minute, will you?"

She frowned.

"And get some wine. For yourself. I've

got to tell you something."

I tried to eat a little as she fooled with the cork in the kitchen, but the first bite was dry and tumbled into my stomach like a rock. I set it aside and was relieved to see she had brought two glasses. She poured them both. "What is it, Ferenc."

I cleared my throat. It was a theatrical gesture that allowed me a moment and a bit of pain to distract me from what I was preparing to say. "This morning I went over to Stefan's apartment and found him dead. He'd been shot."

She finally got to her wine. Her hands did not shake. She said, "That's not possible."

"I know."

"You've got to be lying to me. Joking."

I waited.

"Come on," she said, then stood up. She looked down at me. *"Stefan?"* Then she walked into the kitchen.

The affair was nothing to me. My oldest friend was dead, and the man my wife loved was suddenly gone. We had been together too long for me not to feel some of the pain she must have felt.

When she reappeared she was wiping her red eyes with a dish towel. She said, "That's why you called me." Her glass was empty, so I filled it up in her hand and watched as she walked over to the radio set, put her hand on it, and looked out the window. "You said he was shot?"

"Yes."

"Many times?"

"I don't know how many."

"He died quickly?"

"I don't think so," I said, and wondered why I hadn't lied.

She nodded at the window and finally came back. The glass was empty, and when she sat down I refilled it. "I'm sorry," she said. "He was your best friend."

"I'm sorry, too."

She held my gaze. We were fixed like that for a little while, as if we both had a lot of words that we could not say.

She stood. "I'm going to bed now. But would you rather me stay up with you?"

"I'll be all right. What about you? Do you need me to be with you tonight?"

"Do you need to be with me?"

We looked at each other a moment more.

"I'm okay," I said.

She nodded, first slowly, then resolutely, and wandered back to the bedroom.

I went for the sheets and wondered selfishly if her decisions were now finally made.

# 51

The next morning was a Friday. There was an abundance of housewives out in the street, stocking up for the weekend. I leaned into the fogged tram window and hated myself for not having woken up in the same bed as my wife.

Feder was in a subdued mood. He had left Stefan's body in the drawer so that no one would have to look at him unnecessarily. He told me when I arrived that the other inspectors had already filed through his office — no one was willing to wait for anyone else. So he repeated his performance for me in his empty lab, without having to read from the clipboard in his hand. "Nine millimeter in the stomach. Two shots. I can't be sure how long it took, but by the signs in the apartment, the smear of the blood, I'd say he was conscious for several minutes."

"What about the blood on the stairs?"

"Stefan's was B — this was O-positive. Couldn't say whose it was."

"And fingerprints?"

He looked at the clipboard. "Stefan's prints on the outside and inside of the front door."

"And the window?"

Feder frowned. "What about the window?"

"The bedroom window. It was open."

He tapped his pencil on the clipboard. "Well I'm glad I've finally been told. All the lab did was the front door."

"Have them do the dishes as well. Someone was eating with him when he was shot, and I want to know who."

"Yeah," said Feder. "I would, too."

There was a note from Moska on my desk, and when I went to see him Sev was in the office. I waited outside until they finished, then watched Sev watching me as he left. "Enter, Ferenc."

I sat across from him and told him what Feder had reported. "I want to see what comes of dusting for more prints."

Moska stared at the pencil in his hand. He twirled it awkwardly. "Look, Ferenc. I've got to talk to you about this. It's not something I like."

"Tell me."

"A month or so ago you attacked Stefan, didn't you?" He was still looking at the pencil.

"In a bar," I said. "Yes."

"Can you tell me about it?"

"I'd rather not, unless I have to."

He used the flat end of the pencil to scratch his scalp. "You don't have to tell me anything, Ferenc. I'm just trying to clear things up. I've got a dead inspector on my hands, and I want to know who killed him."

"And you think I killed him."

He aimed the pencil at me. "Ferenc, don't get self-righteous."

"Is that why Sev was here? Is he investigating me now?"

"Just tell me: Why the hell did you attack Stefan?"

"Because he was sleeping with my wife."

He dropped the pencil and inhaled. Then he shut his eyes and pressed them with his fingertips. "Damn," he said. "Damn. Just get out of here, okay?"

I sleepwalked the rest of the day with Emil, helping him canvass the residents of Unit 21. A plumber accurately described Nestor Velcea entering the building around 6 p.m. Wednesday. "You notice a guy like that," he told us. A nine-year-old boy verified the story. Only one gunshot had been heard by the neighbors.

"One shot," said Emil, as we walked to a bar.

"When there were at least three bullets fired. Two for Stefan and a third into Nestor, who ran down the stairs."

"Nestor was using a silencer. It's the only answer."

"So who shot Nestor?"

Over our silent drink no ideas came to us, and afterward I returned alone to Stefan's spattered apartment to stare at the terrible walls. After a while, I lay down in Stefan's bed and tried to sleep. The exhaustion was too much. The ceiling went in and out of darkness as I blinked, but when it went black I saw everything, in pieces. Broken shins and femurs, porridge, beaten faces, and bowls of fish soup. And I saw Stefan's bleeding forehead and the cracked mirror I shoved him into.

Stefan never really recovered after Daria left him. The reason for the break was a mystery — he'd only said that a man can only get so fat before his woman searches for a thinner man. But what else could he have said? If someone asked why my marriage was crumbling, my answers would have been just as ludicrous. Such things cannot be paraphrased.

I rolled over and forced my face into his pillow. It smelled like him, or I imagined it did. Dirty. The smell of the east, as the

Frenchman had said. We stink, and we mutilate one another. The clothes we wear and the words we speak are just masks. We take our revenge because we can't let the past go. Because in the past we were no better — we ate each other like wild, starving dogs.

Maybe it was then. Maybe later, after I drifted off and woke from uncomfortable dreams about a genius painter who becomes, by way of betrayal, a mad killer. Sometime in that restless night the storyteller in me put it together. Antonín's rise to fame with the help of Josef Maneck, nearly simultaneous with Nestor's demise. Nestor, the eccentric who wouldn't even sign his work. And the things Stefan had fretted over: Josef's sudden conversion to alcoholism because, as Martin had said, he *couldn't live with himself,* and Antonín's shift into the banality of state art. Then I knew it. I knew, with utter clarity, why Nestor Velcea had killed Josef, Antonín, and Zoia. I knew it in a flash, like a vision from God. It was art. It was all about art.

# 52

I washed in Stefan's grime-laden tub, dried off with his mildewed towel, used his toothbrush on my teeth, and drank coffee from his cup. I looked out his window at the gray blocks he saw every morning and paused at the same door he opened each day.

At home I pulled out my dress uniform. All inspectors had one, but only brought it out for celebrations or funerals. I was mildly astonished that mine still fit. Magda and Ágnes wore identical black dresses, bought from the same sale. Magda had told Ágnes about Stefan, and she seemed to be taking it well. On the drive she asked if dying hurt.

"Depends on how you die," I said.

She shifted in the backseat, looking out the window. "I think when I die, I want it to hurt a lot."

Magda looked at me. I said, "Why on earth would you want that?"

"Because. That way I know I'm dying. I don't want it to be a surprise."

I looked at her in the rearview and wondered if I should be worried.

With the pleasant exception of Kaminski, everyone was there, in uniform, both Moska and Sev with little rows of medals on their chests. It was as if our office had lost its walls and desks, then grown crabgrass and tombstones. A ring of trees separated us from the city, and Lena, in an impressive black gown, toyed with a leaf. Beside Moska stood his wife Angela, a tall, thin woman with a round face that seemed unable to smile.

She was a good woman, everyone agreed, but she seldom spoke to any of us. Ágnes and Magda shook hands with everyone, Magda a little shamefully — she hadn't seen most of them in a long time — and Ágnes boldly. Ágnes gave Leonek a big hug, which surprised Magda. She pulled Ágnes back, blushing, and said, "Hello again, Leonek."

Leonek left a hand on Ágnes's shoulder and smiled back.

Emil's uniform looked too big for him, but it was better pressed than anyone's. I assumed Lena had taken care of that. "Can I take your husband away a moment?" I asked her.

She smiled and let go of his arm.

We'd made it to a fresh grave not yet covered with grass before he said, "What is it?"

"Nestor Velcea. I know what he's doing."

"Then please, for Christ's sake, tell me."

I took a breath, then spoke it aloud for the first time. "Antonín Kullmann turned in Nestor so that he could steal his work. All of it. Antonín signed his name on the paintings, and Josef Maneck, the curator, showed them. The guilt turned Maneck into a drunk, and when Zoia learned of it she left Antonín."

He patted his schoolboy hair. "It's a stretch."

"Not entirely. Take a look at the early Kullmann paintings and compare them with the newer ones. Even Stefan saw the difference. Kullmann ran out of Nestor's paintings and had to make his own finally. I'd been trying to figure out why Nestor had mutilated Antonín, had put him through such pain. It's because he took his whole life away. He took everything. And I'll bet that if we look into it, we'll find that Antonín had been supporting Josef's life-style, in order to keep him quiet about it all."

"It's too simple," said Emil. "How could this kind of thing remain secret?"

"Nestor never showed his work. No one knew it."

"Somebody must have known."

"Zoia did. Because they all lived to-gether. Maybe someone else did, too, but this at least gets us moving."

"But why did he kill Stefan?"

"That, I don't know,"

He shook his head. "Good job, Ferenc.

Really. I wish I'd come up with it."

"Don't worry, I'll teach you a thing or two before this is over."

Georgi brought Vera. I shook Georgi's hand and gave Vera a hug as my family loitered with the others. "What are you doing here?"

The corners of her lips twitched into a sneer. "You don't think I remember Stefan? I knew him."

"Years ago, and you only met a couple times."

"I didn't want Georgi to be all alone. He needs a shoulder. By the way, the uniform suits you."

Vera and Georgi greeted my family. Occasionally during the ceremony I shot glances back at both women standing beside one another, Magda erect beside Vera's slouch. Beneath my fear I noticed how different they were — their looks, their characters, the way they made love. I was their only shared attribute.

We stood stiffly during the reading, and now and then I caught Sev's gaze wandering over to evaluate my grief. The casket was open, and Stefan's uniform was too tight on him, pulling around the belly. Magda was surprisingly dry-eyed, while Ágnes clutched her hand and gaped. We

were all surprisingly dry-eyed. All except
Leonek, who wept quietly.

# 53

The guys invited me out for drinks, but I
looked back at Magda and Ágnes and declined. We drove in silence, and silence
reigned at home. Ágnes turned on the radio,
then sat with Pavel on the floor, while
Magda prepared dinner. I watched Ágnes for
a long time, but thought only of Stefan.

Ágnes bored of Pavel and found a newspaper crossword puzzle to work on. Pavel
climbed into my lap. There was a docu-
mentary on the radio — not American, but
ours — on the history of the nation and
the ethnic diversity that made it an ideal
home for socialism.

I scratched Pavel's ear absently.

Stefan could no longer ease his pain by
confessing to me, and I could not sit him
down and forgive him. I pressed my eyelids,
remembering moments of our childhood in
Pócspetri, and later, after Daria left him. I'd
distanced myself from him, and with his
mother's death Stefan's life was empty of
almost everything, except regret.

Magda wanted to know if I preferred potatoes or fried cornmeal. I looked at her a while before answering.

"It's a simple question, Ferenc."

"Cornmeal. Yes, cornmeal."

She returned to the kitchen. No wonder he had jumped at the chance to be with her again. He had nothing else.

The radio told me that Comrade General Secretary Mihai wanted us to revel in our history, to learn from it the possibilities for our future.

Ágnes scribbled letters into boxes.

When I came back from the war, I was nothing to look at, nothing to consider, nothing to be. Magda thought she recognized me at first — I looked the same and spoke the same — but soon she knew better. All I would do was sit on the sofa and ask for water. She always brought it, but there wasn't anything else I wanted. There had been a week in the trenches when we did not have fresh water, and in the middle of a dry field, pinned in by mortar fire and explosions puncturing the sky, we thought we'd die the way sailors once died — scurvy, salt water on the brain. What was she to think? She offered what she thought I wanted. Hot meals, a warm woman. But all I wanted was fresh water. Finally, she talked me into sex. It

340

was a revelation. Beyond water there really was something. There was flesh and warmth and that tremor of the glands that I hadn't thought of since I'd seen glands and flesh exploded by German mines, and the glands and flesh of my parents when I imagined their small house obliterated by that German bomb. My emotions were suddenly in reach after so long; I felt human again.

We had dinner with brief moments of conversation. Ágnes wanted a bicycle, which I at first said we could not afford; then, as she pressed, I told her I'd see what I could find. Magda was melancholic, but not the way I'd expect from someone who had just seen her lover buried in the earth. How well did I know her? Perhaps I had lost track of her in the provinces, just before we moved to the Capital, when she cared for me like a nurse. Perhaps she began hiding hard facts from me then, beginning with her night with Stefan, and had steadily built her own, secret world.

The idea of Magda's leaving had come to me on and off over the years. Married people do this. In a small part of their minds hides a secret world of independence, and in that parallel world there are other companions. Some beautiful, some less so, and for a while it seems these others are more or less the same as the one that you have, in the real world, devoted your life to. How different are the breakfasts and dinners, the weekends in the country, the lovemaking, the conversations? Not so different, in the end.

But when troubles begin, this secret world grows. It is visible on the horizon. It takes roots in reality. I thought about the other women I knew. Vera, sure. Seductive and strong. There was something there. Roberta, a stenographer who visited the office now and then, had been single for the last five years — I imagined how her famished and ample body would be in bed. She would have the virtue of gratefulness. I even wondered about the bodiless voice from the Militia radio: Regina Haliniak. There were others whose names I didn't know, women on the street who held my gaze for a few seconds longer than polite — and within the brackets of these flirtations a new future presented itself.

This is the first stage, the hopeful stage. Promiscuous fantasies without the burden of responsibility. When I thought of Ágnes, I ignored the unavoidable custody worries. Although she seldom appeared in my fantasy life, it was granted that Ágnes was with me, waiting at home.

In this first stage, divorce seemed surviv-
able, maybe even a little invigorating — the
building of a new life always is. But then it
approached from the horizon, moved close
enough that I could make out its barren
details. The second stage is knowledge.
While sleeping with other women had its
virtues, I couldn't imagine what would
follow.

What had we to say to each other? I
couldn't eat breakfast with these women,
and the thought of taking a weekend trip
with any of them was unbearable.

I realized then what I'd always known:
Magda was in every action I took and
shadowed every thought. A life without her
was no life at all.

When Ágnes asked me to pass the salt, I
had been staring blindly at her for a while.
"You all right, Daddy?"

"Fine, honey."

"You don't look so good."

"It's been a hard day."

Magda looked questioningly at me, and I
smiled and shook my head. "I'm going to
have to take off after dinner. I've got something to do."

"Will we see you again tonight?"

"Yes," I said, then repeated it. "Yes."

# 54

I parked on the dark, empty street outside her block and went over the words in my head. I took a breath, wiped my face, and got out.

She wore slacks and a white blouse that hung loose and transparent over her breast. She wore a smile as well. "Ferenc, I didn't think you'd come. Give me that coat."

I gave it to her and watched her take it through the kitchen to the bedroom to toss it on the bed. She noticed my hesitation when we kissed.

"I was going to whip up something to eat. You hungry?"

"I just ate."

"Then I'll wait."

I sat on the sofa. She stood in front of me a moment, then straddled my knees. "Tell me, Ferenc."

"Yes, we should talk." I moved her off of my knees — she was light, easy to lift — and onto the cushion beside me.

Frowning, she left a hand on my thigh.

"It's over. From this moment. It's over."

"Us?"

"I'm sorry," I said. "Look: I have to make things work with Magda. It's what I have to do."

Vera looked at her hand on my leg, then began to stroke. "You don't have fun with me?"

"That's not it."

"You don't like what we do?"

"You know I like it."

"Well then," she said. "You keep working on Magda, and at the same time keep working on me."

"It's not that easy."

"Sure it is. I do it all the time, and I can tell you how easy it is."

I took her hand from my leg and put it on her own, but her other hand fell upon mine and pressed it to her thigh.

"Listen, Ferenc."

"I can't listen."

She drew my hand up into her groin, and though I could have resisted, I didn't.

"I should go now."

"Don't be a bastard," she said, but her voice was soft. She put her free hand on my crotch. "She won't do the things I'll do, you know this."

As she massaged me, she leaned up to my ear and whispered what she would do. I looked at her, momentarily shocked, then easing into it. But the fears of a life of regret flashed back, and I took her hand off me. "I really should go."

"You know what your problem is?"

I should have stood up and left. But I said, "Let's pretend I don't know."

"Simplicity."

"Thanks for the insight."

She shook her head. "It's true. You're desperate for simplicity. It's why you've held on so long to a dead marriage. You want to think you understand everything, but you'll never understand yourself until you accept your contradictions."

I stood up, but didn't walk away.

She said, "You need to learn that specific actions do not yield specific results. Just because you're good to your marriage doesn't mean it'll be good to you." She grabbed my arm, but I pulled it away.

"You don't get it," I said. "It's . . . it has to do with Stefan. With my daughter, with everything."

She pulled her lips back and showed me her teeth.

"Where's my coat?"

"You know where."

I didn't want it like this, but my explanations had turned to smoke. I went back to the bedroom and took my coat from the bed. It was the right decision, I knew this, and I had to see it through. When I turned, she was standing in the bedroom doorway, blocking my exit.

"Let me see something," she said.

She took the coat from my hand, tossed it back on the bed, and sank to her knees. When she started to take off my belt, I reached down to stop her, but she slapped my hand.

"Don't touch me."

She unbuttoned me quickly. I was excited despite myself. She looked at it, almost curiously, then put it into her mouth.

The telephone woke us. Vera turned on the bedside light and looked at the clock — a little after five in the morning. She walked naked to the living room. "Yes? . . . No, he's not . . . okay, all right. I'll get him." Then: "Ferenc!"

"I won't say a thing, okay, buddy?"

"I'm not worried about that, Georgi. What do you need?"

"Not me. Magda. She called over here looking for you. She was worried."

"About me?"

"No, not you. At least she didn't say that. Someone was banging on your door."

"Who?"

"She doesn't know. A man. She thinks he's gone now."

"When was this?"

"Fifteen minutes ago. Something like that."

It was cold, and the car took a while to start. My breath steamed the windshield. I bounced through the holes and crevices of our parking lot. The block looked empty. I climbed the flights, pausing to listen and check the color of the steps. Then I listened at the door and used the key. "It's me," I whispered as I pushed it open.

# 55

I put the car through more than I should have, cutting across the parking lot and flying up Tashkent Boulevard, out of town. I'd rushed them through the packing, answering all Ágnes's questions with a hysterical *It's a trip! We're going on a trip!* Magda had thought I was overreacting.

"What are you saying?"

"That man might have killed you both, like he did Stefan. Get your bag."

She stood by the bathroom door with a towel in one hand, and nodded.

As dawn grew, we passed the outskirts,

the final unfinished blocks falling away, and the earth leveled into fields. Magda pointed out that I was going the wrong way. "We need to go south."

"I don't want to drive through the city."

"Why not?"

"I don't want to get into a wreck."

She smiled a little strangely.

"I'm just terrified."

She reached over and held my free hand.

After a while, Ágnes passed out, sprawled across the backseat, Pavel stuffed under her arm. Magda yawned. Teodor and Nora would watch them for however long was needed, but I couldn't see any further than dropping them off.

Teodor was in town sitting in on an informal collective meeting, and Nora was scrubbing the wood floors in the kitchen when we arrived. She smiled at the front door and gave us all kisses, but looked apprehensive when Ágnes ran across her clean, wet floor. "Let's sit around back," she suggested.

The shrubs around the garden had thinned considerably, and now you could see directly through them to the orchards leading to the horizon. A cold wind blew, so we crossed our arms over our chests for warmth.

"You're looking good," Nora said.

"No we aren't, Mama." Magda grinned. "We both look worse than we have in a long time."

"Oh, I don't know about that." She touched her fat fingers on her arm, as if playing a piano.

"I'd like them to stay here a few days," I said.

She picked a white puff of something off her blouse and flicked it away. "Are we still a family?"

"Of course," said Magda.

"No. The three of you. Are you still a family?"

"We've never stopped being a family," I said, and Magda, to my surprise, gave a smile.

I helped Teodor unload half a lamb from the truck — a Czech Tatra the new local commissar let them use — and as we walked he asked what the hell was going on.

"It's a case," I said. "They'll be safer here."

"When are you going to get out of that work, Ferenc? Be a writer."

"Don't you want me to support your daughter and granddaughter?"

He huffed as he propped open the door. "I'd rather they were poor than shot dead by one of your suspects."

A little later we told them about Stefan, and after the required moment of reflection Teodor told me again to find another line of work.

We ate a dinner of potatoes and lamb swimming in paprika and listened to Teodor mutter about the new directives to get rid of private plots for farmers. "They expect us to buy the food we grow *back* from them! That just makes no sense. I've got the land here, you can be damn sure I'm going to keep some of it for myself, so I can grow what I like."

Ágnes rolled the fork in her hand. "It's been a record year for crops."

Teodor eyed her. "They say that?"

"Best crops in twenty years."

"Well, don't you believe a word of that, darling."

After dinner he pulled out the brandy, and though I tried to feign sleepiness, he stood and looked squarely at me. "Ferenc."

I got up.

We could no longer see the apple trees in the blackness. He handed me a glass and stood beside the shrubs. "Nora tells me there's been no progress. Is that true?"

"In a way, yes."

"Is it worse?"

I wanted to tell him that his daughter's lover was finally out of the way, but could think of no way to express it without telling him. "Some of it's gotten better."

"I suppose that's something."

The brandy warmed me, then cooled me off, so I had to keep drinking.

"How long are they staying?"

"Maybe a week, I can't be sure."

"And Ágnes's school? Magda's factory?"

"Magda will call them both."

He seemed satisfied with that and turned to look over the orchards he couldn't see. "Nora and I have been talking about leaving here."

"Where would you go?"

"Where else? The Capital."

"Ah." I imagined them moving into our same building, one of the floors below us, always appearing with dishes of Nora's dull meals. A part of me hated the idea, and another part wondered if it could help. They wanted us together, and they would fill Magda's ears with reasons to love me, or at least reasons to stay with me. "Could you afford it?"

"It's almost time for my pension, Ferenc. Not much, it never is. But maybe it's enough."

"Won't you miss it out here? It's a different life in the Capital."

"Of course it is," he said, and came to sit beside me. He found the bottle and refilled us both. "A lot of our friends have moved away, and now when we go to the cooperative's social club we know fewer and fewer people. They're all leaving," he said. "That, or dying off."

# 56

Magda and I slept in the guest room. It was a large bed, and we didn't touch, didn't say anything. I put my hands behind my head and stared at the ceiling, just visible in the light from the porch. She rolled on her side, away from me. After a while, I heard her heavy breaths, but it wasn't the sound of sleep. I touched her bare shoulder. "What is it?"

She shook her head and didn't look at me. "I was just thinking of Stefan."

I withdrew my hand. "It must be hard on you."

"Not so much. I was thinking about how his life was. He must have been so lonely."

"He had you."

She quieted, then rolled over so she faced me. I couldn't quite see her face.

"What does that mean?"

"Come on, Magda. There's no more need."

"No. What are you talking about?"

I took a breath. We were finally having this conversation, but in a bed that didn't belong to us. "You were having an affair with Stefan. I've known it for a long time."

She didn't say anything at first. I heard a couple sighs, as if she was going to speak, but nothing would come. Then she said, "You're such a fool sometimes, Ferenc."

"Maybe I am."

"I slept with him once, many years ago, and I've never stopped regretting it."

"And now?"

"What *now?* I never touched him again."

I took this in gradually. "But I saw you go to meet him. At that Turkish bar. It's his favorite."

"You *followed* me?"

"When you believe your wife's having an affair, you're allowed some improprieties."

"I can't believe you followed me."

"Give it a rest, will you?"

She rolled away again, and after a minute sat up on the edge of the bed. She looked at the floor while I waited for something to come. "It's Leonek," she said finally.

"It's —" I started to repeat, then didn't.

"We've been together, on and off, for a month and a half now. I don't have any excuse. I've wanted to tell you for a long time, but I wanted to know what I really wanted first." She was still looking at the floor, and her voice was clear and strong. "At the beginning it was just desperation. It looked like everything was over between us, and I wanted something for myself. Can you understand that?"

I said, "Yes, I can," but I was in a fog.

"And I've broken it off with him I-don't-know-how-many times. Remember that night when you came back from Georgi's party, and I wasn't there? Stefan called. He'd been drinking, and he wanted to apologize for telling you about what he and I had done during the war. That's how I found out you knew. It was such a shock. I immediately went to Leonek and told him it couldn't go on. I broke it off." She shook her head. "But you remember how I was when you saw me later that night. You wanted to talk, and I couldn't. I was confused. The next morning I called him, and we started it all over again. On the Sixth of November."

I remembered that day, and remembered her inexplicable panic when I asked her who had been listening to the Americans.

It had been him — it was the only station he listened to. "So," I said, "what is it he gives you? What does Leonek give you?"

She finally stopped looking at that goddamn floor. I could just make out some of her features. She looked old. "I've told you before, Ferenc. You're different. You're not the man I married. Leonek . . . I always know how he feels about me. With you I'm never sure." She took a breath. "And he does love me."

"You love him?"

"Maybe. I don't know. He's good to me, but I don't know if he's good *for* me."

I finally moved. I sat up and leaned against the headboard. But I didn't know what to say.

"Are you going to leave me?" she asked.

"I was going to ask you the same thing."

She didn't answer.

"Do you love me anymore?" I asked.

"I don't know."

"Not even a 'maybe'?"

She nodded. "Maybe."

I brought my hands to my face and breathed into my palms. The shock was starting to fade, but slowly. All my emotions were a shadow of themselves now, though I could pick them out and count them where they floated just out of reach.

I got up and put on my clothes. Magda didn't say a word as I walked out and found the brandy bottle in the kitchen and took it to the freezing garden. Teodor had left his cigarettes outside, and I began to smoke them, one by one.

# 57

In the morning I walked to the cooperative office at the top of the hill because Teodor and Nora's phone only dialed out locally. I showed my Militia certificate and watched the lame man behind the desk stumble for the telephone and pass it to me. Then I called Moska and told him I was going to the Vátrina Work Camp in order to look up information on my suspect. He sighed and accepted this.

Magda and Ágnes were in the kitchen with Nora, making breakfast. The smell was heavy with grease. Magda looked at me with an expression that said everything without saying a thing.

After breakfast I threw my bag into the car. She followed me outside.

"You're going back home?"

"Tonight, or tomorrow. I've got to check on some things first."

She squinted into the breeze.

"What is it?"

She said, "Don't hurt him."

"What?"

"Libarid."

"Who?"

She shook her head. "Leonek, I mean. Libarid's his birth name."

"Oh."

"His mother made him change it when they came here. She even called him Leonek in private. *Damn*." She looked at the dirt. "I'm babbling, and *that* was a secret. But listen." She looked at me again. "I don't want you to get the wrong idea. This wasn't his fault. It was mine. I was looking around and he was just there."

I took a step away from her. "I can't promise anything."

She looked at the ground again and when she looked back, her eyes glimmered. She was crying so much these days. "Just don't put all the blame on him. I want to be fair."

"Fair," I repeated, then went in to say good-bye to the others.

Vátrina was forty minutes to the north and, entering the small farming town with its tiny train station, it was difficult to believe there was a work camp there. Old men dotted the side of the road, walking past fences and puffing on barely visible cigarettes, and three fat women with babushkas huddled around a well. The central square was small, with a grocer's, a post office, and a modern hotel that didn't belong — a wide concrete bunker with a sign that proclaimed HOTEL ELEGANT in peeling red paint. I first tried the post office, but there was a long line of young, sunburned men with slips of paper leading up to the one open window, where a woman with dyed black hair smoked and stared at them. So I went into the Elegant. A worn red carpet stretched to the end of the faux-marble lobby, past the entrance to a dark bar, to where a younger black-haired woman sat behind the counter, smoking and reading a paperback. I leaned beside the guest book. "I'm looking for the Vátrina Work Camp, number four-eighty."

She held up an index finger, read for a second longer, and closed the book on her other finger. It was a novel by someone I'd met a few times at Georgi's. "They don't put work camps in main squares, idiot."

She had a nice, round face with an expression that didn't match what she'd called me. "I don't have a lot of practice with them."

She sighed and turned her book flat on the counter. "What business do you have there anyway?"

I started to reach for my Militia certificate, but instead patted my coat for cigarettes. I pulled one out and lit it. "My own business. That's what business I've got."

She rolled her eyes as if she'd heard this a million times, and that's when I realized this was how she flirted. Stuck behind a desk in a dead-end town, you learn strange ways of getting a man's attention. "And you think your own business is important?"

"I expect it's more important than chain-smoking in a flea-infested hotel all day."

Her face brightened, and she tapped the counter with a fingernail. "Tell me, come on. I know how to keep a secret."

I leaned closer to her face. "How can I trust that?"

"You'll just have to," she whispered.

"But keep it quiet, you understand?"

She nodded again, seriously.

I told her I was a novelist researching a book on the history of the Vátrina Work Camp, number 480.

She leaned back again. "You're giving me a line. That probably works on a lot of girls. But not this one."

I shrugged. "What can I do if you don't believe me?"

"You write any other books?"

"*A Soldier's Tale*. It was a few years ago."

She hesitated, then smiled broadly. "Really? I read that! *No*."

I showed her my transit identification papers to prove who I was, and she leaned close again, her voice back down to a whisper.

"I thought it was *extreme*ly good. You know that? You're a very good writer."

I suspected she had never read it, but didn't press. She told me to drive down the eastbound road six, seven miles. "It's as plain as day. You staying the night?"

"I don't know yet."

"I'll be chain-smoking here until six."

# 58

It lay on the left-hand side of the dusty road, in a flat expanse of harvested wheatfield. The watchtowers were visible first — five wooden columns connected at their bases by barbed wire — and inside lay five long, low buildings. It was as basic as you could imagine, no signs, no indication of purpose.

The towers were empty, but when I turned off the road and took a gravel path to the front gate, a guard in a heavy coat wandered out to meet me, patting his arms. He opened the gate and stuck his head in my window. "What can I do for you?"

His rancid breath quickly filled the car. His teeth were like overthickened fingernails. "I'm here to talk with the commander."

He looked around the inside of the car. "Are you from Yalta Boulevard?"

"I'm from Militia headquarters. This is part of an investigation."

He licked his discolored teeth and inhaled deeply. I braced myself for the exhale. "Mind if I see some evidence?"

After I showed him my Militia certificate he waved me inside, closed the gate, and pointed to a space between two buildings. He walked me down to the back of the camp, where a muddy field opened up. In the far corner, beside another gate leading out of the camp, was a small building with a smoking chimney and a telephone cable connecting its roof to a tower. That, the guard pointed out, was the commander's office.

I walked the rest of the way alone. The guard was the only person I'd seen, and the long buildings, which I assumed were used to house prisoners, were silent and, I also assumed, empty.

There was a muddy window on each side of the front door, and before I knocked I tried unsuccessfully to see inside.

*"Enter,"* came an unpleasant voice. For a moment I was confused.

Like Moska, the commander sat in a dim room at a disorganized desk surrounded by stacks of files. Some open steel cabinets revealed piles of letters that had been read and stored there. Against the back wall and beside a sooty Mihai, a small iron stove burned, its open grille revealing a few half-consumed papers on the coals. The commander was bald and surprisingly short — his jacket and slacks were too large on him. When he introduced himself as Comrade Captain Gregor Kaganovich, it was with a voice dirtied from a lifetime of cigarettes and shouting. A coal drawing of the captain hung on the wall — well-done, but severely romanticized.

"I've come to ask some questions relating to a case I'm working on." I handed over my certificate.

He slipped on a pair of round glasses, turned the certificate in the weak light from the window, then handed it back. "What kind of case are we talking about?"

"A homicide."

"One of my pets get killed?"

"One of them is doing some killing."

He clucked his tongue, as though we were talking about one of his own children. "I've heard of this happening before. Some wolves just can't help but follow their instincts. You can beat them as much as you like, but they can't be domesticated. Some coffee?"

"I'm interested in a particular one. Nestor Velcea."

He looked at me as he poured a cup, but I couldn't catch his expression. "No, I'm afraid I can't remember all my pets. But look around," he said, waving at the files. "There's bound to be something." He handed me the cup and squatted among some stacks. "I tell you, the Comrade Prime Minister could have given us a little *warning* over this Amnesty, if you know what I mean." His fingers flipped through the files at an alarming speed.

"No, I don't know what you mean."

"I mean, he announces it, and the next day — not in a week, not a month, but *the next day* — all my boys are out of a job. A lot of them are from the other side of the country, and were transferred here when we needed them. And we *did* need them. Then one day they weren't needed."

"Then they get transferred somewhere else."

"That's what you'd think, wouldn't you?" He lifted a file to the light, opened it, then shook his head and closed it. "It wasn't until the end of the summer they realized they hadn't followed through on that small point. That's a lot of men to suddenly transfer. My guess, though, is that they just didn't know if they'd change their minds and need the boys all over again."

"I don't quite understand."

He stopped searching and turned to me. "By the end of the summer they had put through transfers for all the camp guards throughout the region. But nothing for our camp. So I made calls, and after weeks of this, finally got some answers. Number four-eighty is going to reopen in the spring." He smiled.

"So what are you doing in the meantime?"

"I'm cleaning up the old files to make room for new ones. But my boys, they're the ones in a tough spot. They have to wait around in that hole they call a town until spring."

"What kind of work did they do here?"

"The guards?"

"The prisoners."

He tilted his head from side to side. "Everything, really. We'd take them into town to build things — you've seen the Hotel Elegant?"

"Yes."

"Our work," he said, tapping his chest. "We have them farm the wheat around the camp, and during the winter they work the gravel up at Work Site Number One."

"The gravel?"

"Sure. About two miles away there's a quarry, and my pets bash it to hell. But I've got some better ideas up my sleeve for when they return. Some *digging.*" He raised his eyebrows.

As he leafed through the files, I nodded at the cabinet of letters. "Mail from your admirers?"

He looked confused, then the smile came back. "Oh *those!* No. Just letters my pets wrote while we put them up. To the family and that sort of thing. Want to read some?"

I didn't.

Velcea's incarceration file was interesting. I had my own theory about how things had unfolded, but this at least settled a few facts. On 17 February 1947, an anonymous call to Yalta Boulevard reported that Nestor Velcea, a painter, had been seen handing out an underground broadside called *Independence*. On 25 February, a handwritten letter arrived at Yalta Boulevard, unsigned, claiming that one Nestor Velcea had been overheard at a party criticizing Comrade Mihai's foreign policy initiatives in particularly disturbing and violent terms. Then, on 1 March, another call came through. This one said that Nestor Velcea would, on the evening of 3 March, go to the central rail station to meet with an agent of foreign imperialism in order to give away sensitive national information.

Armed with this knowledge, state security agents waited in the station on 3 March. According to the report, Nestor Velcea arrived at 7:12 p.m. and sat on one of the benches near the ticket windows. He did not purchase a ticket, and he regularly looked around at arriving passengers. At a quarter to eight, he got up to leave, and that's when he was arrested.

The rest of the file contained signed transfer documents and arrest paperwork, and some reports on his behavior in the camp over his ten years. Other than various instances of falling ill, his behavior had been exemplary. The final sheet was his amnesty certificate, a form letter with his name scribbled in a blank space, signed and stamped by the camp commander sitting across from me.

"So what does this tell you, Comrade Inspector? If I can ask."

The file told me that Antonín Kullmann had framed Nestor in as methodical and precise a way as he kept his old letters. "Not a lot. I was told he's missing a finger, that it was cut off by a guard."

He winked at me. "They like to spread stories. It gives them a thrill."

"What do you remember about him?"

"I've had a lot of pets here, it's hard to remember the quiet ones. The ones you remember are the ones who shout all the time, and keep returning to this office for their reprimands."

"It looks like Nestor was all right, then."

The captain shook his head. "None of them is all right, Comrade. And what he's done on the outside just proves it."

I took my hat from his desk and stood up. "Thank you, then."

When we shook hands he held on to mine a little longer. "You get him, now. Make sure you get him alive so we can have him back."

"You want him back here?"

"I'll make up a bunk for him today. I like to have all my pets back at home . . . who wouldn't?" Then he frowned. "Hey — you didn't touch your coffee!"

# 59

It was only four, but I needed a drink. I'd heard enough about the work camps to know I had walked across soil with a heavy blood content and had talked to one of the most brutal sons of bitches that state security could find — because that's who you put in charge of work camps, the ones who could stomach it.

Along the road to the center there were more bars than anything else, so I parked and entered one at random. Young men leaned against high tables and cupped their shot glasses with thick fingers. The bartender smiled thinly at me. "You need a coffee?"

"Palinka."

He poured it and looked me up and down. "You one of the new ones?"

"The new what?"

"You know. The new guards."

I sipped my drink. "New guards? I heard

there were plenty already."

He leaned close so he could whisper. "That's the word. New guards are being shipped in any day now. What are these boys going to do?" He nodded at the drinkers. "They've waited long enough as it is."

"Well, I'm not one of them."

"That's good for you," he said with a wink.

I leaned on a free table and gazed at the photographs that covered the wall. Shots of "old Vátrina." The only difference between old and new Vátrina, the photos told me, was the Hotel Elegant, and the camp.

A thick man with a close-shaved head set his drink next to mine and looked up at the photos, as if unaware of my presence. The back of his neck was swollen with wrinkles where his excess flesh had collected, and his puffy cheeks were riddled with gray pockmarks and stubble. "You come in from the Capital?" he asked the wall.

"Yeah."

"Horia says you're not a guard."

Horia watched us from behind the bar. "That's true."

"It's all right if you are," he said to a

photograph of a woman and a horse in front of the feed store. "We're not vindictive here. Everyone's in the same boat."

"I'm still not one."

"Then what are you?" He turned to look at me. His eyes were light blue, and below one of them was a scar.

I said it before I could think it over: "I'm a writer."

"What do you write?"

"Novels."

"You mean, stories you make up?"

"That's it."

He considered this as he finished his shot, walked back to the bar, and returned with two more. He put one in front of me.

We raised our glasses to each other.

"So why aren't you in some café in the Capital right now? Why are you on the stinking edge of the world?"

"Research."

"Working on a story about *this* town?"

"About the camp."

His mouth opened, but then he closed it. He noticed someone at another table. "Hey, Krany!" A little dark-haired guy with a cigarette in his mouth looked up. "Krany, come over here."

Krany sauntered over with his glass and leaned on our table without looking at me.

371

"This guy wants to know about the camp. He's a writer."

Krany put out his cigarette and frowned at the lingering smoke. "Why're you writing about that, Comrade?"

"Because somebody's got to."

The thick one nodded his agreement, but Krany still wasn't convinced. "What are you going to say about the camp?"

"I'll know when I learn more."

"You some scaremonger who's going to say we're a bunch of thugs who like beating up on people?"

"Are you?"

He smiled then, and I pulled out my cigarettes. I offered them to the guards and left the pack on the table.

Krany, it turned out, was primarily a tower man. He had spent his days, summer and winter, up in one of the boxes overlooking the camp and the farmland surrounding it. He was one of the best shots in the camp, and once killed an escapee from a distance of five hundred yards (though his friend disputed that figure). "And he went down. I wanted to get his leg, just stop him, but it ended up going through his head." He took another of my cigarettes.

The first guard's name was Filip. He

worked down in the mud with the prisoners. Each morning he would herd them out of their cots and march them to the quarry. "It was all about following orders," he told me. "They were ordered to walk, and if they didn't, we would hit them. Usually in the stomach and chest, because we didn't want to break their legs."

"Come on, Filip," said Krany. "You broke some legs. I could see you just fine."

"So you get carried away."

"It was easier up in the tower. You didn't have to smell them, you didn't have to do that kind of work."

I bought another round and asked if they knew Nestor Velcea. Krany shook his head, but Filip thought it over. "A small guy? What was he . . . an artist?"

"That's the one."

"Sure, I knew him. An okay kid. He thought we didn't know about all those charcoal drawings he did. But when prisoners clean up a wall, you notice. The wall's dirty already, and then you've got this big clean spot." He smiled grimly. "Some of them were real idiots."

Krany nodded. "Yeah, the artist. The one who did Gogu's portrait."

"Who's Gogu?"

"The commander," said Filip, and I remembered the portrait on the captain's wall.

I passed out cigarettes, emptying the pack. "But Gogu said he didn't remember Nestor. Does that make any sense?"

"Of course he remembers Nestor," said Filip.

"He was pulling your leg," said Krany. "He damn well knows who Nestor is."

"But there were a lot of prisoners. Why would he remember Nestor?"

Krany looked at Filip, as if asking something. Filip shrugged. "What does it matter?"

Krany turned back to me. "Last spring, this gray Citroën comes up to the gate. Cosmin checks it, but the driver doesn't have the right paperwork to come inside."

"Who's Cosmin?"

"No one. Another guard. Pay attention, okay?"

I nodded.

"So Cosmin won't let him inside. And this guy gets out — a big guy, kind of oily hair — and starts shouting for Nestor through the fence. Only it's daytime, and all the prisoners are off at Work Site Number One. He was a foreigner, maybe he didn't know any better. So he's shouting to an empty prison."

"What kind of foreigner?"

"Don't know," said Krany. "But you could tell there was an accent. What a hothead he was. Finally, Gogu had to come out and deal with him."

"I heard about it that evening," said Filip.

"We all heard about it," said Krany. "And this is why Gogu will swear he doesn't know Nestor. Because the foreigner bribed him with a stack of koronas the size of my fist. Gogu tried to cover it up, he told him to put it away, and they went back to the office to take care of it. But we all saw it. Bribing's no big deal, just as long as you keep it quiet."

"So what happened?"

Filip said, "I brought Nestor back from the work site and into Gogu's office. Gogu stepped outside for a few minutes to leave them alone. Then Nestor went back to work, and the foreigner left."

"But — what was it about? What did he want?"

Filip finally lit the cigarette I'd given him. "No one knows. We asked Gogu, and he told us to keep out of his business unless we wanted to end up as one of his pets."

"And Nestor, too," said Krany. "He wouldn't say a word, would he, Filip?"

"Not a word. I punched him a few times

because I was so curious, but the lump just wouldn't speak."

# 60

It was after seven when I returned to the Elegant with my small bag of clothes. There was a different clerk at the desk, a young man who took my papers and wrote the information in a ruled notebook. In the middle of writing, he squinted up at me. "You came in here before?"

"For information."

He tossed his head in the direction of the bar. "Tania's waiting for you."

I had forgotten about her. My mind was stuck in the realm of barbed wire and mud and beatings, and spending the evening with a woman just didn't fit in. So I took back my documents and key and walked directly to the stairs, not looking up as I passed the doorway to the bar.

The stairs and the doors and the corridor and the tiny room — all of them had been built by cracked and bloody fingers, slumped backs and sore stomachs. I lay on the bed, my feet hanging off, and stared at the beige ceiling.

There was a knock at the door, but I

didn't get up. I was wondering what was said in Gogu's office last spring.

The knocking started again, so I got up, grunting, and opened the door. Tania smiled at me. "Think you can get rid of me that easily?"

"Look. I'm tired."

She put her hand on my chest and pushed me back. I noticed an open bottle of wine in her other hand as she closed the door. "You don't look so tired to me."

There was a certain prettiness to her, but I couldn't see it then. She got two glasses from the bathroom and filled them up. There was no other place to sit than the bed. She tapped my glass against hers and winked.

"You kept me waiting so long I almost found myself another victim. But then I remembered this," she said, touching the rings on my right hand. "And this." She touched my chest. Then she set her glass on the floor and moved her round face up to mine. "And this," she whispered, before kissing me.

The kissing was enough for a while, and we rolled on the bed, a mess of tongues and saliva. Sometimes she got up suddenly, leaned over the edge of the bed as I rubbed the back of her thigh, and took a sip, then returned with wine-reddened lips. But when she started to take off her clothes I stopped her. "No," I said, and she frowned, took another sip, and began kissing me again.

This was all I wanted, something simple and almost childlike, and that's all we did until we were lying together on the bed, both very tired.

Tania was twenty-five, had grown up in this town, and the only outsiders she met were connected to the work camp. "I like this, meeting people from all over. Most of them are pretty nice, and sometimes we can have ourselves some fun."

"So you do this a lot?"

She stretched an arm over her head. "Now and then. There are a couple guards I see regularly, but we all know I'm not the kind of girl to settle down." She looked at me. "It's too fun, isn't it?"

"Fun, yes." I poured the last of the wine into her glass and asked if she wanted to stay over.

"Think there's enough room?"

There wasn't, but I wanted to sleep with a warm body tonight. "We can make it work."

The room was getting cold, so I checked the radiator, which didn't seem to do a thing. Tania banged on the knob a few times. "This hotel is a joke."

As she undressed, I noticed the black, shiny spot on her stockings, where she'd used nail polish to repair a hole. I turned out the lights.

It was difficult, but she curled up with her back to my chest, and I wrapped my arms around her. She talked steadily through the next hour, mumbling about how she'd had offers from men to take her out of this town, but she would never go. "Here I'm somebody. What would I be in the Capital? Just another peasant. Just another slut." She said she'd even had offers from state security men. One of them sent her packages of Swiss chocolates on a regular basis. "He's in love with me. That job must have screwed up his brain. You can see it in them, those security types are all a little off."

"You should watch out for them."

"Me? No, *they* should watch out for me."

"Maybe you're right."

Her hair shifted against my nose. "I'm serious. One told me that he was frightened of me."

"A little girl like you?"

"I didn't believe it either, but," she said, then paused, trying to remember exactly.

"He said he was afraid of my inability to commit to one man. Not that it scared him, not *personally*, but he said that more and more people were like me, and if you couldn't commit to a single person, how could you commit to a state?"

"That sounds like state security."

"I even get the occasional foreigner."

"Foreigners?"

"Well, not many. So you remember them. The last one was French. Nice enough guy. Big and fat, but not so jolly as he looked. He was trying to get a friend out of the work camp. I could've told him it wouldn't work."

My arms around her twitched, but she didn't notice. "Remember his name?"

"Louis. Yes — Louis something. Nice guy." I felt her fingers grip my elbow beneath the covers, as if for support. "But he wasn't such a gentleman as you."

# 61

I drove home with the first light, having whispered a farewell to Tania's sleeping form. I showered and changed, and by three was at the station. Emil was in, so I sat on his desk and took one of his cigarettes. He winked.

380

"Got some interesting news for you."

"Me first," I said. "Watch out for yourself and Lena. Nestor found out where I live."

"You saw him?"

"He tried to break in while I wasn't there."

Emil frowned.

"I took Magda and Ágnes out of the city. You might consider the same thing for Lena."

He nodded very seriously. "Okay."

"Another thing: A Frenchman named Louis Rostek saw Nestor last spring at the camp. The commander won't tell me anything, and the guards don't know what it was about. But I think he told Nestor that Antonín had put him away."

"A Frenchman?"

"Someone I know. Through Georgi."

Emil dragged his fingers through his hair. "I think my interesting news will stand up to yours."

"Tell me."

"The lab came back with prints on Stefan's bedroom window and those fish soups. Guess who his window-climbing dinner guest was."

"Don't make me guess," I said, as his phone began to ring.

He reached for it and winked. "Nestor Velcea. Matched his work camp fingerprint card perfectly."

I watched him lean into the telephone. Stefan and Nestor Velcea, sitting at the same table eating fish soup — why? Was Stefan involved in the crimes? No. Then who came to the door? I didn't know how to put it all together.

Emil hung up. "Sorry, but that was Lena. She's vomiting everything she takes in. And," he said with a grimace, "she's a little hysterical." He got up and went for his coat.

I stared at the empty doorway after he left, then wandered slowly toward my own desk. Louis's role made sense — the scene at the camp was of one man's loyalty to another, of a friend who had put some clues together. I remembered that Antonín Kullmann's paintings had even made it to Paris — his success enabled his downfall. But the scene in Stefan's kitchen over fish soup —

On my desk was a phone message from Georgi.

I met him in the café attached to the opera house on the corner of International and V. I. Lenin. It was another of those Habsburg monstrosities that seemed not to have changed in the last fifty years, with the exception of its nonplussed waiters, who smoked in the back corner and watched you wait.

Georgi handed me a list of names of people who might know the whereabouts of Nestor Velcea. As I looked it over, he said, "They're all writers. Nestor didn't like painters."

"So I heard." I pocketed the list. Georgi was looking good. He had a new hat, something a friend had brought from Vienna — not Louis, though. "Tell me more about him."

"What do you want to know?"

"Everything."

It was a tough thing to ask, but Georgi was up to it. "I met Louis some years ago. 'Forty-seven, -eight? He was spending some time here at the expense of the Writers' Union. He was thinner then, that's for sure. The women went wild for him. French accent and all. You can imagine."

"Sure I can."

"My book had just come out, and they had me read a little bit. Louis was impressed. I can't say I liked *his* poems — he was a little too didactic in those days."

"In what direction?"

"You know, glories of world revolution and all that. He's calmed down a lot since then."

"Did he know Nestor Velcea?"

"Apparently they'd met each other during the war. 'Forty-four or so. I'm not sure. He knew Nestor was a basket case, but thought he was talented."

"Did you think Nestor was talented?"

"I never saw his paintings, never met him until he came to my party." Georgi gave an elaborate shrug. "Nestor was already in the camp when I met Louis."

A waiter appeared and reluctantly took our order. Then he returned to the smoking group, the order still on the notepad he had dropped into his pocket.

"You should have seen it when they met again at the party. They embraced and cried like father and son."

"Before I showed up."

"Yeah. Before."

I noticed my thick fingers were pulling at my rings, sliding them up a knuckle, then back. "What did Louis think about Nestor's imprisonment?"

Georgi pulled out a cigarette. "He wasn't in the country when they took Nestor away. He was supposed to come in on the same day Nestor was arrested, but something kept him — some visa problems, I don't know."

Nestor went to the train station to meet a foreign agent, but the foreigner didn't arrive.

"Anyway, Louis didn't hear about the arrest until maybe six months later, when he came through again. That's when I met him. And, of course, he was angry. When Louis is angry, you don't want to get in his way."

"He has a temper?"

"Not at all. That's what makes him so tough. If you've done enough to get Louis angry, you know you're in for big trouble."

"What did he do then?"

"When?"

"When he found out Nestor had been taken away."

Georgi puffed a couple times, spreading smoke. "He lodged a complaint. He felt sure he could get Nestor out, maybe because he was a foreigner. But he went directly to Yalta Boulevard, to the Office of Internal Corrections. Can you believe it? Walked right in, alone, and came out a few hours later, furious. They hadn't let him talk to anyone. They had him sit in the waiting room for something like two hours, then told him the officer had left for the day."

"Who was the officer?"

Georgi shook his head. "No idea."

I wondered what had happened that day. It was hard enough to get into Yalta Boulevard, particularly a foreigner. And then expect to free someone? Louis knew that. The only way he could have expected to have any pull in Yalta Boulevard was if he was connected to state security. Probably as an informer.

The waiter finally appeared with our coffees and placed the bill under the sugar bowl. Georgi scooped a spoonful into his coffee and stirred.

# 62

Driving to Vera's block that evening was instinct. It didn't occur to me to go home. By now my desire for her was its own separate thing that turned the wheel and applied the brake like another, more sure Ferenc, to whom I had not yet been introduced.

I knocked on the door. Her voice came from the other side, but it wasn't directed at me. It was quieter, as if for someone else in the apartment. Then I figured it out, but too late. The door opened and Karel stared back at me.

His surprise was evident in his thick brows and the big, flaccid mouth peeking out from his beard. He'd gotten fat as his poetic success increased, but he had never lost his youthful inability to hide his emotions. Then he smiled and glanced back at Vera, who looked stuck to the sofa. "How about this! Ferenc Kolyeszar, what a surprise!"

Outside of Georgi's parties, he and I never talked, but he had always been one of the many who made halfhearted promises to meet for dinner or drinks. He waved me in. Vera stood up and gave me her cheeks to kiss politely.

"I was just telling Vera about Yugoslavia. What people! Incredible."

"That's why I came over," I said. "Georgi told me you were back, and I wanted to hear all about it." I noticed a plate of food on the coffee table. "I should have called, though, and it's late. How about tomorrow?"

"*Nonsense,*" said Karel. He pushed me toward the sofa, and Vera moved over to give me plenty of space. "I have photos! You better believe I've got photos. Vodka?"

I forced a smile and nodded, and he disappeared into the kitchen.

Vera and I communicated with our eyes.

Wide, round, surprised eyes. Half shrugs.

Karel asked about Magda and Ágnes, and I said they were out in the provinces for a little while, staying with Magda's parents. He winked at me. "Be sure and behave yourself!"

He had more photos than anyone I'd ever known. A heavy stack of black-and-whites of drab, gray-clad poets and professors standing stiffly for group portraits against blank walls or beside tables covered with books. He had some underexposed shots of Belgrade and Zagreb, and overexposed ones of Roman ruins in Dubrovnik and the beaches of Split, leading to the Adriatic. And he had stories that went on for too long. He laughed a lot and rubbed the back of his neck. The experience had invigorated him. He was a national emissary brought in to exemplify the best our little country could produce in a man of letters, and this was the role he felt most comfortable in. He said this without modesty, then followed with, "Those Serbs eat up stuff like that. Next we'll send them our country's finest garbageman, and they'll build a statue to him."

The stories became duller as the night wore on, and as he was relating an anecdote about Tito's brand of cigarettes, I finally gave a yawn and thanked him for the enthralling description of our socialist friends. When we shook hands, he said, "This was great, Ferenc. You should come over more often."

I kissed Vera's cheeks again as Karel smiled radiantly at us.

The apartment was stuffy, so I opened the windows, which only made it cold. I closed them and poured myself a brandy, then turned on the radio. For once, it was not set to the Americans, just an easy Austrian waltz. I had a copy of Karel's first book of verse, published five years ago, and settled on the sofa with it. His lines were as dull as his stories, loose rhyming statements about the open-ended quality of life, the ambiguities that make it a pleasure despite the hardships. They were optimistic poems, and I wondered if he could write such happy drivel if he knew what I had been doing to his wife, or what that Swiss philosophy professor had done to her before their marriage.

I woke to a dim room. Then I heard what had woken me: a knock at the door. Although a large part of me knew, I grabbed my pistol. "Yes?"

"It's me," she whispered.

I set the pistol on a table. We didn't embrace when she came in. She looked cold.

"I thought he'd be gone a few more days," she said. "That was weird."

"A drink?"

We sipped our wine in the kitchen. "I told him I needed to stay with a girlfriend tonight. His head is too far in the clouds for him to be suspicious." She looked at me. "Is that all right?"

I put my arms around her and kissed her deeply on the mouth.

The climbing rope that Ágnes had been awarded was knotted every foot-and-a-half so that the Pioneers could use their feet to climb up into trees. I found it rolled up beneath her bed and brought it to the bedroom.

I told Vera to take off her clothes. She looked at the rope suspiciously, but seemed to like not being the only one to give orders. Once she was naked, she lay back and I tied a knot around one of her ankles, then around the other, so that she could spread them a couple feet, but no farther.

"What are you —"

"Quiet," I said. I tied the other end to her wrists, so that when she brought her hands to her face she was forced to bend her knees. She did this once. When she pulled her hands away, her smile was dreamy.

I did not take off my clothes. Instead, I unbuttoned my trousers and aroused myself in front of her. She watched me, the smile fading into a heavy-lidded gaze as her hands moved slowly up and down, her knees bending and unbending, sliding the knotted rope between her legs. I watched her as she watched me, but although I wanted to badly, I did not touch her.

She came very quickly, but quietly, her face convulsing as if in pain, mouth falling open.

I took off my clothes and lifted her by the rope, so that her feet and hands, red from constriction, wavered above her thin body. Then I lowered her to the bed and finished inside her.

I began to untie her wrists, but she shook her head, eyes closed. "Not yet."

So I lay beside her and drew my finger over her damp body, over the rough fibers of rope, over the knots. It was a long time before we slept.

# 63

Lena had gotten over her illness, and Emil and I went to see the few people on Georgi's list. As I drove and Emil spoke about the long night spent nursing Lena, I mulled over the previous night. I'd never done anything like that before, but while doing it I'd known exactly what to do, and how long to do it. But it hadn't been me — it had been that other, more sure Ferenc, the one I'd met on the drive to Vera and Karel's. It was the Ferenc born of the recent past, amid deaths and work camps and infidelities, the Ferenc sick of being able to do nothing. I still didn't know how I felt about this strange man.

". . . was the best thing to do," I heard Emil saying.

"I'm sure it was," I said.

Tamas Brest, surrounded by books I suspected he went out of his way to keep dusty, said he hadn't heard from Nestor since that party for Louis. "Once word got around that my camp book was going to be state-printed, everyone dropped out of touch. As if I'd *done* something." He puffed on a pungent cigar when he spoke. "And now I've got two militiamen in my home. How is *that* going to look?"

Stanislaus Zambra just wanted to tell me that his series of poems remembering the end of Stalinism was finished. "Four months, and all straight from the heart," he said proudly, then nodded at Emil. "Is he a writer, too?" Emil shook his head.

"Well, that's all right. Nothing to be ashamed of."

"I'm not," Emil muttered.

"But Nestor," I repeated. "Can you help us find him?"

He couldn't, and neither could Bojan Kuz, though he did suggest we talk to Kaspar Tepylo, which I assured him I'd already done.

On the way to Miroslav Olearnyk's home out in the Seventh District, I told Emil not to let these writers get to him. "I avoid them as much as I can, and when I can't, I fall silent."

"They're amusing," he said. "They don't bother me."

"But something is bothering you."

He looked at the windshield — not through it, but at it — and nodded. "What do you think about love, Ferenc?"

I changed gear as we turned into a narrow street cluttered with traffic. "I think I'll need a drink to answer that."

He didn't say anything for a few minutes, and I stopped behind a line of cars, then moved slowly forward with it. "I reread your book last week."

"Glad to hear it's worth a second read."

"It's good," he said, but without enthusiasm. "There's a line in it that always stuck to me. I don't remember the exact words, but it's about love of your country. Something about the love of a soldier for his country is the most mature, because it's about sacrifice. What was it? *If your love is mature, you will not hesitate to sacrifice yourself if the object of your love will benefit.*"

"Yeah," I said. "Something like that."

He nodded into his chest, and I stopped again behind a truck filled with bags of onions. "You said it was the same whether the love was for a country or a woman."

"I remember."

He turned from the windshield finally. "I've been thinking about this, and about Lena. I'm not sure I'm any good for her."

"That's a load of crap, Emil. It's obvious even from the outside that without you she'd go off the deep end."

He shook his head. "Wasn't always that way. She used to be the strongest woman I knew. Then we married, and she became steadily more terrified by life. And when she leaned on me, I was happy to support her."

"Just what I'm saying."

"But now she doesn't know how to stand on her own. I can see it getting worse each day. And it will get worse, unless she's forced to stand on her own."

"Well, force her."

"I can't. If I'm there, I'll help her. I can't do otherwise."

I turned onto an emptier street and got going. "Listen, Emil. I'm not one to give marital advice, but if you truly believe this — if you think your presence is doing Lena more harm than good — then I suppose you're thinking the right thing."

"If my love is mature."

I didn't answer.

"What about you?" he asked, looking back to the windshield, and through it. "Would you leave Magda if you found out you were bad for her? Would you leave Ágnes?"

"Sure," I said, but I just wanted to sound decisive. "If I was bad for them, I'd leave."

Emil let the subject rest. We soon appeared at Miroslav Olearnyk's block, but he was not in.

# 64

At the station, I saw Leonek for the first time since before the provinces. His hair was a little long, and oily, and he looked pale. But he was smiling about something, and that smile kept me from being able to focus on anything. He pulled up a chair. "Not only has Kliment found Boris Olonov, but he interrogated the son of a bitch. The transcript should arrive tomorrow."

I stared at him, expressionless. "Did he kill Sergei?"

"Kliment didn't tell me much, but he did say that while Boris isn't my man, he *was* one of the soldiers who killed the girls. There's something else in the interview. He wouldn't tell me what it was — he wants it to be a surprise. But he said it should begin to bring everything together."

I continued to stare at him.

"Kliment's very interested in this case."

"Of course. It's his father."

"Yes," said Leonek, nodding, his smile wavering. "Look, I'm going to give the Jewish quarter another try. If I tell them we've got one of the girls' murderers, maybe I can get something more. Come along?"

I shrugged.

On the drive, he began telling me about how he had almost given the case up. "So many blind alleys. I thought it would have been easier. What about your case? How's it coming?"

"It's coming."

Leonek patted a dark hand against the horn, frightening an old woman in the middle of the street, and I couldn't help but think of all the things that hand had touched. "He mailed the interview transcript, it should arrive by tomorrow."

"You told me that."

Leonek gave me a look I'd seen before, and only now did I understand where the shame had always come from. "You all right, Ferenc?" He spoke quietly. He didn't want to ask, but there was no choice. "Is there something wrong?"

I turned to watch a group of workers with pickaxes walk by, their breaths coming out like smoke. "Maybe it's the thing I had to learn from my wife."

He brought a hand down from the wheel. He seemed to recognize how close we were in this car, and that he was trapped. Then an ounce of courage came into him, and he put the hand back on the wheel. "I'm not proud of it, Ferenc. But I do love her. Honestly."

"That makes me feel better."

"I don't mean it that way. But I do love her, and I love Ágnes as well."

He had no right to love my daughter. I shifted, just to watch him lower his hand again. "You know, I would be fully justified in beating the hell out of you. No one would argue this."

His voice was a whisper. "I know."

I stared at him as he drove. He had nothing to say — or, he probably had a lot to say, but knew none of it would come out right, so he kept quiet. I didn't have anything more to say. I only wanted him to know that I knew, and to be afraid. I would not hurt him — I could not do that to Magda — but Leonek didn't need to know that.

When he came to a stoplight, I placed my hat on my head and opened the door. "Good luck in the Jewish quarter." I stepped out, and the bright light made me sneeze.

# 65

I called Magda from home. It was a brief conversation; we did not speak of Leonek. Ágnes had become bored by the second day, and her parents were starting to drive Magda crazy. "When are you going to take care of this guy so we can come home?"

"Home?" I asked. It seemed like a word we were no longer allowed to use. "Soon. I'll bring you back home soon."

Vera did not come over that night, and on Thursday morning when I arrived at the station, Sev was waiting for me. He waved me over. I moved stiffly. "Ferenc." He paused. "The morning you discovered Stefan's body, why were you there?"

I looked at his hands on the desk. "To talk with him about our case."

Sev moved his hands so his thumbs touched, a movement I remembered from Lev Urlovsky. "I'm just doing my job, Ferenc. You know this."

"I know."

"So please tell me the truth." The absence of emotion in his face always gave it a dull strength.

"What are you getting at?"

He glanced around the empty office. "I am aware of your animosity toward Stefan, and I also know it was unfounded."

"I know that now, too."

"Good. So tell me. Why did you go to Stefan's that morning?"

Just talking about it made me feel as I did when I stood looking down on Stefan's body — weak. I pulled up a chair. "To talk, Sev. That's all. I just wanted to talk it out."

"And you wouldn't have attacked him again, like you did in that bar?"

"I don't think so. Leonek is still alive, isn't he?"

Sev nodded at his thumbs. "Thank you, Ferenc."

I stumbled back and shuffled through the papers on my desk from the past few days. Among the circulars about new penal codes from the Politburo was a scribbled phone message. Kliment had called.

I struggled with the Russian operators, using the words I knew and listening to them use all the words I didn't know. I gave them the direct number Kliment had left. *"Da?"*

"This is Ferenc Kolyeszar."

"Ferenc. Thanks for calling. Look." He paused. "I've got some terrible news, you're not going to like it."

"I've gotten a lot of bad news lately. I can probably take it."

"Two days ago Svetla Woznica was killed in her village. She was shot once in the chest and once in the head. They found her body in the woods outside town."

I took a long breath. "I can't believe it."

"Believe it. And it's clear enough who did it."

"Was he seen there?"

"He didn't hide. He arrived the day before by train, spent a lot of money in the hotel, and disappeared just before the body was found. He crossed over at Turka."

"I can't believe it," I repeated.

"I've seen it before. Some men are that

way. If they can't have their woman, then no one can."

I fogged over, thumbing my rings until they hurt, remembering that battered face at the train station, kissing my hands. But he was speaking again.

"— can't do anything about it now. With the proper papers, I could follow him there, but it's not the sort of thing they'll sign for. I wish I could."

"You've done enough, Kliment. Thank you. I'll take care of it."

"I figured you would, Ferenc. Watch out for yourself."

As I hung up I looked over at Sev looking back at me. I think that was the closest I ever came to killing Brano Sev, even though he had nothing to do with Svetla's death. But he was one of many — like the missing Kaminski — whose positions made them feel they could not be touched. I filled his empty features with all the evil in the world. He blinked. I stood up. But instead of ending everything right then, I made myself walk out the door.

# 66

The Canal District was colder than the rest of the city. The water seemed to suck any heat from the air, and wind funneled through the empty passageways. In Augustus II Square, where long before I had found a black shoe, the water level had dropped, and I arrived relatively dry at number three. The chalk X had faded away. The inner room was still a pool, the small well still dry, but the blemish from Antonín's body was completely gray now, with spots of black corroded by the wet air.

I could not find Nestor, and Louis was in another country. I was no longer sure who had killed Stefan, but I was convinced I would never figure it out. And it didn't matter how valiantly I protected my family — my marriage was slipping away. Now, my only virtuous act in recent memory — the only one that I had followed through on — had been erased. No action I took seemed to stick. I wanted to sleep.

In the mosaic beneath the water were chalices, wine, debauchery — a satyr leaned, grinning, over a white-robed young woman with a breast exposed. In the corner, a platter of wild berries and the head of a pig gazed up at me.

The Romans had themselves a time in their day, putting everything into their mouths like children. They slaughtered whole civilizations and sowed lands with salt. These were a people of extremes, but somehow over time all the extremes had been bred out of humanity, so that we wore ties and took busses and trams and clocked in and out of the jobs that fed our family. We spoke with calm, responsible detachment and made words that seemed to show what logical beasts we were. But the only important words are those that result in action — Vera knew this. And so did I. In the war I learned who I was — not by the words I spoke, but by the things I did.

We were captured near Humenne on a bleak, dry hill that had become our home for a week. We ran out of ammunition, and our commander, a young man from Hust, announced that the fight was over. Then he went behind the hill and shot himself in the mouth with his last bullet. The Germans came over the hill in a cloud of dust and their bold helmets, well fed and scornful. They arranged us into lines and walked us westward.

Before shooting himself, our commander had told us about the camps set up by the Germans. They were for Jews, Gypsies, and Slavs. The Germans, he pointed out, were a people of extremes. His stories were difficult to believe, and some of us laughed at him, though since then his descriptions have seemed mundane. But on that dusty walk, as we starved on blistered feet, we began to suspect the truth.

Each day we stopped so the Germans could rest, and during one of these breaks I escaped with a couple other soldiers. I've written about this. I've written about the calculations we made, the old trenches we dropped into in order to escape snipers, the grass we ate to hold off starvation, the peasants' homes where we rested and received nourishment. What I never wrote down was the bitterness between us when we stopped over a clump of grass and tried to divide it up. I used my size to force the largest portion, and once when another escapee — Yakov Teddi, a skinny boy with long hair — tried to take his fair share I kicked him in the face. This is something I never wrote about. My boot broke his nose, and I didn't care. But he stayed with us until the end.

# 67

Vera was in a mood when she arrived. She didn't tell me what it was, but the mood was evident by her silence, and the way, in bed, she held my big hand up to her face and turned it to see it from every angle. She brought the palm up close to her eyes, as if to read my future, and kissed the hair on the back of it. She smiled, then quickly sank her teeth into my middle finger. The pain shot through me, and I instinctively slapped her, harder than I would have wanted. When she got up on her elbow there was a bright red spot on her cheek. But she was still smiling.

At the station, Leonek was busy struggling through Kliment's interview of Boris Olonov, in Russian. "Why didn't he translate it?" Leonek muttered to himself. "He could have translated it."

"Get Kaminski to do it," I muttered.

Leonek looked up at me, unsure if I was joking. In case I wasn't, he said, "Kaminski's got the flu. That's what Brano says."

Brano didn't seem to notice his name being said.

Leonek tried a smile. "Maybe we can get Kaminski for sabotage."

Through his open door, I saw Moska eating a sandwich at his desk. "Come in, Ferenc. Haven't seen you much lately. A bite?"

I shook my head.

He set the sandwich down and cocked his head. "I heard about the Woznica woman."

"What about her?"

"That she was found dead in her home village."

"Who told you?"

"Brano," he said as he lifted the sandwich again. "She was officially one of ours, so Moscow sent a report. Brano didn't think you'd tell me. Was he right about that?"

"I don't know. I would've gotten around to it."

"Are you going to follow up on it?"

"Any reason I shouldn't?"

"Of course not, Ferenc. It's your job. I'll see if I can get some clearance for you to work on international cases. It'll take a week or two, so wait before arresting him. He won't go anywhere."

"Okay."

"And I'm closing down the other investigation. I told Brano this morning. I know you didn't touch Stefan. He knows it, too."

"Thanks," I said, then looked at him. "Really."

He took a bite, pulling his lips back to expose the two holes where teeth had once been, then dropped the sandwich again. "Is there anything you need to talk about? You seem a little weird these days."

"You know about Magda and me."

"That's been going on a long time."

"It's worse."

His sympathetic smile made me wonder if he, also, knew about Leonek. But he said, "Ferenc, everyone's marriage is rough. Don't think you're alone in this."

"I didn't say I was."

"I never told you about Angela and me, did I?"

"I knew you had some problems."

"I don't gab about it, but it wasn't pretty. It got bad enough that I started sleeping with some young girl from the administrative typing pool. Exceptional girl. She's married now, with two kids. Very happy."

"Good for her."

"The point is, Angela and I finally sat down and talked. There were a lot of

407

things she had never said to me, and a lot of things I hadn't said to her. Nothing easy about it, marriage. You've got to make some sacrifices. How long have you been married?"

"Seventeen years."

"Not long at all. We'll talk again when you get to twenty-five years, and I'll have some more advice for you."

I grinned. "I can't wait."

# 68

Emil asked where I had been the previous day, but didn't wait for the answer I didn't want to give. "You should've come out with me. I had a grand time talking to old women who didn't want to say a thing."

"In Stefan's building?"

"Yeah. And Antonín's. Nothing of use. But then," he said, sitting on the corner of my desk, "I started thinking about this Frenchman. This Louis Rostek."

"Did you?"

He looked at me.

"Go on."

"There's a French school over on Yalta Boulevard."

"The one I'm going to send Ágnes to."

"Exactly. The head didn't know anything about Louis, but he suggested I check with their consulate. They host parties for French nationals."

I sat up. He'd actually been working while I moped in the Canal District. "And?"

"And I haven't been there yet. Want to come?"

It was west of Victory Square, along the tree-lined streets of the diplomatic area. Three identical Mercedes were parked behind the gate, and the guard, a local boy, picked up the telephone in his little guardhouse for permission to let us enter. Then he opened the gate and watched us walk up the stone path to the front door, where another guard stood waiting. This one was French. He took us into a large marble entryway with a board covered by posters for upcoming events and a front desk where we signed in. Another man arrived: thin, white hair, an eye that twitched. His name was Jean-Paul Garamond. He shook our hands. "Good to meet you, Inspectors. Please, please."

He waved us down a marble corridor to his office, then waited until we were inside before entering and closing the door. The chairs opposite his desk were old and comfortable, and he held out an open box of cigars. I shook my head, but Emil, intrigued, took one. "Thank you."

Garamond lit it for him, then settled behind his desk, looking very pleased to have us both there. "Now what is it I can do for you gentlemen?"

Emil was puffing frantically on the cigar to keep it lit, and the smoke began to bother me. I said, "We're here in connection with a homicide investigation. Evidence has turned up a connection to a French national who frequents our country. A Louis Rostek."

Garamond didn't seem to know the name. "Rostek?"

"His family was from here originally, years back."

"I see," he said, eye twitching. "And you think he killed someone?"

"No. But he's connected to our suspect, and he certainly has information that could help us."

Emil was finally satisfied with the ember at the end of his cigar, and began waving smoke away. "Do you have," he said, then blew some smoke from his face. "Do you keep records of your citizens when they're here?"

Garamond smiled, but this was a smile I

didn't trust. "Well, we don't run things *your* way."

"Our way?"

He shrugged expansively. "We don't follow our citizens down the street taking notes."

"And if you did," I said, "you wouldn't give such notes to the local authorities."

"That would be our prerogative."

Emil had gotten rid of most of the smoke. He took a normal draw of the cigar, crossed his leg over his knee, and exhaled. "Can you tell us, then, why a French national was seen at a labor camp last spring trying to get inside?"

"Maybe he was a journalist."

"He's a poet," I said.

Garamond took one of the cigars for himself, but didn't light it. He rolled it between his fingers. "I think you should be going through other channels for this kind of information. Here at the consulate we're more interested in protecting the privacy of our citizens than divulging their secrets. Your people can talk to the embassy."

"We'd rather not do it that way," I said. "For Louis Rostek's good as well as our own."

His eye twitched when he lit his cigar. Three short puffs, and the ember glowed.

"I'm afraid I can't help you men. I can point you to our cultural and language programs if you're interested."

I did consider it briefly, for Ágnes, but said, "No thank you," and stood up.

# 69

She had told Karel she would spend the weekend with her sister, so I watched her make dinner in my apartment, standing where Magda would stand when I got home from work, turning to lay plates on the kitchen table. I went through some papers while she cooked, old notes for a second novel that had never come together. A lot of ideas, but no words, sentences, or paragraphs. I only had the pages I'd written about Magda and me. I picked up my old novel and gazed at it.

The French consulate had been just one more dead end — one more that convinced me that I had no control over the case, or my life. So I sat there with my book — shoddy, as Stefan had called it — wanting the strength to take control of something, anything. But more than that, I wanted the complete silence of solitude and the ease of a life without responsibility.

She was bent over the oven when I came in, but I didn't touch her. This was something I'd noticed. As our relationship progressed, we touched less outside the bedroom. The distance maintained a tension between us — we both understood this. Our time outside the bedroom was spent preparing for the bedroom.

As she plated the food she told me that she had come upon a fresh understanding of herself. "It's through failures. After enough of them you can look around and see what's left to you. Not Karel, that's for sure. And my career is dwindling before my eyes. My friends are all distant, and even you," she said, setting the plates on the table. "I don't really know about you, do I?"

I didn't say anything.

"So when I look around, what's left standing? Only one thing. Recklessness. It's the only thing that makes me feel like I'm becoming."

"Becoming what?"

"Just becoming."

"Recklessness, huh?"

"Yes. Recklessness."

While we ate I mentioned the visit to Vátrina. She didn't seem interested until I told her it was a camp town. "Were there prisoners?"

"There will be once they get it going again. The guards sit around drinking and waiting for them."

She touched her fork to her lower lip, then went back to eating.

"I slept with a woman there."

She laid the fork beside her plate. At first the expression was confused, then it settled. "Did you?"

"She worked at the hotel desk."

"How was she?"

"All right. Interesting."

I wanted her to ask more, because I was feeling reckless, too — I could stretch the truth or simply lie — but she didn't ask anything else. She finished her plate and put it in the sink, then went to the bathroom.

I threw away the food I hadn't eaten and turned on the radio. She came out before I could sit and asked me to turn it off.

"You don't want music?"

"I don't think so."

I checked her eyes for any sign of tears, but there was none. She walked up to me and nodded at the radio.

"You going to turn it off?"

"No."

She slapped me. The burn slid down my cheek and over my neck. When she stepped back I snatched her arm, jerked her to me, and bit her cheek.

She punched my stomach — a light thump — and I grabbed her waist and half carried her into the bedroom. She slapped me again in the darkness until I held her down, ripping at her buttons. She got a hand free and tore at my shirt.

It was more violent than before, more anguished. Her teeth drew blood from my shoulder and I bruised her wrists holding her down. It was angrier than it had ever been before, it hurt. I could tell by her whimpers in the dark.

I rolled over on my back. We were both covered in sweat.

She lay a while, facedown in the pillow, making low, grunting noises. I didn't know if she was crying or not, and I didn't ask. Then she flung herself on me. When she kissed me, her teeth chipped against mine and her tears rubbed into my cheeks. After a while, she calmed and settled her head on my chest.

As she dozed a fresh wave of dissatisfaction overcame me. The recklessness I had tried with her satisfied nothing. But I didn't know what else to do.

In the middle of the night, she woke me with her mouth. She rose on her knees, and from the lights of other apartments I saw that she had Ágnes's knotted rope in her hands. She presented it to me and lay down. I didn't understand at first, but she smiled and said, "I want to sleep like this."

So I tied her wrists behind her back, then her ankles. In the dim light the shadows on her thin body made her seem emaciated, starved. I gave her a kiss on the mouth, then another one between her legs.

I slept deeply until seven, when a nightmare woke me. I couldn't remember it all, but one detail floated through and settled in my mind: Malik Woznica on top of Magda, trembling. It was strong enough to give me the feeling I was still dreaming, and when I sat up and went to put on my clothes it was with a gliding, dream-walk across the rug. I washed my face and returned to Vera staring up at me, her wrists bound behind her. Her eyes were very big. "Are you going somewhere?" Her voice was dry. *Yes,* I said. *I'm going somewhere.* "How long?" *Not so long. I'm not going to untie you.* She seemed to be looking inside me. "Okay."

# 70

I drove to the Fourth District and parked a street in from the river. The Saturday morning sun was just beginning to come out, casting everything in a gray shroud, and a cold wind swept up the Tisa. I quickly found the door to his building. I hadn't really looked at it before, but now I had time. It was large, polished oak, with a bronze handle in the center. His wide, riverview window was on the top floor. The light was on.

I could have gone right up and taken care of it, but that would have been unnecessarily risky. The deaf woman below him could be up early, and might see me going up or down the stairs. So I buttoned the top of my coat, sniffed, and leaned against the railing by the Tisa, fooling with my rings.

I did not think as I waited. I did not reflect on the past or the future; I did not plan. So many of the things I'd planned and committed to had fallen apart, and now I was finished with that. I simply waited, and would act according to the moment. When some early risers passed — merchants on their way to work — I did not think about them. All I noticed was the light changing from gray to yellow, then gray again as clouds filled the sky.

He opened the door a little before nine, and I turned toward the water to hide my face. Once he was halfway down the street, I followed.

He moved slowly, his white hair and sun-burned head bobbing over his heavy body, and tugged now and then at the lapels of his trench coat. His shortness was apparent when he passed others on the slowly filling street. He stopped at a newspaper kiosk and bought the day's *Spark*, then scanned headlines, his pace slowing more until he turned into a café two streets east of his building.

I waited outside, holding down my thirst. I didn't need the coffee — adrenaline kept me awake — but my mouth was parched, and I needed a bath.

He was in there for three-quarters of an hour, then returned to his apartment. When it was clear where he was heading, I stopped at a kiosk and bought cigarettes and a bottle of water. I moved my post to his side of the street, so that if he decided to look outside, he wouldn't notice the big man who did not take his eyes off the front door.

It occurred to me as I waited that I did not have to hold my emotions at an arm's length anymore. They were too far away to matter.

I was lucky. In less than two hours he

was on the street again. He turned the west corner and began looking through his keys while standing beside a green Sachsenring P240, a new model I admired. Once he found his keys I had passed behind him and was getting into my Škoda.

We drove westward, following the Tisa out of town, then north. There weren't many others on the road, and I had to keep a good distance. We passed Uzhorod and moved into a long stretch that slid slowly up into the mountains. Pine trees popped up around us, and with one hand I took my map out of the glove compartment. The only major town along that road was Perechyn, but it wouldn't appear for another hour and a half. We were the only ones on the road.

I imagined he was heading to the dacha where he had taken his wife to find out what all he could do to her. But I didn't want him to arrive — I didn't want to leave clues in an obvious place.

He was a slow, careful driver, so it was easy to change gear and close the distance between us. The road curved as we gained altitude, and trees kept us from seeing what lay around each turn. I pulled the sun visor low and tailgated him. In his mirror I could vaguely make out his nervous face checking for the reckless driver behind him, but I stayed close. Finally, he did what I wanted: He slowed, drew to the edge of the road, and stuck his hand out to wave me around. I took his offer, and as I passed turned my head in the other direction.

Shadows of trees hung over the road as I took the turns abruptly, wanting to give myself enough space. The road was narrower than in the plains, and now and then a warning sign told me that it could not accommodate two-way traffic. At one of these points I stopped and placed the car at an angle. I got out, opened the hood, and leaned underneath it.

I heard him come up behind me, apply brakes, then honk. I kept my head beneath the hood. A second honk. Then, the sound of his door opening and his heels crunching pebbles.

"Is there some trouble? Maybe if you'd slow down, you could —"

I straightened and faced him.

Sometimes when people are stunned, there is a hesitation before the actual recognition. For Malik Woznica there was no pause. I saw the shock, then the back of his head as he ran to his car.

But his legs were short. I caught his coat

as he was pulling the door open and jerked him back, then kicked the door shut.

He was saying *No, no,* but there seemed no reason to reply. I pulled him, kicking, away from his car, turned him toward me, and punched him hard on the brow. His head buckled back, flesh trembling. I ignored the pain in my knuckles and gave him another one that knocked him out and sent blood dribbling down his face. I dragged him to my car, opened the trunk, and stuffed him inside. It was difficult getting his legs in, but after a couple tries I could fold them properly. I slammed the door shut. I jogged to his car and drove it off the edge of the road, into the trees, wiped off the wheel, gearshift and handles with my shirt, then returned to my own car and closed the hood. I turned it around and began driving south again.

# 71

Not everyone knows the history of the Canal District. It was originally attached to the southern bank, a waterlogged narrowing of the Tisa, and until the founding of the Hungarian principality in the ninth century, it was uninhabited. After the coronation of

Saint Stephen I at the millennium, the Canal District itself was used as a base for collecting tolls from boat traffic along the Tisa. During that time the region suffered attacks from the Byzantine and Holy Roman Empires, and in 1241 fell into the hands of the Mongolian-Tartian hordes under Batu Khan, who only left when their khan died. Anticipating another attack, King Béla IV donated large areas of the Carpathian basin to encourage the building of forts to protect from another eastern attack. That was when the Canal District was separated by a defensive canal from the southern bank of the Tisa, connected by only one stone bridge — the Béla Bridge. But this engineering feat also had the effect of flooding the buildings that had been there for the previous couple centuries, and the residents were forced to cut smaller canals into the island to control the water. As trade in the region increased, the Capital grew into a wealthy city that then fell to various nation-states — now an outpost of Transylvania, then a victim of Ottoman conquest, and until the Great War an insignificant piece of the Dual Monarchy of Vienna and Budapest. After that war our independence was finally gained, and now we acted as if we were a real nation, with a long and epic history — though in reality we were less than forty years old.

I crossed the Béla Bridge, which deposited me among rotting wooden scaffolding put up half a decade ago to shore up the buildings against sinking, then abandoned when money was funneled to other, more practical projects.

I parked in gravel, then took a breath. An unsure map of the Canal District appeared in my head, and I charted my way, trying to recall where the waters had blocked paths, and where haphazard repairs had recovered them. The gray sky was bright and cold. I looked around, then put my ear to the trunk. A heavy, wheezing breath. Another. I opened it and saw him lying there, scrunched up, his face blue, struggling for air. He was only half-awake, dazed and sick, and I realized a broken pipe must have leaked carbon monoxide into the trunk. He was heavy and limp over my shoulder. His feet splayed in front of me, and I used a hand to hold them together, to keep balance. Against my back, he coughed.

On the straight paths it was easy enough. I leaned to the right in order to accommodate his weight. But the insecure arched bridges gave me trouble. I had to reach out my free arm, grab railings, and watch where I stepped. In one square I caught sight of a prostitute limping home. She looked at me, I at her, then she nodded at my load.

"Too much fun," I whispered.

She sneered. "Me too."

I walked through flooded squares because there was no avoiding it, and by the time I reached Augustus II Square, I was cold and wet. But I wasn't feeling much by then. I wasn't feeling the soreness in my shoulder that would settle in by the next day, nor the confusion that would come afterward. For now, there was no confusion and no doubt.

My feet crunched broken glass. I dropped him on the soiled spot where Antonín had died, stretched my arms, then lit a cigarette and waited on the other side of the pool for him to come to.

He was the kind of fat that, in the end, gave him a false look of health. His face cleared up, shifting back to its sunburn, purple emerging on his brow and nose around the crusted blood where I had punched him. He muttered something, then fell quiet. He woke with his eyes first, looking at the walls, not remembering, then his gaze moved over the water. When I brought the cigarette to my lips, he scrambled back against the wall.

"W-w —"

"*What* am I doing here? Is that what you're trying to ask?"

He shut his mouth and nodded.

"You just come back from a trip, Malik? Looks like you've gotten some sun."

He leaned forward on his hands and vomited.

I squatted in front of him. "I worked hard, you know. It was a real chore to get your wife out of the country and back to her own. Not to mention expensive. I hate to see all my good work ruined."

He wiped his mouth with the back of his hand and nodded.

"What did you think you'd accomplish?"

I could hardly hear his reply: "Get my Svetla back."

"But she didn't want to come back, did she?"

He couldn't answer that one.

"Tell me, Malik. Did you think I wouldn't find out? Did you think, perhaps, that after all my hard work, I wouldn't be a little angry about this? Or did you think that my anger wouldn't matter?"

He had backed into the corner again, and his arms were crossed in front of him, as if he could ward off an attack.

"Look beneath you, Malik. See that stain? A man was brought here, his legs and arms broken, and set on fire. Right where you are."

He looked down.

"How would you like it done?"

"No," he said. "No."

"Really," I said with a bright voice. "We both know you have this coming. There's really nothing else you deserve. So how would you like it?"

"No."

I stood up, reached through his fluttering hands, and pulled him by the collar into the water. A few loose pieces of mosaic — grapes and nipples — threw me momentarily off-balance, but I got him quickly to the center. I was starting to feel the cold up to where the water reached my knees. His feet splashed, his mouth finally producing shouts: "No! No! Help!" Then I shoved his face into the water to silence him.

He was easy to hold down. His hands pressed on the floor, his feet kicked water into my face, but all I had to do was look up at the ceiling and hold his neck and head down with my two hands. I'd never noticed the ceiling before. It was blackened by centuries and ribbed with arches that met in the center. I imagined there had been another image there at some time, more scenes of pleasure, but I really didn't know.

I let go of him. He coughed, red-faced, slime spilling from his mouth and nose. The sound of his labor filled the room and echoed back down on us. He made a half-hearted attempt to run, falling into the water as I grabbed an ankle and dragged him back. He came up again, a mess of hands and feet splashing.

"You see," I told him, "you might have gotten away with this, were it not for the rest of my life. Things have been very difficult for me lately — I don't expect you to have known this — and right now, you . . . you're the least of my worries."

"I —" He coughed. "I'm sorry."

"Thank you, Malik."

"No," he said, finally finding sentences: "I can help you. Tell me what, I can help you. Don't — just don't kill me."

I made a show of thinking about this. But I knew from the outset there was nothing he could do for me, and nothing I would ever want from him. It had all gone too far.

I looked around and noticed the dry well. I'd had no plans for it — I had no

427

plans at all — but the sight of it seemed fateful. "Take off your coat."

He hesitated.

"I'm not going to kill you."

He got up on his knees and took off his trench coat and handed it to me. Underneath was a gray jacket and a white shirt grayed by water.

"Come on, let's get out of this pool."

I held on to his arm to help him up to the ledge, water pouring off of us.

"The jacket, too."

He took it off. I used my teeth on the stitching of the shoulder until a few threads broke. Then I forced my fingers into the hole and tore off the arm. I did the same with the other arm as he watched, his imagination making the worst images he could come up with.

"Come here."

I used one jacket arm to tie his wrists behind his back. The knot was awkward, but strong.

"Sit down."

He hesitated again, because this was not what he had hoped for, but finally crouched and dropped back on his butt. I took off his shoes, then unbuckled his belt and took off his pants. "It's pretty cold here," he said as gaily as he could manage, but a quick hard look from me shut him up. I forced his underwear off. "Hey," he said, squirming a little, so I punched him on the chin. He didn't pass out, but he wavered a little between waking and sleep, waking more when I stuffed the underwear into his mouth. His eyes gaped, and he tried to yell something through the fabric. I took the other arm of his jacket and tied it around his mouth. He was completely awake now, his breaths harsh through his wide nostrils. His eyes rolled back and forth in panic.

Did I want to kill him? Yes. But I wasn't ready to do that. What he'd done to Svetla was so much worse than simple murder, and my real impulse was to put him through a fraction of the hell he'd put that poor girl through. I wanted to skin him alive.

I picked him up again, the way one holds a bride when crossing the threshold. When his shirt rose, his hairy, shriveled member came into view. His legs kicked now and then, but he couldn't see where I was taking him until we were right over the well. I sat him on the edge so his feet dangled inside. It was wide enough for him to fit, but just barely. He was screaming something through his gag, the veins in his head popping out beneath the welts, and then I pushed him forward.

At first he didn't fall because his hands tied behind his back caught on the wall of the well, twisting upward, all his weight focused on his burning elbows. He screamed louder; this time it was only pain. I lifted him by his shoulders, centered him, and let him drop.

He scuffed the walls on the way down, and in the darkness I could barely see him when he settled, could just hear his muffled moaning.

# 72

It was after three when I left the Canal District and drove back to the southern shore, then crossed the Georgian Bridge, back over the Canal District and into town. I didn't want to go home. The reason eluded me at first. It was Vera. I didn't want to let her go just yet. I wanted to control, with precision, the moment of her release.

Georgi had just returned from lunch with some friends, with whom he had talked poetry and politics and the search for the new socialist man. I hardly heard a thing he said until I took off my jacket and he stopped abruptly: "Is that blood on the back of your shirt?"

"It's nothing. Just a fight. Can I use your shower?"

"Going to tell me the details?"

"I don't think so."

Once the water was hot, I relaxed into it. Instead of Malik Woznica, I thought of Vera. She lay in my bed, probably terrified of what had become of me. Perhaps she thought I was never coming back. I wondered what that thought did to her and how she would react when I returned and made love to her.

Georgi opened the door as I was toweling off. "By the way, I finally got hold of Louis."

"Tell me."

"You're not going to arrest him, are you?"

"I've no plans to."

"Well, he's coming into town tomorrow morning, the ten-twenty from Vienna."

"Did he say why?"

"I didn't ask. You be nice to him, all right?"

"I'm nice to everyone, Georgi."

"I don't imagine you were nice to the guy whose blood is on your shirt." He smiled. "I tell you, it's going to be good to have him around again. This city's become a goddamn *bore*."

I went to dress.

Georgi found a shirt that barely fit me. "You hear Karel's back in town?"

"Yeah, I talked to him."

"Did he show you those awful photos? That's what I mean about this city. A goddamned *bore*."

At least Georgi could still make me smile.

# 73

I paused outside the door and listened. From down the stairs came Claudia's high, irritating voice squealing at someone over the phone, so I leaned closer, but heard nothing.

I let myself in quietly, then moved to the kitchen and drank a glass of water. No hurry. In the icebox lay a leg of cold chicken from last night. I took a few bites, which only increased my hunger. Each time I made a noise, I stopped and listened for a reaction that didn't come. So I left the chicken on the counter and stood next to the open bedroom door. I heard it then: the high rasp of labored, wet breaths. She was just as I had left her, tied at the ankles, wrists behind her, large mouth open in her sleep. There was a strong smell of urine — a dark spot had spread on the sheets. The last rays of evening sun through the windows glimmered on the curve of her stomach and her eyelids where old mascara had run from the edges: She had been crying. She looked beautiful.

I ran warm water over a hand towel in the bathroom and began to clean her. She woke with a start, then saw it was me. "What time is it?" she croaked.

"You wet yourself."

"My wrists hurt."

"Hold on."

I finished cleaning her and took off my pants. The smell was still strong, but what I saw and what I smelled came together and filled me with desire. I entered her slowly. She was dry at first, but soon wasn't, though at one point she shifted beneath me and repeated, "My wrists hurt."

Afterward, I cleaned her again and untied the rope. Her hands were purple when she took them out from behind her and started rubbing them. I kissed them before she went to the bathroom.

When she finished her shower, she dressed and ate the rest of the chicken, then watched me as I sat listening to the radio. "What time is it?"

"It's almost five."

"*Five?*" She sat in the chair. "What the hell were you doing all this time?"

"I had some work to do."

She looked at the floor. "I thought you weren't coming back."

"Did you call out for help?"

"I would have once it got dark."

"I'm glad I didn't leave you that long."

She got up and turned off the radio. "You're a real bastard."

"What?"

"You heard me."

She went into the bedroom and closed the door.

I waited a while before following. It says something about me that I could not understand. I could not see that I'd done anything wrong that day.

She was sitting on a dry corner of the bed, crying. She had opened the window to air it out; the room was becoming cold. I stood over her and watched her shoulders tremble. If she had been Magda, I would have embraced her. But she wasn't.

"I can't believe this," she said through her sobs.

"What?"

"Myself." She uncovered her swollen eyes and looked at my knees. "I can't believe what I've done to myself."

"You didn't do it. I tied you up."

"I feel so humiliated."

I touched her shoulder then, and she shrugged me off.

"You know," she said very quietly, so that I had to lean closer to hear, "my mother always said to me: *Vera, you're just like your father. You never know how good you have it.*"

I followed her into the living room, where she found her purse and the small bag with her change of clothes. "Let's talk about this," I said halfheartedly.

"I can't."

I opened the door for her. "Where are you going?"

"My sister's." She stopped and looked up at me, as if deciding whether or not to kiss me. She decided against it.

# 74

I changed the sheets and closed the window, then made myself a drink. I browsed my old book, finding the passage that Emil had been affected by. But it did not affect me. My own writing bored me.

I still could not see what I'd done. I knew I should, but the fact that I couldn't did not trouble me. Every feeling was beyond my reach. I had given in to the recklessness that Vera claimed was all she had left, but the problem with recklessness is that there are other people in the world. They lie in the path of your recklessness, and you inevitably run them down. I understood this later. But on the sofa, gazing into the murkiness of my empty wineglass, I only understood that I had continued a game that Vera had started — a game she had first learned in Switzerland; and as for Malik, I had shown him the inevitable result of his own recklessness.

Once I was drunk I settled deeper into the sofa, closed my eyes, and tried to think over the case. Antonín Kullmann had used the state security apparatus to get rid of Nestor Velcea, then stole his paintings. Zoia became aware of the scheme and left Antonín in disgust. Yes — and Josef Maneck was caught between turning Antonín in and keeping his own prestige. The tension had turned him into an alcoholic.

Nestor, when he was arrested, had been waiting for a foreigner in a train station: Louis Rostek. Louis tried in vain to get him out. Then, years later, he figured out what had happened. So he went to the camp and told Nestor, then returned again after the Amnesty, when he told me of that most glorious of human desires: revenge.

And tomorrow Louis would return.

My first impulse was to call Emil, but there was a possibility of gunplay, and I didn't want him hurt.

"Hello?"

"It's me, Leon."

"Oh. Hello, Ferenc."

"Look, I need your help tomorrow morning. Can you meet me at the central train station at ten?"

"What is it?"

"We're going to get Nestor."

He paused. "Ten o'clock?"

"Don't be late."

# 75

Around one in the morning, I drove over the Georgian Bridge and parked in the Canal District. There were no lamps, so I had to feel my way, unsure, through the narrow alleys. I kept stepping in puddles, but pressed on. I had woken with a head cleared by a wave of remorse. For Vera, first of all. I had gone too far — this was now apparent. It may have begun as her game, but I had changed the rules and turned a simple enjoyment into torture. Then I remembered Malik Woznica, stuck in his hole. I had no remorse for him — just remembering Svetla justified anything I could do to him — but again, I knew that this was going too far. It could only end in prison. After what I'd put him through already, he wouldn't risk turning me in. I had proven that I could track him down, even in the mountains, and end his life.

Halfway there I started to worry about how to get him out. He was heavy, and the well was deep. I had brought along the knotted rope that still smelled of Vera's urine. He could tie it around himself, but I wasn't sure I had the strength to pull him out on my own.

Like Vera, he wasn't calling for help. No doubt he'd tried earlier in the day, moaning through his underwear, but no one in the Canal District came to anyone's rescue. My eyes had adjusted over the long walk, and stars shone through the shattered ceiling on the mosaic. "Malik," I said as I approached the well. "Malik Woznica, it's time to go home."

The well was too dark to see into.

"Malik? You there?"

I lit a match and saw Malik Woznica's bound head tilted back, his dead eyes staring up at me. The match slipped and fell onto his shoulder, where it glowed brightly before going out.

My first scattered instinct was to get rid of the body. I uncoiled the rope and ran it down into the darkness before realizing that this wouldn't work. I sank my hand down into the well, but fell just short of his head. Then I tried to see all of my options, but it was hard to see anything with a dead body beneath me. I went out to the square and sat on a step. My knees were shaking, so I walked.

A heart attack made sense. That or suffocation — if his nose stopped up, it was the end of him. But that possibility had never occurred to me as I was tying him up and shoving him into that black hole. I pulled my rings off and slipped them back on, one at a time. That other Ferenc — reckless and sure — had been unable to see the simple consequences of his actions. But now I was back.

I had killed a man.

I could not move the body, and so I would leave it. That seemed the only option. When found, it could be another murder to add to Nestor's tally. But this one did not fit. A victim outside the group of art friends, one already known to the Militia. One that could be traced — by Sev and Kaminski, or anyone — back to me.

I returned and looked for something that could help me, but the place had been cleaned out years ago by vagrants. I lit another match. He was naked except his shirt, its collar loose and high around his ears. I climbed on the lip of the well, lying across it and bracing myself with my waist and my head. I reached down. My fingers groped, just reaching the hair, the top of the ear, then the shirt. I had to tilt my head to grip it fully, then use my neck, straining, to tug him up a little. My veins were ready to burst. He stuck to the walls, then slid up a bit. I grunted, rolled, my rising shoulder pulling him farther. It took a lot of sweat, but finally I had his upper half folded over the lip of the well. I gasped at him in the darkness.

Burning came to mind, but there would be smoke — Nestor had been lucky when he burned Antonín. And the canals weren't deep enough to cover him for long.

I collected the rest of his torn jacket, his pants, and shoes, and lifted him over my shoulder, covering him with his trench coat. Then I started for the car. A smaller man couldn't have pulled it off, and I almost didn't make it. I stumbled through puddles, tripped over loose stones, and dropped him twice, his body making a wet thud when it hit the ground. The sky was still black when I folded him back into the trunk.

Once his car was found up in the mountains, they would search the area for his body. So I drove southeast, where the forests near the Soviet border would be out of their reach. The woods were thick there, and the roads empty. The sun had begun to turn the night a bluish gray. A dirt road turned off to the left, and at the end of it were the ruins of an old dacha that had burned to the ground. I carried Malik Woznica deeper into the forest, using my free hand to push aside thorns and vines. Finally, I looked back. I was out of sight of the ruins. I dropped Malik and his extra clothes on the dry leaves, covered him ineptly with a few more, and stumbled back to the car.

# 76

I arrived at the train station at nine-thirty as the rain began. It was a strange bit of luck that no one had seen me when I returned home. I had only had time to wash in the sink and change out of my clothes, which I put into a small trash bag. I then drove to the outskirts of town, where I added stones and dropped the bag into the Tisa. It sank quickly.

The station was busy enough — the regular throng of weekend travelers going to and from the Capital or stopping along other journeys, farmers and clerks alongside one another. I had a brandy in the bar, waved away a Gypsy muttering about all the children she had to feed, then returned to the main hall. A woman's voice over speakers told me that the ten-twenty from Vienna, headed to platform six, would be fifteen minutes late. She repeated the announcement in Russian.

I looked at my empty glass.

At exactly ten, Leonek arrived, hunched and dark, almost a Gypsy himself. He crept over with a nod.

"You look like hell. What happened to your hand?"

It was covered in thorn scratches. I stuffed it into my pocket. I smelled like hell, too.

"So you going to tell me?"

I nodded at the arrivals board. "The ten-twenty from Vienna. It's late."

"Who are we waiting for?"

"A Frenchman. I don't want to stop him. I want to see where he goes."

"Where's Emil?"

"At home with his wife, where he should be."

Leonek looked up at the arrivals board to avoid showing me his expression. Then he looked back. "Do you want to talk about it?"

"I've told you. A Frenchman. The ten-twenty."

"Not that."

He seemed to want to discuss it. But I didn't think I could converse right now, and I saw no need to help calm his guilt. "Let's wait over by the bar."

We leaned on the counter, looking through a window over the platforms and drinking slowly. He said, "I learned something very interesting."

"Did you." I looked past him at families chatting about times and places and people.

"I finally made it through that interview. Had to use a Russian dictionary for half the words."

"Should've had someone translate it for you."

"I'm stubborn."

"I guess you are."

He looked at his coffee. "Turns out this Boris Olonov knew quite a lot. He told Kliment the names of two of the other three soldiers who killed the girls."

"What about the third?"

"Wouldn't give it up. But more importantly, he knew about Sergei's murder, because there was a witness to it."

"Someone saw Sergei killed? How did he know about that?"

"Because another soldier knew the witness," he said. "Now ask me his name."

"The soldier's?"

"No, the witness's."

"Okay. What's the witness's name?"

Leonek smiled. "Nestor Velcea."

"Nestor —" I began, but stopped. "That's impossible. Isn't it?"

"I didn't make it up."

I reached for my drink, but it was empty. I couldn't believe the coincidence. It couldn't have been a coincidence — that was obvious. But I couldn't see anything clearly yet. "So what's the connection?"

"I've told you all I know."

"Nestor witnesses Sergei's murder," I said, thinking it through slowly. "And soon after goes to a work camp." But I couldn't follow the thought through because it was time for us to meet the train.

# 77

It crawled to us and stopped, its brakes gasping. The rain had given its hull a bright sheen, washing away a little of the dirt. The doors opened and spilled passengers onto the platform. We each took a side of the crowd, watching faces under newspapers held like umbrellas. As the crowd thinned, I saw Louis holding a small, beaten suitcase. I motioned toward him, and Leonek nodded.

Leonek retreated to the other side of the engine as I sat on a bench that faced the opposite direction. I wanted to hide my height. Then I leaned forward as if to tie my laces and looked back between my legs. His feet shuffled past. Ten seconds more. Then I stood slowly and turned around. His back disappeared into the main hall, followed by Leonek's.

I tossed Leonek my keys and waited by the front door. As he started my car and swung around to get me, Louis climbed into a taxi.

We followed it south. Leonek had to speed up suddenly at some corners, nearly running down irate pedestrians, and below the passenger's seat I pressed my foot into the imaginary brake. "Turn on the wipers."

"Rain's not so bad."

"Turn them on."

The streets narrowed, and the taxi stopped at the Hotel Metropol. Louis went inside.

I said, "Let's give him a minute to get to his room."

Leonek parked across the street, and we checked our pistols for cartridges.

The lobby's low ceiling gave the white room a feeling of immense breadth. The men lounging on the upholstered chairs with issues of *The Spark* didn't seem to notice us, but I still wondered how many of them were state security men — this was a hotel that housed foreigners, after all — and if they knew anything about Louis. The clerk was a young man who set his fingertips on the counter when he spoke; "Good evening, comrades! Two rooms or one?"

"We're looking for one of your guests."

I showed him my certificate, and that made him more eager. "Well of course, Comrade Inspectors. Do you have a name?"

On a hunch, I tried Nestor Velcea first.

He went through a ledger, tapping his

fingers happily on the page, but found no Velcea.

"I'm sorry, comrades. Perhaps," he said, then lowered his voice. "Perhaps an *alias?*"

Leonek looked at me, but I shook my head, "Maybe you've seen him. About this tall." I held my hand at shoulder-height. "Blond hair. Missing a finger on his left hand."

"A *finger* missing? Oh, that's good. But no, no one like that."

I leaned on the counter. "All right. Let's have Louis Rostek, then."

# 78

I knocked, and Leonek waited beside the door, so that he could not be seen through the viewhole. I knocked again and waited. The light in the viewhole darkened a moment, then brightened. I knocked and said, "Louis? This is Ferenc. Georgi's friend. Maybe you don't remember me —"

A crash came from inside the room. I pounded with a fist.

"Louis? You all right in there?"

Something fell to the floor; Louis groaned.

I threw my shoulder into the door, and the second time it popped open. The room was empty. I ran to the bathroom and found Louis climbing to his feet. The window was broken. I helped him up. "What are you breaking things for, Louis?"

His face was deep red, and the fear popped into his eyes when he saw Leonek over my shoulder. "Oh God, Ferenc. Oh God."

I put a hand on his shoulder. "Calm down. Nothing to worry about."

He shook his sweat-damp hands and came with me back into the main room. Leonek was trying to latch the broken door shut, but couldn't, so he leaned against it. I set Louis on the bed.

"What do you think I'm here for? To kill you?"

Louis looked up at me, his big eyes shivering in their sockets. "Well . . . what *are* you here for?"

I sat and put my arm around him; he flinched. "Well I'm certainly not here to kill you. Where would you get an idea like that?"

He looked at Leonek, then at me, the terror just beginning to subside. "Nothing."

"You're on the fourth floor," said Leonek. "You would've broken your neck out there."

Louis looked at the open bathroom door,

then shook his head and, unexpectedly, laughed. "You're right about that one. I'm not cut out for this."

"Is there a bar in here?" I asked, and Louis nodded at a cabinet. I poured him a vodka. He took it quickly, so I poured him another. "Better now?"

Louis nodded. "You were the last person I expected to see on the other side of that door, Ferenc. How's the writing coming?"

"We'll talk about that later. First, let's talk about our mutual friend."

"Georgi?"

"Nestor."

He made a valiant attempt to hold my gaze, but the color rushed back into his glistening cheeks as he dropped his eyes to the bedsheets. "I don't know who that is, Ferenc."

"Sure you do, Louis. He's why you've come back here, isn't he?"

Louis shrugged. "Nah. I've got to go to some Union meeting. International cooperation and all that." But he was still staring at the sheets.

"Let me tell you a story," I said.

Louis finally looked up, but at Leonek. He nodded in my direction. "*Writers.* Always a story."

Leonek nodded a polite agreement.

449

I got up and poured myself a vodka. "In this story, there is a brilliant painter. He's ahead of his time, way ahead of his time. But no one knows this, because he's also an eccentric. He doesn't show his paintings to anyone, he doesn't even sign the paintings. He's *that* eccentric. Well, he is sent to a work camp. Happens to a lot of people. But after a while another painter — an untalented painter who can't make any headway on his own — comes up with a brilliant idea. He takes those paintings, signs his own name, and gladly shows them off. He's not so eccentric, just a little unethical. And this works. It works so well that his shows even travel into Western Europe — to Paris, even."

"Paris?" said Louis, his fingers tapping his glass uncontrollably.

"This is bad luck for the unethical artist, because a very close friend of the jailed painter lives in Paris. He recognizes the work, and quickly deduces what happened. He decides that this artist sent his friend to the work camp, then stole his paintings. So what does he do?"

I watched Louis chew the inside of his mouth. But he did not speak.

"He returns here and goes to the work camp. He's such a good friend that he even risks himself by bribing the camp commander to have a word with his friend. And there he tells his friend the story of his incarceration. Because, like anyone, this Parisian wants justice for his friend. And not only that, he wants to nurture the most glorious of human desires: revenge."

Louis squeezed his eyes shut, as if they hurt. He remembered telling me this, and hated himself for the slip.

"Once the painter was amnestied from the work camp, the Parisian returned to the Capital to see him — that, by the way, is when I met the Parisian. I imagine he gave his friend the address of the art curator who had shown the stolen paintings — Josef Maneck."

"No," said Louis, shaking his head. "I gave him nothing."

"Okay," I said. "But either way, the artist began killing. Before killing the art curator, he got the address of the unethical artist out of him. Then he tracked down the unethical artist and tortured him. He broke his bones and dragged him into the Canal District, where he set the man on fire."

Louis looked up at me.

"Then he killed the artist's ex-wife, who had nothing to do with the crime in the first place."

He blinked at his hands, which were

scratching his knees through the pants. He didn't seem to know about Zoia.

I sat on the bed again. "The Parisian's heart was in the right place, at least generally so, but mistakes were made. The ex-wife, for one. She actually left Antonín Kullmann in disgust when she realized what had happened. And I'm not entirely convinced the curator knew about it at the beginning. I think he found out later, and the guilt turned him into an alcoholic — Antonín supported him to keep him quiet. But that's the least of the Parisian's mistakes. The biggest one is that, while Antonín Kullmann stole those paintings, he did not turn in Nestor Velcea. Someone else did."

"What?" That was Leonek's low voice by the door.

Louis stared at me, baffled. "That's not true! It's obvious."

"It seems obvious," I said. "I believed it, too. But before Nestor was sent away he witnessed the murder of a militiaman in 1946. And that's a much more plausible reason to send someone to a work camp — to keep them quiet. The man who put Nestor away killed my partner a week and a half ago, and I think he tried to kill Nestor as well."

"W-who?" said Louis.

"I don't know." I nodded at Leonek.

"It's the same person who killed Sergei Malevich, ten years ago. That person didn't care about art, he only cared that Nestor Velcea had witnessed him shooting a militiaman on the banks of the Tisa. And as for Antonín, he was an untalented painter left with an apartment full of his roommate's brilliant paintings. He only took advantage of another man's tragedy."

I let that settle in while I poured vodkas. I gave one to Leonek, who, red-faced, nodded at me. He was trying to comprehend what I had only begun to put together myself. The second vodka I gave to Louis. He took it without looking at me at all. The third I drank, feeling the burn slide down into my stomach. I was sure now of all I had said — it felt right. The act of speaking is like the act of writing; it makes ideas real. But only Nestor knew who had killed Sergei and Stefan.

"So, again," I said. "Why have you returned to our country?"

Louis set his drink on the floor unfinished and mumbled something.

"What?"

"I brought Nestor's papers. To get him out."

"To France?"

He nodded.

"What did he tell you?"

"Just that he needed papers. It was a telegram."

"And when are you meeting him?"

He looked at Leonek at the door, then at his hands.

"Come on, Louis. We're the only ones who can keep him alive."

"But you'll put him in jail, won't you?"

"I don't know yet what we'll do."

Louis finally looked at me. "Day after tomorrow. Tuesday."

# 79

It gave us forty-eight hours to watch Louis. Leonek took the first shift. He paid for another room one floor up and took Louis to it. The hotel staff would notice the broken door and window, but there would be no one left in that room to blame.

Before I left, Leonek pulled me aside, and whispered, "Let's keep this between us for now."

"We could call in Emil."

"I trust him to be quiet, but he won't keep it from Lena, and she doesn't know how to keep her mouth shut. Then Brano Sev will know. Wasn't he the one with Nestor's file?"

I thought about that, but admitted that, despite everything, I still found it hard to believe that Brano Sev would kill Stefan.

"Believe it. That man has no friends."

This was true. "But I also haven't noticed any bullet wounds on him. Have you?"

Leonek shook his head. "Brano Sev is a machine."

And I'd been wrong about plenty of things already.

At home I sat beside the radio set and considered giving Vera a call. The apartment was lonely without even her bleak company. But she hated me now.

So I drank in the empty apartment and wondered what Malik Woznica's body looked like now, if it was covered or if the wind had blown the leaves off of him, exposing him to the elements. I closed my eyes.

The sound of the ringing telephone made me reach, instinctively, for my pistol. But I'd left it in the bedroom. I walked into the kitchen and picked up the receiver.

"Yes?"

"Ferenc?" My legs tingled. She was crying.

"What is it? What's wrong?"

"What happened to Leonek?"

"Nothing. Why?"

455

"I tried to call him all day."

"He's fine. He's working."

"I have to speak with him."

"I'm not going to be your liaison, Magda."

"You don't understand."

"What don't I understand?"

"I was calling him to end it. I can't believe what I've done to you."

I let that hang between us.

"Ferenc?"

"I'm here."

"Can you . . ."

"Can I what?"

"Can you forgive me?"

I hadn't thought of that before. There had been no reason to. All I'd known was that my wife was leaving me, and that there was no decision to make. I could either accept it or go crazy. "I don't know what to say."

"You're right. We can talk about it later."

"Where are you calling from?"

"Dad has a key to the cooperative office."

"Oh."

"Goddamn."

"What?"

"Do you have a number where I can reach him?"

"I'll get him to call you. How about that?"

"Thank you." Then she started to cry again.

I wondered afterward if it had been a dream. Almost two in the morning — it seemed impossible that this had just happened. There was no evidence, except the sweat on my palm.

# 80

I showed up at ten the next morning under a clear sky, and as Leonek left I told him to call Magda. He stopped at the door. "Magda? You want me to call her?"

"She's been trying to get in touch with you. I'll give you the number she's at."

He held up a hand. "I've got it. See you at noon tomorrow."

I had brought coffee and rolls, and as we ate, Louis said he would write an epic poem about this. "It's quite a story, isn't it? I mean, are the paintings any more or less valuable because they've got the wrong signature on them? I wonder what the galleries in Paris would say."

He was talking again the way I remembered him. "Does it matter, Louis?"

"Sure it matters." He brushed crumbs off his shirt. "Though Antonín didn't send

Nestor to the camp for his paintings, he could have. So is a painting as valuable as a man's life? For that matter, is anything as valuable as a man's life? Or is everything that valuable?"

I wasn't in the mood to listen to this. It made me wonder what was equal to Malik Woznica's life, and I didn't want to think about that.

"What do you say, Ferenc?"

"I don't say anything."

Louis grunted. "You were more engaging at Georgi's party. Maybe we need to get you drunk."

"Did you know Georgi was interrogated at Yalta Boulevard?"

Louis's smile faded, and he gave a sharp nod. "I heard."

"What if he didn't come back? Would you still be asking if a painting was as valuable as a man's life?"

Louis patted the air. "Point taken. No more, okay?"

I finished my coffee.

"Tell me about those, then." He nodded at my hand. "You never told me about those rings before. It's a lot for any one man."

I flexed my fingers. "They're from the war."

"Most people get medals."

"Well," I said, then touched the one on my left index finger. "This one belonged to Friedrich Schultz, captain second-class. He was born in Hamburg in 1915. I killed him on 28 April 1939."

Louis leaned back. "You — *all* of them are from Germans you've killed?"

I nodded at my hand, touching Hans Lieblich, Franz Müller and Heinrich Oldenburg. "Except this," I said, and touched my wedding band, which had its own story.

"Forgive me, Ferenc, but that's pretty morbid."

I crushed my coffee cup. "Sometimes I need the reminder that I won't live forever."

We shared the bed that night and I lay on my back, hands on my chest, staring at the ceiling. I wanted to be home in case she called again. I wanted to hear her voice. I was sick of this world of men who loved revenge and other men's wives. I didn't want to puzzle through bloodstained walls or the shallowness of love. But it strikes me now that that is the only world there is, and all I wanted to do was lie and dream.

In the morning, I called the front desk

for more coffee, and as we drank it I said to him, "You were an informer, weren't you?"

He looked up from his cup. "What?"

"After the war, when you came here. You informed on your friends."

"What makes you say that?"

"When you found out Nestor had been sent away, you went directly to Yalta Boulevard. Most people would go to the Militia office and file a complaint. But not you. You went to the heart of state security and demanded your friend be released. Georgi said you were tough, but you're smart, too. You wouldn't walk into Yalta Boulevard unless you thought you had some pull with the people inside."

"I," he began, then set his coffee on the bedside table. "I knew they wouldn't do anything to a French citizen."

I shook my head. "A lot of spies were being arrested back then, a lot of foreigners. And I've never heard of a foreigner, other than a Russian, being allowed in there. No. You knew someone at Yalta, and thought that because of your services you could get your friend out. He wasn't political, after all, and you thought they would trust you. So you went directly to the Office of Internal Corrections. But you

460

were wrong. They wouldn't even see you, would they?"

Louis got up and took his tie from a door handle. He put it around his neck and began to knot it. "They made me wait in the front room for two hours. I left them my name, and periodically went to the desk to ask what was going on, but they told me nothing. I had to give up."

"Who were you going to see?"

"Just the office. I only knew the field operatives I'd meet in the parks around town. I'd never been in Yalta Boulevard before."

I looked out the window to the busy street. "And when Nestor was picked up, he was waiting in the train station to meet you."

"But I didn't show up," he said, fixing his tie in the mirror. "I couldn't get past Hungary."

"You told Yalta Boulevard that you were coming. They knew, didn't they?"

He left his tie alone and turned to me. "Yes."

"And when you came back last September you talked to them once more. You gave them a description of Nestor for their files, and used the code name 'Napoleon.'"

He looked at me, his mouth chewing air, and I felt close to something big. The

Office of Internal Corrections had stalled Louis when he came to plead for Nestor a decade ago. It was the one office that knew when he would come to meet Nestor in the train station, and it also had the power to stop Louis at the Hungarian border. I picked up the phone and dialed.

"Yes?"

"It's me, Leonek."

"Oh," he said. Then: "I talked to Magda."

"What did she want?"

"You know damn well what she wanted."

"We'll talk about it later. Before you come over here, try and get hold of some files — Brano's and Kaminski's. They should be over at the Central Committee."

"Kaminski?"

"He's been out sick," I said, but didn't elaborate on my suspicions.

He arrived early, while Louis was in the bathroom. He hadn't gotten any sleep, and it showed in his red-rimmed eyes and slack mouth as he handed over the file. He seemed to be laboring over the words before they came out: "I'm still shaken up about this."

"The files?"

"No."

I took out two cigarettes and offered him one. He shook his head.

"I don't know exactly what to say."

I took the files to the bed and settled down. "There's nothing to say."

His eyes were focused on nothing in particular. "Maybe not. I wasn't lying before. I love her. I love them both. I always will. But if she's made her decision, then it's done."

"I'm glad you understand."

"Can I have that cigarette?"

I lit it for him.

Because of the nature of their work, both men's files were minimal: Yalta Boulevard would store the details of their own men. These files contained a brief biography, photos, associations, and a page that listed assignments. Brano's assignment had been our own Militia office for the last decade, but Kaminski's listings gave me pause: Chief of the Office of Internal Corrections of the Ministry for State Security, March 1946 to December 1948.

So Brano Sev was not our man after all.

"Are you going to take her back?"

I closed the file. "I don't think that's your business."

"You're right," he said, nodding. "Just be good to her."

"I've always been good to her. And I've always been good for her."

As he took his cigarette into the hall, too distracted to ask about the files, it occurred to me that, despite what he said, Leonek was still hopeful. Magda had shown she could change her mind. She had chosen me years ago, then she chose Leonek. She had probably, in our bed, told him she would leave me for him. And now she was choosing me again. Neither he nor I knew which decisions were final, or if any would be, ever.

# 81

I waited inside the café window, while Leonek walked a few paces behind Louis into the October Square market, where round peasant women sold wormy apples and soft potatoes. Along the edge, the Romanians Ágnes disapproved of stood in a semicircle playing fiddles. A couple uniformed Militia watched them a moment, then checked their papers. In the center of the crowd, Louis rose on his toes to see over heads.

"You going to just stand there?"

"Yeah, Corina. I'll just stand here for now."

She went back to the tables, and I watched the militiamen give the Romanians their papers back and move on, out of the square.

He arrived at five minutes after noon.

Like the gum-chewing teenager had said, he was short, but not a real shorty. He limped through the crowd from the east side of the square, pausing for women to pass, taking his time. I could only see his head and sometimes a shoulder. Blond hair and a gaunt face. Cheekbones sharp and clear and white, eyes set deep into his skull. He noticed Louis, but didn't alter his slow, steady pace. Louis's face lit up in one of his bright smiles as he pushed through bodies to get to Nestor.

Leonek remained a couple people back, glancing in their direction only casually, and I stood at the window with my face half-exposed.

"Sure you don't want a coffee?"

I didn't look at her. "Give me a few minutes, will you?"

"Whatever you say."

They talked a moment, and Louis motioned to the café. I slid farther out of sight as Nestor turned in my direction and considered it. Then he shrugged and limped forward. Leonek kept close behind them. Then Nestor stopped. So did Louis and Leonek. He turned and said something to

Louis, and Louis's face melted, his lips opening and shutting rapidly. Nestor turned back then, quickly, and used his hands to part the crowd. But Leonek caught his arm and stuck a pistol into his ribs. All three turned back to the café. I waved to Corina and pointed at an empty booth. "Four coffees."

He did not struggle. I noticed this immediately, but I didn't know what it meant, if anything. I sat at the booth and watched them enter, Leonek still gripping Nestor's arm. Louis's face looked like pain as he whispered into Nestor's ear. I only heard a little of it once they were at the table: ". . . *the only way . . . no choice . . . just listen . . .*"

Louis sat beside me and Nestor across from me, Leonek beside him. "Hello, Nestor," I said.

His thin face moved beneath the surface, his jaw shifting. "Good afternoon, Ferenc." His voice was high but coarse, as if his throat had been put through a lot.

"Nestor, please give Leonek your gun."

He kept his eyes on me as he pulled it out of the inside of his jacket and passed it beneath the table.

Corina arrived with our coffees and looked significantly at me before walking away.

"Tell me about Stefan."

Nestor frowned. "Here?"

"Yes. Then we'll go somewhere else. Right now, Stefan."

The other customers didn't notice us. They smoked and ate and talked loudly with one another. When Nestor lifted his trembling cup to his mouth, I saw the missing finger — just a pink stump. "I didn't do it," he said.

"Tell me what happened."

He set the cup down. "I went to see him. To turn myself in."

"What?" said Leonek.

"Let him," I said.

Nestor looked at Leonek, then at me. "Stefan didn't believe me at first either. He kept his gun on me, and we talked. I told him why I had killed Josef and Antonín and Zoia. The paintings, and —" He frowned at his missing finger. "And my time in the camp." He looked at Louis. Nestor couldn't hold his gaze still. "He was all right, that militiaman. After a while he made some fish soup; he knew I was hungry. He kept his gun with him, but we talked and ate, and he asked why I was turning myself in."

"What was your answer?" I asked.

He turned to me again. "Because it was

467

done. I had killed them, and I didn't care anymore what happened to me. But then he arrived."

"Kaminski," I said.

"Kaminski?" That was Leonek.

Nestor blinked a few times, then nodded. "Stefan asked who it was, and that's when I learned his name. I didn't know it before. Stefan told me to wait in the kitchen, so I did. Kaminski asked Stefan about me. He wanted to know if Stefan had found me yet, and that when he did he should give me to him. To Kaminski. But as I was listening to his voice, it sounded familiar. I hadn't seen him yet, so all I had was the voice. I stuck my head around the doorway. It was so stupid of me."

"He saw you," I said.

"And I saw him. And I recognized him right away. When you see a man commit murder, his face never leaves you. It was the same face I'd seen in that crowd of four Russians who were talking with those little Jewish girls. The same one who killed that other militiaman, Sergei Malevich. And I knew it then: Antonín hadn't sent me to the work camps after all. I knew it immediately."

"You're right."

Nestor nodded. "Kaminski recognized me,

too, and he was quick. Stefan was taking out his gun, but Kaminski turned and shot him twice. So fast. But quiet, with that silencer."

"But you had a gun too."

"I'd taped it to the small of my back; I didn't know if I could trust this Stefan. I shot Kaminski in the shoulder. But he jumped back into the corridor before I could get him again."

Leonek gaped, "So it's true."

Nestor nodded at him, but his face was pale and unwell. "It's true."

"And you got out through the window," I said.

"I thought he would be waiting at the front door."

"He probably was. Did you come to my apartment a few days later?"

"But the woman wouldn't let me in. Your wife?"

I waved to Corina for the bill.

Louis finally spoke. "Nestor. Good god-*damn. Nestor.*"

# 82

Leonek and I walked on either side of Nestor, holding his arms. We left October Square by the north road and climbed into my car, Louis and I up front. I had to stop continuously in the traffic and honked when a broken-down Moskvich blocked my way, the men pushing against the spare tire on the back shouting at me for patience. It took a half hour to make it to the Ninth District, and the whole way I tried to decide what I was going to do.

The first thing, of course, was the interrogation.

We climbed to my apartment, and I got a bottle of brandy and four glasses and filled them and handed them out. Louis's brandy shook when he brought it to his mouth, but Nestor, settling into the sofa, had calmed. He had the ability to accept his situation and wait for his opportunities — learned, no doubt, from a decade in the work camps.

Leonek put his glass down. "All right, Nestor. I want to know what happened to Sergei Malevich."

Nestor took a deep breath that stretched his thin cheeks, then he exhaled and began. "Sergei Malevich had talked to a friend of mine, Osip Yarmoluk. He was a good guy, a Russian soldier who'd had enough of things. I'd known him ever since they marched in. Did you know he was killed, too?"

Leonek looked at me. I shook my head. "We've never heard of him."

"Well, he was the only one I'd told about the four soldiers taking those little girls into the synagogue. There were a couple other witnesses, but they kept quiet. I can't blame them, particularly after all that's happened to me."

"But you saw it?" asked Leonek.

"I saw enough. They took the girls in there, and I heard them scream. I tried to find some help, but everyone was too frightened. I was, too, or else I would have gone into that synagogue. I told all this to Osip. He knew some of these men. He thought I should go to the Militia about it. But I wasn't sure. I mean, I didn't know who I could trust and who I couldn't. Finally, this Malevich guy started asking questions. He didn't get anything until he finally came across Osip. Osip told him about me, and he set up a meeting that same night. At the Tisa. Jesus," he said, shaking his head. "With that fog, I knew something had to go wrong."

"So you showed up," said Leonek.

"I showed up, all right. And I found him. He was on the bank, waiting. But Osip had never really described what he looked like. He'd only told Sergei what *I* looked like.

471

So I came closer, to let him get a look at me, and Sergei did see me. He started to step forward, then a man's voice called his name. I could tell this was unexpected because he quickly stepped back into the fog and looked away from me. It was thoughtful of him. The last act of his life was to save mine."

Leonek leaned back, hands on his knees, and nodded. "And you saw what happened afterward."

"I had no choice," he said. "I was afraid that if I started walking, this second guy would hear my footsteps. And I didn't know anything about him. So I stood a little bit away, not moving, and watched a tall man — Kaminski — come over and start talking with Sergei."

"What did they say?"

"I don't know. It was all in Russian. I know some now, but back then I didn't know any. Kaminski was very calm, it seemed to me. And at first Sergei was calm, too, but then he wasn't. Because Kaminski had a gun on him. He must have told Sergei to lie on the ground, because that's what he did. He lay facedown, and not once did he look in my direction. Then Kaminski squatted and shot him in the back of the head."

I remembered it myself. The thick fog and the sound of the gunshot echoing off the water.

"When the Russian heard more footsteps, he stood up. That's when I recognized him, from the Jewish quarter. Then he pocketed the gun and ran off. I did, too."

Leonek was flexing his hands in his lap, staring. He looked at me. We were both remembering the running footsteps that echoed back at us as we stood over Sergei's dead body, immobile.

"My mistake was that I told Osip about it. He didn't turn me in, nothing like that. But somebody must have suspected he knew something — he was dead a week later. I didn't know if they knew about me or not, so I kept myself hidden just in case."

I said, "You stayed in your apartment with Antonín and Zoia."

"They were the only ones who knew where I was, so it only made sense that they had turned me in."

"They weren't the only ones," I said. "Louis knew."

Louis was pouring himself a second shot, and at the sound of his name spilled some on the table. He started shaking his head vigorously. "No. That's not it. That's not how it was at all."

Nestor stared at Louis.

I said, "Louis didn't turn you in on purpose. But whenever he came into town he notified the Office of Internal Corrections. He also told the office who he was going to meet. But Louis couldn't know that the man who killed those girls and Sergei not only ran this office, but had also probably learned Nestor's name by beating it out of Osip Yarmoluk before killing him. With all this information, Kaminski didn't have to track Nestor down at all. Didn't have to kill him. All he had to do was plant a couple anonymous accusations against him, then connect him with a foreigner coming into town. That's all that was needed."

"But I didn't show up!" said Louis. "They had nothing on him!"

Nestor, sunk deep into the sofa, arms crossed over his chest, stared at Louis. "Accusations were enough back then."

Louis's face was red and damp. "You don't understand! I tried to get him out. I *tried.*"

"You did," I said, then turned to Nestor. "He's not lying. He went straight to Yalta Boulevard, to Kaminski's office, when he

474

found out. Kaminski didn't even open his door."

Nestor said to Louis, "But why would you tell them anything in the first place?"

Louis chewed air, eyes rolling as he tried to find the right words.

"He was an informer," I said. "It was his job to tell them when he was in the country. All for the glories of world revolution."

Nestor stood up and went to the bathroom. Leonek stood too, as if to follow, then settled back down. He looked at me and shook his head. *"Christ."*

# 83

There was a knock at the door. I pulled out my gun and stood beside it. Leonek had his gun out as well, and Louis shrank into his chair, terrified.

"Ferenc?" It was a woman's voice. A high squeak.

I put my gun away and opened the door a little. Claudia peered up at me. "Hello, Claudia. I don't have a lot of time —"

"It's not that," she said, and glanced down the stairwell. "I just thought you should know. There was a man here last night."

"A man?"

She lowered her voice to a whisper. "A *Russian*. He knocked on your door, I could hear him from downstairs. *Loud*, that one. Loud."

"Do you know what he wanted?"

"How should I know? But he was calling your name. He said he knew you were in. Then he left."

"That's all he said?"

"That's it. You weren't there, were you?"

I shook my head.

"That's what I thought. I'd heard you go out earlier. But I wasn't about to open my door and tell him. I'm not that kind, you see." She smiled and patted my hand on the door to assure me of this.

"Thank you, Claudia. I appreciate it."

She tried in vain to peer past me into the apartment, then rocked back on her heels and shrugged. "We're neighbors, Ferenc. It's nothing."

After I'd heard her footsteps descend the steps and her door open and shut, I sat across from Louis. "Did you tell them about this trip?"

"Them?"

"Yalta Boulevard."

He shook his head. "I stopped that after my last visit. They've tried to get me back, but I haven't done anything for them since."

476

Leonek pocketed his pistol. "Louis checked into the Metropol, and the hotel sent in the daily registration report. Of course they know he's in town."

I walked over to the radio set. "And when Kaminski went to Louis's room, the lock was broken and the room was empty. But he didn't think to check for our names on the register." I looked at Leonek. "The three of us were very close to death in that hotel."

# 84

He had been in there a while, so I knocked on the bathroom door, then opened it. Nestor was on the edge of the tub, wiping his nose with the back of his hand. He looked old and exhausted. I came in and closed the door. "What is it?"

"Nothing." That's when I realized he'd been crying. He said, "It's just that I've ruined everything. I thought that when I got out of the camp I could make everything right. I would make some justice where there hadn't been any before. But look at what I've done."

I sat on the toilet and folded my hands on my knees. The bathroom was very white, and it hurt my eyes.

He said, "It was luck, at first. At least that's how I thought of it. I was in this stinking bar, wondering how I could get back at the people who had put me away for so long, and there was Josef Maneck. Like a gift from God. He was so drunk, I hardly recognized him. I'd met him before, and Louis had told me he was connected to all of it, so I waited outside for him. He'd gotten into a fight with another drunk, and was finally thrown out. So I helped him home. He had no idea who I was. He was just grateful I wasn't hitting him. I got him up to his place and made some coffee, and started to question him."

There was a knock at the door. Leonek looked in, saw the two of us sitting morosely in the white bathroom, and left again.

"Go on."

He rubbed his hands to keep them warm. "I didn't plan to kill him. I really wanted Antonín. But when I told him my name, he went wild. He hit me and tried to run out of the apartment. So I dragged him back. And made him tell me what he knew. He believed the same thing I did, that Antonín had sent me to the work camp in order to steal my paintings. He said he didn't know for a long time, until Zoia told him. He cried and apologized and finally gave me Antonín's address."

"You wrote it on Josef's notepad."

"I guess I did."

"Go on."

"Well, once I had what I'd come there for, I didn't leave. I couldn't leave. Something kept me there, kept me hammering at him. I wanted to know why, once he knew the truth, Josef hadn't gone to the Militia. He said he would have been implicated, because by that point he'd been showing the paintings for months. And he pointed at the apartment and said that it was what he'd been reduced to, because he couldn't take the guilt. But that wasn't enough for me, you understand? It was as if I were someone else for an hour. I wanted to take from him what had been taken from me. So I gave him one more punch that knocked him out and dragged him over to the oven and turned on the gas. Then I left."

I rubbed my own hands together. It seemed very cold in that bathroom, like the cold of the Canal District, and the cold that comes from an hour of being someone else, and looking back at what you've done. "Then you found Antonín."

"You saw the body. You know what I did. With him I was an entirely different person. I don't —" He shut his eyes. "I don't know how to explain it. By that point I had gone to the Canal District and bought a gun. I arrived at his apartment, and when he opened the door I held the gun on him. At first we talked. He admitted to stealing the paintings, but swore he had not turned me in to Yalta Boulevard. And for a moment I did believe him. He was so earnest. He offered to split everything he had with me, he said I deserved it, but he kept swearing he hadn't turned me in. But by then I'd already collected three opinions against him — Louis thought he had turned me in, and so did Josef and Zoia. So I was sure he was lying. Because he knew what I would do to him. But I don't think he could have imagined it — what I did to him." Nestor shifted on the edge of the tub. "Do you have a cigarette?"

I got two out. The bathroom quickly filled with smoke, but I didn't open the door.

"I don't know if you can understand what I did without having lived in the camps. Even having lived in the camps, I still can't believe what I did, but I at least understand it. The things that they do to

480

you, the power they have over you. It throws off your sense of right and wrong." He shook his head. "I can't explain it."

"Just tell me what you did. I'll see if I can understand."

He took another drag. "I gagged him, then tied his hands and feet together. Then I sat and talked to him for a while. I described my life in the camp, I told him how I'd lost my finger, how I'd gotten my limp, and the kinds of things I saw on a daily basis. I told him that what I'd do to him would not be as bad as all that. But I told him exactly what I would do to him. I said I would break his arms and legs with a hammer, drive him to the Canal District in his own car, and then drag him by his broken arms to a place where I would then set him on fire. And that's what I did."

I coughed into my hand. The sound reverberated in the small room. "Why did you tell him?"

"That's what they did in the camp. Sometimes they would tell you in the morning that they would kill you, and by the afternoon you'd be dead. They had ways to make even death worse."

"But you didn't put Zoia through all of that, did you?"

He shook his head. "I had pity on her. I

broke in over the weekend and waited in the basement for morning. I didn't want Mathew around. So after he left I came up behind her and strangled her. Josef had told me she left Antonín because of what he'd done. But still, she — like Josef — hadn't turned him in. *That* was what I could not accept. Why did they remain silent when I was stuck in hell for a decade?"

"Because they didn't want to join you," I said, and he squinted at me through the smoke.

"But I got it all wrong in the end," he said. "Antonín stole my art, but he couldn't have done that if this Russian hadn't gotten rid of me. It seems like human nature that if you give someone an opportunity for easy criminality, he'll take it. Kaminski gave Antonín the opportunity."

"Do you regret it?"

"What?"

"The murders."

His eyes wandered into the smoke, focusing on something I could not see. "Ferenc, all I know is that I've failed. I used to be a human being. But now, with what I've done, and the mistakes I've made, I don't know if I can call myself human anymore. That's why I tried to turn myself in. Because it no longer mattered what happened to me." He focused on my eyes then. "Do you understand what I'm saying?"

My cold hands froze and my feet tingled. "I know exactly what you're saying, Nestor."

# 85

*"Ferenc?"*

It was Emil calling. "What's going on?"

"Malik Woznica."

"What about him."

"He's gone missing."

I opened my mouth and, after a long exhale, said, "Maybe that's best for everyone."

"They've given me the case. He was supposed to visit a relative in Perechyn on Saturday, but didn't, and he didn't show up at the office yesterday. I've checked the apartment; it's empty."

"Any sign of a struggle?"

"None. His car is gone, but it doesn't look like clothes are missing."

"Maybe he was in a hurry."

"We did find a store of drugs. Opiates. Pills and liquids."

"All for his Svetla."

He paused. "Ferenc, you didn't . . ."

"Didn't what."

"I don't know. Did you threaten him?"

"He threatened me. But I never said a word to him."

"Okay. I just want to know why he'd leave."

"He left because he murdered his wife."

"What?"

"He followed her to Moscow and killed her. Kliment told me last week — Sev and Moska know about it, too. But that's all I know."

"Okay, Ferenc. Thanks. I'll let you know if I come up with anything."

When I hung up, I leaned against the wall and tried to measure out my breaths. It was difficult. The kitchen seemed to be underwater, and the icebox shivered, but that was because I was shivering. I made it out to the living room, where they were all sitting, looking up at me.

"You all right?" asked Leonek.

"Keep an eye on them. I need to lie down."

I got into bed with my shoes still on and pulled the blankets over me. But I couldn't get warm. I kept seeing Malik Woznica in that well, his bloated, dead eyes staring up at me. I had felt nothing then. I had been confused, yes. I had been worried. But I had felt no guilt. And there had been no guilt when I returned to Vera tied up in her own filth and watched her rush with all that self-hatred out my door. I hadn't known what I had done wrong.

I twisted the blankets tighter around my legs and tried to still myself. But I couldn't make the past go away any more than I could bring Malik back to life. I had killed him and brutalized a woman who loved me. And throughout it all, my feelings had remained just out of reach. I was an automaton.

Nestor had an excuse. He had struggled through a decade of terror and had come out the other side a machine of vengeance. I had been through so little in comparison, but I had acted the same. Both of us had watched our humanity slip away with a cool eye, and only after it returned could we understand what we had done.

I lay for an hour, stuck in the cycle of these thoughts. They repeated, and I turned each fact, each crime, around in my head, trying to find the justification. There was none, not even in the elegance of well-chosen words. I had always known what I was doing, and I knew that I would do it all over again.

Only after that hour, when I heard a tap at the door and saw Leonek's unsure face peek through — he looked so young, and so good — did I understand what I needed to do to begin to right what had been made wrong. It was the only mature decision left to me.

# 86

It was simple and complicated at the same time. If it went wrong, I would not see them again. Leonek wanted to go. "This part is my case. He killed Sergei."

I said, "Tell me. Do you still love Magda?"

He paused. "Yes. Yes, I do."

"And Ágnes?"

"I adore her, Ferenc."

"That's all I want to know."

I drove everyone to Emil's apartment. He answered the door, and though I had called to warn him, he was stunned by the sight of Louis and Nestor. Lena had prepared some small sandwiches. Louis and Nestor were surprised and very polite. It was a funny thing to see, in retrospect: a murderer and an informer sitting under Lena Brod's expansive, approving gaze, eating her sandwiches. She went to the bar and began lining up drinks.

Emil and I took the reel-to-reel recorder back to my place. Although I explained everything on the drive, the whole sequence of events, by the time we were climbing my stairs he still looked back, and said, "But I don't *get* it, Ferenc. What's going on again?" It was only the rush of too many new facts that made his head spin.

Emil set up the reel-to-reel under the kitchen table. We put blankets over it to muffle the sound of the motor and tested it until it was silent. Only the microphone peeked out. Then I used a tablecloth over the whole thing. We walked around the table to make sure it was hidden.

"I'll hide in the bedroom," he said.

"No. He'll check everywhere. He won't want to be caught like he was at Stefan's."

"But you need some help."

"You've helped enough, Emil. I'll call when it's over."

He was still confused as I drove him home.

I arrived a little after eight, as the entertainment, two brothers who called themselves the Tatra Twins, was preparing to perform. The Crocodile was half-lit so that all the attention would be on the stage, where the brothers — who were as far from twins as one could imagine — strolled on wearing self-consciously large suits with bow ties and hats with the brims turned up. The large one, Bálint, spun a wooden cane as he walked, while short, fat Boris waddled behind him, weaving in order to avoid getting hit. At the center they stopped and introduced themselves.

I didn't see him, and I wasn't completely sure he would come. The round tables were filled with groups of Russians dressed in fine eveningwear. My suit was noticeably cheap among them. I took a table near the stage because I wanted light to fall on me. This was imperative. The waiter looked at me strangely when I asked for a martini, so I instead ordered a palinka. The Twins began a rapid back-and-forth debate about their poverty-stricken village childhood, Bálint sometimes shaking his head in apology to us all for his brother's ignorance. They argued about who had less to eat, who was beaten more by their drunkard father, and which brother lost his virginity first. Each argument culminated with Boris receiving a slap and the audience convulsing in laughter.

The palinka was gone in no time, so I waved to the waiter for another.

Periodically, I looked back over the smiling faces raised to the stage. The women were a mix of Russian and local girls, but the men were all Russian. Their conversations mingled with the comedians' hysterics and left me in a state of utter incomprehension.

He arrived with a very young woman, almost a girl, who held his arm at the elbow and laughed obligingly when he whispered to her. They took a table in the middle of the club, ordered, and watched the stage. The girl leaned into him and settled her head on his shoulder.

They both burst into laughter with everyone else.

I could be overt — it would certainly do the trick. But I wanted to make it back home. So I turned back to the brothers' antics — Bálint was using the cane now, bringing it down heavily as Boris skittered out of the way — but I couldn't understand the humor at all.

When I looked back to the audience, I lost him for a moment. Then I found him because I was looking into his eyes. He had recognized my large form from the back, and was staring, no trace of smile left on his face.

I had been calm until then. I'd turned the plan over so many times that I knew it was the only thing to do, and in that surety there had been no fear. But looking into his eyes, the reasons for fear came back, and my hand was shaking when I raised my palinka beside my head, then nodded at him and turned back to the stage.

I drank it quickly because I did not think I could remain there much longer without screaming. So I walked out, hunched below the lights, and did not look over at him again, though I felt his eyes following me through the dark streets all the way home.

# 87

I didn't have to wait long. Twenty minutes passed before I heard the steady footsteps in the stairwell, rising. I ran to turn on the machine, then covered it again. It was silent. Then there were three knocks on the door. "Ferenc?" He had a sparkling, happy voice. He sounded like an old friend.

I opened the door and saw what I hadn't noticed before: how his left shoulder bulged beneath his jacket. The bandages over Nestor's bullet. When he walked in he showed no sign of injury, but he took his hat off with his right hand a little awkwardly.

"How are you, Kaminski?"

"Mikhail, Ferenc. I think we can be on a first-name basis."

"All right, Mikhail. Want something to drink?"

He shook his head. "I had one at The Crocodile. What were you drinking?"

"I asked for a martini, but couldn't get one."

He winked. "That's because it's an imperialist drink, Ferenc. I'm surprised at you." Then he cocked his head. "Well, maybe I'm not. Tell me," he said as he wandered to the kitchen and glanced around. "What is it you want?"

"What I want?"

"Well, you come to a regular spot of mine and wait until I see you, then you leave. You like vaudeville?"

"My favorite."

"Pretty good, aren't they?"

"I thought so."

I had left both bedroom doors open, and he stood between them, glancing around. "Nice apartment," He opened the bathroom door and sniffed. "Smoking on the crapper, huh?"

I smiled.

"So what did you want, Ferenc?"

"I was going to ask the same of you. You were here last night."

He wandered back into the living room. "And you didn't answer the door."

491

"I wasn't here. But we all have our informers. What did you want?"

He reached into a pocket for a cigarette, and when he lit it I noticed the unsteady left hand, which made the lighter flame wobble. "I came to talk to you about your case. Have you made any progress tracking this Nestor Velcea character?"

"He's hard to find."

"I expect results from you," he said. "Didn't I tell you that already?"

I nodded.

"Before Stefan was killed, I chatted with him about the case. He seemed to have some ideas."

"Before he died?"

"Seemed to think he was close to finding Velcea."

"I wish he'd have told me. Why are you so interested, Mikhail?"

He settled on the sofa, the trigger finger of his right hand tapping the cushion. "Me? I'm interested in the security of this country. I care about all levels of security. This Velcea character strikes me as a real threat, and I'd like to see him stopped."

"You were interested enough to demand answers from a friend of mine."

"Oh," he said, lipping his cigarette. "Georgi Radevych. He's a funny guy. He wanted me to think he didn't really know you. *Funny.* Tell me — who's Gregor Prakash?"

"And then you came to my home at night, when you could talk to me in the office anytime you wanted."

"Well, you weren't in the office yesterday, Ferenc."

"Maybe you don't want to talk about this around other people."

"Why wouldn't I?"

I sat across from him and looked deep into his eyes. "That is the question, isn't it?"

Kaminski leaned forward, tapping his knee. "I think you're trying to scare me, Ferenc Kolyeszar. I think you believe you're a threat to me. Did I tell you I had a talk with a certain Malik Woznica a couple weeks ago? He told me an interesting story. It includes you and a lot of bribery. Seems he learned it all from his wife in Moscow."

"Before he killed her."

He shrugged. "He didn't tell me that part of the story, though I learned it on my own. But as for you, my friend, this is just one more thing I have on you. I've got you on a string. All I have to do is drop you." He took his hat off the chair and stood up.

This was not how it was supposed to go.

I took out my pistol.

"Now, Ferenc," he said, smiling at it. "You've gone from dumb to moronic."

"Maybe a little stupid," I said. "I just want to know why you killed Sergei Malevich."

"Where did this come from? First it's Nestor Velcea, and now it's Sergei Malevich? You're all over the place. Do you have a fever?"

"I'm well enough."

"What about the others — Leonek and Emil? Are they suffering from similar delusions?"

"I haven't told them anything yet. First, I want to know why."

"Always a loner, right?" He looked at his cigarette. "Well, if I had killed Sergei Malevich, I suppose there could have been some good reasons. Security reasons. He was trying to cause more scandal for the liberating army. There had been enough scandals by that point, and public opinion was turning against us. Sergei, from what I've heard, was a little like you. He never cared about the larger picture."

"Public opinion was always against the Russians."

He raised a finger. "No, Ferenc. *Private* opinion was always against us. It's public opinion that is the danger to stability. Once hating Russians becomes a public opinion, you've got what you had in Budapest. You've got busses set on fire and windows broken. You've got tanks in the street. No one wants that."

"That sounds admirable."

"It is what it is."

"But it's not true. You killed Sergei because you were one of those four Russians who took those two girls into the synagogue. And the night you killed him, he was meeting his one witness, Nestor Velcea. You got rid of Sergei, then needed to get rid of Nestor."

He smiled.

I steadied my pistol. "But it was hard to find and kill him on your own, because he went into hiding. So you used the machinery of state security and a French informer to put him away. It must have been a surprise when you were in Moscow and found out that not only had he survived ten years in a work camp, but he was going to be released. You requested a transfer so you could finally take care of him personally."

He brought the cigarette to his lips and took a slow drag.

"But you won't get him."

"So you do know where he is."

"He's safe," I said.

Kaminski's smile returned, and he shook his head. "Nestor is not safe — he's a dead man. And you, Ferenc, you're walking and breathing, but you're also dead. Remember, I have plenty to use against you."

"I know."

"So what are you going to do about it?"

I raised the pistol so he could see into the barrel. "Lie down."

"You wouldn't shoot me."

I shot a bullet past his ear that buried into the wall. He got on his knees. "Down," I said. "Arms out."

With his nose in the rug and arms spread, I found in the lining of his jacket his pistol — a nine-millimeter with a long silencer attached to it — and tossed it into the kitchen. I knelt beside the chair where I had left Ágnes's knotted rope and bound his hands behind his back. He wrinkled his nose when the rope passed near his face. "Damn, Ferenc. That thing smells like piss." I stood in the doorway to the kitchen, watching him as I phoned Emil, but he made no move. When I hung up, he said, "This is it, then. You understand, right? Once I'm in custody, I'll tell everything about November the sixth, and about Svetla Woznica. If you put me away, I'll

496

put you away. That will be the end of you."

I sat in the chair. "Then we'll go down together."

# 88

All four of them arrived, Leonek and Emil with guns drawn. Kaminski smiled at everyone. I wanted more from him. I wanted some kind of pleading, something to let us all know that now he was finished. But he only smiled as I gathered the audiotape and Emil and Leonek lifted him and took him out to the car. Louis and Nestor sat together on the sofa. Louis said, "What about us?"

"What do you think?"

Nestor was tipsy — Lena had kept him drinking. He smiled grimly. "I suppose it's time for me to pay back society again."

Louis was a French national, and I wasn't sure I wanted to charge him with anything. He was a fool, but that had never been much of a crime in our country. So I drove him back to the Metropol. He and Nestor hugged on the dark street, and Louis kept apologizing, but Nestor was serene. The alcohol must have helped.

As we got into the car, I glanced back at the hotel. A white-haired man in the lobby stood and approached Louis. Jean-Paul Garamond did not look happy.

Kaminski was already in a cell, and Leonek and Emil were waiting for me. They stood to the side as I filled out forms for Nestor's detention, then Moska showed up. He was tired and confused and a little angry that he hadn't been told what was going on. But he got over it. After Nestor was taken away we went to a bar. I wanted to be drunk, to gain Nestor's serenity, but intoxication only made me feel sick. I couldn't quite hear what the others were saying. One thing I did make out was Emil's confusion over something Kaminski had said. "He told us that by tomorrow no one will give a damn about him, or Nestor, or anyone. He said tomorrow everything is going to be different."

"What does that mean?" Moska asked.

Emil shrugged. "I wish I knew."

Leonek wagged his head over his glass. "I don't wish I did. I'm very glad not to know a thing."

I felt the same way. I wanted to forget Kaminski's last words to me — *That will be the end of you* — but memory and knowledge are the killers of serenity. Then, around one, when we were all too drunk to read a thing, a heavyset woman came in, red-faced, frantically waving a special late-night edition of *The Spark*.

"*God, oh God,*" was all she could get out, repeatedly.

Leonek swiped the paper from her, and as he moved it back and forth, trying to focus, he looked baffled. "It's Mihai," he muttered, maybe to us, maybe to himself. "He's dead."

# 89

It rained most of the drive. I had not had the patience to clean up the house; all I wanted was Ágnes and Magda. I wanted them with me immediately; there could be no delay. I splashed through craters of rainwater and flew past hitchhikers stumbling through the mud, the sputtering radio teaching me more about the life of Mihai than I would ever have wanted to know. All I learned of his death was that lung cancer had taken him.

I ducked beneath my coat to stay dry and banged on the loose front door. Nora looked surprised.

"Where are they?"

"Inside, dear. Eating lunch."

Ágnes threw herself into my arms, weeping. It was strange to hold my daughter again, and I had to adjust my arms to accommodate her. Maybe she'd grown in the past week. But her tears weren't for me. "He's *dead*, Daddy! W-what can we . . ." She broke down again.

Magda was easier to hold. I sank my face into her shoulder and held her for a few seconds longer than she expected. Then she pulled back. "Are you okay?" She wiped my cheek.

"Me? Oh, sure. I'm fine."

"Your hand is scratched."

"It's nothing. I'm okay."

It took a while to relax, a meal that tasted better than any Nora had ever made before, and a long smoke with Teodor. We discussed Mihai's passing and speculated without knowledge on what would follow. No one that week had any idea what would happen. "Ágnes is a wreck," he said. "Does that surprise you?"

"Maybe those Pioneer meetings had their effect."

He asked about the case.

"It's over."

"And it went well? You got your man?"

"I got him."

"And what about you two?"

"What about us two?"

"Mag told me she asked you to take her

back." He put out his smoke. "Are you going to do that?"

I didn't know how to answer.

All five of us took a walk across the wet communal plots and greeted farmers who stood smoking in empty, long-harvested fields. We made it to the social club, a low wooden building where a couple men played guitars in a corner while drunk farmhands danced with young girls. I didn't like it when one of them covered us with his atrocious breath and asked to dance with Ágnes, but I was pleased when she declined.

At the farmhouse Magda and I took the room where she had once told me about Leonek. But this time she examined my hand with concern, then told me again how sorry she was. I kissed her to keep her quiet, and we made love in a way I'd not done for a very long time: simply, and without any motives other than love. Afterward she told me she could never leave me, because a man as pure and true as me was a once-in-a-lifetime find. "Pure?" I asked her. I was standing naked by the opened window, smoking.

She put herself up on an elbow, and in the darkness she might have been any woman. "I know you, Ferenc. Your impulses are pure. You've proven it to me all these years."

"I'm not pure, Magda. I'm so far from that."

"But you are."

"No," I repeated, then told her about Vera. I told as little as possible.

She was quiet for a moment, then whispered, "I knew something was going on. All those nights out." I noticed her breaths were uneven. "But what else should I expect?" she said. "I'm surprised you didn't do it earlier."

I flicked the cigarette out the window and latched it tightly.

# 90

Magda was disheartened by the apartment — I hadn't cleaned a thing while they were gone — and peered closely at the bullet hole in the wall. Standing with her and seeing it through her eyes, shame overcame me. Ágnes ran with Pavel to her room, and Magda leaned against the radio and sighed.

"Look," I said. "I'll help."

"You're damn right you'll help."

So we spent that afternoon cleaning. She dusted and mopped; I swept and washed dishes. Both of us went through the apartment with rags, wiping down all surfaces, and by the afternoon it was done. We bathed together, washing each other's backs, and when we were done I suggested we go to a puppet show. "That's a nice idea," she said.

But the theater was closed in deference to Mihai, and on the front door was a twenty-line poem extolling the virtues of that great patron of the arts. We ended up at a restaurant where I told them to get whatever they wanted. Ágnes chose fried potatoes. I tried to get her to add some meat to her order, or vegetables, or even ice cream, but she shook her head firmly. "You said whatever I want."

"Fair enough."

We put Ágnes to bed and undressed in our bedroom. I watched Magda slide out of her clothes as if I'd never seen her do it before in my life. Her face and shoulders were brown from a week in the country, and I touched an old scar on her shoulder, white against her tan. We shut off the lights and kissed for a while and made love without speaking. Then, as we lay beside each other in the dark, she finally began to tell me.

"Remember how it was when you came

503

back from the war?"

"Yeah. I do."

"You were a different person. Really, you were. The Ferenc I married was bright and happy. God, you could make me laugh. You did it without effort. You saw the humor in everything around you, and you always pointed it out to me." She shifted, and her hand slid up to my chest. "I was never like that. Then when you came back it was different. Of course, at first you couldn't do anything. You'd been through something I couldn't imagine, and I was willing to work with you through it."

"I remember that. You were so good to me."

Her fingers weaved through the hair on my chest. "Why wouldn't I be? Your family was dead, and you'd been through a war. I loved you. So we moved to the Capital when Stefan got you the job. I knew why he wanted to help you — we both felt guilty. But I swear it only happened once."

"I believe you."

"Once you were working again, you started to come out of your shell. I can't tell you how excited that made me. I was looking forward to greeting the boy I'd fallen in love with." She paused then, her fingers continuing to stroke.

"But he didn't appear, did he?"

Her hand flattened just over my heart. "Not really. I saw moments of it now and then, particularly after Ágnes was born. But you were a different man. I had to realize that. And when you started writing, it seemed to take you away even more. The only time you were like your old self was with Ágnes. I was jealous of her for a long time."

"Of Ágnes?"

"She was the only one who got the old Ferenc. I wanted that Ferenc for myself."

I considered that decade and a half with a man she hadn't married. "Was it so bad?"

"What?"

"Being with me."

She stroked the stubble on my cheek. "Of course not. There were moments, I have to admit, when I was scared of you. You'd get into one of those moods, you'd go silent, and I didn't know if I could trust you. With me. With my body."

"What do you mean?"

"I mean," she said, then paused again, "you don't realize what your size does to people. You could snap someone in half. You could snap me."

"But I'd never do that. Not to you."

"I know you wouldn't. But sometimes I'd look at you, mulling over your brandy, distant, and wonder if you could. I wondered what would happen if I did something to really provoke your wrath." She removed her hand. "And then I did. I did the most provocative thing imaginable. And you . . . you didn't touch me. Not once. Not many men are that way, Ferenc." Her hand returned, this time to my scalp. "Maybe this is what I realized at my parents'. I was throwing away my family because I didn't have enough faith. God," she said, placing her hand on mine again and squeezing.

I could hear the tears.

She said, "I found that letter you wrote."

"What letter?"

"It was in your jacket. You said you were going to leave me and take Ágnes with you."

"No," I said. "You don't understand —"

"Don't explain." Her hand tensed on mine. "I deserve it. But please, consider growing old with me."

I held her with my arms and legs for a long time until, the crying done, she fell asleep. To the sound of her soft snores, I tried to figure out what I wanted now, now that it had all been exposed. I was numbed by the prospect of decision.

But what numbed me more was my impotence: My decisions did not matter. Kaminski's threat still resonated in me, and reminded me that any life I chose had a fast-approaching expiration date.

The next morning, over breakfast, Ágnes smiled at us — she could tell we were better. Then she asked the question: "Daddy, do you know where my rope ladder is? I can't find it."

# 91

Friday morning I typed up the paperwork on the Nestor Velcea case. I listed off the victims — Josef Maneck, Antonín Kullmann, Sofia (a.k.a. Zoia) Eiers, and Stefan Weselak.

Then I outlined the understood sequence of events, from Sergei's case in 1946 to the art fraud in 1948 to its discovery in Paris by Louis Rostek and Nestor Velcea's attempt to right history. Were there a place in the report to mention such things, I might have noted that history can never be made right, but the forms did not ask those kinds of questions. Nor did they allow me to observe that if there was a God, His aims were inconceivable: He gave

507

Svetla an unlocked door, and He also handed Nestor a chance meeting in a bar with his first victim.

I wasn't far into the report when Leonek approached me. Nestor and Kaminski had been moved up to Ozaliko, but Leonek had gotten a call from a friend who was a guard there. "Tells me they took Kaminski away. A couple state security guys."

"They're going to want to know everything he knows," I said.

Leonek smiled. "I hope he makes it difficult for them."

I felt my eyes glazing over. Leonek was saying something. "What?"

He had settled in a chair beside me. "That night. Before you went to The Crocodile. You asked me if I loved them. Why did you do that?"

Part of me wanted to smack him, another part to embrace him. "Insurance," I said. "Now get out of here. I've got to finish this report."

I didn't get much further before Emil pulled up the chair that Leonek had vacated. "Thought you'd like to know, they found Woznica's car on the road to Perechyn. It had been rolled into the trees."

"Did he have a wreck?" I asked with surprising calmness.

"Don't think so." He scratched his chin. "Haven't seen it yet, but the local Militia told me the fender only tapped a tree."

"You haven't seen it yet?"

"I'm going now. Want to come?"

I looked at the half-written report in the typewriter. "No. I don't think so."

He didn't move, and I noticed he was grinning.

"What?"

When he told me, my grin matched his.

"For Christ's sake, Emil. Congratulations!"

"We'll get it confirmed by the doctor, but she's pretty sure. I just hope it works this time."

"When's the due date?"

"Twentieth of August."

"So you've decided," I said.

"What?"

"Not to leave her."

He touched the corner of my typewriter. "I suppose my love's not that mature, Ferenc."

He went to his desk as I looked at the report, dazed by the white paper. Emil's new life was just beginning as my new life was preparing to end. Then, on cue, two men entered the station. They were obvious — the long leather jackets, the low-slung hats — but they walked as if no one knew they were state security. They paused in the doorway. This had come sooner than I expected. I took my fingers off the typewriter and reached for my bag. But then they noticed Sev, smiled and walked over to his desk.

Not yet.

So I continued, working with the sticky T to make the name *Nestor* and being gentle with the carriage return so the roller would not shoot out of the machine. I was almost finished when I heard his footsteps behind me. "Ferenc?"

I turned to Sev.

He looked at the report in the typewriter, then at me. "Can you tell me, generally, what you did after the riot on November the sixth?"

I looked past him at the two men waiting by his desk. "I walked back to the station and drove home."

"And did you receive any telephone calls at home?"

"No," I lied. "I went to sleep."

Sev blinked, no expression cracking those features. "Thank you, Ferenc." He returned to his desk.

Through the rest of the report my hands did not shake. My stomach was steady, and my mind was focused. It didn't matter that everything was closing in on me. I was still able to work like an automaton through the details of my life, grab my hat, and go home to my family as if each hour did not lead nearer to my demise. I had taken so many steps toward my own end that by now the steps were easy. I could believe in fate or not; it no longer mattered. Nothing mattered. I sat with Ágnes on the floor, helping her fashion a new knotted rope out of one she had found on her way home from school. I smiled at her and joked as though I were still a man with human feelings. Magda touched me in bed and I made love to her as if I still knew what that meant. And she believed it. Both of them believed it.

# 92

The crowd lined the entire length of Yalta Boulevard, sprouting out of Victory Square and growing straight and sure past state security headquarters at Number 36, out to where Yalta terminated in the middle of the Seventh District. We were somewhere in between. The announcements had been plastered on walls ever since Wednesday, and the radios had broadcast unending reminders of the time and place, but I never imagined so many would heed the call. After the Sixth of November, this kind of turnout seemed impossible. But here they were, all the discontented of the Capital alongside the satisfied and even the apathetic. And they were all weeping.

Children sobbed on fathers' shoulders; mothers clutched their heads whenever anything appeared on the cleared boulevard. Banners fluttered down from windows, announcing that MIHAI LIVES FOREVER IN THE HEARTS OF THE WORKING CLASSES and quoting him: "THE PATH TO FREEDOM IS TREACHEROUS, BUT WE ARE GREATER THAN MERE TREACHERY." His younger portraits hung from lampposts like Roman standards and filled shop windows. Magda grabbed my hand as we were pushed forward. The motorcade began with white Militia cars, their aerials bound in black ribbons, then came the long hearse. Magda slipped as the crowd surged, but steadied herself on my arm. Bullhorns on the hearse's roof bellowed a slow dirge and a deep voice listing all his titles: *Liberator of the Nation; Friend to the Young and Old; Fount of Impenetrable Knowledge* . . . Wails shot up around us.

On a family vacation we once drove to Baia Mare to see Mihai's childhood home. It was a letdown — a two-room shack outside the city, with portraits of him everywhere, looking down on the ratty BED WHERE HE SLEPT and the clay oven in the KITCHEN WHERE HE ATE. I didn't understand until Magda sighed, and said, *He really is one of us, isn't he?*

Magda's fist covered her quivering lips, and her red eyes tried to see past shoulders and heads. Then she buried her nose in my chest. I turned to my other side. "Where's Ágnes?"

Magda's face was twisted. "What?"

. . . *Seed of the Land; Thunderstorm in Times of Drought* . . .

"Ágnes!" I shouted. "She's not here!"

Magda unlatched herself and pushed people aside to see for herself. "Ágnes?"

We split up and threaded through the crowd. I shoved women and men aside and kneed children who stood in my way as the worry became frantic. "Ágnes!"

. . . *Academician of Worldwide Acclaim; Friend to the Animals of the Planet* . . .

As I pushed I imagined her trampled beneath feet, dragged away by molesters, knifed by Nestor Velcea or tortured in a wet Canal District mansion, her corpse carried to the mountains for disposal. Not once did I imagine the most evident scenario, which was proven as the Politburo cars slid slowly by and Magda caught up with me, dragging our daughter along: She had

513

squeezed her way to the street in order to cry and wail where she could better see the object of her adoration.

# 93

We were eating dinner when they came. The buzzer went off, and Magda got up from the table to open the door. I followed her when I heard his voice, monotone: "I'd like to speak with Ferenc, if you don't mind."

He was already inside the apartment when I got to them, and through the door I saw the other two men. Leather coats, hats. They did not come in.

"Ferenc," he said, and squinted as if faced with too bright a light. He stuck out a hand and I took it. "Comrade Kolyeszar," he said to Magda. "Would you mind if Ferenc and I talked alone?"

Ágnes stood in the kitchen doorway, frowning. Sev noticed her and tried a friendly smile, but no one was convinced of it, him least of all. Magda took her back into the kitchen.

We sat — him in a chair, back straight, me on the sofa. He touched the mole on his cheek. "Listen, Ferenc. I'm going to have to take you over to Yalta

514

Boulevard. Some questions."

"Questions about what?"

"The case. The Nestor Velcea case."

"You have my report."

"And other things."

"I'll come by Monday."

"Ferenc," he said. "Let's not make this ugly. There's no reason."

"I suppose there isn't."

Somewhere inside me, in a small soft place, I was terrified.

"My wife and daughter know nothing about any of this. You realize that, right?"

He glanced back toward the kitchen. "I know that."

"Then let's go. I'll tell them good-bye."

"Listen," he said. I looked at him chewing the inside of his mouth. "This," he began. "This is not my doing, what's going on right now. Comrade Kaminski talked to other people, and they want to know more from you. I'm following orders."

I wasn't sure if I believed that or not.

Ágnes was sitting at the table, and Magda stood by the sink, chewing the nail on her little finger. "What is this?"

"It's nothing. Just some questions. I'll be back soon."

"Questions? Questions?" She shook her head, and her kiss was salty. She held my

515

lower lip in her teeth. "Don't go," she whispered. "Tell them you'll go in tomorrow. Or Monday."

"I tried. If you need . . ."

"What?"

"If you need anything, call him."

"Who?"

"Libarid."

"Oh God, don't say that."

"Where are you going?" asked Ágnes.

I pulled away from Magda, but she clutched my hand as I leaned over the table and kissed Ágnes's head. "Just to talk with these men. It's nothing. I'll be back soon, but if I'm not back tonight, you go on to bed, okay?"

She smiled a moment, then her smile disappeared. Perhaps she saw it in her mother's face, because she started to cry quietly. "Are you going to be all right?"

"I'll be fine, honey."

Magda squeezed my hand until the rings pinched my fingers, then walked with me into the living room and helped me into my coat. Then she said to Sev, "Bring him back soon. Do you understand?"

He pressed his lips together. "Of course, Comrade Kolyeszar. I will do my very best."

*You hear this later.*

*You hear that the Magyars have it worse than anyone this year. Nagy is lured out of hiding from the Yugoslav embassy and over a year later is executed deep inside the Empire. Thirty-five thousand Hungarians are arrested and three hundred executed.*

*You hear that after the death of Mihai, after the convulsions of grief and homages to his immortality, the nation goes on. It is announced that a joint leadership is now in power, because how can such a man be replaced with just one? There are three: Bobu the Professor, Kozak the Engineer, and a name you've not heard before this, a name no one has heard: Tomiak Pankov, a Party apparatchik from before the war. Less than a week later, Bobu is arrested by state security at his mistress's apartment in the Fifth District. The next morning* The Spark *explains all: He is guilty of financial improprieties. Kozak and Pankov shake hands on the balcony of the Central Committee chambers before a crowd that fills the entirety of Victory Square. They wear identical greatcoats to symbolize their accord, and then the arrests begin to riddle the Capital with holes where men once stood — you're only one of many. The empty prisons swell as they did a decade before,*

517

*after the war, and the trains lumber under the weight of the dispossessed on their way to the provinces and the camps. This is what you learn much later.*

*You learn that once the Capital is cleansed it is time to fumigate the Central Committee. Chairs in the great hall go empty, two, three at a time. Emergency elections bring in new, quieter men, younger men with a lifetime of service before them. Then, in February, Kozak delivers a speech to these new young men, says that he will resign his position for a quiet life in the provinces. He holds his hand up and tells them, tears in his eye, that it is the hardest decision of his career, as well as the wisest. Tomiak Pankov shakes his hand and smiles, then opens his arm to the Committee members. This movement lets them know what to do next: to give the poor old engineer a rousing farewell. Which they do, all standing and hollering. You never see the newsreels of this meeting — no one sees them. But you can imagine the fear in Kozak's eyes and the desperate sound of all those shouting voices, wanting nothing but to live and to go on.*

# WINTER

# 1

I look back over weeks and months in an attempt to give them order, but time can only be given shape by time. Fall had been my season of irresponsibility, and I had moved steadily through it, accumulating mistakes and fears and tragedies, and in the winter I was paid back for it.

The beginning was a white, four-door Mercedes. Brano Sev sat in front with the driver, and the second man remained in the back with me. Brano had not talked in the stairwell and maintained his silence all the way to Yalta Boulevard, where the shops were closed, their metal blinds like mouth braces holding the buildings straight.

Sev walked ahead of us as the guard opened the heavy door of Number 36 without a word. I couldn't remember if he was the guard from Georgi's visit. The inner doors parted, and we were in a cavernous, institutional green room, where two uniformed women sat behind a wide desk. Sev talked to the heavier one, and the other, her thin face revealing the shape of her narrow jawbone, watched me. The hawk on her shoulder patch matched the one on the wall above them: a copper sculpture five feet tall, the hawk at rest.

Two doors on either side of the desk led from this room. We took the left one through a low corridor, not unlike the Militia station's corridors, but what I noticed was this: There were no names on the doors' translucent windows, and no numbers. And that is when I became afraid. The unmarked doors of Yalta 36 were part of a world that was beyond my understanding.

We descended a concrete stairwell at the end of the corridor, and I wondered if Georgi had followed this same path. I tried to remember the details of what he'd recounted; but the growing panic was making me forgetful. Three levels down, Sev knocked on a steel door and waited for the tiny barred window to open and close. A series of locks were worked on from the other side, and then the door opened.

The guardroom was just big enough for a desk holding a telephone and a copy of *The Spark*. Hooks on the wall held keys. The guard was a meaty man with round glasses. He smiled and asked me to empty my pockets. All I had was some loose change, my wallet, and my Militia certificate.

"Laces?" he said, and waited as I knelt and unthreaded my shoelaces. He spoke to Sev while looking at me. "Which one?"

"Seventeen." Sev's voice was flat.

The guard handed over a key and used another one on the next door. It opened onto a narrow, concrete corridor lined by more steel doors.

"Is this really necessary?"

Sev acted as if I'd said nothing as I followed him to the ninth door on the left. Here, at least, were numbers, but they were drawn with chalk — at any moment they could be wiped clean and changed. Sev worked with some effort on the lock, but got it open, then glanced at the guards who waited back with the jailer. In the dim light his face had lost all its color. "We both know it's necessary. At least for now."

I followed the direction of his hand, and the door closing behind me filled the cell with darkness.

# 2

When we were captured in the trenches near Humenne and marched westward, I had wondered what the prisoner-of-war camp would be like. My imagination had come up with details of a hypothetical cell: dirt floor, bunk, a slot in the door for food, maybe a hole in the corner for a toilet, and certainly a barred window one had to stand on one's toes to look through to see the sun. None of these details matched the cell on Yalta Boulevard. It was extremely small, like — as Georgi had said — a soundproof water closet; unlike Georgi's cell, this one was unlit. The ground was rough concrete, and there was no hole in it, only a small pot in the middle of the floor. No bunk and no window, no matter how high I reached my fingers up the wall. Then I remembered: I was under the earth.

The darkness settled on me with real weight. It became thicker with time, and after a while I could only sit in the corner, lacking the strength to climb up through it. I touched the dead German soldiers on my fingers and repeated their names. I think it helped, because it reminded me that in the war people died indiscriminately, and I was back in that world. That was at least familiar. I would live or I would die based on the whims of people I could not see, could not argue my case with. Fatalism settled into me with the fog.

But with time either the darkness sheds its weight, or you shed yours, because I began, without realizing it, to pace. Three steps took me to the back of the cell; two crossed its breadth. But I was able to make a kind of lap by using infant steps. Sometimes I ran into the wall — the concrete left a scrape on the tip of my nose — but I learned to sense the wall by the movement of air along it, and turned, quickly, to continue my lap.

The tiny cell stank of mildew and my sweat and urine. I held off defecating as long as I could — how long, I don't know — then gave in. I used my undershirt to cover the small pot, but that didn't help the stink.

My fatalism wavered over the hours. It wasn't as strong as it had first appeared. I was still healthy — physically, at least — and could stand up straight. That in itself seemed enough to assure my survival. I was strong, and it didn't make sense that a man as large and strong as I was could simply be erased.

This is the irrationality of darkness. You begin to grasp at little things. Just the sound of your footsteps on concrete give hope: They are so loud in the absence of all other sounds, they are godlike.

The hunger that came on and off and twisted my stomach into knots seemed like the only way to track time. I could go without eating for a couple days, which perhaps meant I'd been there two days. I considered banging on the steel door and calling for food, but I doubted my voice would make it through. And this was what I knew they wanted, for me to panic.

At some point a slot at the base of the door opened, filling the cell with a dim, painful light. This, at least, was something I had imagined while walking under German guard: an opening in the door for food. A tray slipped through, spilling soup from a tin bowl. Bread, and a brackish, chunky liquid I could not identify. By the time the slot closed again, I had almost finished it.

# 3

They came four meals later, while I was sleeping. I had slept so much in that cell, though sleep never rejuvenated me. There was the shock of light, the aching eyes, and two sets of hands pushing my shoulders as I stumbled through the steel door and up three flights of stairs, which, I remembered vaguely, placed us on the ground floor, where there were two doors. The one on the right led to the long corridor without numbers and out the front; the left one led, as I learned, directly outside, into a wide courtyard, where vans and cars sat in rigid lines. It was night, and a light blanket of snow covered the ground. They threw me into the back of an empty white van, locked the door, then climbed into the front. I pressed my face against the metal screen. "Where?"

The driver, the one with the mustache, looked at me in the rearview. "Don't worry so much. You'll give yourself a hernia."

The other stuffed my shoelaces through the screen. "Put these back on."

I tried to remain standing in order to see out the back windows. I thought we were driving south, but when we passed Unity Medical and entered the Second District, I realized we were headed west. The van jostled, and I hit my head on the ribbed ceiling, then squatted. I hadn't noticed the cold until then; it burrowed into me.

When I checked again, we were in the Fifth District, stately Habsburg homes sliding past. Then a right-hand turn took us to our destination: the Fifth District train station. Unlike the central station, this one closed at ten every night and reopened at six. We drove through the empty lot and into a corner, where a ramshackle building stood hidden in the shadows, smoke trickling out of a smokestack.

We left prints in the fresh snow up to the door. Inside, it was too warm, and a fat man with bristle on his cheeks dealt cards to another fat man at a desk. The dealer smiled at us. "Guests?"

My clean-shaven guard took some folded papers from his pocket and handed them over. The dealer set down the deck and read thoughtfully. Then he leaned on his knees, grunted, and stood up. The keys on his waistband made a racket when he walked to another door and unlocked it.

"Get in," said my clean-shaven guard.

The one with the mustache said, "Good luck, Inspector."

This cell was huge — a paradise. There was a bench attached to a wall, and when I stood on it I could just see through the barred window to the overcast night sky. The cold didn't bother me, and for the moment I didn't worry about what would happen next. For the moment I could take long strides and even jump, which I did, many times.

# 4

I woke to the first sunlight I had seen for a long time. But the elation drained away as I looked down on my blackened hands and soiled clothes and tasted the decaying teeth in my mouth. My own grime and smell were intolerable.

The fat card dealer brought some soup that I ate while standing and staring at the sky. When he came to take the bowl, I asked where I was going. He waved the bowl as if it were a little flag, "You're going to put yourself to use for once, Comrade. You're going to *work*."

"Which camp?"

He shrugged.

Three hours passed, then five, and I watched the sun set through the bars. My time didn't come until after I'd fallen asleep on the bench, and I woke to the dealer standing in the doorway with three soldiers holding rifles. "It's your big moment!"

The train was already sitting on the tracks. I was led to its rear, to a cattle car that held three young men — no older than seventeen — with bruised faces. Dirty straw covered the floor, and when the door was pulled shut the darkness and smell of decay covered us. One voice said something about concentration camps. Another told him to shut up.

The train whistled and started to move.

They introduced themselves, and in passing lights through the high barred windows I could connect names with faces. Gyula, his ear crusted with dried blood, was the one who was afraid of concentration camps. Florian, with a purple, swollen right eye that remained shut, had no patience for such talk. He asked what I'd done to end up here. When I told them it was connected to a case, and that I was a militiaman, they fell silent again. But I enjoyed the sound of their voices. "What did they get you on?"

"Nothing!" said Johann, the third, who blushed beneath his bruises. "They didn't tell us anything. They took us from our homes, beat us, and brought us here. It's unbelievable!"

They were students who had helped draw up a little manifesto during the height of the Sixth of November fervor, then quietly returned to their studies. But their names had appeared alongside their classmates', and these signatures became part of the long lists of the condemned.

When the sun rose, we could see through the high windows that we had reached the countryside. Then we stopped at a station that Gyula believed was Ricse. When we arrived at Dombrand, stopping just before the station, I was sure of our destination. Soldiers opened the doors and walked us to another train. Some travelers with luggage watched from the platform, hands shielding their eyes. They put us on another cattle car that was connected to a regional train with passenger cars up front. There were other prisoners there, young and old men, some with no marks on them at all. One held on to his blood saturated pant leg. I moved to a corner and watched them talk among themselves. Then the train pulled up to the station and, pulling myself up to the window, I could just make out the very clean travelers climbing into their cars.

From there we stopped often, letting travelers on and off, and when we reached Vátrina, which must have been the end of the line, the final regular passengers disembarked. The soldiers waited until the platform was empty before opening the cattle cars. There were about sixty of us in all, from three cars. An officer approached, a tall man with buzzed hair who held a black truncheon, and he told us to assemble on the edge of a field that bordered the station. Once we were collected, the officer motioned to the soldiers, who began to herd us across the field and away from town.

I knew this route. We were heading east, and to our right was the road I had driven to the camp. Six, seven miles. A cold wind came over the field, arching the grass and slowing us down. My dirty shirt stuck to me. In a wheatfield just in sight of the five towers of the camp, the prisoner with the bloody pants stumbled and dropped into the grass. A guard wandered over and shouted at him, but we could not see his reaction through the grass. Twice he kicked the prisoner, looking down and shouting, then he took a pistol out of his belt holster and shot him.

Gyula kept looking back over his shoulder. I thought that he was trying to catch my eye. But he was looking farther back, to where the dead man lay.

We reached the barbed wire and waited while the guards conferred by the front gate with Gogu. He looked healthier now that he was in business again. They handed him a file full of papers, and he spoke to his men, his flushed bald head bobbing as he joked. Then the guards ran about, shouting, rounding us up into lines like soldiers on display. Gogu put his hands behind his back and waited until we were ready.

"Welcome," he shouted, his dirty voice

on the edge of breaking, "to Work Camp Number Four-Eighty! I am Captain Gregor Kaganovich and you are my *pets!* I reward and I punish — I am your last recourse before your god!" He raised his thumb. "Only one rule here — this is simple, now — *work!* If you want to eat, you work! If you want to sleep, you work! If you ever want to leave here alive, what must you do?"

A couple prisoners in the front answered him, and two guards came over and slapped their faces.

"Work," said Gogu. "Not talk."

The blows began. Each guard had a truncheon that he used with fervor, beating us in the general direction of the gate. I caught sight of Filip, the excess skin collecting on the back of his neck, his scarred face twisted into screams as he swung. They beat us into five groups in front of the five buildings. My back and arms stung, and my ear was bleeding. The guard who struck me on the ear shouted, "It's the big ones that go first, bastard! It's the big ones we liquidate!"

He was the one who ordered us to strip completely, except for our shoes, and throw our clothes into a pile. We were marched around the side of the buildings, where four guards stood with razors to shave our heads. We froze in that line, waiting for the guards to dump water on our heads and then chip at our scalps. The barber took my hand. "What are these?" He tugged a ring — Hans Lieblich — off my left pinkie. "Hey, Filip!"

Filip came over and called me a bourgeois pansy, then the two of them worked each ring off. Not once did Filip recognize me, and I never saw my German soldiers, nor my wedding band, again.

We waited, arms around ourselves, shivering. Beside the barbed wire were two full burlap sacks. The guard shouted for our attention and walked over to one. He opened it so we could clearly see the dead man inside, his battered face lumpy and purple.

"This!" the guard shouted. "This is the only way out of here!"

Under a rain of more truncheon blows we ran inside the barracks. On the rotting hay was a pile of soiled, striped prison clothes. The guard screamed at us to dress.

It's hard to say what I was feeling at that point. A certain terror, yes, but a part of me was sure I would make it out alive. The extremity of my surroundings was almost too deadly to comprehend, so I held on to the only thing I could understand: Gogu's one rule: work. I was still a strong man, and could at least keep up with that. And this was my mistake: I still thought that rules had a power of their own. I thought that camp rules would ensure a path of safety.

# 5

That night the weary veterans, who had been out at Work Site Number Two all day, returned to the barracks. Some became angry when they found their bunks occupied by newcomers, while others, too weary to shout, simply dropped into a free shelf. Some questions were answered. We would know when to do what by a bugle call. When to wake, eat, and work. The work at Site Two — the new project Gogu had mentioned a long time ago — was digging: They were building a canal to the Tisa, about five and a half miles away.

The bugle sounded early, and I woke to the cold and a sweet, sickening smell. As I climbed down from the bunk, I asked a veteran who slept below me. He was an old man with a permanent look of worry on his face. "The pus," he said. "You'll smell like that once you've been hit enough. You'll get worms, too, but don't worry, they'll clean those out in the infirmary."

There were more truncheon blows when we gathered for the morning roll call behind the barracks. The sun had not yet risen, and in the darkness a guard with a wavering, young voice called the names and we each yelled "Here *here!*" as loudly as we could. Gogu looked on from the door of his office. Halfway through the names a heavy, bearded guard reached forward and pulled one of the new prisoners — a student — out of our ranks and dragged him to an electrical pole. As the names continued, he shouted at the student to hold on to the pole, and as he did so, began beating the student's back. Whenever the student screamed, he delivered a blow to his head. This went on until the student passed out. Roll call was over.

We had the same kind of soup and bread I'd had in Yalta 36, sitting outside in the cold, and were then marched through the predawn night out of the camp and farther east. I was hit a couple times by the barracks guard, and the old, worried man was hit three times. It impressed me that, despite the blackening welt that showed when his shirt rose from his hip, he could keep moving. There were about three hundred of us in all, being beaten across the wheatfields, two miles to Work Site Number Two.

The work on the canal had not been going on long. A crevice about fifty yards wide and a quarter of a mile long had been dug, and we were told that our daily quota was ten cubic yards. If we did not reach that quota, we would be punished. Each of us was given a shovel and a wheelbarrow and sent into the hole. They had picked a sandy area, and as we hefted the heavy wheelbarrows sand spilled out. The guard standing by the truck where we dumped it looked at each load critically, asked our name, and marked down an estimate. This went on.

The first day was the hardest. It was unbelievable how heavy those wheelbarrows were, and how undependable the sandy wall of the canal could get. Often I would make it halfway up, only to slide and see my entire load turn over. A guard would scream at me from above, accusing me of sabotage, while I tried to focus and fill it up again. I didn't make the quota at all the first week, and each night, after a dinner of more soup, I cut wood outside, under the glare of the camp searchlights.

Although they sometimes made excuses, it became evident that the killings had no logic other than the logic of terror. Those who did not collapse on their own could at any moment be pulled out of roll calls, out of our dinner huddle, out of work details or bed. Sometimes a guard approached a prisoner in the morning and held a small mirror in front of his face. "Take a good look — this is the last time you'll see yourself alive!" Then he handed the prisoner a burlap bag to carry to the work site, and that night the bag carried him back.

By the second week I was terrorized into submission.

I talked with the other prisoners during the rare instances when exhaustion did not make me mute. There were all kinds: students, Gypsies, factory workers, and even some who had been in the Party — the old worried man had been the head of his metalworking collective until he was turned in. "I know who it was, though," he whispered to me one night, the worry suddenly fleeing his face. "Wlodja Stanislavsky. He's one of the machinists, and for the last five years he's been in love with my wife. But she would never touch that dirty Pole. So he decided to get rid of me." He shook his head. "That bastard will only have her if he rapes her."

His name was Tibor Petrescu. He had been in the camp for a month when I arrived, and each Sunday when we were allowed to rest he wrote his wife long, convoluted letters. At first I wrote letters, too. I wrote to Emil, asking him to find a way to get me out, and I wrote to Magda, in order to reassure her of my health and love. I had been a fool to let her and Ágnes go — given the chance again, I would have sent Leonek to The Crocodile that night. How could I have hesitated when she asked to be taken back? In the camp I found the limits of my maturity. But after a while, I stopped writing altogether. I had asked Tibor if he ever received answers from his wife, and his *no* reminded me that mail did not leave this camp. Everything remained stacked in that steel cabinet in the commander's office to be read over brandies and cigarettes, for a laugh.

I gave up, and gave in to the regime of work. I watched the other prisoners fall, and once brought back a burlap sack filled with Gyula, the student, thinking only that his fear had reached its end.

Despite all the sand we dug, the canal seemed to make no progress. Gogu arrived with a uniformed officer, shouting at us from above, and the next day the quota was raised to twelve cubic yards. I was just able to keep up, but Tibor fell short often, and at night I'd hear him grunting in the yard as I tried to sleep, then the thud as his ax hit wood.

# 6

Two and a half months into my stay, I was at the work site, collapsing beneath the weight of a wheelbarrow filled with snow-damp sand, when the mustached barracks guard — the Cosmin I'd heard of in another life — appeared at the edge of the canal. He put his hands on his hips. That morning he had pulled a boy from the roll call, ordered him to strip naked, then made him sit in the snow and cover himself with it, like a blanket. When we marched off to work, the boy was still there, rasping through congested pipes, turning blue. "Kolyeszar!" I looked up, my empty stomach tightening. "Get up here, Kolyeszar!"

I left the wheelbarrow and climbed up the embankment. Cosmin grabbed my ear and started walking forward — I had to bend so it wouldn't tear off. He walked me to another guard, who kept his machine gun pointed at me.

"Take care of him," said Cosmin.

I could hardly walk back across the wheatfields. I didn't know why they hadn't killed me there, in front of the others. Shooting me in secret just didn't make sense — it was the one thing I felt must make sense — and only when we were in sight of the camp did I begin to suspect that I wasn't going to die.

We went in through the back gate and stopped at the commander's shack. The guard knocked and waited. By the fence was a burlap sack. I knew, by glancing over to the empty yard, that the frozen boy was in it. *"Enter."* The guard opened the door and pushed me inside before closing it again. The warmth enveloped me as my eyes adjusted to the darkness. Gogu sat at his desk, fanning himself with a file, while beside him, impassive, stood Brano Sev.

He said, "Hello, Ferenc."

"Hello."

"Can you excuse us, Comrade Commander?"

Gogu stopped fanning himself and looked at Sev. He seemed about to protest, but then lumbered out, muttering to himself. Sev took the commander's seat and motioned to a chair. I collapsed into it.

"You don't look good, Ferenc. Camp life doesn't suit you."

"You're right."

"And that smell."

"It's the pus."

"Well, let's see if we can get you out."

I didn't answer, afraid that anything I said might ruin this one tenuous possibility.

"I should tell you," he said after a moment. "You should know that I never knew about this. About Kaminski. He was sent to help me with my work, and for a while he did just that. I was grateful for his help. But when he started showing interest in Nestor Velcea I became suspicious."

He paused, so I ventured an observation: "But it was you looking at his file."

"Yes," he said. "After Kaminski had already been through it. I wanted to know why he was so interested in an ex–camp prisoner, and so interested in your case. The only connection seemed to be that he was running the Office of Internal Corrections at the same time Nestor was put away. But I didn't know enough to understand everything. Maybe if you had been more honest with me in the first place, I could have helped."

I looked at my blackened fingernails. "But you did know about Sergei."

"Of course," he said without inflection. "I knew about the execution in 'forty-six.

You have to understand: Back then we were still fighting a war. It wasn't as relaxed as it is now."

"Relaxed?"

As he talked, he arranged his hands on the desk, as if plotting out moves. "People forget. I learned of Sergei's execution just after Kaminski performed it. It was a necessary thing. Sergei's investigation threatened to undermine the entire Soviet presence in the country. We still had Fascists in the hills, and foreign instigators were spread throughout the city. They could have used the investigation to devastating effect."

I didn't want to argue. "What about Nestor?"

"That was what I didn't know. I didn't know there had been a witness to the synagogue murders — no record was kept of it in our files. And I certainly didn't know how Kaminski was connected to those girls. One expects more of state security." He shook his head. "But Kaminski finally admitted it all. In the interview room."

"Oh."

"I might have turned a blind eye to some of this, but I could not allow that Kaminski had killed Stefan. That was entirely beyond imagining."

"Where is he now?"

Sev looked at his own fingernails, which were very clean. "He's dead, Ferenc. His body was found in the Tisa. He'd been shot in the back of the head."

I leaned forward, not quite understanding. "He —"

"Don't ask, Ferenc."

I took a deep, wavering breath as I leaned back again.

"Nestor Velcea is in a work camp in the east. He's a miner. And now to you." He straightened in his chair. "I've spent the last months arranging an amnesty. It was not easy. I couldn't defend your actions on November the sixth, but I did talk with them in more depth about the situation with the Woznica woman. Emil was useful in this, as he knew the whole story. I was hoping that Malik Woznica himself could verify some facts, but he has not yet been found."

I noticed my cold hands were beginning to shake.

"The best I could arrange was internal exile. You won't be allowed in the Capital again, not without proper authorization."

I remembered to say, "Thank you."

"One condition."

"What?"

"A confession. It's bureaucratic, a simple

thing. But they want an in-depth confession of your crime, as well as a full report on the case. You will deliver this to me."

"And what will you do with it?"

"I'll put it in your file. Type it up in the proper format, numbered, and wire me when you're finished. That's all they want."

Later, I would think about how he used the word "they" instead of the more appropriate "we," but at the time I just looked at my hands, at the red and black sores that covered them.

He said he would be back in a week with the release papers, and that in the meantime I should stay alive. I asked him how I should go about doing that. He shrugged. "Work hard."

# 7

Over the next week I saw two more inmates shot, one of them Tibor Petrescu. He was killed in the wheatfields at twilight, on our way back to the camp. That day Tibor's wheelbarrow had slid back on top of him, crushing his leg, and he spent the rest of the day up by the truck, helping collect sand that spilled out. In the fields he fell three times, and Cosmin, without hesitation, walked over and put a bullet in his head. He knew that Tibor and I had been friends, so he tossed me the burlap sack, and said, "He's all yours, Kolyeszar."

I collected Tibor as well as I could, at first trying not to look at the hole in his forehead. But then, as I folded his legs to make him fit into the bag, I paused to look directly into his face. He'd made it through a lot, but in the end a wheelbarrow signified his death. I hadn't told him or anyone else about my impending release, because I didn't want to face their agonizing, jealous stares, but I wished I had told him.

The next morning, which I later learned was the twentieth of February 1957, Cosmin came into the barracks before wake-up and called my name. Everyone moaned, half-awake, and I climbed down. "Now!" Cosmin shouted, and I hurried over to him. He quickly swung his truncheon against my arm, sending a bright, wakening pain through me. "Let's get going."

I followed him to the front gates, where a guard handed me a clipboard with a form on it. I couldn't read it in the darkness, but signed where he pointed a finger. He lifted the sheet and had me sign another. Then a third. Cosmin grabbed my shoulder and pushed me forward as the guard opened the gate. "I better not see you again," he whispered in my ear.

The gate closed behind me.

What I hadn't seen in the darkness was a white Mercedes moving slowly up the long dirt path from the main road. Its lights leapt as it bumped along. Then it stopped about ten yards from me, and the driver's door opened. A figure stood up and waved.

My legs no longer supported me. It was Emil.

# 8

"Jesus, Ferenc. What did they do to you?"

I didn't answer. I couldn't even smile. Because I knew this must all be a dream. And I would wake soon to the bugle call and rotting mattresses and truncheons.

The female desk clerk at the Hotel Elegant — not Tania — was reluctant to give us a room when she saw me, and Emil had to use his Militia certificate to persuade her. "Don't destroy the place," she said as she handed over the key.

I took a long bath. Emil had been speaking ever since he picked me up, pausing only to puzzle over my silence and try to think of something else to say, but I hadn't heard a word. The water blackened very quickly, so I emptied and refilled the tub. My sores hurt when I squeezed them dry, then scoured them. My hair had been shaved again the previous week, but the lice had returned to infest the little hair that had grown, so I used a razor to shave it off again. As I dried I caught myself in the mirror and understood Emil's horror.

He was talking again when I came out, something about how he'd had to drop the Malik Woznica case because there were no clues, but I only said, "Did you know prisoners built this hotel?"

They were the first words I had spoken, and by the look on his face I knew they were the wrong words. "No. I didn't know that, Ferenc." He spoke the way one speaks to an injured child.

"I've got to admit," I said, trying to sound human again, "I haven't heard a thing you've said all this time. I'm sorry."

He dropped onto a bed. The sun was beginning to shine through the cheap curtains. "I didn't say anything important. Anyway, I bet you'd like to sleep on a real mattress."

"Oh God," I said, and fell into the other bed.

When I woke up, groggy and aching but rested, it was nighttime. Emil was out, but by the time I had gotten up and washed another time, he appeared with a small suitcase. "What's that?"

"You're not going to live in those striped rags, are you?"

Inside were clothes I could hardly remember after these months of prison garb. They were clean and pressed — perfectly. "Where did you get them?"

"Magda packed it all."

"Did she try to come with you?"

He looked at the bed. "No. I suppose she didn't think she could take it."

"Leonek?"

"What?"

"Is she with him?"

He scratched the back of his neck. "I don't know, Ferenc. No one tells me a thing."

"But you've seen them together."

He looked away, nodded.

I didn't ask anything more, because a part of me knew this all along.

In my clothes again, I almost felt like a man. My face was still battered, but my suit covered the sores, and when I walked the chafing reminded me that I was back with the living.

In the hotel restaurant I ate too much and had to vomit in the bathroom. When I returned I passed Tania at a table with a camp guard. She noticed my face and muttered something to the guard, who looked at me and nodded. But as I sat down I realized that she had no idea who I was.

The next morning we drove south, to Pócspetri. Emil didn't tell me until we were halfway there that Lena had lost the child. "Emil. I'm sorry."

He tugged down the sun visor. "I suppose we should just stop trying."

"Has she been checked out by a doctor?"

"A dozen times. She's physically fine. It could be her nerves, or the drinking. Probably the drinking."

"Then try it again after she stops drinking. That's all you can do."

"Pick yourself up and try again? We'll see."

We reached the farm by eleven, the sun bright over the rolling orchards, lighting the dirt road winding past the cooperative offices and down to Teodor and Nora's house. I could just make out Nora standing on the front steps, hand shielding her eyes, watching us approach.

"You're going to stay here?" Emil asked

as he looked ahead along the road.

He was smiling as if the question were funny. I wasn't sure why, until I looked ahead to where Nora was waving beside the Škoda I hadn't noticed before. I reached to twist a ring that wasn't there. From a distance it looked like Nora, but it wasn't.

# AFTERWORD TO THE 1978 EDITION BY GEORGI RADEVYCH

Ferenc Kolyeszar began writing his confession on 12 March 1957 and finished it on 5 November, three days after Khrushchev launched Sputnik II — a relatively short time compared to the years it had taken him to write his first book, *A Soldier's Tale*. It was composed at both Teodor and Nora's Pócspetri farm and their dacha near Sárospatak. When he returned from the dacha on its completion he called me, but made no mention of the book. He only wanted to know what I knew about this satellite orbiting the earth, and about the dog inside it. "What's going to happen when it runs out of air?" he asked, in a panic. When I told him the dog, Laika, was going to die, he fell silent.

It took another month for him to put together the "official" version that he turned in to Brano Sev. By that point Laika was dead. In his official confession, Ferenc cut out all references to the crimes of others. For example, there is no mention of anyone other than himself listening to

Radio Free Europe, and the station-house strike that followed the Sixth of November demonstration is put down as his idea. But what no one, least of all Brano Sev, suspected was that Ferenc would confess to killing Malik Woznica. There was no evidence against him, and Woznica's body had not been found. When he told me what he'd done, I asked him why on earth he'd confessed. He said, "Sometimes, Georgi, you've just got to be an adult." He gave this version to Brano Sev on 11 December 1957.

It surprised Ferenc that he was not arrested after turning it in. He expected that within the week a white Mercedes would pull up to the farm and take him back to Vátrina. But he finally understood, and wrote me in a letter, "They will hold it over my head, Georgi. All I have to do is open my mouth and say something they don't like, and I will be back with my friends in that camp."

Ferenc only told me about this uncensored version of his *Confession* eight years later. He had waited long enough so that no one besides himself would be punished for its contents. He changed the names of the characters and used a pseudonym, like most underground writers at that time. In

June 1965 I put out the first edition as a simple typed manuscript, five copies that we passed around to our friends and read in groups. The Russian word *samizdat* had just come into vogue, and this was the lowest form of *samizdat* you could find: a stack of pages stuffed into a folder.

It wasn't until 1971 that we found the means and will to bind *The Confession* into a box of nine serialized pamphlets — known as "the Box" to those who looked for it. I asked Ferenc if he could compose some words to remind people of the political situation in those days, because some younger readers, I worried, would not remember exactly how it was. Ferenc answered with the second-person interchapters found in the present edition.

*The Confession* gained a life of its own. It was discussed in living rooms and kitchens all over the Capital, and a few copies were smuggled to Poland and Hungary. The Hungarians, with their own rich *samizdat* history, translated it into their difficult language and began printing it madly. From there his book spread like a beautiful malady.

But this popularity was the very thing that Yalta Boulevard was waiting for. On 1 February 1972, the white Mercedes did arrive at the Pócspetri farm, where Ferenc had lived with his wife and her parents for the last decade and a half, and took him to another work camp, on the eastern side of the country. The charge was murder, and Ferenc seemed, according to Magda, to have been waiting for that moment all his life.

He was released in 1975, during another wave of amnesties, in part because voices outside the country were demanding to know his whereabouts. He was returned to Pócspetri. His lungs were weak from working in the mine shafts of the Carpathian range, but Ferenc went immediately back to farming. "It is," he confided to me once, "the only thing that gives me satisfaction."

— March 1978

# ABOUT THE AUTHOR

OLEN STEINHAUER was inspired to write his Eastern European crime series while on a Fulbright Fellowship in Romania. His first novel, *The Bridge of Sighs*, was shortlisted for the Ellis Peters Historical Dagger Award. Raised in Texas, he currently lives in Budapest.